Also by Julia Stagg

L'Auberge
The Parisian's Return

About the author

Julia Stagg lived in the Ariège-Pyrenees region of France for six years, where she ran a small auberge and tried to convince the French that the British can cook. Having done her bit for Anglo-Gallic gastronomic relations, she now divides her time between the Yorkshire Dales and the Pyrenees.

You can find out more on her website www.jstagg.com or on Facebook www.facebook.com/staggjulia and follow her on Twitter @juliastagg.

JULIA STAGG

The French Postmistress

HODDER

First published in Great Britain in 2013 by Hodder & Stoughton
An Hachette UK company

This paperback edition published 2013

1

A CIP catalogue record for this title is available from the British Library

ISBN 978 1 444 76596 0

Printed and bound by Clays Ltd, St Ives plc

Hodder & Stoughton policy is to use papers that are natural, renewable
and recyclable products and made from wood grown in sustainable forests.
The logging and manufacturing processes are expected to conform
to the environmental regulations of the country of origin.

Hodder & Stoughton Ltd
338 Euston Road
London NW1 3BH

www.hodder.co.uk

For my Maman

Thanks for filling the house with a world of books . . .
and the music of Fats Domino.

I

High above the verdant valleys of the Ariège-Pyrénées, in the very corner of France where it snuggles up to the borders of Spain and Andorra, a man sat waiting at the edge of a small clearing, his long limbs folded uncomfortably, his breath swirling in white clouds around the brilliantly coloured foliage that concealed him.

To his right, rising out of the mist far below, a range of magnificent peaks serrated the morning sky, Mont Valier king of them all, snow-capped and glistening. The vista, which had tempted many a visitor to Fogas, was not enough to seduce this man. Indifferent to the best that the region had to offer, he was concentrating solely on the surrounding woods.

The sound, when it came, would have been inaudible to most men. But he wasn't most men. Recognising the snap of dry twigs under immense feet, he raised his weapon. He'd only get one chance and after three days he wasn't prepared to miss. Leaves rustled underfoot as she approached and he forced himself to be still. Totally silent.

He felt a tremor of excitement when she emerged from the dark mass of trees, an expanse of tufted grass and rocks between them. Young, no more than four years old, her body was compact, ready for the coming hibernation, hindquarters powerful. The early morning sun rippled across the dense brown fur of her coat. She was beautiful.

And if he wasn't mistaken, she was pregnant.

He eased out from his cover, feet placed instinctively where they would make no sound, body arched ready for flight. He was the best at this. That's why he'd been given the job. Held his job despite his unorthodox methods. He took one more step, gun pressed tight against his shoulder, and then he pulled the trigger.

'I'm telling you, it's a wild boar print!'

'You wouldn't know a wild boar from a goat when it comes to tracking!' René puffed up the hill after his brother-in-law Claude, leaving the more substantial figure of Bernard lagging further behind. 'What makes you so sure?'

'It had dewclaws. And look, Serge is definitely on to something.' Claude pointed at the beagle which was racing ahead of them, bell jangling on his collar. He stopped, nose to the ground, circled a couple of times and then took off again.

'That dog is about as useful as its master,' scoffed René, glancing back to see if Bernard was still there. 'Come on, slowcoach. Your Serge seems to have found a trail.'

Bernard halted, hands on his ample hips, rifle hanging from his shoulder, face puce under his orange beret and chest heaving. 'You . . . carry . . . on. I'll . . . catch . . . you.'

'Catch a cold more like,' muttered René as he turned back into the hillside, wishing not for the first time that he'd been born down on the plains around Toulouse where hunting was so much easier than on the steep slopes of the Pyrenees in the commune of Fogas.

The sharp yap of the dog pulled his attention back to the chase. Perhaps Claude was right? Maybe they were on to something? What a change it would make if the three of them actually caught a boar! For once, they wouldn't have to endure endless ribbing back at the lodge from the merciless Henri Dedieu, club president and ruthless hunter, and there'd be *civet de sanglier* aplenty, washed down with a hearty wine from the neighbouring Languedoc region. René licked his lips, a rumble of hungry anticipation rolling through his stomach, and started tackling the arduous path once more.

Back in the safety of the hide, the man heard the bark carry clear across the autumnal air. She heard it too. She tensed and raised herself onto her hind legs, tottering slightly.

It had been a perfect shot. The shoulder. Just behind the thick mass of neck muscle. She'd twitched, as though stung by a bee, the dart hanging from her. Looked like it had penetrated far enough. In five minutes he'd be able to tell.

But now this.

Hunters. It was Saturday. He should have known. But the signs were supposed to be up, marking out this territory as a no-entry zone. Should have been up for the last week. So what on earth were they doing here?

They would kill her if she made any move towards them. It was a tailor-made excuse for a group of people predisposed to hate her. And she was in no position to defend herself, the strong drug already in her system, shutting down reflexes, sending her to sleep.

He reached for another dart. He only had one left but it might be enough. Failing that . . . He laid a hand on the rifle lying beside him, loaded with live ammunition as a precaution the authorities insisted upon. No fan of hunters, he wouldn't think twice about resorting to it if necessary.

The dog was the first to appear, dashing into the open space, whipping round to chase its tail a few times, totally oblivious. Then it froze, fixated on the looming shape before it, and its ears flattened. He expected a growl. An attack. But the dog merely whimpered and lowered its belly to the floor.

'Serge? Here Serge. Where's that bloody dog got to?'

'There, he's through there.'

The bushes parted and they were in the open. Two men. Both typical of the region, short legs and barrel chests, the older of the two panting as he leaned against the trunk of an oak, head down, eyes closed and face scrunched in pain.

'Christ, Claude. Think my heart's about to give up.'

But Claude wasn't listening. He was staring at the mass of fur and muscle that reared above him.

'René . . .'

'Just a sec. Let me catch my breath.'

'René . . .'

'Not sure all this is worth it, you know. Tromping up and down the mountain, nigh on killing myself and for what? To see Bernard's daft beagle writhe around on the floor. I mean, for goodness sake, what's with this dog—'

'*René!*'

It was a whisper laden with fear, enough to make him look up from where Serge was lying prone on the ground. To look up over the stout frame of his brother-in-law and beyond to . . . what was that? Silhouetted against the sun it looked like . . .

'*A bear?*'

Claude nodded. And gulped, the sound unnaturally loud in the tension of the clearing.

'*It's a bear?*'

'*Yes!*' hissed Claude.

René's mouth dropped open and his legs started to tremble as he beheld a sight that was at once terrifying and magnificent. In a patch of forest he knew better than his own garden was the biggest beast he had ever set eyes on. Standing tall on its hind legs, it was watching them intently. And it looked like it was developing an appetite.

'*What do we do?*' the younger man demanded.

'St-t-t-tay c-c-c-calm,' stuttered René. '*And whatever happens, don't run!*'

Seconds passed with animal and hunters locked in a pastoral tableau that could have graced many a château's hallway. For René, less than twenty-four hours into yet another bid to give up smoking, it felt like an eternity as his petrified brain tried to formulate a plan of action but failed to produce anything more concrete than an overwhelming desire for a cigarette.

And then he noticed something. The bear's focus had shifted, its gaze had become less threatening, body less rigid. In fact, if he didn't know better . . .

'*It's falling asleep!*' he hissed. '*Look!*'

Sure enough, the bear seemed to be going into a trance, eyelids drooping, head starting to loll. Exploiting this sudden drowsiness, René took a couple of steps backwards, provoking no reaction in the somnolent animal.

'*Slowly does it.*' He beckoned Claude to follow him. '*No sudden moves and we should be okay.*'

As the two men began easing towards safety, it would have been beneficial if René had shared even a fraction of the innate abilities of the man hiding just metres away. Then he might have heard the approach of something from behind. But as it was, every fibre of his body was concentrating on the imminent danger in front of him. So naturally, when a fat paw landed on his left shoulder he did what any other red-blooded Ariégeois hunter would have done.

He screamed.

And Bernard Mirouze, finally having caught up with his friends and not knowing why his casual greeting had been met with such terror, screamed too. Then he saw what was in the clearing and screamed a second time.

The shrill notes shattered the quiet truce, jolting the bear out of her slumber and she staggered, stretched up on her hind legs and then crashed towards them, mouth wide open. It was too much for the hunters, who promptly ignored everything they'd been taught about surviving an encounter with a wild beast.

'RUN!' René shouted, turning tail. Claude scampered after him, leaving Bernard and Serge the beagle to bring up the rear.

From his refuge, the man watched their hasty departure as the bear finally crumpled to the ground, oblivious to the crash and thump of the escaping hunters who were making their way down the hill a lot faster than they'd made it up. Swapping the airgun for the rifle, he approached the now sleeping animal with caution. With twenty minutes to complete his work before she started to come round, hopefully he'd have no more interruptions.

On a hillside across the valley, a narrow track, largely forgotten by the present inhabitants of this forested region, afforded an excellent view of the tiny settlement of Picarets where houses clung to the mountainside in stubborn resistance to the ever-encroaching woods. But the two men standing on the gravel path were not concerned with the spirals of smoke from early-morning fires drifting out of a scattering of chimneys. Nor with the small blue car winding its way through the hamlet, descending towards the main road.

Instead, one of them had his binoculars fixed high above the stones and slates of the Pyrenean homes, up beyond the old quarry which had been closed longer than most could remember. There, at about the point where the unmade road ended abruptly in a circle of forest, he was focused on three figures who were loading equipment into a four-wheel drive, their activity punctuated by frequent rests and the odd dash into the trees.

'They're breaking camp,' he noted. 'They look pretty sick.'

'You haven't killed them?' The fear in the second man's voice prompted a derisory laugh.

'Just incapacitated them. They'll recover.'

'And the fourth one?'

'No sign of him. Damn it! He must have slipped the net!'

He lowered the binoculars, revealing a steel blue stare, the pupils pinpoints of darkness.

His comrade shivered. It was nothing to do with the temperature, which was mild for the time of year. And he was suitably clothed for the outdoors, even if his combat trousers still bore the creases of the packet and his Le Chameau boots were straight out of the box.

The trill of a mobile sounded loudly.

'Yes?' the first man barked. He listened intently and then smiled. 'Excellent. See you at the lodge.' He shoved the phone back in his pocket. 'Good news. We have a positive sighting of the bear. That clown René and his mates.'

'They saw it?'

'Stumbled across it in a clearing apparently.' He rubbed his hands in anticipation. 'It's about to begin.'

'And the fourth member of the team? The tracker? Won't he get in the way?'

'I'll take care of him.'

'You won't harm him?'

The cold gaze swept over the man who would never be a hunter, no matter his attire and came to rest on the pristine boots with a sneer.

'Having doubts are you, Pascal? Thought you wanted to be part of this?'

'I do . . . I'm not . . . I mean . . .' He was out of his depth. His wife had warned him. This man was dangerous. But it was too late now.

7

'Well grow a backbone. This is the perfect time for us to make our move. And that bear is the key.'

'It's just . . . I didn't think . . .'

'You didn't think you'd have to get your hands dirty?'

Pascal had no reply.

The other man raised the binoculars once more, the sunlight shining on the boar's-head signet ring that graced his left hand, and he watched the four-wheel drive, government logo emblazoned on the door, bounce down the dirt track and off into the distance.

'I'll be in touch,' he said, once the vehicle was out of sight. 'And if you don't lose your nerve, six months from now you'll be Mayor of Fogas.'

2

'It was a bear!' René Piquemal reached for his beer, still trembling. 'Enormous. Came at us. Thought we were done for.'

He took a long sip, and wiped his moustache with the back of a hand covered in scratches from the unconventional route the three hunters had taken down the mountain. With René leading, they had fallen through bushes and over rocks, stumbling and lurching in their desperation to get away. At one point René had been overtaken by Bernard whose forward momentum, greatly abetted by his hefty paunch, had caused him to lose control and he'd tumbled head over heels to the track below.

Once back at the safety of their cars, Bernard and Claude had decided to go home, overcome by their adventure. René however, in need of company and an audience, had driven straight down to the bar in La Rivière.

Unlike the villages of Picarets and Fogas, with which it had been bound in a triumvirate of political discord since Napoleonic times, La Rivière was situated on the valley floor, thus forming the midpoint of the geographically challenged commune of Fogas. Hence it was a natural meeting place – some would even say 'neutral' given the rivalry between the other two villages, arising out of the sense of superiority Fogas had retained purely because it had given its name to the district – and on a Saturday the modest bar was crowded with regulars partaking of a pre-lunch drink after a long morning at the market.

'You didn't think to shoot it?' asked Philippe Galy, sitting at the large table which dominated the room. Around him the usual hum of conversation had fallen quiet as the locals absorbed this latest news.

'Shoot it?' Plumber by trade, woodsman only by hobby, the idea hadn't even crossed René's mind. He didn't analyse what kind of hunter that made him. 'Didn't have time. It moved like lightning. Covered the ground in colossal strides. We were lucky to escape.'

'You couldn't shoot something like that!' exclaimed Josette, busy drying glasses behind the counter. 'Not a bear. They're too majestic. And anyway, they're protected. You can't just go round killing them.'

'But if it was attacking someone?'

A derisory snort came from the only other woman present. 'Probably wasn't even a bear. Probably just a wild boar with long legs!'

The plumber scowled as the place erupted into laughter. 'Joke all you like, Véronique! But when it comes down here and runs amok you won't be laughing. And it will. Mark my words. There are already rumours that the bins at the Sarrat bridge have been raided. Most likely the same beast.'

A rumble of consternation greeted his news about the bigger, more affluent commune that lay across the river, its sloping fields basking in sunlight. Then he indicated the archway behind him which opened up into an épicerie, shelves stocked with croissants, bread and fresh vegetables, the pervasive scent of saucisson filtering through.

'Wouldn't be surprised if you go through there someday, Josette, and find one rummaging around in the shop. They're a menace. And you've got more to lose than all of us,

Christian. Know how many sheep were taken last year alone by rogue bears?'

Christian Dupuy, the large man with the mop of blond curls who'd been sitting quietly, enjoying the mayhem, shrugged. It was a complaint he heard all too often at the Farmers' Union meetings. And one he was sorely tired of.

'Over one hundred and fifty, that's how many,' René continued. 'It's wrong is what it is. Releasing them up in the mountains on some conservationist whim and expecting farmers and hunters to shoulder the costs.'

'But they're not shouldering the costs,' cut in Véronique. 'Farmers get compensated for any stock killed by bears.'

'And even some that isn't!' added Christian with a cynical smile. As someone who took livestock up to the mountain pastures every summer, he was expected to disapprove of the government policy; to take part in the regular protests, many of them violent, which were organised by his fellow farmers who were outraged at the danger posed to their untended animals. But in fact, he didn't understand why they couldn't live side by side, the way they had for centuries before the bears were hunted out of existence.

'I know of a few who've had the benefit of the doubt when it comes to claiming compensation,' he said. 'Paid in full for a ewe that was probably killed by a stray dog. And bought new fencing and a couple of Pyrenean mountain dogs courtesy of the grants available.'

'Pah!' René thumped his fist on the bar. 'Those grants are just a sop to make us swallow yet another piece of legislation thought up by some Parisian intellectual who knows nothing about life in these mountains.'

'And even with a *patou* in place, sheep still get taken,' added an elderly shepherd from the back, using the affectionate term for the dogs the government was promoting as a suitable bear repellent. Traditionally bred to be a guard dog rather than a sheepdog, the *patou* lived its life amongst the flock, its shaggy white coat and tail making it resemble the very animals it was designed to protect. As a result, there'd been many a tourist over the years who'd claimed to have been chased down a hill by a barking 'sheep'.

'What galls me the most,' continued René, 'is that there was no local consultation. None!'

'They held talks up in Toulouse,' Christian said.

'Since when was Toulouse in the Pyrenees? Bloody Paris bureaucrats! The lot of them should be made to face what I had to this morning. See how they'd like to stumble upon a bear in their back garden!'

A murmur of support reverberated through those listening and Philippe Galy's voice surfaced from it.

'René's right! My hives are up in those hills and I've lost enough bees this year without them being attacked. And while I can make use of the electric fencing the government provides, a *patou* is no good to me!'

'Don't let Maman hear you say that!' Véronique Estaque laughed, thinking of the two massive Pyrenean mountain dogs that were the centre of her mother's life. 'She's been inundated with calls to breed hers since the reintroduction programme started.'

'She should take them up on it. About time someone bene-fited from this travesty,' grumbled René.

'So, going back to your encounter,' said Véronique with a mischievous twinkle, used to his mercurial temper and know-ing he wouldn't be able to resist resuming the tale. 'How did you get away?'

'With difficulty! It was up on its hind legs, towering over us, jaws open wide.' The plumber slid off his stool and assumed the position of the threatening animal, short arms raised in the air, teeth bared, even his moustache looking vaguely menacing.

'Was it wearing a beret?' asked Christian to smothered giggles.

René glared at him, whipped off his orange hunting beret and continued.

'Claude was next to me. Terrified, he was. Shaking so much I was afraid his gun would go off! So I calmly told him to take a step back.' He eased himself away from the bar in the manner of the besieged hunters, facing his audience, back to the entrance to the shop. 'So now there's a distance of a few metres between us, and this beast is still snarling.'

'You must have been petrified!' said Josette, tea towel abandoned as she got caught up in the excitement.

'Claude was. I just had this wave of calm wash over me. Like Jean-Claude Van Damme before he goes on the rampage. It was as if every sense was razor sharp, every reflex ready to fire.'

A stifled snort came from the back of the room.

'So then what?' asked Philippe.

'I persuaded Claude to take another step.' René edged back again, totally in the moment now and carrying his audience with him. 'It was like trying to get marble to move. Frozen solid with fear, he was. And all around, this eerie silence, as if nature was holding its breath.'

Tension permeated the bar, every eye on the fearless plumber who stood crouched in the doorway.

'We'd almost made it. We were right at the edge of the clearing. But then . . .' he paused dramatically. '. . . Then Claude made a noise. And just like that the bear roared and lunged towards us. We didn't have time to think. It was a matter of life and death. I threw myself in front of Claude and I—'

But the dramatic conclusion was never reached. For the

second time that day René's 'highly honed' senses betrayed him as, without warning, a large hand descended heavily onto his shoulder from behind, scaring the living daylights out of him.

And for the second time that day, he screamed.

'Christ, René!' Christian mopped up the beer that was swilling around the table, the result of René's high-pitched yelp, which had jolted more than one member of the audience into spilling their drinks. 'What happened to the Van Damme reflexes?'

'I can't help it if people keep creeping up on me,' René groused, as he glared at the cause of the commotion.

He was huge. A mountain of a man, taller even than Christian, easily as broad across the chest but with a panther-like quality that the awkward farmer would never possess. And that hair! It was as black as a night sky on a new moon and flowed over his collar in thick, luxuriant waves. No need for special shampoos in that house, thought the plumber as he ran a hand over his own balding pate.

'Sorry. Didn't mean to scare you.' The stranger's voice was deep and had the rough edge of disuse and although there was nothing explicitly offensive in his words, René got the sense he was being mocked.

'You can't scare him,' said Véronique with a laugh. 'He's just confronted a bear.'

'Has he now?' The man directed a warm smile at her and then focused on the plumber. 'Around here?'

'Up above Picarets. We came on it in a clearing and it went for us,' explained René, returning to his place at the bar and noticing, as he got closer, the musky scent of the forest emanating from the man. He hadn't been near a shower for a while.

'Sounds like you had a lucky escape.' The man paid for the beer Josette had placed in front of him but his gaze never left René's face, causing him to feel like a butterfly pinned to a mounting board.

'He was just telling us about it when you came in,' said Véronique. 'So what happened next, René?'

'Nothing. It doesn't matter.' The unrelenting scrutiny had dampened René's enthusiasm for his exaggerated tale and no longer wanting to be the centre of attention, he took his drink and made his way to a seat next to the elderly shepherd who immediately started reminiscing about how much better things had been in his day.

'So what brings you to these parts?' asked Josette and the man dragged his eyes off the retreating figure of René and turned to face her.

'I'm working here.'

'What kind of work?'

'Research.'

His reply was met with scepticism. It wasn't a common profession in the area and for those present who'd never met a researcher before, which was the majority, the newcomer's grubby clothing and mud-streaked face weren't quite what they'd expected from a man of science.

'Into what?' asked Véronique.

But the man mustn't have heard, as he responded with a query of his own. 'Can anyone tell me where I can find the mayor?'

Philippe Galy let out a dry laugh. 'Now there's a question.'

'He's not always around these days,' said Véronique. 'Perhaps we could help?'

The man graced her with another smile and a blush stole up her cheeks. 'I'm sure you could. The town hall is supposed to have arranged accommodation for me.'

As one, everyone turned to the big farmer who had shown no inclination to join in with the conversation. Now, however, Christian stepped forward and Josette noticed he was standing straighter than normal, as though making an effort to appear even taller.

'Accommodation? Are you sure?'

The man reached into his pocket and pulled out a bundle of papers. He separated a page from them and passed it over, the town hall crest visible on the top. The farmer read quickly, heart sinking. It seemed there had been yet another administrative glitch in the commune of Fogas.

'When was this arranged?'

'A few weeks ago.'

'Well, it wasn't mentioned at the council meeting last week. And there are four of you?'

'There were. But things have changed. It's just me now.'

'At least that's something.' Christian ran a hand though his curls in exasperation.

'What is it?' demanded Josette, leaning across the counter and pushing her glasses up her nose as she peered at the letter.

'This man, Monsieur . . .'

'Petit,' the man volunteered, a hand held out to the farmer. 'Arnaud Petit.'

Christian grasped it and felt the strength of a fellow outdoorsman. And calluses. Not the soft hands of a researcher.

'Christian Dupuy, deputy mayor of Fogas.' He turned back to his audience. 'Monsieur Petit has been promised community housing for the duration of his . . . research.'

'That wasn't approved by the council,' barked René.

'Serge must have forgotten to raise it.'

'Huh. That's becoming a regular occurrence,' muttered Philippe. 'He forgot to submit my new building plans and I had to take them down to the office in St Girons myself.'

'He has just lost his wife. We must remember that.' Josette's tone held more than a hint of reproach.

'It's nearly a year ago, Josette,' countered Véronique. 'And while we should make some allowances, the commune still needs to be run. I'm having the same problem trying to get him to contact La Poste to demand a meeting. Every time I ask I feel bad for pestering him but it's ten months since the fire and we still don't have a post office.'

'Going to ruin, this place is,' grumbled René. 'Maybe we ought to be thinking about voting in a new mayor!'

'Now, now.' Christian held up his hands to silence the growing discontent. 'Serge is doing his best at a difficult time. It's our place to support him, not criticise him.'

'Serge?' Arnaud Petit was looking confused, having last heard the name applied to a beagle on the hillside above Picarets. And not a very bright beagle at that.

'Serge Papon,' explained Christian. 'He's the mayor of Fogas.'

'A bloody useless one,' came a mutter from the back.

'Well, at the moment he's all we have so we'll just have to make do and sort this mess out.'

'Sort what mess out?'

The voice came from the same doorway that had already yielded one surprise that morning. But for those residents of Fogas who had been born and bred in the sleepy commune, it was a far cry from the booming sound that used to echo around the hills. Much quieter, almost tentative, it was still enough to startle them into silence.

'I said, what mess?' Serge Papon stepped forward into the crowded bar, face markedly thinner than a year ago, clothes baggy on his once stocky figure.

'Serge,' Christian said awkwardly. 'Bonjour!'

How long had he been there? wondered the farmer. Had he heard?

'Bonjour.' Serge flicked a dismissive finger at the letter. 'What's this all about?'

'Apparently we're supposed to be housing Monsieur Petit while he carries out research.'

'Monsieur who?'

'Monsieur Petit,' said Arnaud, stepping forward, hand outstretched, his huge frame making the older man seem even frailer.

'Serge Papon.' The reply held something of the resonance of times gone by and was accompanied by an expansion of his chest like a proud rooster. 'Mayor of Fogas.'

'An honour to meet you. My department spoke to you a fortnight ago.'

'They did? I mean, they did. Yes.' Serge glanced back down at the paper, still looking unsure, and then he seemed to dredge something up from the inky depths that had become his memory. 'Of course! I remember now. You're the man from the bear reintroduction programme!'

Shock rippled through the bar, closely followed by a wave of dark mutterings as the residents of Fogas reassessed the newcomer. Little wonder, thought Christian, that he had been coy about the nature of his research. It was such a volatile topic and for the likes of René and the old shepherd, Arnaud Petit represented the very government that was forcing them to adapt the way they lived for a reason they just couldn't accept. He was the enemy.

Aware of how easily their open curiosity could turn into hostility, Christian moved to put himself between Arnaud and the now restless natives, noting with irritation that Véronique was regarding the man with a look of awe.

'You've agreed to put up a bear researcher in the commune?' René was the first to find his voice.

'Technically, I'm not a researcher. I'm a tracker. If that makes any difference.'

Arnaud Petit's droll interjection did nothing to alleviate the escalating discord. But Serge, normally fine-tuned to the shifting moods of his electorate, seemed not to notice the growing rumble of discontent and continued blithely on.

'Yes. Just for a few months.'

'A few months? Are you mad?'

'Far from it,' Serge replied curtly. 'We're getting handsomely paid in rent and the bears are good for tourism.'

The elderly shepherd had heard enough. Getting to his feet, he shook his walking stick in the general direction of the tracker. 'Since when was tourism the only concern? What about our livelihoods? Those bears and the likes of him are ruining our way of life.'

His outburst was met with a roar of approval which couldn't fail to register on Serge's political Richter scale and he stepped forward to smooth the ruffled feathers.

'I think we're all getting a little overexcited,' he said, the authority from years of uncontested power bringing order to the bar. 'It's only a temporary measure until the monitoring project is finished. Then Monsieur Petit will be on his way.'

'What monitoring project?' René's voice was laden with suspicion.

'They're tagging some of the bears to find out which one is causing the problems.'

'What problems?'

'Oh, I don't know. Something to do with a bear being seen down by the Sarrat bridge. Probably wasn't even a bear but you know how it is. Ever one to pander to his electorate, Henri Dedieu was immediately on the phone, squealing to the relevant agency.' Serge shook his head in disgust. 'So, thanks to the mayor of Sarrat, we have a team of researchers in the area for the next few months.'

It was vintage Serge Papon: a skilful shift of responsibility onto the neighbouring commune which was held in universal contempt by the people of Fogas. But the side-step, worthy of all his years in power, had come too late.

'I told you!' exclaimed René, stomping to the front to wag a finger at Christian and Véronique. 'I told you that animal would create havoc.'

'There's no evidence that the bear you saw is the culprit.' Arnaud had moved past Christian to face the room, the combination of his deep voice and his immense stature quelling the opposition. 'Once I have the results of her DNA sample we'll be able to tell.'

'And how do you propose to take her DNA?' asked Christian.

'I already have. Took it this morning.'

'This morning?' René queried. 'Is that why it attacked us, because you'd provoked it?'

Arnaud chose not to notice that René was getting more and more puffed up, fists clenched, inching closer to the tracker with every word.

'No,' Arnaud said, as Christian put a restraining hand on his friend's shoulder. 'I took the sample just after you left. When the drug I'd injected into it before you arrived had taken effect and the bear was fully asleep.'

It was said so quietly. With such understatement. But it had the desired impact. René's bravado collapsed like a popped balloon and the room erupted into hilarity, the burgeoning friction dissipating as the truth of the epic adventure was disclosed.

'And that final roar, by the way,' concluded Arnaud, driving the definitive nail into René's bear-shaped coffin. 'That was a yawn.'

René shook off Christian's hand and stormed out of the bar with laughter ringing in his ears. He was barely two steps away before he lit a cigarette. Today was not the right day to be giving up.

'But that doesn't solve the problem,' Christian pointed out once the noise in the bar had abated and the figure of the furiously smoking plumber had disappeared from view. 'Where are we going to house Monsieur Petit?'

Serge stared at his deputy mayor, his composure of moments before replaced by confusion. 'We discussed this, didn't we?'

It was pitiful. Almost pleading.

He's an old man, thought Christian with a wave of unexpected sympathy for this behemoth of local politics who had ruled Fogas for a quarter of a century, so often an adversary rather than a friend. And Christian, not having a duplicitous bone in his body, had no relief to offer him.

'Er . . .'

'Yes, you did.'

Christian turned to Véronique, eyebrows raised.

'You told me about it,' she continued, staring at the farmer and willing him to play along.

'I must have forgotten. Remind me what we decided again?'

Véronique smiled. 'You suggested Monsieur Petit stay in the flat next to mine. It's vacant for the foreseeable future.'

'Excellent idea!' Serge Papon slapped Christian on the back before he had a chance to protest. 'Let's take Monsieur Petit over there right away.'

'Arnaud, please call me Arnaud,' insisted the tracker as Serge Papon threw an arm around his waist, not being anywhere near tall enough to reach the man's shoulders, and ushered him out of the bar before the locals turned again.

'I'll go too,' Véronique said, bustling after them.

'Probably for the best.' Christian addressed her with rather more bite than he'd intended. 'Seeing as it's your plan after all!'

'This doesn't bode well,' said Josette as the bar door slammed shut and they watched the three figures head down the road to the old school building that now housed two flats owned by the commune. 'I can see the farmers and hunters being up in arms over this. And the man who's going to be at the centre of their protests is staying right here in La Rivière!'

'You're right. Look what they did in the village of Arbas when the mayor signed up to the reintroduction programme,' said Philippe Galy. 'Group of anti-bear protesters damn near ruined the place. Wrecked the town hall, threatened to kill the mayor too. Last thing we need is trouble like that. Serge should never have agreed to accommodate this man. We need to call a council meeting, Christian.'

'Sorry?' Christian pulled his attention away from the sight of Véronique smiling at something Arnaud Petit was saying to her.

'I said we need to call a meeting. This situation could be a real problem.'

'I agree,' said Christian, not quite understanding why he was so vexed at the arrival of the big man in his town. 'This could be a problem indeed.'

3

It didn't take long to settle Arnaud Petit into his flat. Serge could tell he was a man used to living without luxuries, which was fortunate given the condition of his new abode. Somehow, the routine clean organised by the town hall at the end of each tenancy had been overlooked and there were tracks of rodent activity punctuating the scratched wooden worktop in the kitchen, while a strong smell of damp was corroborated by the fungus blossoming in the shower.

The tracker hadn't seemed perturbed. He'd brought in his rucksack and declared himself at home. Serge had offered the services of Bernard Mirouze, the *cantonnier* for Fogas who took on all the odd jobs in the commune, but Arnaud had said that he was happy to get the place into shape himself. Which was probably just as well as Bernard was a bit of a liability when it came to anything more taxing than changing a light bulb. And even then, he'd been known to stick a finger in a live socket. Not that it seemed to give him any more spark!

Serge chuckled as he walked back towards the épicerie. But his flicker of good humour was extinguished as he approached the building and heard the lively sound of voices inside. They were all still in the bar. Probably talking about him again.

He threw a wave as he passed the window but didn't stop for his customary pastis. He had no desire to walk in there. Plus, his favourite tipple no longer tasted the same, the sharp anise tang almost indiscernible to him of late, rendering the opaque drink as tempting as a glass of cloudy water. So where now? He couldn't face the thought of going home. Their house, or rather, his house, felt so alien without Thérèse.

Across the road, the entrance to the garden centre was ablaze with colour; reds and purples and yellows were spilling out of the pots lined up in tiered rows outside. Weren't they chrysanthemums? They only appeared once a year in these parts. He checked his watch for the date and slapped his forehead.

'*Toussaint!*' he muttered. How could he have forgotten? Tomorrow was All Saints' Day. Thérèse had followed tradition every year, visiting the graves of her ancestors with bunches of chrysanthemums and bringing extra to place on the tombstones of his family to make up for his neglect. But this year it was up to him to observe the ritual. And he really ought to take some flowers to his wife.

He crossed over, trying to decide which colour Thérèse would have chosen. Something delicate. A pink, perhaps? He'd got within touching distance of the first rank of flowers when he saw a flash of flame-red hair through the crowd of people inside the gates.

Stephanie Morvan. His heart sank. He couldn't face her today. She'd been hassling him for months about providing more parking in the village to accommodate the growing number of people visiting her garden centre and he hadn't got around to it. He watched her dealing briskly with the long queue of customers and then he turned and walked empty-handed back to his car. Despite his reluctance, he decided to head for home, hoping that the drive would shake off the feeling of being lost that was always with him these days.

Depression, the doctor had said when Serge had gone in to get his blood pressure checked. Normal given the circumstances, apparently. He'd sounded so blasé about it, had tried to

24

give Serge a prescription for some pills that would supposedly make everything all right again. But Serge had refused to take it and had bought himself some vitamin tablets instead, confident they would do the trick and give him back his energy. The container remained on the table in the bag from the chemist's. He'd not even had the enthusiasm to open it.

He put the car in gear and took the narrow road which twisted around the back of the village towards the Romanesque church that marked the beginning of the meandering climb up to Fogas. As he passed the burnt out ruins of the post office, he felt another twinge of stress. He still hadn't chased up plans to reopen a branch in the commune following the fire last New Year's Eve. Véronique Estaque had asked him several times about the situation, desperate to resume her duties as postmistress. But he'd got no further than thinking about it. He'd meant to do it but lately . . .

For twenty-five years he'd ruled the commune as head of the Conseil Municipal, the local council made up of eleven elected councillors that was in charge of Fogas, and for several before that, he'd been deputy mayor. The political heartbeat of the place had been his life. Nothing had happened in the three villages that constituted his fiefdom without his knowledge. He liked to think that he'd governed with a paternal care – and that included doing some things without the knowledge of the very people he was leading. But he'd always had their interests at heart, even when it came to his more scheming side.

Recently, though, he found it difficult to raise enthusiasm for anything. He no longer fussed over what he ate, consuming mass-produced rubbish that Thérèse would have been mortified to have grace her table, and had to really summon an effort to have a shave of a morning. He, who'd once taken such pride in his appearance and had been rewarded with the attention of many a young lady from the surrounding valleys.

Which shamed him now. The way he'd let some of those women turn his head. More, even. He couldn't shake off the belief that his infidelities had driven Thérèse to an early grave.

Ironically, it was a lack of the very passion that had caused him to behave that way which was now afflicting him. And others were starting to notice. They'd been complaining about him when he walked into the bar, saying he wasn't up to the job of mayor. And he'd heard René suggest that they ought to get rid of him.

He knew René well enough to know that the stocky plumber was all bluster. He'd been on the council for several years and had always voted with his conscience, even if he was some-times a bit hot-headed. So Serge didn't really perceive him to be a threat. But there were plenty of his fellow councillors who wouldn't hesitate to get their knives out if they knew that Mayor Papon was vulnerable. And the good-hearted Christian Dupuy would only be able to protect him for so long.

What a valuable deputy he'd turned out to be. Serge had fought the farmer's election onto the council as ruthlessly as he could and done plenty over the intervening time to limit Christian's power, simply because he knew the man was incorruptible and therefore a threat to the position that Serge didn't want to give up. In the last twelve months though, he'd grown to respect his young rival. Would have been proud to have him as a son if God had thought to grace him with one.

But God had chosen to ignore Thérèse's frequent pleas for children, her countless novenas to St Gerard, patron saint of motherhood. A cynic when it came to religion, Serge hadn't even attempted to pray, knowing that if there was a deity look-ing over them, there was no way it would listen to a rogue like him. And so he was on his own now. He'd thought he could cope with that. Thought his obsession with Fogas politics would be enough to sustain him.

That, however, didn't seem to be the case. He just didn't care anymore.

He'd had to bluff earlier when reading the letter that he'd sent to Arnaud Petit. If he hadn't been staring at his own signature scribbled across the bottom of the page, he wouldn't have believed that he had been in contact with the man's department. He had no recollection of it until he made the connection with the bears. Then it had come flooding back. But too late.

Perhaps most galling of all was Véronique Estaque stepping in for him like that. He wasn't a man to take sympathy from anyone, but provoking it in her was even harder to bear. Known for her caustic tongue and straight-talking attitude, Véronique didn't suffer fools and he respected her for that. But he didn't want her charity.

Still, it had been quick thinking by the postmistress. And part of him had been amused to see Christian struggling to play along, guile not being an inherent part of his nature. Didn't make Serge any less embarrassed though. Having younger members of the community come to his rescue.

He crunched the gears down into second as he approached a particularly steep section of road, taking the turn to the left on automatic pilot after years of negotiating his way up and down the sides of the mountain that was home to Fogas, largest of the three villages in the commune. But today, as he turned the bend, veering too far over on the narrow strip of unmarked tarmac, he came face to face with a cattle truck.

There was a squeal of brakes on both sides and they came to rest millimetres apart, the other driver issuing a stream of expletives accompanied by subtitles in the form of gestures. Serge put up a shaking hand in apology and reversed the car into a small patch of verge that served as a passing place. He raised a hand again as the lorry started off, the driver still ranting, and waited a few moments before pulling back onto the road. And as he did so, he came to a decision.

He would serve out the end of the year but in January he would resign from his post as Mayor of Fogas and step down from the council. It was time.

The bar in La Rivière was quieter now, the midday rush of people returning from St Girons having decreased to a trickle. Christian Dupuy, however, was making no move to go home for lunch as he reasoned that no one could be expected to endure his mother's cooking twice a day. René had once quipped that Madame Dupuy was the only cook in the world who had misunderstood the concept of 'fusion' and had opted for the nuclear version. It was a fair enough comment seeing as the majority of dishes that emerged from her oven were reduced to black, smouldering lumps.

'He's slipping,' he said, referring to the events of the morning. 'Letting things slide.'

'It's to be expected.' Josette placed three coffees on the table and took a seat, glad of the chance to rest her legs. Her business had recently undergone a major expansion and while the new layout of the épicerie and bar was proving a success, sometimes Saturdays were almost too much for her to cope with. She was really beginning to feel her age. And, although she was loath to admit it, she was missing the company of her nephew, Fabian, who now spent every weekend across the road helping Stephanie get her fledgling garden centre off the ground.

Young love, she mused. She could remember it well. Which was why she had sympathy for the mayor of Fogas, despite their past history.

'Serge has suffered a huge loss. He's bound to feel adrift.'

'But you weren't like this when Jacques died! I mean, you kept this place going all on your own.'

Josette took a sip of coffee to avoid answering. If only people knew, she thought. She'd been just as racked with grief when her husband had suddenly dropped dead of a heart attack the year before. The difference was, she'd only had a few days in which to mourn him. Because on the day of his funeral, he'd reappeared. Not in a Christlike rose-again kind of way. More in a ghost-sitting-in-the-fireplace kind of way.

She cast a glance over to the inglenook where the spectral presence of Jacques was inclined to spend his time, watching life in the commune pass by. His white hair was vibrant against the soot of the chimney and the outline of his slender body was indistinct, as though someone hadn't coloured him in right up to the edges. He was listening intently to their conversation and no doubt fretting that he couldn't contribute, his after-life existence not coming equipped with the ability to talk.

'Everyone's different,' she said, with massive understatement.

'I'll have to take your word for it,' Christian continued. 'I can't imagine what it's like to spend your life with someone special and then lose them. Especially as I've reached the grand age of forty-one without finding anyone who remotely fits that description!'

Annie Estaque, the third person at the table, emitted a gruff sound that locals knew was her version of laughter, imbued with the broad accent of the Ariège region.

'Norrr will you,' she said. 'Not stuck up a mountain farrrm-ing all yourrr life. Takes someone special indeed to want to take that on.'

'Touché!' Not wanting, or needing, yet another lecture from a well-meaning soul on his disastrous love life, Christian steered the conversation back to Serge Papon. 'But not every-one will be so understanding of our mayor's plight. It was clear he had no idea this Arnaud Petit was arriving and even less of an idea as to where to accommodate him. But for Véronique's quick thinking, Serge would have been left looking like a fool.'

'She gets her wits from you, Annie!'

'I wouldn't bet on it,' Annie muttered enigmatically into her coffee.

'Talk of the devil.' Josette tipped her head towards the door where Véronique was just coming in. 'Coffee, love?'

'I'll get it.' Véronique put a gentle hand on Josette's shoulder to prevent her getting up. 'Anyone else want a refill?'

Annie held out her cup with an unapologetic grin.

'Might have known you would, Maman!' Véronique dropped a kiss on the weathered cheek of her mother as she passed.

'You know which blend to use,' cautioned Josette. 'Don't want her climbing the walls this afternoon.'

'So what's he like, then?' Christian asked, deliberately focusing his eyes on the black and white photos of Fogas in times gone by that lined the wall behind the bar as Véronique bent over to deposit the old coffee grounds in the bin. He'd noticed a tendency of late for his gaze to linger over the contours of her backside whenever the opportunity presented itself and it was a habit he was determined to conquer. In the last twelve months she had become a good friend and she deserved better than this uncharacteristically lecherous behaviour.

'Arnaud? He's lovely.'

'*Arnaud*? On first-name terms already are you?'

Immediately regretting the words, Christian wondered what it was about the newcomer that made him feel thirteen all over again. But if Véronique sensed the petulance in his question, she chose to ignore it.

'The flat was a bit of a mess though. Turns out Serge didn't get round to organising a clean-up after the last tenant left. Yet *another* thing he's let slip.' She raised an eyebrow in Christian's direction as she approached the table with the drinks. 'It's not good enough.'

'I hearrr you werrre standing up forrr him earrrlierrr. Why so harrrd on him now?'

'I don't know. He was so defenceless and confused this morning. It felt like attacking a lame rabbit.'

Annie snorted. 'Now that's one descrrription of Serrrge Papon I neverrr thought I'd hearrr!'

'I think we're overreacting.' Josette pushed her glasses up her nose and rounded her shoulders as though expecting to be shouted down. 'After all, apart from forgetting that Monsieur Petit was coming today, what has he done that's so dreadful?'

'Well, he failed to tell everyone about the problem with the bears in the first place,' Christian began. 'Even if the sighting was in Sarrat, he should have mentioned it at a council meeting. Otherwise he infuriates the likes of René.'

'And he's made no move to sort out the mess with La Poste,' said Véronique. 'People are getting really frustrated about it. But what can I tell them? It's ridiculous. I'm still getting paid to be the commune postmistress but I have no post office to run!'

'Have you trrried contacting them yourrrself?'

Véronique shot her mother a glance that would have disconcerted many a woman. But Annie Estaque was made of sterner stuff.

'Yes, Maman, I have. And much good it's done me. I was on the phone to them this morning but they pass me from pillar to post, then tell me I need to send copies of any documentation they can think of. In triplicate. If I didn't know better, I'd say they were stalling. But I can't think why.'

'I'll try to have a word with them next week,' offered Christian. 'See if my position on the council pulls any strings.'

'That'd be great. I've asked Pascal several times but he's always so dismissive. I come away feeling like I've been patted on the head from a great height!'

Christian nodded, well acquainted with the arrogant ways of his fellow deputy mayor. But Josette wasn't convinced.

'It still seems like we're making a drama out of nothing. I mean, it's rather harsh to be judging the man on these trivial matters when he's given us twenty-five years of good service. Even if we aren't all fans of his methods.' She looked towards her husband with her final words. Jacques had long disapproved of Serge Papon's machinations – a disapproval he'd managed to carry over into the hereafter, as his scowl now testified.

'Actually, something else came up when I was at the flat. I was opening shutters to air the place while Arnaud sorted out his rucksack and I heard him talking to Serge. I didn't mean to eavesdrop—'

Annie snorted for the second time and even Christian and Josette had to laugh, Véronique's reputation as the fount of all Fogas gossip not having been gained through an aversion to listening where she shouldn't.

'Okay! Guilty as charged.' Véronique grinned good-naturedly. 'So, I heard Arnaud ask why there hadn't been any signs up in the forest to warn hunters away from the area where he was conducting his research. Serge didn't seem to know what he was talking about. Then when Arnaud produced a copy of the letter his department had sent explaining that it was the responsibility of the town hall to mark out the area, Serge reacted as if he'd never seen it before.'

Christian let out a low whistle. 'So that's how René and his colleagues stumbled upon the bear! It's a wonder no one was hurt.'

Véronique nodded. 'And guess who'd be responsible if

someone had been? From what I can gather, the town hall would have been liable.'

'So we'd all end up footing the bill.' Christian turned to Josette. 'Still think we're being unfair?'

'No, I suppose not. But what are our options? Getting a new mayor isn't that easy. We'd have to apply to have Serge removed and that would be a lengthy and acrimonious procedure. As a member of the Conseil Municipal, I don't want to go down that route.'

Christian put an arm around her frail shoulders. 'Neither do I. But after today, there will be some on the council who are prepared to. Word will get back to Pascal and he'll be sure to make the most of this.'

'Huh! You mean his vixen of a wife, Fatima, will.' Annie drank the last of her coffee, its acrid undertones no match for the bitter taste that was already in her mouth. This was a business she had no stomach for, her long-standing enmity towards Serge Papon having mellowed in recent months.

'Maybe one of us ought to have a word with him,' Josette volunteered.

'And say what? "We think you're past it. Resign as mayor"?' Christian ran his hand through his hair, leaving curls sticking out in all directions. 'Sorry. I just don't need this at the moment. But you're right, Josette. One of us should talk to him. Give him a chance.'

'So, who's going to put the bell on the cat?' Véronique turned to the other women and then, as one, they all looked at Christian.

'Oh no! Not me. No way. You set me against him not long ago and that was bad enough.'

'You can't ask Maman and Josette to take this on. Not at their age.'

'Thanks!' The two older women spoke in disgruntled unison.

'That still leaves you, Véronique,' Christian countered. 'You've got more reason to push him than the rest of us.'

Josette added her voice to his argument. 'And perhaps it would be better coming from a woman. Given his history!'

'You think so? Well, I could try—'

'No!' Annie's strident tones cut Véronique short. 'Not Vérrronique.'

'Why ever not?' asked Christian.

'Because she's—' Annie swallowed the words that had been on the tip of her tongue. '—She's not on the council.'

'Good point, Maman. Things like that count with Serge.' Véronique turned back to Christian and he felt the full force of her gaze, her hand warm on his bare arm. His resolve evaporated.

'Okay, okay. I'll do it. But if it backfires . . .'

'It won't,' Josette said adamantly. 'It'll turn out to be a fuss over nothing. You wait and see.'

'Bonjour, anyone serving?' A farmer from Sarrat poked his head through the archway and, spotting the deputy mayor, crossed the bar to shake hands. 'Christian! Haven't seen you in ages.'

'Bonjour!' Christian greeted him warmly. 'Moving your cattle already?' He indicated the truck parked outside, the soft noses of cows protruding through the slats.

'Yeah. The forecast isn't looking great so I'm bringing them over from Fogas. Damn near came a cropper on the road down, though.'

'Some young lad going too fast?'

'Just the opposite. Your mayor driving in a daydream. Came round the corner on the wrong side and nearly took both of us into the gorge. Seriously, he's not fit to be on the road. You ought to tell him to quit before he kills someone.'

Christian turned to Josette. 'See now why we're worried?'

'All the more reason why you should talk to him!'

'It wasn't appropriate.'

'What do you mean it wasn't appropriate? What can be more appropriate than carrying out orders—'

Arnaud Petit held the phone away from his ear, reducing his ranting boss to a squawk, and stared out of the window at sleepy La Rivière. It was pretty, he had to admit. The road winding down parallel to the river, the stone houses with their slate roofs, the épicerie and bar with the lovely terrace, and the statuesque church at the back of the village, its simple belfry more Spanish than French.

It had been a stroke of luck finding the flat. The department had tried plenty of other villages in the area, none of which had been willing to take in four researchers from the bear programme, afraid of the protests it could unleash. And the violence. Although he got the impression that Mayor Serge Papon wouldn't have been swayed by such fears, even if he couldn't remember signing the letter of consent in the first place.

Of course, in the wake of today's events, the other researchers wouldn't be coming. Arnaud had got a text earlier to say they'd broken camp and were heading back to headquarters, all three of them struck down by a bout of sickness which they'd attributed to something they'd eaten. Possible, given they'd been camping rough for a week. But the bottle of *eau de vie* which a local had given them the night before was more likely to be the cause. The tracker had resisted the temptation of the homemade hooch, opting instead for a walk in the forest. And considering how things had turned out, he was grateful. Not only had his colleagues been obliged to leave prematurely, after what he'd done this morning they would have no need to return as had been planned. At least not until the spring.

The bells tolled the hour and he let his eyes follow the sides of the mountains which rose up from behind the church, trees in hues of red and gold covering the slopes. She was up there somewhere. Hopefully none the worse for her enforced sleep.

'—Arnaud? Arnaud? Can you hear me?'

'Sorry . . . poor reception . . . line . . . cut . . . off.' Arnaud ended the call and placed the phone on the table. It rang again almost immediately but he ignored it. His boss needed time to see that the right decision had been made, even if it went against regulations. But then Arnaud Petit had never been a man for abiding by the rules. Which was why he was so good at his job.

Tracking was his life. He'd acquired his skills living among an Iroquois tribe in Quebec, stalking caribou, learning to blend into a forest, to live for weeks on only that provided by Mother Nature and to move as imperceptibly as the wind. He'd become so adept they'd given him the name Silent Bear, in acknowledgement of both his ability and his size.

Returning to Europe, he set up as a freelance, employed by wildlife agencies across the continent, tracking wolves in Sweden, wildcats in Scotland. He'd even been enlisted to help find missing people. And then he got the call from France.

He'd debated not taking the position, not being in any hurry to return to the land of his birth. But the job interested him. Overseen by the government agency which had been given the unenviable task of reintroducing brown bears to the Pyrenees, he was to work alongside researchers, using his skills to find the bears they wanted to study and to interpret evidence at the sites of alleged bear attacks.

His new colleagues were wary at first. Resentful of his presence and the implication that they were inferior trackers, they

36

were also outraged at his lack of a scientific background, his lack of a formal education. It was only as they worked with him that they began to appreciate his talents. And when they heard that he'd even been known to find his prey in the dark, they demanded to put the claim to the test.

They'd blindfolded him and dropped him in the woods to track another man. Not wanting to appear too arrogant, he'd had to make it look harder than it was. He'd spent a long time running his fingers over the compressions left in the man's tracks. Made a big show of finding the man's trail through broken branches. They'd been amazed when, still blindfolded, he walked up to the man and placed a hand on his shoulder in what they considered record time. What he never told them was that they'd made a fatal error. They'd forgotten to tell the prey not to wear aftershave. With a sense of smell more developed than the best sommelier, for Arnaud it had been like following an arc lamp through the trees. But his reputation in the unit had been established.

They wouldn't be so impressed with him today. Not when word got round about his actions.

Earlier that month, his department had dispatched a team to the Ariège to investigate claims of a rogue bear in a couple of neighbouring communities. When efforts to locate the animal had proved futile, Arnaud had been sent for.

His orders had been clear: find the bear that was causing all the problems. Once found, it was to be tagged with a radio collar and then monitored from the flat in La Rivière. After that, it would decide its own fate. If it continued to enter villages and attack sheep, then the bear would be exterminated.

Arnaud had arrived in the Fogas valley a week ago and things had started off well. Down at the Sarrat bridge, about a mile out of La Rivière on the road to St Girons, he'd discovered a rear left footprint in a soft patch of mud next to the bins. It had been trampled on by several people, the heel portion rendered almost indistinct, but even so, from the length of it and the size of the pads, he was certain it was the print of an adult male bear.

But the bear had proved elusive and when Arnaud next picked up a trail, in the forest above Picarets, it was that of a female. Which was when the problems started. Despite there being no proof that she was their culprit, his colleagues had overruled his objections and insisted that he track her so that she could be fitted with a radio collar.

Based on half-prints left in dried puddles and bark tattered by sharp claws, Arnaud dutifully studied her pattern of behaviour and set up a hide on a high plateau where the team spent their days. Watching. Waiting. But thanks to the mystery illness which had befallen his colleagues, when the female bear had finally made her appearance that morning, Arnaud was alone. Already uneasy about what he was being asked to do, realising she was pregnant was the last straw. So on approaching the sleeping animal, he'd made a snap decision. He would take a sample of her DNA, but he wouldn't subject her to the tracking collar.

For him, it was clear-cut. Miel, as he'd officially christened the bear in his report owing to her dark-honey-coloured coat, was innocent until proven guilty. And in his court, the evidence to date was not sufficient to warrant such an intrusion on her life. Or her first pregnancy. Plus, given her condition, she would soon be going into hibernation high on a hillside, at an altitude well removed from any temptation to steal food from people's bins or rustle the odd chicken. Therefore, let her have her winter sleep in peace and let the hysteria that always surrounded any sightings of bears in these parts die down.

Knowing he'd be on his final warning after his stunt today, Arnaud had worked out a way to mollify his boss. Making use of the flat that had been rented for the now redundant monitoring team, he would offer to stay on in the area to find the male bear that he was convinced was the real offender. He'd promise to do everything by the book, including monitoring the ridiculous little cameras the researchers had installed in various parts of the forest, and even volunteer to liaise with local media and schools in promotional work which he normally shunned. Then come the spring, when Miel emerged from her den with her cubs, if there were renewed complaints from the adjacent communities and Arnaud had failed to detect the presence of another bear, the DNA he'd taken this morning would quickly ascertain if she were to blame.

The phone rang again and he answered without speaking.

'Arnaud? Arnaud, I know you're there.' A long sigh issued from his beleaguered boss. 'Let's talk about this, okay?'

Arnaud pulled out a chair and sat down. He was more than happy to talk about it. Knowing there was nothing else that could be done.

'I hope you didn't mind me dropping in on you at home like this. It's just the others don't really appreciate the urgency of the situation.'

'No, not at all. That's what I'm here for.' Pascal Souquet, first deputy mayor of Fogas, escorted his visitor into the hallway, aware of a surreptitious movement to his left. An ear being hastily removed from the partially opened door, no doubt. As he watched Philippe Galy put on his jacket, he marvelled at the piece of fortune that had fallen into his lap.

'So you'll persuade Serge to call a council meeting?' asked the bee-keeper.

'Even better than that. I'll get a majority behind me and schedule a meeting myself. This should have been discussed by all of us.'

'I agree. I just don't think Christian has the heart to confront Serge right now.'

Pascal made what he hoped was a sympathetic face. 'Well, that's the difference experience brings you. Christian is letting his emotions get the better of him. He'll learn.'

'I'm sure he will. But I don't want it to be at the expense of my business. This needs sorting. And soon.'

'You have my word it will be.'

'Good. I knew I could rely on you.'

The two men shook hands and as Philippe turned to leave he spotted the boots on the rack next to the front door.

'I didn't know you hunted!' he said, taking in the glossy Le Chameau leather and reappraising the man before him, who was known to be more at home in a Parisian salon than on the hills of the Ariège. 'Didn't think that would be your thing.'

'It isn't . . . I mean . . . I don't. They're for walking.'

Philippe laughed. 'They must be paying deputy mayors too much if you forked out for those just to stroll around here!'

Pascal managed to keep a smile on his face until his guest stepped over the threshold into the late afternoon. With the sun already low behind the mountains, the village of Fogas was bathed in a beautiful mellow glow, the peaks on the western horizon dark silhouettes. But Pascal had no appreciation for the miracle that was nature in the Ariège. He promptly shut the door.

'Did he suspect?'

Pascal leapt in the air. 'Fatima!'

His wife was standing right behind him, her thin face severe, reminding him of a ferret he'd once seen in a pet shop in Paris. Eyes glittering, it had been gnawing on the metal bars of its cage with a demented determination. He'd been terrified. Like he was now.

'Well? Did he?'

'I don't think so.'

'So what are you going to do?'

'What we agreed. Undermine Serge any way I can.'

'Are you going to call *him*?'

'Yes. I have to. This is our chance.'

Fatima stared at her husband as though assessing the quality of the material he was made from. 'You're in over your head. Remember I said that,' she warned before walking back into the kitchen.

How could he forget? He reached for his mobile and dialled the number, clearing his throat in anticipation.

'Yes?' That voice. So cold. Calculated. Deadly.

'It's me. I have news.'

'Just a moment.'

Pascal heard the raucous background noise give way to the gentle burble of flowing water and knew that the man had stepped outside the hunting lodge, a ramshackle building which bordered the river at the far end of the village of La Rivière and was the meeting place for all the hunters in the area.

'What news?'

'The fourth man. The tracker. I know where he is. He's staying at the old school.'

A sharp intake of breath, which Pascal didn't know whether to attribute to surprise or the inhalation on a cigarette.

'You're certain?'

'Yes.'

'Perfect. Just perfect.'

The line clicked and Pascal was left listening to the static of a dead call.

It was falling into place, he thought. The months of preparation, the clandestine night-time meetings. It was all going to pay off. Soon he would be mayor of Fogas and beyond that . . . It was the dream he had been spun. So much loftier than his original ambitions. A position that would guarantee him a place on the regional council and perhaps even more. But it meant having patience and trust.

He picked up the boots which had so nearly given him away and put them in the cupboard under the stairs, out of sight. In the same way, he closed the door on the nagging voices in his head, voices that reminded him his wife was never wrong.

4

Véronique Estaque loved the simple ritual of *Toussaint*. Straight after mass on Sunday, which had been celebrated up in Sarrat this week – the two communes long having been deemed capable of sharing a priest by the diocese no matter how severe their secular differences – she made her way to the church in La Rivière, weighed down by pots of chrysanthemums. Averting her eyes as she approached the charred shell which was all that remained of her former home and workplace, she crossed the road and entered the graveyard.

Wrapped around the rotund church, which was much smaller than its Sarrat counterpart, and all the more atmospheric for it in Véronique's mind, the graveyard was already ablaze with colour. White angels gazed impassively down at the seas of reds and yellows lapping at their feet and the more sombre tombstones of grey granite were bedecked with flowers like tables awaiting guests at a banquet.

Véronique picked her way through the haphazard maze of graves, stopping to greet one or two people as she crossed to the far corner where the procession of granite ended, leaving untended land, earmarked for her peers no doubt. It was at this final frontier that the members of the Estaque family had been buried for generations. They were one of the oldest families in the area and Annie often boasted that an Estaque had built the first house in Picarets. Clearly his descendants hadn't spared much to commemorate the poor man though, as an austere stone cross on a small plinth was all that marked out the last resting place of her Estaque forefathers. Who were in fact the only ancestors that Véronique had any knowledge of, her maternal grandmère having been a refugee from Spain and Maman never having disclosed the identity of the man who had left her an unmarried mother in a small mountain community that had long memories and sharp tongues.

Growing up, it was something Véronique had been painfully conscious of. On the rare occasions when Maman had yielded to her demands that they take part in the *Toussaint* festival, her youthful pleasure in the day had always been tempered by an awareness that she was different. In the single classroom that constituted the village school, she was the only one who didn't have a papa – a distinction never more conspicuous than on the day when ancestors are celebrated.

While her classmates flitted from grave to grave scattering flowers, Véronique would be confined to the restrictive parameters of the Estaque burial plot. Her natural curiosity would then lead her to break the unspoken rule; she would begin to question Maman about her father. Invariably, the day would end badly, Maman annoyed by her pestering on a topic that was out of bounds and Véronique sullen with resentment at a life which already seemed unjust.

Eventually, realising that her lopsided observance of the custom was yet another weapon to hand to the schoolyard bullies who already possessed an extensive enough arsenal to make her life hell, she stopped taking part. And Maman, having no time for gods or spirits or idle gossip, was all too happy to oblige. But on returning to Fogas after college, Véronique had revived the tradition, at first trying to persuade Maman to accompany her. After years of brusque refusals, she no longer made the effort.

So it was with some surprise that when she reached the

stone cross she noticed a simple posy of autumn crocuses already adorning the grave. She put the chrysanthemums on the ground, their opulence looking out of place against this humble, homemade bouquet, and as she straightened up she heard a familiar voice.

'Thought you might be herrre.'

'Maman!' She leaned in to kiss her mother's cheeks, a rush of pleasure catching her off guard. 'Not like you to get this close to a church!'

'Not against thc law is it?' Annie sniffed defensively and then softened her tone, gesturing at the bursting pink and burgundy blooms that Véronique was arranging. 'They look lovely.'

'They brighten the place up.'

'And they'rrre biggerrr than anyone else's!'

'Why, I hadn't noticed!' A wicked grin revealed Véronique to be an Estaque to the core as she knelt to pull up the few weeds that straggled around the edge of the tombstone.

'Yourrr new neighbourrr settling in, then?'

'Arnaud? I wouldn't know. Haven't seen him since yesterday afternoon. He doesn't strike me as the kind of man who'll be round for coffee and a chat on a regular basis.'

'I hearrrd he's quite good-looking.'

Véronique stared at her mother. Had she really just heard that note of curiosity from a woman who for so long had seemed indifferent to the actions of her only child?

'I suppose you could say that.'

'Not yourrr type then?'

Véronique's jaw dropped. 'My type? Since when have you been concerned with my type?'

Annie shoved her hands into the pockets of her fleece, the one Véronique had bought her two Christmases ago and never seen since, and turned away, smarting at the reproach.

Damn it. Véronique yanked the weeds out with renewed enthusiasm. What was it about *Toussaint* that always brought out the worst in them? She shouldn't have been so curt. Not when Maman was making an effort. Ever since the night of the fire when Véronique had almost lost her life, there had been a noticeable thaw in their relationship and the majority of that was down to her mother.

Full of remorse, which in true Estaque style only made her more irritable, she grabbed the last handful of leaves.

'Ouch!'

'That's a nettle.'

Véronique bit her tongue.

'Herrre.' Annie took her hand, which was already coming up in welts, and rubbed it with a couple of weeds. 'Dock leaves. Always worrrk.'

And just like that, Véronique was a child again. Running home covered in red blotches, and Maman breaking off from the milking to apply dock leaves to the worst areas. She hadn't asked how her daughter had got so many stings. Likewise, Véronique hadn't revealed that she'd been pushed into a bed of nettles by one of her classmates as his friends roared encouragement. Or what words he'd used to describe her mother as she lay there, afraid to get up.

She tipped her head forward to shield her tear-filled eyes.

'Come on.' A hard hand brushed softly across her hair. 'Let's go get a coffee. Even the barrr on a Sunday will have morrre life than herrre!'

As they turned to go, they saw Serge Papon standing a few metres away, eyes fixed on a cherubic angel cradling a black granite slab which bore the name of Thérèse Papon in gold lettering. He looked totally lost.

'Bonjour.'

Véronique's greeting startled him.

'Oh! Véronique. Annie. Bonjour.'

He kissed them both and Annie noticed that the pungent smell of aftershave for which he had once been famous was absent. And his cheeks had the rough feel of stubble. Not that she could complain. At her age, it might not be long before she was stubbly herself!

'You well?'

He nodded, a game smile on his face, but she could see the effort it was taking. He didn't look good. The heavyset features of old were gaunt, leaving his brow more prominent than ever.

'Very well. Yes. Very well. Just dropped by . . .' He gestured futilely at the new gravestone. 'Forgot to bring flowers though. Still, some kind soul left a bunch.'

'How curious,' began Véronique, looking at the clutch of crocuses that lay at the feet of the cherub. 'Maman, did you—'

'Lovely headstone,' Annie interrupted. 'Thérrrèse would have liked it.'

'Yes! I hated the thought of leaving her here alone. Wanted someone to watch over her. And the man at the funeral home suggested a baby angel. Thought that was fitting somehow. You know . . . after all our troubles . . . a baby . . .'

His words petered out. Then he sighed.

'Can't believe I forgot the bloody flowers,' he muttered. 'Typical.'

Never articulate at the best of times and sensing that there was no need for words here, Annie remained silent, assessing the man who had altered so much in the last year.

He was unshaven, his clothes were crumpled, and he hadn't been to the barber in a while, strands of grey hair curling over his ears. But it was his shoulders that marked the biggest change. No longer stiffened with the resolution that had made him such a dynamic leader, they now slumped towards the ground.

He was a man with no pride left in himself. Or in the world around him.

She tried not to. But it was instinctive. To compare this shadow of a man with the vibrant deputy mayor of thirty-six years ago. The one with the distinctive jawline, the strong hands, the roguish grin and that easy confidence that springs from self-belief. The one who had women flocking after him. Her included. Although she hadn't flocked. More like she'd been snared. But still, the result was the same.

'Here, take these.'

Annie looked up from her memories to see Véronique handing over the pot of pink chrysanthemums that she had brought for the Estaque grave.

'Are you sure?' Serge already had them in his hands, not waiting for the nod of assent, his face suffused with delight. 'Pink, too! Her favourite colour.'

He placed them carefully next to the small bouquet of crocuses and then embraced Véronique.

'She's a credit to you, Annie,' he said gruffly, as he released her now red-faced daughter.

Annie was lost for words.

'We're going to the bar, aren't we, Maman,' babbled Véronique into the awkward silence that followed. 'Won't you join us?'

'No, no. Not today. Got a few things to do. Up at the town hall.'

'On a Sunday?'

'Yes. I've been getting a bit behind. What with every-thing . . .' He flicked a hand at the cherub, now almost hidden by the profusion of blooms. 'But give my regards to Josette.'

Recognising the dismissal for what it was, the two women took their leave and traced the path through the jumble of gravestones.

'You didn't mind that I gave him the flowers?' Véronique asked once they were out of earshot.

'Mind? Why would I?'

'Because you always made it clear that you didn't care much for Thérèse Papon.'

Annie felt the words like a punch to the stomach.

'I neverrr disliked the woman,' she muttered. 'It's complicated.'

'Clearly,' replied Véronique with the sharp tongue Annie knew she had inherited from both parents. 'So complicated that you left a bunch of crocuses on her grave. Honestly, Maman, I wonder if I will ever understand you.'

And with that Véronique strode ahead, leaving her mother to close the gate.

Complicated didn't even begin to cover it, thought Annie.

She took one last glance towards where Serge was still standing. It was getting more and more difficult to bear, this secret that she'd carried at Thérèse Papon's behest for thirty-six years. Only yesterday in the bar she'd almost blurted out the truth. Which was what Thérèse had wanted in the end. For the truth to be revealed.

'Why can't life be simple?' she grumbled as she rattled the gate into place, knowing herself well enough to recognise that she was afraid. And she was. Terrified. But it had to be done.

'I'll tell them,' she promised to the clouds above, not believing for one moment in an afterlife but not knowing where else to look when communicating with the dead. 'When I see a way how to, I'll tell them both.'

Up in Picarets, in a farmhouse that stood beyond the village where the road climbed steeply up the mountain, Christian Dupuy had made a confession of his own. It had taken him months to pluck up the courage. But finally he'd done it and now he was assessing the impact.

The kitchen table looked no different. Same old length of rough pine, nicked and stained from years of use. His mother's armchair by the woodburner hadn't altered, stuffing spilling out of the side where a dog, long since buried, had attacked it as a puppy. And the oak sideboard which lined one wall still groaned under the accumulated weight of memories that jostled for position across its surface: a snow globe with a plastic skier on the piste from the Alps; a doll in traditional dress from Mont St Michel; an empty tin of Breton biscuits; two toy cows wearing T-shirts proclaiming their love for the Cantal. It was a virtual map of France sent from holidaying sons and daughters and grandchildren, his parents never having ventured much beyond the borders of the Ariège. Tied to the farm, they'd never gone much further than the twin valleys of Fogas, in fact.

But all that was about to change.

After months of fretting and trying to stave off the inevitable, Christian had sat his parents down and explained as gently as possible that they had no option but to sell the farm. That he'd chosen *Toussaint* to reveal to his father he was going to have to forsake his ancestral home, the place where he'd been born seventy years ago, was an irony not lost on the big farmer.

He'd become aware of the problems a year ago when the summer had proven less bountiful than normal, the price he'd been offered for his livestock lower than it had ever been. Meanwhile the cost of feeding the three of them had soared and when he'd got the bill for the heating oil, he'd wondered if they'd poured liquid gold into the tank by mistake. The following spring his fears were confirmed. For the first time ever, the farm had made a loss.

Thinking it was just a blip, he'd consulted Fabian Servat, Josette's nephew who knew a thing or two about accounting, and although the picture the tall Parisian had painted was bleak, there had been the perennial hope of another summer which was just around the corner. Deciding to give the coming season a chance, he'd investigated ways of maximising revenue from his limited acreage, the limits imposed by the geography of the region which made large-scale farming impossible.

It had proven futile. Oh, there were plenty of options, like going organic, which Stephanie at the garden centre had advocated. He'd be able to ask a premium price for his meat and perhaps even cut out the middleman and supply restaurants directly. But the certification process took time. It would be several years before he'd see any return from his investment. And that was the other thing; it required investment. Quite a substantial amount for a man who was already mired in loans and with a bank that was refusing to offer any more.

Problem was, he didn't have time. What he needed was an instant remedy, a magic wand to increase the size of his farm so he could compete with both the giant agribusinesses that dominated the north of the country and the imports of cheap meat that were flooding in from Eastern Europe. And when the much anticipated summer had failed to deliver, there was no point in struggling any further.

Of course, coming to this conclusion didn't stop him railing against the inequity of it all. Having inherited his father's lifelong passion for socialism, Christian was incensed that while local farmers struggled to get fair recompense for their labours as the supermarkets squeezed the lifeblood out of the region, the very same supermarkets were registering record profits as the cost of food escalated. The injustice was enough to drive a man insane. And that was before he even got started on the bankers.

He watched the tabby cat twitching on the armchair,

blissfully unaware of life's hardships as it chased elusive mice through the cobwebs of its dreams, and he would have given all he had to swap places with it right then.

'Everything?' his mother finally asked. 'The house? The farm?'

Christian nodded, noticing the tremble in her left hand as she grasped the edge of the table. His father, who'd taken the news far more stoically than Christian had anticipated, reached over and covered her stout fingers with his own. He might as well have plunged a knife into his son's heart.

'You know Christian adores the place as much as we do, love. He won't have suggested this lightly. If he says selling is necessary, then so be it.'

Josephine Dupuy straightened her shoulders and gave a firm tip of her head in response.

'You're right, André.'

'I usually am,' he replied, which elicited the desired smile from his wife.

'And who knows? Maybe it's for the best.' she continued, with the pragmatism that made her the quintessential farmer's wife. 'God knows, Christian, you've given up more than just years looking after this place, and us into the bargain.'

Christian knew what she was alluding to, although he'd never for one moment blamed his prolonged bachelorhood on the farm. He wouldn't have had it any other way. If by chance he did manage to find the woman of his dreams and, by a second chance he was still a farmer, she would have to learn to live with it, as his passion for his land was stronger than any possible love for a woman. Of that, despite his limited knowledge of the ways of *amour*, the big man was sure.

'So, we should start looking for a smaller place?'

'I'm sorry, Maman. I didn't want it to come to this.'

'You have nothing to apologise for, son! Not to your mother, nor to me. If it wasn't for you, we would have had to sell up years ago.'

His father's voice wavered and Christian felt a surge of affection for the ageing man who had never been cut out to be a farmer. An idealist, he'd been destined for a life in politics, having secured a scholarship to university just as the war in Algeria was fracturing the country and de Gaulle was coming back to power. It was a heady time for anyone who was politically aware and André Dupuy couldn't wait to be in the thick of it.

Then, a couple of months before the start of term, his only brother was killed when his car skidded out of control on a treacherous mountain road. André had dutifully unpacked his bag, cancelled his accommodation in Toulouse and shouldered the burden of running the farm.

He'd made an average farmer. More at home discussing the infighting that blighted French socialism than the benefits of a new milking machine, he'd done his best. But he'd grown to love the place and the land that he'd initially viewed as a millstone. Not wanting to force any of his children to make the choices he'd had to, he'd been overjoyed when one of his sons had shown genuine interest in taking the mantle on from him.

Which was why Christian couldn't shake off the feeling that he'd let his father down.

'Annie was saying that the place next to the Rogalles might be going up for sale,' Josephine said, trying to lighten the mood. 'The cousins who inherited it have finally agreed on who gets what and it should be on the market in a month or so. We should have a look.'

'Old Widow Loubet's house? It's a wreck!' exclaimed Christian, thinking of the near-derelict house with the sagging roof that stood forlorn on the square in Picarets. 'You'll be able to afford better than that once we sell this place and pay off the debts.'

'Well, I know it needs a bit of work, but you could do that. And it's big enough for the three of us.'

'It won't need to be that big,' said Christian gently.

His parents stared at him and then at each other and his mother's eyes welled up.

'You're leaving?'

'What else can I do? There's no work for failed farmers around here.'

'But where will you go?'

'There's the chance of a job at the Airbus factory in Toulouse. I'll try there.'

His father cleared his throat. 'You've got to do what's best son, we understand that. But don't rush into anything you might regret. If I've learnt anything over the last seventy years, it's that this land has a way of getting under your skin and if you leave it, you might never find true happiness.'

'He's right, Christian. You'll have a place with us for as long as it takes you to get sorted.'

'Thanks, Maman.'

A shrill beeping interrupted them.

'Merde!' Josephine leapt up and started wafting a tea towel under the smoke alarm that Christian had fitted only a month ago but which now sounded on an almost daily basis.

'Don't worry about the alarm, woman!' roared André Dupuy with years of suffering in his voice. 'Rescue my blasted lunch!'

As the familiar commotion carried on around him, his mother's inability to cook meaning that no mealtime ever passed unnoticed, Christian headed out into the fresh air.

It had been a long morning. One of the hardest he'd ever known. He was more exhausted than when he'd had to take down the big pine tree in the far field on his own, and more worried than the night Sarko the bull had escaped and nearly killed himself.

Sarko, his Limousin bull, who was just visible down in the lower field, a solid brown mass in stark relief against the mountains in the background. He'd have to be sold, too. But who'd buy him? He was well known to be the most cantankerous beast in the Ariège-Pyrénées and his repeated, and often successful, attempts at escape made him a liability in a society that was becoming litigation happy. Plus he had a vicious temper.

As if in response, a loud bellow came from the distant pasture and Christian felt a tug at his heartstrings. He'd grown to love the old bugger. Couldn't imagine a life without Sarko being part of it.

He took a deep breath of the sharp air which presaged the coming winter and, feeling older than his forty-one years, trudged back into the farmhouse. He was in time to hear the last beeps of the smoke alarm as his father finally managed to turn it off. And to witness his mother producing yet another burnt offering from the smoke-billowing oven.

'So,' she said as she put the casserole dish on the draining board. 'When we move, can I get a new oven? This one has never seemed to work properly.'

André and his son stared at each other in disbelief and then they all started laughing.

'No, that's reverse!'

Gears crunched and the cherry-red Peugeot 308 lurched forward and stalled, the left wing mirror brushing dangerously close to the garage door.

'Sorry! My foot slipped.' Josette fumbled with the ignition while Véronique turned to check the road behind. They were straddling both lanes, Josette's garage being situated almost exactly on the bend that followed the curve of the river through La Rivière.

'Ready when you are,' said Véronique, with a calm she didn't feel.

'Okay, okay. Clutch, mirror . . . do I need to signal?'

'Signal?' Annie barked from the back. 'Just stick the bloody thing in gearrr and get it in the garrrage beforrre we'rrre all killed by a logging wagon!'

'Maman, you're not helping.'

'I'm not trrrying to help! I'm trrrying to surrrvive this orrrdeal in one piece!'

'I don't understand why it's not moving!'

'Handbrake,' said Véronique, eyes on the cattle truck that was coming up the valley at speed, rattling past the Auberge des Deux Vallées, the small country inn that marked the beginning of the village.

'Handbrake. Yes, of course. Oh, it's a bit stiff.'

'Now would be good, Josette.' The cattle truck showed no sign of slowing down.

'I can't shift it. It's stuck.' Josette's petite frame was twisted as she tried to lift the brake with both hands.

'Don't want to worry you, but there's a lorry coming.' Véronique was frantically signalling the driver who was on his mobile, unaware of them.

'But I can't do it. I can't . . .'

The click of a seat belt being unfastened prefaced two strong hands reaching forward to lift off the brake with a sturdy heave. Engine already straining, the car now shot into the garage and just as it seemed inevitable that the Peugeot's front bumper would hit the back wall, Josette slammed on the brakes.

'That was close! Is everyone all right?'

Josette's solicitude for her passengers provoked a string of muffled curses from the vicinity of the gearbox and she was surprised to see the dishevelled head and shoulders of her old friend wedged between the two front seats.

'Goodness! You ought to know better,' she said as she helped Annie sit back up. 'Next time keep your seat belt on until the car is parked.'

'Therrre won't be a bloody next time!'

Willing to overlook her friend's anger as an unfortunate side effect of adrenaline, Josette turned to her instructor.

'So, how did I do?'

Véronique was watching the driver of the truck in the rear-view mirror. Having swerved to avoid them at the last minute, his truck had very nearly gone into the river and he was still gesticulating as he drove off up the valley, shouting something about all Fogas drivers being lunatics.

Then she focused on the stones that formed the wall milli-metres beyond the windscreen and her hand strayed to the small cross that hung at her throat.

'Well, at least your emergency stop doesn't need any practice.'

'Quit yourrr gassing and get me out of herrre!' Annie snapped, terrified Josette might reverse the car out and subject her to another hour of hell.

Bringing Maman had been a mistake, thought Véronique as she opened the back door and watched her hustle towards the bar, no doubt wanting a double espresso to calm her nerves. When she'd said she quite fancied the idea of a Sunday after-noon drive, Véronique had tried to dissuade her. But Maman had insisted. And it had been hard to explain just how bad a driver Josette was when she was standing right next to them, keys in hand.

It had all started a few months ago. Spurred on by her nephew's encouragement, Josette had declared that she was going to learn to drive. Fabian had been behind his sixty-eight-year-old aunt all the way, downloading the application forms and helping her study for the theory exam. But when

Josette had announced that she wanted to prolong her practice by becoming an accompanied learner, Fabian, who'd already experienced his aunt's driving, suddenly became too busy to help.

So Josette had approached Véronique. Feeling flattered, the postmistress had said yes and they'd agreed that every Sunday after lunch the two of them would go for an hour's drive, Fabian being left to look after the épicerie.

It was an agreement Véronique was already lamenting. Josette rarely got the car out of second gear, stopped on every roundabout to yield to the right and refused to overtake cyclists in case she knocked them off. Overtaking another car had so far not proved necessary, given her reluctance to use the accelerator.

'So that's another few kilometres ticked off,' said Josette merrily, as she locked up the garage. 'How many left before I can apply for the test?'

'Well, if we continue to drive at a speed of thirty kilometres per hour for an hour every Sunday—'

'And I've already done three Sundays,' Josette chimed in, choosing to ignore Véronique's sarcasm.

'—that leaves ninety-seven hours before you're eligible.'

'Just under two years then. Isn't that great? Two more years of us driving together!'

Véronique wished she could share Josette's enthusiasm.

As did Jacques, the rightful owner of the beautiful cherry-red Peugeot, who'd only had the car for a matter of months before he'd keeled over dead. Now he was standing at the window of the bar, face pressed to the glass and mouth open in a silent scream, a ghostly replica of Munch's painting. He'd seen it all. The car emerging in fits and starts and almost knocking a passing cyclist off his bike. The screech as it went off up the road in the wrong gear and the squeal of brakes as it returned an hour later and Josette overshot the garage entrance as always.

It was agony. Absolute agony.

He'd always loved his wife. Worshipped the ground she walked on. Still did, despite being dead. But this was too much to ask of a man. Allowing a woman to drive his car was bad enough. Having a woman learn to drive in it was something no man should have to endure.

He pressed himself even closer to the glass, trying to communicate his intense pain so that she would desist, put the keys back in the drawer where she'd found them six months ago and leave his gorgeous Peugeot behind the garage doors where it should be.

Josette, however, was ignoring him. She could see his thin features framed by the open shutters. She could feel his distress. But now that she had discovered the thrill of driving, she didn't think she would ever be able to give it up. When she'd taken her first lesson down in St Girons, her heart had soared as they'd left the town behind and the countryside opened up before her. The long stretch of green pasture, the jagged peaks of the mountains in the distance and the winding ribbon of road which rolled out ahead. The instructor had only let her drive as far as the village of Castillon and back, all along flat valley roads, but even so, it had left her breathless with excitement.

The world was at her wheels.

So she steadfastly turned her head from Jacques' beseeching gaze as she entered the bar behind Véronique.

'Coffee, ladies? Or perhaps something stronger? I hear it was quite an adventure.' Fabian tipped his head in the direction of Annie who was huddled over her second espresso.

'A coffee would be wonderful, Fabian. Been busy?' Josette was already tying on her apron, getting ready to relieve him as he set two cups on the counter.

'Not really. A few people in for bits and pieces but nothing much.'

'Thanks for covering for me.'

'You're welcome, Tante Josette.' He bent down and kissed her cheeks as he passed. 'Sorry I can't help out much at weekends but Stephanie is up to her eyes. Once the garden centre gets established she'll be able to give up her waitressing job at the Auberge and then I'll have more free time.'

'I understand,' Josette assured him.

He said his goodbyes to the two Estaque women and left.

'Not surrrre I'd be so underrrstanding,' commented Annie, once the door had closed.

'What do you mean?' asked Josette.

'It was him who talked you into extending the place and now he's neverrr herrre when it's busiest. Harrrdly herrre at all, in fact.'

'Don't be so hard on him. He's a good lad and Stephanie needs all the help she can get.'

Annie harrumphed, which was her way of conceding an argument.

'But Maman does have a point, Josette. You even considered retirement when Fabian first arrived ten months ago. Now you can't find twenty minutes to put your feet up.'

'I know,' sighed Josette as she sank onto a chair. 'But what else can I do?'

'Close forrr a few hourrrs a day like everrry otherrr buggerrr rrround herrre!'

Josette was already shaking her head. Not since one of Jacques' ancestors had hung strings of his famous saucisson from the ceiling of what had been his dining room and declared the épicerie in La Rivière open, had the place ever closed for lunch. She was determined that wasn't about to change now.

'I might be able to help,' Véronique continued. 'But it would involve a bit of rearranging.'

'What kind of rearranging?' Josette was instantly wary, the nightmare of the building work which had created the new-look shop and bar all too recent.

'Room for a post-office counter for a start . . .'

'The post office? In here?'

'Is that perrrmitted?'

Véronique gestured for them to keep their voices down, even though they were the only ones present. The only ones Véronique could see, that is. Unbeknownst to her, Jacques was leaning in to catch what the postmistress of Fogas was about to say, his hearing not what it once had been.

'Nothing's definite, so not a word to anyone, okay?' Both older women nodded. 'I've been doing some research, talking to colleagues in other communes, and I'm convinced that La Poste is dragging its heels on purpose.'

'You mean they don't want to reopen in Fogas?' asked Josette.

'No one's saying that exactly. Not to my face, anyway. But it seems they're no longer keen to take on the responsibilities of rural post offices for economic reasons. One of the ways around this is to make the communes take on the role of running them.'

'Like in Moulis,' said Annie. 'They only managed to keep theirrr brrranch by rrrelocating it in the town hall.'

'Exactly. So from what I can tell, if we approach La Poste with a plan that removes some of their liability, they may be more willing to come on board.'

'But why here? Why not up at the town hall in Fogas?'

Annie snorted. 'Who in theirrr rrright mind would trrraipse all the way up the mountain to buy a few stamps? This is a perrrfect spot. Think of all the extrrra customerrrs it would brrring in!'

'But I don't know anything about running a post office! And my geography is hopeless. I'd never cope with foreign letters.'

'You wouldn't have to. The town hall would rent the space and supply an employee to run it. Me!' Véronique grinned at her own ingenuity.

'Sounds like a grrreat idea.'

Josette wasn't convinced. 'I don't know. I can barely cope at the moment. The last thing I need is more customers!'

'You're forgetting something,' explained Véronique. 'The post office only opens from nine to eleven. The rest of the time I'd be free to lend a hand.'

At a stroke, Josette's resistance was overcome. She'd have someone around on a permanent basis to reduce her workload. And to talk to. Provided she didn't dwell on the necessary refurbishments and the hassle they would bring, she was tempted to give it a try.

Mistaking her silence for reticence, Véronique continued.

'Like I said, it's not definite. There aren't many post offices operating under this scheme yet as it's relatively new, so La Poste might say no. And of course, I've got to persuade the Conseil Municipal to approve the initial outlay. But I've got a meeting with Serge next week so I thought I'd run it past you first. What do you think?'

Josette knew what she thought. But as the previous proprietor was still present, albeit in a different form, it was only appropriate to get his approval for any changes to the épicerie. She looked at Jacques who was still craning forward, trying to overhear, his aged legs quivering with the effort. He caught her eye and nodded vigorously. It was all she needed.

'It does sound like it could work . . .' she began tentatively.

'Of courrrse it'll worrrk,' said Annie. 'Give you plenty of time forrr prrractising yourrr bloody drrriving, too!'

And as Josette's face lit up at the idea, Jacques snapped upright in horror. His back, never the strongest part of his physique in the mortal world, gave way at the sudden movement and his legs collapsed underneath him. He slid to the floor with a silent groan.

'I hadn't thought of it like that!' exclaimed Josette.

'Neither had I!' muttered both Véronique and Jacques in despair.

5

The view was stunning. A panorama of valleys dipping and rising, covered in acres of vibrant forest interspersed with patches of green pasture and all leading to those mountains. They were amazing.

On a day like today, a warm late-autumn breeze ruffling the red and orange leaves, the sun bright overhead in a cloudless sky, Christian didn't need any expert to tell him the value of the place he lived in. He knew for a fact it was priceless.

'Mountain aspect,' the woman standing next to him noted on her clipboard. 'That'll add a few euros. And your nearest neighbour?'

'Down in Picarets.'

'Excellent. Remote rural property.' She wrote with sharp movements, covering the page in indecipherable flourishes. 'Shall we head inside?'

'Don't you want to see all the land?'

'The land?' She seemed genuinely puzzled. 'No need. It's the house and the scenery that will sell this place, not a handful of fields.'

Christian winced as she casually dismissed the very thing he felt defined him. But she didn't notice. She'd already walked past him and into the farmhouse. He followed her slim figure, trying to see his home through the eyes of a stranger who might want to buy it.

It was a shambles. The dark hallway was cluttered with

boots and coats, a broken chair propped up against the wall and sagging under the weight of a bag of chicken feed, and an old woodworm-ridden chest, which served as an office, was piled high with letters, invoices, bits of baling twine, a couple of screwdrivers and, of course, bank statements.

It was all pretty much as normal. Although he wasn't sure that the brown egg nestling in the pile of bank statements had been there earlier. He scooped it into his pocket and chased the possible offender into the yard, hoping the woman hadn't seen.

'Plenty of character,' she said, casting her eyes over the space before giving herself a quick glance in the fogged mirror which hung above the chest, its glass pitted and yellow, adverts for livestock auctions stuck into its frame. She ran manicured fingers through her sleek black bob and then continued into the kitchen where the lingering acrid smell indicated that Christian's mother had been attempting to bake.

'Madame Dupuy?' The young woman approached Josephine with her hand outstretched. 'I'm Eve Rumeau. From Ariège Estate Agency.'

'Pleased to meet you, Mad . . .' Josephine hesitated, trying to sneak a peek at the woman's left hand.

'Eve will do fine,' said the estate agent sharply. 'I don't care for Mademoiselle.'

André Dupuy let out a gruff laugh, taking in the willowy shape and the immaculate complexion as she turned to greet him. 'You young girls are all the same. Wait until you're older. Then you'll be wishing you could be called Mademoiselle!'

'Papa!' Christian hissed.

'But it's true!' he exclaimed. 'Why, back in the sixties—'

'I dare say you're right. Now, shall we get down to business?' Eve Rumeau clicked her pen, wisely curtailing the discussion of sexual politics which André Dupuy would rather have engaged in than this meeting to sell his home.

'Where do you want to start?' asked Josephine, and Christian could hear the anxiety in her voice.

'This seems as good a place as any. Will the cooker be included in the sale?'

It didn't take long. Fifteen minutes to assess the value of the home the Dupuys could never have put a price on. A quarter of an hour trailing round after the businesslike estate agent as she asked question after question about double glazing, central heating, property taxes, rights of access. She'd made no comment on the moulting stuffed parakeet in one of the bedrooms – a present from a cousin of André's who'd moved to Guadeloupe – or on the array of family photos that spanned the generations from sepia to digital in a procession up the stairs. And if she'd noticed the hand-stitched picture of a fierce tiger in faded stripes which had hung above Christian's bed since his infancy, much to the farmer's relief she didn't mention it.

'Have you got time for a coffee?' Josephine asked as they all re-entered the kitchen.

'That'd be great.'

'And a slice of cake to go with it? Homemade, of course.'

The trepidation her suggestion triggered in the males of the household subsided when Josephine held out a sublime chocolate gâteau that had clearly never been near the inside of her oven.

'Just half a slice,' said Eve, watching carefully as a thick slice was cut and then halved. 'Actually, that's too much. Half again, please.'

Josephine's lips pursed as she wielded the knife once more but she never said a word. Although the plate, with its much lighter load, was put down rather heavily in front of the visitor.

'So, how soon do you want me to market the farm?' Eve asked as she took the smallest morsel onto her fork.

66

Christian scratched his head. 'I hadn't really thought that far. I don't suppose there's any point putting it up before the New Year, not when we're already in mid-November.'

'No point at all. Not even the English go house-hunting in the run-up to Christmas!'

'Do you think it will sell quickly?' asked Josephine.

'Is that important?' Eve looked to Christian. 'Because if so we should price it accordingly.'

'Well, we're not desperate,' he said. 'But then again, we don't want it to take years like some round here.'

Eve nodded. 'It's a slow market all right but the views will make this stand out. And with the outbuildings and the land, it would make an ideal commercial venture. Something like an upmarket bed and breakfast perhaps?'

'A bed and breakfast? You're going to turn this place into a hotel?' André choked on his gateau.

'Papa, it's how it is. There's no demand for farms anymore.'

'Christian's right,' said the estate agent, not perturbed by the older man's indignation. 'I've sold three farms this year alone and not one of them was bought by a farmer.'

'Who bought them then?' asked André, incredulously.

'A Dutch couple turned one into a mountain-biking centre. Another was bought by a man from Toulouse who works in IT. He now works from home. And the third went to a horti-culturist.' She shrugged. 'Things are changing.'

'What a waste of all this land!'

'Well, you could do it yourselves,' suggested Eve. 'Create a bed and breakfast instead of selling. Farm vacations are all the rage. You could even provide home-cooked meals. If this cake is anything to go by, Madame Dupuy would make the perfect host.'

An outburst of coughing around the table momentarily halted the conversation and Josephine steadfastly avoided the gaze of her menfolk until Christian came to her rescue.

'We don't have a choice. It's a matter of putting it on the market.'

'In that case, I'll contact you during the week with my valuation and we'll take it from there.'

Praising the wonderful cake once more despite most of her portion remaining uneaten, Eve said goodbye and Christian walked her to her jaunty Suzuki Jimny. Parked next to his battered Panda 4x4, the contrast between the two vehicles was so great that Christian began calculating whether the proceeds of the farm sale might stretch to an upgrade. And he was instantly swamped with a feeling of disloyalty.

'My details are all on here,' said Eve, passing him her business card. She leaned in towards him, a hand on his forearm, and he caught the heady scent of her perfume. 'Business and personal. Don't hesitate to call me. Even if it's not about selling the farm.'

She squeezed his arm, her long red nails bright against his shirt, and got into the car, providing him with more than just a flash of her slender legs as she did so. With a wave, she was gone, out onto the road and down the hill to Picarets in the distance.

He stood there, card in hand, trying to work out what had just happened.

Josephine Dupuy, standing in the doorway, knew all too well. She didn't need to hear the words. The body language had been enough. But Christian, like his father, was a complete innocent when it came to the dark arts of seduction.

'That was Josette on the phone,' she said, breaking the spell. 'She called to remind you that the meeting starts early tonight.'

Christian groaned and slapped his forehead. The council meeting. He checked his watch. He had plenty of time to get ready. But it didn't make him any more inclined to go.

Backed by a majority of his fellow councillors, the first

deputy mayor, Pascal Souquet, had called the extraordinary session rather hastily and Christian could only surmise that it was going to be some kind of attack on the leadership of Serge Papon. The obligatory agenda, sent to all council members and pinned to the noticeboard up at the town hall, sounded innocuous enough: a discussion of the problems arising from the presence of bears in the area. No reference to the mayor's incompetence. But the rumblings in the commune had been growing in volume and tonight, egged on by Pascal, they would probably get an airing.

The farmer really wasn't looking forward to it. Especially as he hadn't found the time to have the talk with Serge that he'd promised Josette he would.

'She also said that Arnaud Petit has asked if he could have a lift up to the town hall.'

'The bear tracker? He's coming too?'

'Makes sense if the meeting is about the bears, I suppose.' Josephine shrugged. 'Anyway, I told her it was okay. Was I right?'

Christian pulled a face but nodded, still unable to explain his aversion to the big man. In the two weeks since his arrival, Arnaud hadn't attracted any trouble from the anti-bear brigade. He hadn't caused any either, even taking a diplomatic stance for an interview in the local paper. Indeed, he'd barely been seen, doubtless spending most of his time up in the forest. And Véronique hadn't mentioned him. Not that it would be any of Christian's business if she had. Wouldn't be any of his business if the two of them were having cosy chats over apéritifs or—

'Can you take the rest of that cake down to Josette's with you, when you go?'

'Sorry, what? The cake?' Christian got his thoughts back under control. 'Why on earth would I take the cake back to the shop? Are you going to complain it wasn't homemade?'

Josephine whipped his legs with the tea towel she was holding. 'Would you rather I'd served the gâteau I did make?' she demanded. 'Not that Mademoiselle Estate Agent would have eaten any more if I had. Not unless she's on some carbon-based diet!'

'Don't be too hard on her, Maman. She's good at her job. One of the best around and that's what we need to sell this place.'

'I know, son. But it's difficult. Having someone wandering round the farm analysing it as an asset as opposed to the home that it is.'

Christian pulled the short figure of his mother into his arms. 'We'll get through this. I know we will. Now, where's that blasted cake? Not that Josette will want it back.'

'It's not for her,' countered his mother as they walked back into the kitchen. 'It's for Véronique and young Chloé. I'm sure *they'll* appreciate it!'

'Véronique's going to be at the shop? Tonight?'

'She's looking after the épicerie and minding Chloé while Josette's up at the meeting.' Josephine started cutting the cake, making sure there was an extra-thick slice for Chloé, daughter of Stephanie and a firm favourite at the farm. 'Stephanie's working at the Auberge and Fabian is tied up doing someone's accounts so Véronique agreed to help out. She's a good sort, don't you think?'

She was talking to an empty space. Her son was walking down the hall, whistling softly to himself as though life had turned up an unexpected bonus.

So like his father, she marvelled, as she watched his long stride take the stairs two at a time. Neither one of them knew the first thing about the female sex. Still, she thought, as she smoothed her skirt down over hips that testified to her being a woman who didn't take her cake in half-slices,

70

André hadn't fared too badly. Hopefully his son would prove as lucky.

While the Dupuys were coming to terms with their future in Picarets, if a crow had chosen to fly up over the hill that rose directly behind their farm, continued past the old quarry and across the steep gorge which lay beyond it, flapped its wings and crested the steep sides of the next mountain, then it would have come to the village of Fogas in less than five minutes. But as only a crow could make this journey, no road lying between the two villages, then residents of one had to descend all the way down to La Rivière in order to drive to the other. And as Fogas, perched on its ridge with amazing views, was home to the most inconveniently situated town hall in the history of the French Republic, the journey up and down the winding road was one that the residents of the commune made on a regular basis. Just as Véronique had, less than half an hour before.

Still revelling in the freedom that came from being mobile once more, the insurance company having dragged their heels for the best part of a year before paying out on the car she'd lost to the inferno at the post office, Véronique was in a good mood. With Christian's help, she'd found a Renault that far surpassed the heap of rust she'd had before and it was beginning to feel like the catastrophic repercussions of the fire were finally being put right. All that remained now was to sort out her work.

Which wasn't proving straightforward.

Originally planned for the first week in November, her meeting with the mayor on that very subject had been postponed twice, the last time just as she was leaving her flat. The secretary had been very apologetic but had offered no excuse, merely saying that the mayor was unexpectedly not available.

Unexpectedly not available! Huh, thought Véronique, as she sat in the hallway of the town hall waiting her turn. Serge Papon probably hadn't shown up for work again. Rumour had it he was rarely seen in the corridors of power these days. Not that the corridor she was sitting in gave much indication of power. The pine panelling that covered the lower half of the walls was pockmarked with woodworm and above it, the khaki-green paint was chipped and flaking. The mottled stains on the ceiling simply added to the air of neglect.

A door banged and heavy footsteps came down the stairs, accompanied by a furious chuntering as Céline Laffont, long-suffering secretary at the town hall, stormed into view.

'I'm to tell you to go up,' she fumed. 'But I'm warning you, the man's an idiot!'

She marched across the hallway and into the meeting room, her temper crackling the air behind her. Surmising that Serge must be on fine form, Véronique went up to his office. The door was ajar so she knocked lightly and entered.

'Ah, Véronique. Do come in.'

The slight figure dwarfed by the large desk, fingers steepled beneath his chin in an affected manner, was no substitute for Serge Papon. Whereas the mayor matched the stately proportions of the oversized office, his first deputy, Pascal Souquet, was rendered insignificant by the vast space.

'I'm supposed to be seeing the mayor,' Véronique stated bluntly, halting in the doorway and reflecting that Pascal's presence went some way to explaining the secretary's foul mood, their mutual antipathy having already added several chapters to the political annals of Fogas.

'So I understand. However, Serge can't make it. He's unexpectedly—'

'Not available.' Véronique sighed and was already turning

to leave, confident from previous encounters with the first deputy mayor that any further dialogue was a waste of time.

'Perhaps I can help? Is it about the post office?'

The unprecedented interest was enough to make her pause. 'Yes.'

'Well, why don't you take a seat and we can talk it over?' He waved a regal hand at the chairs in front of the desk and her dislike of him overrode her surprise.

'It's okay. I'll speak to Christian tonight.'

'Christian? Oh, I wouldn't go bothering Christian. Not with his troubles.'

'Troubles?'

'You haven't heard? He's had to put the farm up for sale.'

Véronique, lifelong resident of a small community and expert collector of gossip, had whittled down the fine art of surviving life in Fogas to one simple rule: don't react. No matter what they say to you or about you, don't give them the satisfaction of knowing they have hit the target.

In this instance she might have got away with a couple of rapid blinks and she was fairly sure that her sharp intake of breath hadn't been audible. But she couldn't help reaching out for the chair. Couldn't help sitting down in it as her legs refused to support her.

'There's even talk of him moving up to Toulouse,' Pascal continued, repeating verbatim the news his wife had passed on when he'd popped home for lunch. News she'd had from her niece who worked for the estate agency where Christian had placed the farm. 'But I'm sure you know all this already. So, what exactly do you want to talk to Serge about?'

'I just . . . I think . . . erm . . . I may have found a way to chivvy La Poste along. Something that would make them commit to reopening a branch in the commune.'

Véronique was having difficulty focusing, but even in her

befuddled state she noticed Pascal sit up straight, his eyes fixed on her as he reached for a notepad.

'Do go on.'

'It involves the épicerie, and I'd also need the support of the council.'

'In what way?'

Véronique proceeded to outline her ideas for repositioning the post office within the shop and Pascal listened attentively, covering the paper with notes.

'It would mean a slight reduction in services,' she concluded, 'but nothing major really. Nothing that would be missed by my regular customers.'

'And you've spoken to Josette, I take it?'

She nodded.

'Excellent,' said Pascal, standing up. 'Leave this with me. I'll get in touch with La Poste first thing tomorrow and see how viable it is before we put it to the council. How does that sound?'

'Perfect!' Véronique managed to summon a smile as she bade him farewell, amazed that someone in Fogas was finally paying attention to her concerns. She was equally amazed that the person was Pascal Souquet. Who'd have thought that he would be the one to step forward and help her get the post office back in town?

It only took the short distance down the stairs to the hallway, however, for her thoughts to return to Christian. Was it true? Was he really going to leave? She didn't know if she could bear it if he did.

In accordance with her own set of rules, her outward appearance remained sanguine as she crossed the car park. But inside she was in turmoil.

Pascal Souquet, soon to be mayor of Fogas if tonight's council meeting went to plan, watched Véronique getting into her car.

That she hadn't known about his rival's financial problems had been apparent, even though she'd done well to hide it. But the pain that had flickered across her broad peasant's face had been all too clear. And he'd revelled in it.

Fools, he thought, as he watched her pull out onto the road and head down towards La Rivière. All of them. Once satisfied by his ambition to be mayor, he was now anxious to be out of Fogas, impatient to move up the golden ladder that had been so tantalisingly lowered in front of him. And he sensed that Véronique's ideas for the post office could be instrumental to his plans.

How though?

He paced the office, knowing he'd stumbled upon a chest marked 'treasure' but with no idea how to open it and bereft without the wise counsel of his wife. It was a counsel he'd had to rely on less since Fatima had made it clear that she didn't approve of the company he was keeping. Or trust the man he was working with. Her only advice had been to withdraw, have nothing more to do with the scheming; it wasn't too late.

But Pascal, for the first time in his life, hadn't listened to his wife. Actually, if he was honest, it was the second time. The first time had been when he'd invested heavily in a venture that had promised breathtaking returns. They'd been breathtaking all right. Just not in the way Pascal had expected. Last in and at the bottom of the pyramid, Pascal had been made bankrupt overnight. Forced to sell their home in a trendy quarter of Paris, he'd also lost his job as he became too ill with stress to work.

Fatima had saved him. She'd packed up what few possessions remained, put them in storage and brought him back to her mother's hometown of Fogas, where she'd inherited a tiny house. Immediately she'd set about plotting his comeback. They would start small. Courting the votes of the often ignored second-home owners as their power base, they'd got him elected

75

onto the council as first deputy mayor. The next goal, one almost within reach, was Mayor of Fogas. From there, he would progress to the Conseil Général in Foix, capital of the Ariège-Pyrénées. Then on to the regional council up in Toulouse. After that, the holy grail of national politics beckoned.

He'd been game to go along with his wife's plans despite his repugnance for the people he now lived amongst – the very people he represented. They were so bucolic. Obsessed with the price of animal feed and calves; finding pleasure in hunting and playing pétanque. And their idea of good food was a hearty cassoulet washed down with a local red.

How he yearned for the refined lifestyle of the Parisian boulevards, the intellectual social circle he'd been part of, the caviar, the champagne. Perhaps that was why when he'd been offered more than just being mayor of this backward gene-puddle, a fast track to his grander ambitions, he'd jumped at the chance.

He looked out on the street which wound through Fogas, not a soul visible. Why would there be? The only visitors were locals calling in at the town hall and the odd stray tourist. What else would attract people? The road was a dead end which petered out further up the mountain after it had visited several obscure hamlets, and there wasn't a single amenity left in the village. No shop. No bar. Even the *lavoir* had fallen into disuse with the advent of washing machines.

There was absolutely no reason to come up here. Which was why the village was dying.

And suddenly all became clear.

Ebullient, he picked up his mobile. They needed to meet. Tonight. This couldn't wait.

6

'I wish I'd heard it from someone else, that's all. Preferably Christian!'

Several hours on and Véronique was still rattled. But rather than allow herself to contemplate the awful ramifications of the news, she had decided to vent her wrath on the manner in which it had been disclosed.

'I've only just found out myself,' said Josette, as she placed her handbag on the bar and glanced at the clock. 'His mother told me. Although I knew he was having problems.'

'You did?'

'He said something to that effect last winter. Just before we had all the trouble.' Josette nodded enigmatically towards the girl who was sitting at the far end of the big table, homework spread out before her. She didn't need to spell it out. By far the most traumatic time in recent Fogas memory, Véronique knew she was referring to the events that had almost cost young Chloé Morvan her life.

'What did he say exactly?'

'Oh, I can't remember the details. But I know that he ran the accounts past Fabian and the news wasn't good.'

'He's even told *Fabian*?' Véronique didn't try to disguise her disgruntlement. 'At this rate I wouldn't be surprised to discover he told Pascal Souquet himself!'

'Don't be daft. There's no way he would have told Pascal.

It's Fatima who'll have heard it. Her ear is always to the ground when it comes to Fogas gossip.'

'Well he obviously thought all of you were more trustworthy than I am!'

'I'm sure it wasn't anything of the sort.' Josette draped her coat over the back of a chair. With the warmth of the day now dissipating at sunset, the chilly evenings were heralding the coming winter and she would need it. Especially as the heater in Christian's car was temperamental, either working full blast or not at all. 'He probably just didn't want to bother you.'

'Huh!' Véronique started emptying the dishwasher that had been installed behind the bar during the great makeover, thumping everything onto the counter with a ferocity that made Josette fear for her glassware.

'Here,' she finally said, unable to bear the tension of imminent breakages any longer. 'Why don't you let me do that? You go and finish off your coffee. I'm sure Chloé could do with a hand with her homework. Couldn't you, love?'

Chloé, pencil in hand, her youthful forehead furrowed prematurely with the rigours of schoolwork, got straight to the point. 'Are you any good at history?'

'Depends. What era?'

'The revolution. Madame Soum is always going on about it. School would be a lot easier if it hadn't happened.'

Véronique raised her eyebrows in mock reproach. 'How dare you say that about our glorious Republic!'

Chloé grinned and pushed her books towards Véronique as she sat down. The two dark heads bent over the textbook and Josette noticed Jacques, white head propped on wrinkled hands, watching them from the fireplace with a smile.

When Stephanie had asked her to mind Chloé, Josette had jumped at the chance. The ten-year-old was a delight to be around and livened up the slow evenings as she sat at the table doing her schoolwork. But the real joy for Josette was that Chloé Morvan, direct descendant of Stephanie's gypsy ancestors, could see Jacques. It was a secret the two of them had shared for over twelve months and so far, the fact that she could interact with a ghost didn't seem to faze the kid at all. But then Chloé wasn't exactly your average child. Josette had yet to come across any other youngster who thought nothing of throwing herself in the air in a bid to become a world-famous trapeze artist.

'Good grief!' Having read a couple of paragraphs, Véronique sat up and flicked the book closed with derision. 'This is awful! How on earth do you stay awake in class?'

'I stare out of the windows at the mountains,' said Chloé, with her trademark honesty. 'And then I get my knuckles rapped for not paying attention.'

'But it's criminal. This makes the revolution seem so dull.'

'School makes everything seem dull,' moaned the reluctant student who, despite her lack of enthusiasm for the methods employed, was consistently top of the class. Much to Madame Soum's exasperation.

'You've got a point there. But it's a shame. You should enjoy learning about the past.'

'Did you? When you were at school?'

Véronique shook her head. 'No. I studied it later. On my own. And I discovered that the revolution was complicated. And long. But never dull. Take what happened to poor old Marat, for example.'

'Who's he?'

'*Who's he?* Doesn't that old bat Madame Soum teach you anything? He was a founding member of the republic, that's who he was. Before he met a sticky end.'

'What happened to him?'

'He was murdered in his bath.'

79

'In his *bath*?' Chloé's eyes had grown wide, focus completely on Véronique. 'Why did someone murder him in his bath?'

'I don't think they set out to murder him there. It's just that he spent a lot of time in it. He had this bad skin disease which meant he had to bathe a lot.'

'What kind of skin disease?'

'Opinions vary but they all agree that he was covered in blisters and smelt bad.'

'Is that why someone murdered him? Because he was smelly?'

'No. Not quite. Look, why don't I start at the beginning . . .'

The door to the épicerie sounded and the tall figure of Arnaud Petit sauntered into view.

'Bonsoir.' The tracker approached Josette. 'Sorry I'm late.'

'Don't worry about it. Christian isn't even here yet. Must be having trouble getting the hens to bed!'

Arnaud smiled and took a seat next to the postmistress, who had begun her account of the tragic Monsieur Marat, Chloé and Jacques hanging on to her every word.

'—And it was while he was living in the sewers that he got the problems with his skin.'

'Ugh! Imagine living in a sewer! No wonder he needed a lot of baths.'

'What on earth are they talking about?' Arnaud whispered to Josette, who noticed that his gaze was fixed on Véronique's face as the history lesson continued.

'The death of Marat.'

He raised his eyebrows. 'Why?'

'Véronique's helping Chloé with her homework.'

'Wish I'd been taught this in school,' he said with a grin, clearly captivated by the young woman and her narrative.

'—So Marat agreed to see Mademoiselle Corday.'

'Even though he was in the bath? And he was naked?' Chloé was agog.

'He had a special bath that covered up his bits. It had a desk on it and everything.'

'Wow! He worked from his bathroom?'

'Yes. Which was his eventual downfall . . .'

Hearing the rattle of a car pulling up outside, Josette tore herself away from the saga and from her musings about a possible attraction between the tracker and the postmistress, based on nothing more than her female intuition which was hardly ever wrong. She started putting on her coat.

Christian turned off the engine and took a moment to savour the scene before him. The shutters to the bar had yet to be closed and he could see Chloé and Véronique inside. They were sitting at the big table which was strewn with books, the subdued light of the low-watt bulbs falling softly upon them. They looked beautiful, faces animated, Véronique's auburn hair tumbling in waves to her shoulders while Chloé's unruly curls framed her rosy cheeks. And whatever fairytale the postmistress of Fogas was spinning, the young girl was completely enthralled.

For that split second, Christian knew that this was what love would feel like. Coming home to a scene like this. Wife and child abandoning their stories of princes and princesses to run into his arms, the aroma of good cooking coming from the stove.

He allowed himself to luxuriate in the image for a few seconds more and then, with a sigh, pulled himself back into reality: the cold interior of his battered Panda which always smelled of hay or worse, and a future that might lie far away in the big city of Toulouse. He gathered up the parcel of cake and headed towards the épicerie. At least he could enjoy this brief moment, he thought as he opened the door, wishing for all the world he could spend the evening in the bar rather than at a meeting up in the town hall.

'Bonsoir,' he called out, his step faltering as he crossed the threshold and saw the broad figure of Arnaud Petit sitting near Véronique with an expression of rapt attention on his dark face as he listened to the postmistress.

'—And then she plunged the blade into his chest! And with a cry of "Help me, my love!" he slumped over, dead.' Véronique flung herself to her left, head lolling on Arnaud Petit's shoulder, tongue sticking out and eyes crossed in imitation of the hapless Marat.

'Ugh! Did the bathwater turn red? I bet it did!'

'I'll have to look that one up, Chloé,' answered Véronique from her reclining position as Arnaud laughed softly, his strong arm slipping around her waist.

'Bonsoir!' Christian said again, the enchantment he'd felt only moments before souring faster than a pail of milk left out on a summer's day.

'Bonsoir,' came a chorus of replies and Véronique shot upright, face red.

'You ready, Josette?' Christian demanded as he thrust the small parcel across the table towards the postmistress.

'A present?' asked Véronique with a smile as she recovered her composure.

'From Maman. She said you weren't the kind of woman to turn down a slice of cake.' Even as he said it, Christian knew it hadn't come out right. 'And there's a bit for Chloé too,' he gabbled on, trying to cover up his mistake. 'Hers is the bigger one. Just so you don't take the wrong piece.'

Véronique stared at him while Arnaud Petit got to his feet, eyes dancing in amusement, which the farmer suspected was at his expense.

'Thanks for offering to give me a lift,' he said, shaking Christian's hand.

'For the record,' retorted Christian, his mood getting worse by the second, 'I didn't offer. Shall we go?'

Shooing Josette and the tracker ahead like the hens he'd been chasing around the farm, he stormed out of the door leaving Véronique speechless behind him.

What on earth has got into him? wondered Véronique as the car's headlights disappeared up the road to Fogas. The way he was behaving, anyone would think that *she* was the one keeping secrets. But perhaps that was it. Perhaps it was the stress of selling the farm that was making him so grumpy.

She wasn't the only one wondering. Having witnessed the rare display of temper from the farmer who was good-natured to the core, Jacques didn't know what to think. Or rather, he did. There was only one thing that could make a man that crotchety. And that was a woman.

He settled back in the inglenook, deep in thought as Véronique unwrapped the cake and Chloé fetched plates. Who could it be? It wasn't as if there were a lot of contenders in the commune of Fogas, the majority of the female residents being over the age of fifty. Not that age should be a factor. But he couldn't imagine Christian being anyone's toy boy!

No, it had to be someone younger than him. Someone with personality. A woman with a bit of spirit.

'Would you like some cake?' Chloé whispered, offering him her plate while Véronique was busy pouring Oranginas at the bar. Jacques grinned, sensing that the kid hadn't quite grasped the limits of his existence, and silently refused.

'So,' said Chloé in her normal voice as she dug into the unexpected treat. 'What happened after the death of Marat?'

'Ah ha!' said Véronique, approaching the table with a

wicked smile. 'Have you heard about something called the Reign of Terror?'

Chloé's eyes grew round, fork suspended in mid-air. 'Noooo,' she breathed.

And with relish, Véronique launched into the next chapter of French history, much to the delight of both her listeners. It was only as she was reaching the end of her tale, the floor metaphorically littered with the heads of the many who had encountered Madame Guillotine, that Jacques got the answer to the question that had been bugging him.

'Of course!' His mute exclamation went unnoticed but the abrupt movement as he leapt out of his seat made young Chloé jump.

'Are you all right, Chloé?' asked Véronique as she gathered up the pieces of paper that had fluttered to the floor in the sudden draught from the inglenook which seemed to have startled her charge. 'I haven't scared you, have I?'

Chloé gave her a look of scorn and picked up her pencil. 'Can you help me write some of that down? I'll use it for my project.'

'We might have to censor it a bit. For Madame Soum!' Véronique winked and Chloé started laughing.

And as the two of them bent over the books again, Jacques resumed his seat, tired after his short burst of energy. He was soon asleep, a smile of satisfaction on his face. After all these years, Christian Dupuy was finally in love and he, Jacques Servat, despite being dead, had worked out the object of the farmer's affections. What he didn't know was that the farmer had yet to make that discovery for himself.

They'd made the journey to the town hall in record time, Christian throwing the Panda round the tight bends on the road up to Fogas with an abandon that Josette couldn't fathom.

She'd had to hold on to the edge of her seat, so nervous that she'd forgotten about poor Arnaud Petit, scrunched up in the rear. But then he was wedged in so tight, he'd probably not suffered at all as the car whipped around the corners!

When Christian had held open the car door down at the épicerie and gestured for the tracker to get in the back, she'd tried to argue with him, protesting that she was more than happy to give up the passenger seat. But he'd had a gleam in his eye that she hadn't recognised and his face was set, making him look as stubborn as that stupid bull of his. To Arnaud's credit, he'd merely folded himself into the cramped space behind the front seats and hadn't said a word for the entire journey.

Neither had Christian. Nor had he waited at the town hall while Arnaud extricated himself from his confinement. Instead, he'd stormed off towards the front steps, barely acknowledging the greetings of those arriving for the meeting.

It must be the farm, she thought. What a weight his broad shoulders were carrying – selling the fields that had been farmed by the Dupuy family for as long as anyone could remember and making his parents homeless in the process. No doubt he hadn't come to the decision lightly but as far as Josette could see, he was damned either way. If he did nothing the business would collapse and he would lose everything. But in order to avoid that, he had to sell up and move away, which effectively resulted in the same thing. It was cruel. Doubly so as the land was Christian's first love.

He'd been a kid when he started skipping school, spending the stolen time up in the hills helping out his father who didn't have the heart to force him back inside to spend miserable hours learning about things that had no relevance to the farmer he wanted to be. And as an adolescent, he'd already had a demeanour that meant older men deferred to him.

Josette recalled him sitting in the bar at an age when they really shouldn't have let him in, advising a group of locals on stock sales with a confidence that would see him elected to the Farmers' Union as the youngest member ever.

It had taken longer for him to make the move towards the Conseil Municipal. Apolitical and lacking any personal ambition, he'd rebuffed the frequent requests from others in the community that he stand in the elections, only succumbing when he sensed that he could use the position to try to halt the gradual erosion of everything that he cherished. He'd stood on a platform of change, wanting to bring Fogas into a future that was sustainable. A future that meant kids could grow up here and not have to leave to find work. As it was, the ongoing depopulation of the younger generations had resulted in a commune inhabited by the elderly and increasingly run by second-home owners. Led by Pascal Souquet, these infrequent visitors had little time for the grittier aspects of local politics, such as schooling provision, preferring instead to focus their energies on trivialities like the annual summer fête.

His passion resonating with the locals, Christian had been elected with a massive majority and chosen as deputy mayor by the other members of the council. If he did have to move to Toulouse, the loss wouldn't just be felt by his parents; it would resound across the entire community.

'Don't let Christian forget he's giving me a lift home.' Arnaud's comment was accompanied by a droll smile as he held open the door to the large room that always housed the council sessions. 'In the mood he's in, I wouldn't put it past him!'

Josette didn't even try to defend the farmer as Arnaud was several aeons behind in the politics of Fogas and she didn't really feel like bringing him up to speed. Instead she patted his arm reassuringly.

'If his temper hasn't improved by the time we're finished, *I'll* be driving us back!' she said.

Mistakenly thinking she'd set the tracker's mind at rest, she walked through the public seating area to the U-shaped table. Feeling the familiar knot of tension which accompanied her every appearance on the Conseil Municipal, her husband Jacques having left behind a pair of shoes she knew her petite feet would never fill, she took her seat next to the big farmer, glad to see he'd saved her a place despite his tetchiness.

God, what was wrong with him? He was acting like a hormonal teenager. Christian ran a hand through his hair, remorse at his outrageous behaviour already weighing heavily on him as Josette slipped into her seat and gave him a concerned look. He was in no state to deal with the shenanigans that he suspected were about to unfold.

For an impromptu meeting, the room was unnaturally full, a quick headcount suggesting at least fifty people in the public seating. Incredible, considering they were normally blessed with an audience of no more than five. Christian scanned the rows of seats facing him, picking out the handful of locals who attended every session, some out of interest, others out of boredom in a small commune where a political dust-up was high-octane stuff.

Then of course, there was Fatima Souquet, prominent on the front row, notebook to hand. She fell into neither bracket, her sole motivation being a ferocious desire to see her husband succeed. Far brighter than Pascal and possessed of a feral cunning that could give Serge Papon a run for his money, Fatima had never stood for the council herself, much to Christian's bewilderment. But then she had two counts against her: she was a newcomer and a woman and for some of the locals, the latter far outweighed whatever local heritage she could claim through her maternal ancestors.

Perhaps Fatima had appreciated this when she'd stepped aside to let her other half take the limelight, opting to pull the strings from behind the curtains. If she ever let go of them, thought Christian, her puppet of a husband would collapse in a heap.

Apart from the regulars, the public body was further swelled by the attendance of shepherds and farmers, most of whom were normally too busy to be bothered with the administrative aspects of the commune. Given tonight's agenda, however, they had turned out in force, several rows of weathered faces showing a discomfort brought on by a combined dislike of shirt collars and enclosed spaces.

But while the agriculturalists represented a possible source of disruption for the evening's proceedings, the burly men on the back row were far more disconcerting. Numbering about twenty in total, even without their uniform bright-orange berets – worn tonight in an act of provocation – it would be easy to tell they were hunters. What perturbed Christian was that he recognised only a handful of them. Which, given the size of the commune with its permanent population of just over a hundred people, was fairly unusual.

As well as three men from Fogas he'd known since school, there were also a few from Sarrat he knew in passing, one of them sitting to the side talking on his mobile, heavy strapping on his left arm. Although Christian couldn't place the rest of the assembled men, he was familiar with their types. Bull-necked and thickset, they gave off an air of menace that contrasted with their jaunty berets. With Arnaud Petit choosing to stand directly behind them, the farmer sensed that this meeting was going to demand every ounce of diplomatic skill he had. Possibly supplemented by a bit of physical intervention too. And judging by the fact that the *Gazette Ariégeoise* had sent along a reporter, an elderly, bespectacled man sitting towards the back of the room who was already furiously making notes, Christian wasn't the only one who suspected the session might be eventful.

'If I could call the council to order.' Pascal Souquet rose from his chair, its legs squeaking across the tiles having more of an impact in quelling the background chatter than his effete voice.

Glancing down the table at the single empty space that remained, Christian spoke without thinking. 'Shouldn't we give Serge another few minutes? It's only just gone the hour and it's not like him to be tardy.'

Too late, he realised it was exactly what Pascal had been hoping for.

'I understand your sympathies lie with our mayor, Christian, but given his recent behaviour and his frequent dereliction of duty, perhaps it's better if we start? Anyone object?'

Pascal looked around at the other councillors, eyes resting the longest on René Piquemal who normally opposed everything the first deputy mayor proposed, purely on principle. But tonight he offered no resistance.

'So it's only you, Christian. Are you okay if we continue?'

It was masterful. Way too clever for Pascal to have conjured up on his own. From the outset he'd positioned himself on the side of the suffering electorate, in tune with their frustrations. At the same time he'd raised the issue that was really at the heart of the evening's gathering while neatly aligning his closest rival with the mayor who was the root cause of the simmering dissatisfaction.

'Go ahead,' Christian said, laying a discreet hand on Josette's arm as she started to demur. He felt a rush of gratitude for her loyalty but the political axis that had characterised the Conseil

89

Municipal since before he'd been elected had been reforged in the heat of vexation at the recurring ineptitude of Mayor Serge Papon. And protest was pointless.

Pascal gave his best effort at a smile, thin lips pulled straight apart with the merest inflection at either end, and proceeded to address the assembled councillors.

'Firstly I must apologise for dragging you all here for this extraordinary session but when one of the community approached me about the issue I wish to raise tonight, I felt it was imperative that we convene as quickly as possible.'

His opening was met with a scattering of interjections from the public gallery, the hunters muttering and shifting in their seats. Here we go, thought Christian. But to his surprise, as Pascal continued, the noise abated.

'To be blunt, we are gathered here this evening to formulate a strategy to deal with the problems faced by the commune of Fogas. Problems which have been caused by the presence of a bear within our borders.'

Up until that moment, apart from René's evidence which was taken lightly by most who knew him, it had all been rumour. Now the public were hearing for the first time, from the mouth of an elected official, that there had indeed been a bear sighted in their commune. And the reaction was noisy with murmurs growing in volume and shouts of 'Bravo Pascal!' issuing from the back row.

'He's got them eating out of his hand,' Josette hissed in the farmer's ear. 'Whatever he's about to propose will get voted in!'

She was right. Pascal was hitting his stride, outlining the threat bears posed to the local population, his speech punctuated by cheers from the gallery and bouts of applause which the first deputy mayor took with an air of humility Christian hadn't imagined him capable of.

'Only the other week,' he continued, 'one of our own councillors came face to face with the beast up in the forest.' He indicated René Piquemal who kept his head down, cheeks flushed as he heard his own exaggerations rebroadcast. 'It went for him! And yet we are told by Paris that we must accept these animals. That we must learn to live with them—'

'And they're not even French!' interrupted the old shepherd who'd been in the bar when René had recounted his tale. 'Damn Slovenian imports! Much more aggressive than our native bears.'

'He's right!' called out another. 'French bears wouldn't have attacked like that.'

'They're a danger to our flocks . . .'

'Bloody menace . . .'

Even as the commotion grew, Christian couldn't see where Pascal, a man who had never shown the slightest concern about how pastoralism was managed in the Pyrenees, was taking this. He scanned the increasingly volatile crowd, shepherds banging their sticks in agreement, villagers nodding furiously and the hunters stoking it all with well-timed rejoinders from the back. Behind them the tall figure of the bear tracker was curiously impassive, standing erect, arms folded across that massive chest. Sensing Christian's gaze, he gave a slight movement of his head and drew the farmer's attention to the hunter with the wounded arm.

The man was still on the phone. Only, he wasn't holding the mobile to his ear. He was holding it out in front of him as though trying to capture the events. Recording them perhaps? But why? Two seats to the left of Christian, Monique Sentenac's pen was flying across the pages of her notepad as she took the minutes for the meeting. Minutes which would be made public later that week. There was no secrecy. No need for corroboration.

So what then? The only explanation was that he was holding out the phone so someone else could hear. Someone who didn't want to be seen at the meeting.

Christian looked back at Arnaud, a growing sense of unease unfurling in the pit of his stomach. The tracker returned his stare and, as if sharing Christian's premonition of trouble, he rolled his shoulders and twisted his head from side to side, loosening his thick neck. Then he raised his hands behind him and in a deft movement, pulled his hair into a ponytail.

Never do battle with your hair down.

Who'd said that? Was it Chabal, his rugby-playing hero who'd always entered the fray with his hair tied back? Or Conan the Barbarian? Either way, Christian thought, one thing was clear: Arnaud was getting ready to fight.

'There's going to be trouble. Stay here and don't move until it's sorted. Okay?' Christian whispered to Josette, keeping his focus on the back row, the most likely source of any unrest.

Josette nodded calmly, but he noticed her fingers clench round her pen.

'—So, I think we're all in agreement,' Pascal was saying to thunderous applause. 'This bear in our midst represents a threat to our livelihoods, our lifestyle and our safety!'

He paused, letting the cheers die down. Then he raised his fist and shook it at the crowd.

'But what are we going to *do* about it?'

It was a cue. Aimed straight at the men in the orange berets. And like true professionals, they played their part, voices loud above the rest.

'Bears out! Bears out! Bears out!'

Others joined in, making the hall pulsate.

'Bears out! Bears out! Bears out!'

'Order, order,' Pascal called from the front and Christian

caught a slight movement from the bandaged hunter, who now had his mobile pressed to his ear, and the back rows fell silent.

He was controlling them! Christian glanced at Arnaud who nodded his head, clearly of the same impression. Whoever was on the other end of that phone was using the hunter as his second in command, marshalling his troops like a general far removed from the conflict.

'I understand your concerns,' Pascal continued. 'But this is a formal process and I need a proposal.'

He turned to the councillors, his gaze resting on one of them, and Christian finally understood. Saw it all so clearly. And realised that while he'd been absorbed in his own problems, Pascal had been fanning the embers of discontent which Christian had been too busy to deal with.

'I'd like to make such a proposal.' Philippe Galy, still relatively new to the commune and voted onto the Conseil Municipal purely on the strength of his grandfather's name, stood up, provoking one or two murmurs of surprise. Not least amongst his fellow councillors. 'Given his inadequate handling of this situation and his reluctance to oppose the reintroduction of bears in the Pyrenees, I suggest that we take steps tonight to have Serge Papon removed as mayor of Fogas.'

7

Philippe Galy's words fell into a stretch of silence as the locals grasped the significance òf what was being advocated. And in that silence, which was punctuated only by the rasping cough of the old shepherd, lay the possibility of retreat, a return to the harmony that Fogas had known for twenty-five years under the rule of Serge Papon. Christian knew his neighbours. Knew they would prefer to give their mayor another chance. Perhaps in a normal session, they may have done. But then, from the back – Christian could not pinpoint exactly where – a lone voice started chanting and the final piece fell into place. Serge was doomed.

'Papon out! Bears out! Papon out! Bears out!'

The mayor's name entwined with the bears, a juxtaposition that was as damning as it was unjustified, beginning as a mere ripple but then swelling in volume as other voices joined in . . .

'Papon out! Bears out!'

. . . washing over the back rows, bringing in its wake the support of farmers, shepherds, old men who'd known 'the young Papon' since he was a child . . .

'Papon out! Bears out!'

. . . spreading through the hall and gaining momentum, gathering up even those who'd voted for Serge in every election . . .

'Papon out! Bears out!'

. . . and on a tidal wave it crashed against the U-shaped table where the councillors sat nonplussed . . .

'Papon out! Bears out!'

Then in unison, the hunters stood, pulling placards from beneath their seats which they held aloft while several of them started blowing on hunting horns, the shrill notes bouncing off the thick walls.

PAPON OUT! KILL THE BEARS! proclaimed the signs, giving text to the deafening noise.

'Order, order!' Pascal shouted. 'We need to vote.'

But the racket only grew louder.

He flapped his arms. He hollered. To no avail. It was like watching a carefully set hill fire run wild, the man who'd been in charge now panicking as the flames shot beyond the boundaries of his control.

'We must vote!' he screamed at the council who could just about hear him. 'All those in favour—'

Christian leapt to his feet. 'We can't vote in these circumstances,' he shouted, trying to overcome the din. 'We need to ask the public to leave. We have to proceed behind closed doors.'

'No!' Pascal retorted. 'We vote now! All those in favour . . .'

Christian sank into his chair, aghast as hands began to rise around the table, the cacophony increasing as each arm was lifted.

Pascal; his cousin Geneviève; Lucien Biros, another second-home owner; Philippe Galy. Four votes in support so far.

Next was Alain Rougé, an honourable ex-policeman who shook his head and mouthed something at Pascal which Christian couldn't hear over the commotion but thought it related to the marital status of the first deputy's parents. Clearly a no, the first refusal sparked further uproar, the hunters stamping their boots and baying their disapproval.

'This is wrong,' shouted Christian but Pascal ignored him and pointed at Monique Sentenac, the council secretary.

Pale-faced beneath her immaculate coiffure, she stared at the crowd, fear visible in her taut features. But Christian knew that she had faced up to far worse than this when her husband was alive. She drew back her shoulders, shot the hunters a look of disdain and said, 'No!'

Feet slammed on the floorboards, catcalls rained down on the council, horns sounded. It was pandemonium. And Josette was next. Her small hand grasped Christian's, bones fine like a child's. She was trembling.

'No!' she said, flinching as the mob screamed.

'And another no!' roared Christian, pounding the table and making Pascal jump.

Four against. With Serge absent, the first deputy needed the last two council members to vote with him to ensure success.

'René?' Pascal rasped, hoarse from shouting. 'Your turn.'

René, who'd kept his focus fixed on the floor throughout, slowly raised his hand and sent the public berserk.

In that moment Christian felt a strange dislocation from it all. The chanting subsided in his head and his concentration fell on chubby Bernard Mirouze, the last councillor to vote and such an ardent fan of Serge Papon that he'd named his beloved beagle after the mayor.

Confusion evident on his plump face, Bernard was studying the empty chair at the top of the table as though seeking guidance from the one man who wasn't there. Then he looked into the crowd. Christian followed his gaze and saw a white-bandaged arm protrude forward, fingers pointed to imitate a gun which was aimed at the head of the *cantonnier*. The virtual trigger was pulled, the gun recoiled, and with a fat tear sliding down his cheeks, Bernard Mirouze lifted his arm into the air.

It should have heralded mayhem but at that precise moment the double doors at the back of the hall flew open and the unmistakable tones of power cut through the chaos.

'*This* is not how a democracy is run!' roared Serge Papon, hands on hips, face livid. He grabbed a placard from the nearest hunter and smashed it over the back of a chair, the sound of splintering wood echoing among the rafters. Shaking the broken shaft at the gathering, his wrath encompassed them all. 'How dare you profane this system! A system your fathers and grandfathers before you died to protect.'

He strode further into the room and glared at those in the gallery, pointing a thick finger in their direction.

'By order of the power invested in me by the French Republic, I demand this chamber be cleared. *Now!*'

Total silence. Bernard's hand was still raised, the tear suspended on his chin. And then, behind the robust figure that held the room transfixed, a white-bandaged arm lifted a placard and, with calculated precision, brought it down towards the square head.

'He'll kill him!' Christian yelled, leaping over the table to protect the elderly mayor. But he was too late.

With the rectangle of wood millimetres away from Serge Papon's skull, a broad hand shot out and flicked the bandaged hunter on the chin. It was the lightest of touches and yet the man's eyes crossed, his legs buckled and his body concertinaed to the floor at the feet of Arnaud Petit. And that, reported the journalist, who was found at the end of the evening cowering under a bench, was when all hell broke loose.

Enraged at the attack on their leader, the hunters rushed at Arnaud Petit, brandishing their placards as weapons. And equally incensed by the assault on their mayor, the good folk of Fogas, forgetting that they had been calling for his resignation only seconds before, went for the outsiders. Christian caught sight of Bernard and René throwing themselves into the mêlée, Bernard landing a solid thump into the belly of one of the orange-beret brigade, before they were swallowed up in a muddle of arms and legs.

'Let's clear the room,' Christian yelled at the huge tracker who was holding his own, swatting off attackers like flies. 'Serge, man the doors!'

Nimble for his age, Serge darted through the fracas to hold the doors open and Arnaud ejected the first protester, propelling the man head first into the hallway.

Struggling against a surge of fleeing people as the more sensible members of the public took the opportunity to escape, Christian made his way to the worst of the fighting. Dodging flailing fists and poorly aimed punches, the majority of the brawlers too old and too fat to cause serious damage, he decided it was no time to distinguish between friend and foe. Instead the farmer started grabbing bodies indiscriminately from the writhing mass, throwing them through the double doors using arms, legs, whatever came to hand and feeling a certain satisfaction as they landed in the corridor where many of them continued tussling.

'Having fun?' Arnaud was next to him, a grin splitting his face as he held a squealing hunter by a little finger. With a flick of his wrist he expelled the man, who got the added insult of a kick up the backside from Serge Papon as he exited.

'Oh yeah!' laughed Christian, hauling someone up from the floor by the ear.

'Merde! It's me you idiot!' shouted a red-faced René, held fast by the farmer's grip but still kicking the prostrate hunter beneath him.

'Sorry!' Christian released his hold, René shooting him an aggrieved look, and together they hoisted the man up by his arms and flung him towards Alain Rougé who'd joined the mayor at the doorway. With a solid hand in the back, another hunter was shown out of the room.

'Last one!' called Arnaud and the pair of them turned to see the tracker frogmarching the man who'd started the trouble to the door. Still groggy-looking, his white bandage now very grubby, the hunter was howling with pain. Yet Arnaud was using only two fingers on the man's elbow to usher him forwards.

'What is he? Some kind of ninja?' muttered René in awe. 'Did you see him knock bandage-boy out? Touched his chin and wham! How the hell does he do it?'

'Don't know,' replied an equally impressed Christian. 'But I'm glad he's on our side!'

The doors were slammed shut, leaving only the eleven council members and Arnaud Petit in the room. And of course, the journalist, who wasn't discovered until much later.

'Christian, Arnaud, make sure none of those scoundrels make their way back in here!' ordered Serge, leaving the two big men to brace themselves against the thick oak doors which juddered and shook as the skirmish continued outside. 'The rest of you, take your seats. We've got a council meeting to conclude.'

'How did you do that?' Christian asked Arnaud as they leaned against the wood, chests still heaving from the commotion. 'Knock that troublemaker out and then that trick with your fingers?'

Arnaud tapped his nose. 'Let's just say he might be in need of a new set of bandages tomorrow.'

Christian laughed and slapped Arnaud on the shoulder.

'Thanks,' he said. 'For rescuing the mayor.'

A slow smile lit the dark features of the man next to him. 'Does this mean I can sit up front on the way home?'

'Right!' Serge's voice came from the head of the U-shaped table where, as a result of their unscheduled interlude, the reassembled councillors appeared somewhat unkempt: René sporting the beginnings of a black eye, Bernard nursing his bruised knuckles and Monique Sentenac doing her best to smooth her dishevelled hair. 'Let's record whatever you were voting on before this debacle started.'

The councillors looked at each other, guilt stealing into their expressions. Then they looked at Pascal who hadn't moved throughout the fight and stood now, frozen in place, face drawn, eyes unfocused, like a man who had lost everything.

'Pascal!' barked the mayor. 'What were you voting on?'

The first deputy mayor turned his head, mouth working but no sound emerging.

'For God's sake, man!' thundered Serge. 'What was the motion?'

'We were voting to remove you.'

It was Josette. Her calm delivery made the words even more emphatic, the magnitude of their betrayal stark against the singular display of leadership they'd just witnessed.

Serge blinked. He rested a hand on the table.

'Right.' He paused. 'And the outcome?'

'In favour.' Pascal had found his voice.

'Okay.' Serge dipped his head. 'Then let it be noted in the minutes.'

'No!' Josette jumped up, gesturing for Monique to stop writing. 'It can't be recorded.'

'Why ever not?' demanded Pascal.

With a look of triumph that made Christian proud to know her, Josette reached for the notepad that she had been scribbling in all evening.

'Because this session has contravened the regulations as stated in the Code Général,' she continued, beginning to read from the set of rules that governed local councils. '"In the case of an extraordinary meeting being called by the mayor or by the majority of the council members, the meeting shall focus only on those items as listed in the agenda. No other subjects shall be discussed."'

She placed the notepad on the table and held up a piece of paper.

'I have a copy of the agenda for tonight. The one you drew up, Pascal. It lists only one item – a discussion of the problems arising from the presence of bears in the area. Which means, according to the regulation I just quoted, that's what we should have been talking about. Nothing else. As I don't think even you could convince the authorities that deposing our mayor comes under that topic, we have therefore deviated from the agenda and this motion is null and void. *That's* what should be noted in the official record.'

Amid a buzz of confusion, she took her seat, the slightest of smiles playing on her lips.

'Well done!' Christian mouthed across the room, aware of how much it had taken for the normally reticent Josette to confront the first deputy mayor.

'Huh! Never thought I'd be glad to hear someone quoting the Code!'

René's quip raised a few laughs, his usual irritation at the pedantic adherence to the rules, favoured by Fatima Souquet above all others, having been replaced with relief that his part in the notorious vote would not be committed to paper. Likewise, Bernard was blowing out his cheeks at his fortuitous salvation while Monique was giving Josette a thumbs up. Pascal, however, merely looked like he was about to be sick.

'Thank you, Josette.' Serge's voice stifled the beginnings of conversation and he got slowly to his feet. 'Your loyalty means a lot to me. But I fear Pascal will get his way after all. You see, I only came here tonight to tell you that I've decided to resign. I intend to submit my letter to the Prefect in Foix at the end of the year.'

He glanced down at his hands which rested on the table, tracing the twists and knots that had marred them with age as though they would guide him to what to say next. Then, realising perhaps that nothing remained to be said, he picked his way through the overturned chairs and headed out of the door that Arnaud was holding open for him. The hallway beyond had emptied, the unheated space having served to cool the passions that had run high, and Christian's last image of the mayor of Fogas was of him struggling into his coat as he stepped out into the moonless night.

'That,' remarked Arnaud as the outside door slammed shut, 'is not what this place needs!'

Which is precisely when the journalist emerged from under a table to one side of the room, notebook still clutched in his hand, glasses crooked and his hair tousled and laced with cobwebs.

'Is it all over?' he asked, voice quavering and eyes large behind cracked lenses.

'Yes,' said Christian, surveying the shocked faces of the councillors who were still trying to make sense of what had happened. 'In more ways than one, I fear.'

'He resigned? Just like that?'

Christian nodded.

'Wow.'

'Wow indeed.'

The fire crackled, the four figures clustered around the table in the bar flickering in the light it cast over them.

'Wish I'd been there,' sighed Véronique.

'No you don't!' said Josette, still wan from the experience. 'It was awful. Terrifying, in fact.'

'Oh, I don't know . . .' Arnaud gave a sly grin. 'There were some good bits!'

Christian laughed despite himself.

'Wasn't too good coming out to all that damage in the car park,' countered Josette and the two men sobered up like chastised children.

'And you think it was the hunters who attacked the cars?'

'Who else?' replied Christian. 'Luckily they only bent a wing mirror on mine. Which was already loose.'

'Probably took pity on it because of its age!'

Christian scowled at the postmistress. 'They didn't discriminate as far as I could tell. Philippe had his windscreen smashed, Geneviève Souquet's tyres were slashed. In fact, Pascal's Range Rover got the worst of the damage. They scrawled "Bears out" all over it. It'll be a while before he gets that white paint off.'

'Huh! You reap what you sow,' Josette declared primly.

'Still, sounds like he'll be too relieved at how the evening ended to worry about his car.'

'You could be right. His carefully orchestrated protest got out of hand and, thanks to Josette, his plans to overthrow Serge legitimately were wrecked. But just as he thought all was lost, he was rescued by the person he was trying to undermine.' Christian gave a dry laugh. 'By the time we left he was looking like a modern-day Lazarus after Christ had performed his tricks – dazed and a bit disbelieving!'

The biblical reference, coming from a man who had no time for religion, made Véronique smile. 'Didn't know you knew anything about the works of the Lord.'

'After tonight, I think I can claim to have witnessed a miracle first hand!'

'Seriously though, do you really think he planned all this? Pascal? I mean he's not exactly bright.'

'Fatima is,' pointed out Josette. 'She could easily have plotted this little coup.'

'Pascal had help all right.' Christian downed the last of his brandy and glanced over at Arnaud Petit. 'But it wasn't Fatima.'

'What makes you say that?' asked Véronique.

Arnaud replied. 'He was on the phone. The troublemaker who started it all. We both saw him.'

'So? He was on the phone. What does that have to do with anything?'

'Everything,' stated Christian. 'We're pretty sure he was getting directions from the person on the other end.'

'You mean someone was coordinating it all from afar? Who on earth would want to do that?'

'No idea. It doesn't make sense. But someone was giving orders to those hunters. Orders which played into Pascal's hands. And I can't think for the life of me who it could be.'

'The question you need to be asking,' Arnaud interjected, 'is *why*.'

'Go on,' said Christian.

'Well, something has been puzzling me all night. Okay, we all know hunters, shepherds and farmers want rid of the bears.'

Christian raised his hands in protest.

'*Most* farmers,' Arnaud continued. 'So you'd expect them to be there tonight. Expect them to cause trouble, maybe. I've seen it before. People get fired up and demand I leave. Demand I take the bears with me. But what I can't understand about this evening is why the hunters were calling for Serge to be dismissed. If they were genuine protesters, they would have focused on the bears. And on me.'

'It doesn't make sense,' muttered Christian for the second time.

'Yes, it does!' Véronique, her mind genetically predisposed to cope with the machinations of local politics, leaned forward excitedly. 'Someone was using the anti-bear protest as a ruse for getting rid of our mayor. So if you find out why

Serge's downfall would benefit anyone other than Pascal, then you find the person who was on the other end of that phone.'

Arnaud nodded agreement but if Véronique's words had encouraged any sense of optimism among those around the table, Josette's reply quickly quashed it.

'It's all irrelevant,' she said, gathering up the glasses and stacking them on the bar. 'Because with Serge resigning and every possibility that we might be losing you, Christian, there's not a thing we can do. Come the New Year, Pascal Souquet will be mayor of Fogas.'

'You imbecile.'

Pascal stared out at the night. There was nothing else to see, the moonless sky rendering the landscape before him indiscernible.

'You almost ruined it.'

'I didn't know—'

'That's your problem, Pascal. You don't know.' The man inhaled on his cigarette, the end glowing bright in the dark, and then he exhaled and Pascal fought the cough that rose in his throat as the smoke swirled between them. 'If it hadn't been for Papon's decision to retire, all our plans would have been for nothing.'

'But . . . but it's okay,' stuttered Pascal. 'And with Christian Dupuy leaving too . . .'

'Yes, that is fortunate.'

'And there's the post office. Once I've sorted that . . .'

'It will be the end of Fogas.' A staccato of laughter completely devoid of mirth and then a voice weighted with intimidation. 'Just don't mess up this time. Or you'll be dealing with far worse than paint on your precious foreign car.'

He flicked the cigarette into the void in front of them and

turned to go. It was only as Pascal made to follow, that he realised he was trembling from head to toe.

When the earth had turned sufficiently to shift the position of the stars in the ebony sky, and the dust that had been raised in the town hall had settled back onto the varnished floorboards, Jacques was still awake, standing at the window of the épicerie and mulling over the evening's events.

Stephanie had collected Chloé just after eight and Véronique had passed the remaining time reading a book about the Russian Revolution, no doubt preparing herself for when her history protégée reached that particular epoch. Jacques himself had spent the hours snoozing in the inglenook, dreaming about the time he and Serge Papon had cornered a wild boar up in the hills above Fogas. Massive, it was, with fearsome tusks and a short, powerful body. Must have weighed nearly 150 kilograms.

In real life the boar had charged and Serge had only just dragged Jacques out of the way, both of them slipping on the damp leaves underfoot. They'd been left sprawled on their backs as it thundered down the mountain. In his dream, however, Jacques was lining up to take the shot, rifle pressed into his shoulder, his hands miraculously free of the tremors that afflicted them in his waking hours. The beast was his.

And then the shop door had crashed open and Josette had rushed in, all of a flutter after the eventful council meeting, and the boar of his dreams had evaporated into the billow of smoke that was sucked out of the fire on the draught of her arrival. Arnaud and Christian had sauntered in after her, much more amicable than when they'd departed hours before, and over several glasses of brandy, they'd filled Véronique in on the details. Jacques, from his ringside seat, had soaked up every word.

How he wished he could have been there. Much as he'd

fallen out with Serge Papon in the later years of life, the close friendship of their youth not surviving into adulthood and marriage, he wouldn't have hesitated to join in the fray.

It had been ages since there'd been a good altercation at a council meeting. Last one he could remember was between Monsieur Sentenac and old Henri Estaque, Annie's father. Monsieur Sentenac had turned up drunk and accused his wife, Monique, of having an affair. With everyone expecting him to point the finger at Serge Papon, whose philandering was legendary, the councillors had been agog when Monsieur Sentenac had instead named Henri as the guilty party, despite his advanced years. Henri had denied it, truthfully as it had turned out, but the jealous husband had lunged at him anyway. With a hunting knife.

Jacques couldn't recall all that followed. But he did remember that the knife had been a rather beautiful item, hand-forged by a smithy somewhere past St Lary on the route over the Portet d'Aspet. He'd picked it up off the floor while Serge held the drunkard down and had been mesmerised by the intricate woodwork on the handle. Wonder where that had ended up?

Anyway, it had transpired at a much later date that Monsieur Sentenac had had every right to be indignant; he just hadn't got the right person. Many years later when he burst in on his wife and the curé – needless to say not in church – he was brandishing a rifle. The curé was last seen leaping from the bedroom window and fleeing down the back path towards the vestry in a state of undress, having left a lot more than his clerical collar behind.

So that had been the last time a fight had broken out in the town hall. But tonight sounded a lot more serious. From what Christian had said, the rabble-rousers had been highly organised and well prepared. And from outside the area.

Which was the bit that concerned Jacques most.

He cast an idle glance down the street, knowing he should retire to the fireplace and get some rest but too wound up to go to sleep. Pressing his nose to the glass, he could just make out a light in a window of the old school. Arnaud Petit's flat. So he was still up too. Given the angle the buildings were at, it was impossible to see if Véronique's windows were similarly lit. But then, she could be in with Arnaud. Now *that* would annoy Christian!

Jacques chuckled softly, the *Fermé* sign lifting on his exhalation.

The farmer had been vexed enough to see Véronique heading off into the night with the big tracker without having to contemplate them having a tête-à-tête into the small hours. Oh, what fun he'd have with this knowledge if he was alive, thought Jacques, his great affection for Christian never having stopped him from teasing the young man when it was merited.

And this merited it.

Jacques was about to turn in for the night when headlights pierced the dark, coming up the valley from the direction of St Girons. Someone was up late. Curious to see if it was anyone he knew, he remained in the window as the full beams lit up the interior of the shop, him included. But of course, he couldn't be seen. It had taken him a while to grasp that. Back in February when he'd started his nocturnal vigils, driven by a sense of impending danger which threatened Chloé and her mother, he'd dived to the floor every time a vehicle went past. Now he knew better.

As the car came round the corner in front of the épicerie, its lights moving across the shelves of cassoulet, the empty breadbaskets and the collection of knives above the till, it started to slow and eventually pulled up midway between his vantage point and the old school. The passenger door opened and someone got out.

Whoever it was waited for the car to drive off. Then he, for Jacques was sure it was a he by the way he moved, crossed the road in quick strides and walked towards the bar. It took a few steps before the sulphurous glow from the street lamp across from the épicerie was enough to show his features. But when the man finally entered the weak circle of light, Jacques shrank back from the window despite himself.

For the person was none other than Pascal Souquet.

Peering cautiously around the window frame, Jacques watched the first deputy mayor of Fogas walk up the alleyway to the church and he couldn't help remembering something. A memory from last spring. Pascal Souquet getting out of a car in the dead of night.

If it had been yesterday he might have persuaded himself that Pascal was capable of cheating on Fatima. After all, no matter how improbable given the man in question and his ferocious wife, what other explanation could there be?

But after hearing about the goings-on up at the town hall, Jacques was confident that this was no mere dalliance. In fact he was convinced that it was connected to Pascal's attempts to overthrow Serge.

It took a few moments for the significance of this to hit home.

Whoever had been driving that car was probably the person Christian was trying to identify. But for the life of him, Jacques couldn't recall a thing about the vehicle or its driver.

With a groan, he turned and headed for bed, thinking, as he settled beside the dying embers of the fire, that for once it would be good if someone else in Fogas would take on the mantle of guardian angel. He, for one, was sorely tired of it.

8

In the same way that the cuckoo heralds the coming spring, so the struggling engine on the Panda 4x4 was a harbinger for the onset of winter. Blowing on his freezing fingers in an attempt to restore sensation, Christian turned the key in the ignition once more and was rewarded with a spluttering cough that finally sparked into life.

'Good girl,' he muttered, patting the steering wheel, his breath condensing in front of his face. Leaving the car running, he got out and began scraping the ice off the windscreen.

A week and a half on from the fracas at the town hall, and the weather, just like the atmosphere in the commune, had taken a turn for the worse. Snow now covered the mountains and most mornings began with a hoar frost that glazed the bare trees, the roofs, the grass and of course, his car, in a thick layer of white. Under the blue sky that stretched across the mountains, it was breathtaking, almost making the inconveniences it brought with it worthwhile.

Almost, thought Christian, as he shook his hands which were now raw with the cold.

Visibility restored, he got back behind the wheel, the interior barely above freezing as the fan rattled and chugged in an effort to raise the temperature. With a sigh, he released the handbrake and pulled out onto the road, turning the hiccuping vehicle towards Picarets, as reluctant to make this journey as the Panda seemed to be.

It had been a long ten days, the fallout from the council meeting still causing tension even amongst those who had once been friends. Alain Rougé and Philippe Galy had argued bitterly about Philippe's decision to support Pascal and the two men were now not speaking to each other. As a result, part of the commune was boycotting Philippe's honey and applying pressure on Josette to stop stocking it in the épicerie. So far she'd stood her ground, saying that Philippe had acted within the law, but she was feeling the strain.

Meanwhile, René and Bernard's outing with the hunting group the weekend before had been fraught as they were still sporting bruises inflicted by the very people they were hunting with, who were also the worse for wear. As everyone had been carrying a rifle, it hadn't made for the most harmonious of Saturdays and René had declared afterwards that he was contemplating setting up a rival lodge. So far, potential members numbered two: René and Bernard. The thought of spending most Wednesday afternoons and every Saturday in the company of just the *cantonnier* had been enough to make René change his mind. And go back on the cigarettes.

As for Christian himself, in the intervening days the political wrangling had been overshadowed somewhat by events at home. Eve Rumeau, the estate agent, had dropped by with her valuation, her personal visit being the subject of much teasing from his parents, and although the figure she'd quoted had been far higher than the Dupuys had expected for their ramshackle farm, seeing the numbers on the page had brought home the awful reality of what was about to happen.

While his father had wandered around the place muttering about the ethics of a society that was willing to pay a farmer over the odds for his buildings but begrudged him a fair price for the produce that came off his land, Christian's mother had been far more practical. Firmly believing that action prevents despondency, she had started packing, the contents of the house gradually disappearing into cartons that she brought back from the supermarket in St Girons. Consequently, Christian and his father now spent their days tripping over boxes marked 'Café Grand'Mère' or 'William Saurin Coq au Vin' and were forever having to ask her where things were.

So it was hardly a surprise that it had taken him this long to arrange a meeting with Serge Papon to discuss the future of Fogas. And now as he drove down the road that led to Picarets, taking the bends with extra caution given the likelihood of black ice, he was wishing he'd taken a bit longer. Because when he thought about what lay ahead for the commune he was filled with dread. Not only that Pascal would be in charge, but also that he, Christian Dupuy, would not be around to witness the changes that would bring. He'd be up in Toulouse in some soulless one-bed apartment that faced onto a brick wall instead of a mountain range, and working inside a noise-ridden factory instead of walking his fields in the fresh Pyrenean air. And when he thought about not seeing his parents, Josette, René, Véronique . . .

Depression wasn't a word he'd ever had much use for. Although convinced that his prize Limousin bull, Sarko, suffered from the ailment when he was separated from the cows, it wasn't something he'd ever applied to his own mental state. He'd never had need to. A walk in the hills cured most problems and a dose of Estaque-tonic dished out liberally by Annie or Véronique tended to rectify everything else. Now though, with his heart slowly tearing apart, he didn't think either remedy could heal him.

With a mood as black as something pulled out of his mother's oven, he approached Picarets. Even the familiar sight of Stephanie's cottage on the outskirts of the village, its eye-catching shutters thrown wide open and dazzling in the winter sunlight, failed to cheer him. But the small bundle of energy in a bright orange coat that came bounding down the path on his approach raised an instinctive smile.

'Christian!' Chloé waved her arms frantically, wanting him to stop.

Christian pulled up and wound down the window, letting the precious pocket of warm air that the heater had laboured to produce seep away.

'Bonjour, Chloé!' He kissed her cheeks, surprised at how cold they were. 'Have you been outside practising? In this?'

'I'm still working on the aerial cartwheel,' she said solemnly, her ambition to be a famous trapeze artist not something she ever joked about. And after the events of the last year when her passion had saved the lives of herself and her mother, it was no longer a laughing matter in the commune either. 'I'm just not getting the landing right.'

She showed him her back which was covered in frost.

'And your mother knows . . . ?'

Chloé grinned. 'Of course. Fabian's over and they're both in the kitchen watching me. Well, they're supposed to be watching me but they seem to be looking at each other a lot!' She made a kissing noise and rolled her eyes.

'They're still happy then?' Christian asked, and she nodded, black curls bouncing. 'So what can I do for you?'

'I need some bear poo.'

'Some what?'

'Bear poo. You know. S-H-I-T.' She spelt out the adult word.

'I know what bear sh— poo is, Chloé! I just wondered why on earth you need some.'

'It's for my project at school.'

'Does Madame Soum know what you're including as a part of this project?'

'It's a surprise.' Christian didn't comment on this understatement. Perhaps sensing his reluctance to get involved, she continued, 'I read that you can tell what bears eat from their poo. So I'm going to dissect it and list all the ingredients. And that way I'll be able to prove Miel didn't kill any sheep.'

'Miel?'

'The bear René saw in the woods. They wrote about her in the paper.'

'Right.' Christian stroked his chin in contemplation; her naive enthusiasm was contagious. 'So tell me, how exactly am I supposed to get this for you?'

'Oh, I don't need you to get it. It's far too dangerous. I want you to ask Arnaud the Bear-Man to get me some.'

Just like that, the ray of sunshine that had illuminated the dark interior of Christian's soul disappeared behind a cloud.

'Ask Arnaud, eh? I'll see what I can do,' he promised, not wanting to reveal to the young girl how wounded he was by her casual remarks. And not quite understanding why they had hurt so much, either.

'Brilliant!' She threw her arms around his neck and gave him a farewell kiss before scampering back round the cottage to the garden.

'Bear-Man indeed!' Christian muttered as he drove off. 'Too dangerous! Huh. As if I couldn't do his job. Don't see what's so special . . .'

His grumbling lasted through the village, continued the entire length of the road past Annie's farm and all the way to the T-junction opposite the Auberge on the valley floor. As he turned his head to check for traffic he caught sight of himself in the twisted wing mirror which was hanging drunkenly to one side, the hunters not having succeeded in wrecking it completely. The frown that creased his forehead seemed to have become a permanent feature and the dark shadows under his eyes were getting more pronounced with each successive sleepless night.

He gave himself a mental shake.

There was enough going on without getting stressed about Arnaud Petit. Especially as he couldn't for the life of him work out why the man got under his skin so much. He'd thought they'd formed a friendship of sorts at the town hall but a few words from a ten-year-old and he was all worked up again.

It would do him good to call in on the man. Put Chloé's request to him and see how his work was faring. He'd go over to the old school right away. Although . . .

He looked at the clock on the dashboard. It was only eight. Would he be up? And what if . . .

What if Arnaud opened the door and a pair of slender bare legs, legs which the farmer had once had the privilege of seeing, were visible in the background? And what if in the foreground the floor was littered with items of clothing? And in case he had any doubt as to the owner of those legs, his mind added a small cross on a chain, thrown over the arm of the couch. What if . . .

A toot on a horn roused him from his agonies and he saw Stephanie's blue van behind him.

'Stop daydreaming, Christian!' Stephanie called out, her words loud in the morning silence. 'Whoever she is, I need to get to work!'

He raised a hand in acknowledgement, gave a sheepish grin and pulled off onto the main road.

What if, indeed!

He passed over the small bridge that spanned a stream which ran into the much larger river to his left and as he approached the épicerie, he saw none other than Arnaud Petit, breakfast baguette tucked under his arm. Glad to be spared a visit to the flat, Christian parked and got out.

'Bonjour, Christian! Not stuck the wing mirror back on yet?'

Christian shook the extended hand. 'Out of tape. I'll pick some up when I'm next in town.'

'I've got some in the flat. Do you want to come and get it?'

'No! Erm . . . I mean, no rush. I'll fix it later.'

Arnaud shrugged.

'I do have a favour to ask though. Bizarre one, really. On behalf of young Chloé.'

He explained the nature of the request along with the reasoning behind it and the tracker burst into laughter, a resplendent sound that made Christian smile too. We could actually be good friends, he thought. Given time.

'I'm heading up into the hills today so I'll see what I can do,' Arnaud promised. 'Although it's the wrong time of year as Miel will be in hibernation by now. But I'll find something for Chloé. Can't have that enthusiasm dashed!'

'Thanks!' Christian was about to head off into the shop when inspiration struck. 'Did you get some of Josette's scrumptious croissants to go with your baguette?' he asked, all innocence.

With a look of disdain, Arnaud patted his lean waist. 'Not good for the figure,' he said and strode off towards his flat. And when he got there, he would open the door and the room would be empty. No bare legs. No clothes. No cross. Of that Christian was sure. For if he knew anything about Véronique Estaque, he knew that she wasn't the kind of woman to go without croissants in the morning.

Feeling much lighter in spirit, he entered the shop and headed straight for the wicker basket which was filled to the brim with the moon-shaped pastries. He popped two in a bag and was halfway to the counter to pay when his hand, without any conscious thought, patted his hips.

He froze. Then he walked back to the basket, emptied the bag and picked up a baguette instead.

'Watching your weight are you, Christian?' commented Josette as she took his money.

'No!' he retorted. 'Just don't need the extra sugar.'

Leaning against the window, the ghostly figure of Jacques slapped his thigh and started laughing uncontrollably. Christian was halfway to Fogas before Josette managed to get her husband to calm down and when he finally stopped chuckling and settled in the inglenook for a snooze, she was left wondering what that had all been about.

Whatever reluctance Serge Papon had felt on entering the town hall, a place he hadn't set foot in for the last ten days, the aroma of coffee wafting from his desk had helped put him in a better frame of mind. And when he saw the croissant on a plate next to it, the pastry golden and flaky, he felt his appetite return for the first time in months.

'Thanks, Céline,' he said, popping his head back through the open door to acknowledge the secretary in the office beyond.

She looked up from her computer and smiled, a rare sight for the inhabitants of Fogas. 'I called into the épicerie on my way up and couldn't resist.' She held up a plate to show her complicity. 'Decided I'd corrupt you too!'

He laughed and turned to go.

'Monsieur Mayor,' she addressed him with the formal title that only she and Bernard Mirouze ever used. 'Is it true what people are saying? That you're going to resign?'

'Yes. At the end of the year.'

She scowled, a return to her normal demeanour. 'You'd better take this then.'

Reaching into the top drawer of the cabinet next to her, she pulled out a sealed envelope and thrust it across the desk at him. He slit it open, quickly scanned the letter it contained, and then he sighed.

'Céline, you don't have to do this. I appreciate your loyalty but—'

'Loyalty?' She almost choked on the word. 'I'm not stupid

enough to give up a state pension for loyalty! But even the promise of being well cared for in my old age can't persuade me to work for that snake Pascal Souquet.'

'But there's no saying he'll be the next mayor. You seem to be forgetting Christian Dupuy.'

'And you,' she said, her eyes narrowing, 'seem to be forgetting that Christian Dupuy's farm is on the market and he's looking for a job in Toulouse. Which pretty much means, between the pair of you, you've handed Fogas to that odious Parisian and his insufferable wife.'

'What did you say?' Serge leaned a hand against the doorframe, suddenly light-headed.

'I said, you've handed—'

'Before that. About Christian.'

'He's leaving. Apparently. He's putting the farm up for sale in the New Year.'

'So Pascal will be mayor . . .'

'You didn't *know*?'

'No. Not a clue.' He wandered dazedly back into his office, closing the door on the open-mouthed stare of his secretary.

That put a different slant on things. He collapsed into his chair and stared blankly at the croissant, which had lost all its appeal.

Could he do this? Walk away from his position and leave the commune in the hands of the self-serving man who was his first deputy? Because without Christian Dupuy around, that's what would happen. No one else on the council was capable of commanding enough support to overthrow Pascal and his second-home-owning faction. And it seemed as if he'd already made inroads on Christian's power base if the vote the other night was anything to go by.

Serge reached down and scratched his legs, his eczema having flared up again with the onset of winter. The doctor had given him ointment to apply daily but without Thérèse to remind him, his skin was suffering. Which seemed only fitting when the rest of him was suffering too, almost as if the permanent itchiness were a manifestation of his internal unrest.

This latest hiccup was making life no easier.

It was a difficult decision. When he'd contemplated the future of Fogas, it was with Christian Dupuy at the helm. Céline's news rendered that impossible. But was the thought of leaving his fiefdom to Pascal dreadful enough to make him stay on as mayor?

No.

Because in his present state, he, Serge Papon, wasn't what this commune needed. Far better that he stand aside and let those who were genuinely concerned about local affairs take charge.

Even if that meant Pascal Souquet. And, of course, a new secretary for the town hall.

He read Céline's letter again and noticed the date in the top right-hand corner. The letter was over two years old! She'd had it in her drawer all that time, in preparation for the day when the leadership changed and the worst, in her opinion, came to pass. Which meant that after only two months of working with him, for Pascal had been elected in the spring of that year, Céline had known she hated the man. Enough to give up a state pension.

But even that wasn't sufficient to change Serge Papon's mind.

He reached for the croissant, despite knowing that he would taste nothing, his entire life being devoid of flavour of late. He broke off a corner and began to chew mechanically, his thoughts drifting back to the last council meeting and the motion he had interrupted.

They'd turned against him. René. Bernard. Christian too, perhaps? Without a record of the vote he couldn't be sure.

He felt a spark of the old passion ignite, indignant that he should be treated thus. But it was quickly smothered under the suffocating blanket of depression that was permanently over him. He took one more bite and then, unable to derive any pleasure from it, pushed the croissant to one side.

Christian wouldn't have supported Pascal, would he? Surely he would have seen through the man and his intentions? Not that the farmer owed any loyalty to his mayor given recent history, Serge would be the first to admit that.

But still. Not knowing how Christian had voted bothered him. And he wasn't sure why.

Feeling the familiar irritation flare up again on his legs, he vowed to search out the ointment when he got home.

Christian took the steps two at a time in a fit of youthful energy, startling the town hall secretary when he bounded into her office.

'Bonjour, Céline. Is he here?' he asked, trying not to be worried by the fact that his heart was rattling in his ribcage, telling him that he wasn't as young as he felt.

'Yes.' To the point and laced with disappointment.

'Everything okay?'

'Fine!'

Christian, despite his naivety in the ways of women, sensed all was not fine. He equally knew, thanks to some innate instinct, not to enquire any further. Instead he hurried across the room, knocked on the door to the mayor's office and entered.

'Suppose you bloody voted against me too!' barked the squat figure behind the desk before the door had even closed.

'Bonjour, Serge. Glad to see you and Céline are in such good form!'

Serge grumped, pointed at a vacant chair and held out a letter. Taking his seat, Christian quickly read the single page.

'She's quitting?'

'Because of us. She says with me resigning and you going, she has no option. Is it true? You're leaving?'

'Probably.' Christian shrugged, trying to downplay his problems. 'Can't see a way around it, really. Know anyone who'd like a nice farm? Complete with bull.'

'Sarko? You're selling him too?'

'What else can I do? I can't take him with me to Toulouse. So far I've had no takers though. Apart from the knacker's yard.'

Knowing that the pain was visible in his face no matter how lightly he tried to treat the subject, he glanced down at the letter. Which was when he noticed the date.

'Christ! Céline must really hate Pascal!'

Serge chuckled darkly. 'Amazing, isn't it? That he can inspire such passion, even of a negative sort. Which brings me back to my question . . .'

'Did I vote to remove you? No, I didn't. But do you care?'

Serge was rather surprised to find he did. A lot. He pulled the croissant back towards him and took another bite, flakes of pastry melting in his mouth.

'Mmm . . .'

Christian tore his gaze away, stomach rumbling loudly. 'And as for Bernard—'

'I know about Bernard.' Serge took a mouthful of coffee, the bitter taste complementing the flavour of the pastry, and he found himself wanting more. 'He came to see me in tears. Wanted to explain his actions.'

'Did they threaten him?'

'Worse than that. Bernard would have stood up to them if it was *his* life in danger.'

'What then?'

Serge rubbed his temples, a flash of anger pulsing blood

into his head. 'The bastards threatened to kill his dog if he didn't vote to depose me.'

'Merde!' Christian exclaimed, the white-bandaged hand holding the imaginary gun suddenly making sense.

They contemplated each other in silence, contemplated the future of Fogas, and their twin acts of betrayal lay unspoken between them.

'What can we do?' Serge finally asked. 'I can't go on as mayor. I just can't do it anymore. Not since Thérèse . . . And you, it's not as if you have a choice.'

'We need time. If we can delay the elections for a few months, we may be able to scupper Pascal's plans.'

'And by then something may have turned up which means you don't have to leave.'

The hope in Serge's voice made Christian smile wryly. 'Now that would take a miracle. But it should be long enough to get a decent campaign organised.'

'Perhaps persuade Josette or René to stand for mayor?'

Christian nodded. 'And find out who is so eager to get Pascal elected. And why.'

'So you want me to delay my resignation?'

'Would you?'

'I'll give you until March.' Serge reached for the remaining morsel of croissant and popped it in his mouth, aware finally of the farmer's focus. 'Sorry, only had the one,' he explained, licking his lips to catch the last vestiges of pastry. 'From Josette's. You should pick some up on the way past.'

'I think I might do that,' said Christian as he rose to leave. 'Don't suppose you have another exit out of here? One that doesn't pass Céline?'

Serge grinned at the big man before him. 'There's always the window!'

★ ★ ★

While Christian Dupuy was seriously considering squeezing his body through the window of the town hall, Arnaud Petit was walking slowly uphill, labouring under the heavy load on his back. But he didn't mind. The sun was out. The temperature had risen, the morning frost long since burnt off. And up above the trees, a canopy of blue stretched overhead.

It was his version of paradise. Not another person in sight. Just the rustle of dead leaves beneath his boots as he climbed ever higher, noting tracks and spoor with the ease of a man reading a newspaper over his morning coffee.

Forty minutes into his hike, when the forest began to give way to small clearings and scraps of pasture, he stopped in a thicket of trees. Letting the sounds of the woods settle around him, he waited, alert for anything out of place. Anyone who shouldn't be there.

He'd been careful, leaving his car in Picarets at the foot of the track that led up to the old quarry and on to Fogas. He'd made sure he was seen setting off up the path, greeting Fabian and waving to Madame Rogalle as she ushered her twins into her car, late for school. Then, once above the village and hidden from view, he'd doubled back, cutting across the mountainside on a narrow trail and scrambling down to the main road above Annie Estaque's isolated farmhouse. He'd crossed the road undetected and then started up the opposite side, climbing steadily, the Estaque farm soon out of sight.

Perhaps he was being overcautious. But it didn't hurt. Not with the levels of hostility he'd witnessed at the town hall. He couldn't shake off the feeling that something terrible was going to happen in the commune of Fogas and that Miel was going to be at the centre of it. All the more reason why he had to make sure no one had followed him. That no one *could* follow him. The last thing he wanted was to lead someone to her door.

He eased away from the rock he'd been standing on, careful to leave no impressions, no evidence of his visit, and half an hour of fast walking later he arrived at the first of his destinations. A circle of barbed wire strung around a group of trees about fifty centimetres off the ground and in the middle, suspended from a branch, a plastic container giving out a noxious odour of fish and blood. It was ingenious, Arnaud had to admit.

Despite his initial aversion to such methods, having monitored the research team's traps for over a month he was beginning to see their use. Attracted by the foul smell, the bears ducked under the wire and in the process left behind precious fur which the researchers could then collect and use to build up a DNA database and a record of behaviour.

But it didn't end there.

Once inside the enclosure, the bears aimed straight for the bag of corn hanging above the stinking lure. And in doing so, set off a motion-sensitive camera hidden in the trees, the resultant images being beamed straight to Arnaud's laptop down in La Rivière.

So far, it hadn't made for spectacular viewing: several curious wild boar, a passing deer and a couple of lost hunters who'd had more difficulty getting out of the trap than any of the wildlife, thus vindicating Arnaud's low estimation of their intelligence. There had been a few grainy images of a bear however, captured at night by a camera up above the old quarry.

It had been hard to say exactly how large the animal was as it shuffled past with an unusually lopsided gait, but it was enough for Arnaud to know it wasn't Miel. In fact, he was pretty sure it was the elusive male that he'd been searching for since his arrival – the same bear that had left its mark down at the bins by the Sarrat bridge.

He'd gone up to the trap the next day and retrieved a cluster of hairs which he'd sent to headquarters for analysis. But he'd found no decent tracks leading away from the camera, nothing that he could compare to the print he already possessed. Faced with only broken branches and snapped twigs, he'd soon lost the trail when it had led into the quarry, the stony ground yielding no further clues. Still, he had the bear's DNA so he'd had to admit that the cameras served a purpose.

With five such traps installed in the area, one of the conditions for Arnaud being allowed to remain in the region was that he check them every week or so, changing batteries when needed and recharging the bait. As he reached into his rucksack and dug out a bottle of turpentine which he sloshed onto a tree as a further ursine enticement, he wondered how many more trips he'd need to make this year.

Given that it was late November, his last few visits had produced little of interest. A few boar bristles but that was it. With the onset of winter the woods were beginning to quieten down, small rodents curling up in their nests and the bears making their way to their dens on the mountainside. Which was where Arnaud was heading next.

Checking once more that he was alone, he swung his rucksack onto his back and, without recourse to compass or map, effortlessly picked up the route he'd hiked only weeks before. He walked stealthily, using every technique he'd learnt in the art of being invisible as he headed ever higher, until he emerged between two outcrops of rock onto a small plateau way above the twin valleys of Fogas. In front of him a flat expanse of rough grass and boulders stretched to the edge of a pristine tarn, its surface rippling slightly in the breeze. Behind it, curving up out of the water, were the steep slopes of the mountain. And it was on the other side of those very slopes, south-facing and remote, that he would find Miel.

The smile that began at the thought froze half-formed as a clatter of stones came from on top of the outcrop to his left.

He'd been followed!

Slipping the rucksack silently to the floor, he flattened himself against the rock face. Another clatter, this time pebbles trickling over the edge. Whoever it was didn't care if they were heard. Which probably meant they were armed. And he was a sitting duck.

Idiot. After the unrest at the council meeting, he should have been more careful.

Stretching his arms overhead to grab hold of the top of the crag, he pulled himself slowly upwards, trying not to make any noise. If he could surprise them he might still have a chance. But as he peered over the edge, he only had time to register multiple legs before he was attacked, a compact body hurtling towards him.

Losing his precarious hold, he tumbled backwards as a silver flash of hooves soared over his head, closely followed by a second set. With a tremendous rattle, they landed on the rocks behind him and hurtled away over the plateau.

Izards! Two males, long horns arching over their backs and so engrossed in their annual battle for supremacy that they'd been unaware of his presence. From his prone position he watched as they chased each other across the open space and up the far side of the mountain, their hooves barely touching the ground as they leapt upwards, agile and surefooted like their alpine cousins, the chamois. He waited until they were out of sight before picking himself up, grabbing his rucksack and walking towards the tarn. The terrain was hard underfoot, rain not having fallen for a while and the frost now mere droplets clinging to the odd blade of grass. It wasn't the best of conditions for tracking. But Arnaud didn't need assistance from the elements. He stopped at the water's edge, where the soil gave way to soft silt.

There. Part submerged but clear nevertheless. A bear's footprint, claw marks pronounced, the broad pad of a front paw well defined.

He crouched next to it, careful to leave no tracks himself, and took measurements. Then, with his fingers, he smoothed out the ridges and indentations until all that remained was a muddy smudge.

Having scanned the shore until he was satisfied there were no other telltale signs, he started cautiously down the incline. He was still some distance from the spot when he heard something between a snore and a grunt. He hadn't expected this. She was supposed to be asleep.

Arriving at a ledge that overlooked her den, he shuffled forwards on his stomach until he could see through the bushes, down into the small clearing that she had made her own. And there she was. Bathed in the sunlight poured onto the grass, Miel was standing outside the deep crevice that she had chosen for her winter sleep.

Still carrying her weight from the autumn feeding, she looked fantastic. An exquisite specimen of bear, coat thick, body solid. And unencumbered by a radio collar! Something he was proud of, especially as it wouldn't be long before she gave birth.

She grunted again, took a few paces forward, staggering left and right like a drunk on a Saturday night, and then lazily scratched her back against a boulder, her face held up to the sun. After a few more scratches, she stumbled towards the den and disappeared inside.

It was the bear equivalent of sleepwalking, a mid-hibernation stroll without being fully awake. Arnaud had heard his colleagues talk about it but had never witnessed it before. Not wanting to risk interrupting a repeat performance, he let an hour elapse before he moved. Then, when he was sure she had settled back to sleep, he slipped noiselessly down to the clearing and crept across to the rock she had been using as a backscratcher. Lodged on one of the sharp edges was a clump of fur. Exactly what Chloé wanted.

Well, not exactly. But a suitable replacement!

Securing it in a plastic bag, he reluctantly left his post and set off for Picarets via a circuitous route, determined that no one would discover Miel's hiding place until her cubs were born and raised. He would see to it that she was protected from the violence that was brewing in Fogas. By whatever means necessary.

Croissants. His car fragranced like an early-morning bakery and his stomach grumbling in protest, Christian drove stoically up the Picarets road. He'd called in at the épicerie, pleased to see Fabian behind the till rather than Josette, thus avoiding any comments on his rapid about-turn as he laid four croissants on the counter. Then, with a spring in his step he'd walked over to Véronique's flat, intending to share his mid-morning break with her.

But there'd been no answer.

He'd loitered outside Arnaud's for a few minutes. To his shame, he'd actually put his ear to the door but he'd heard nothing. Which could be either good or bad. And was none of his business either way.

Finally accepting defeat, he'd decided to head home.

So as he turned the last bend before the Estaque farmstead, his stomach was in revolt as, having anticipated the sweet taste of pastry since eight o'clock that morning, it was still being denied.

'Not long now,' he muttered, swinging the Panda to the left, and there, in front of the small house that served Annie's farm, was Véronique's car.

He wasn't aware of making the decision. One minute he was driving home. The next, he was walking up Annie's path, paper bag held high above the inquisitive noses of the two Pyrenean mountain dogs that had bounded over to greet him.

'Chrrristian!' She'd beaten him to the door, her dogs letting her know the moment he pulled onto the track. 'Lovely to see you!'

'Bonjour.' He stooped to kiss her, disentangling his legs from the dogs.

'Pourrr anotherrr coffee, Vérrronique,' Annie called out as they entered the kitchen. 'Chrrristian's herrre. And he's brrrought crrroissants!'

Christian, who was a couple of steps behind his host, didn't see the transformation on the face of the younger woman who was sitting at the table. But her mother did. She watched with a shrewd eye as her daughter reached up to kiss the farmer, trying to work out whether it was the man or the pastries that had caused the colour to rise to her cheeks.

'We werrre talking about you,' said Annie as she placed the croissants on plates. 'Is it trrrue you'rrre selling?'

Christian sighed and sank onto a chair. 'Sorry. Meant to tell you myself but . . .'

'It doesn't matter how we found out,' said Véronique with a magnanimity that earned her a glance of amazement from Annie who had just endured a disgruntled rant from her daughter on that very topic. 'What matters is whether or not it's true.'

'Yes.'

'So, you'll be leaving then.' Annie accepted the terrible future that awaited Christian with typical pragmatism. 'You'll have trrrouble selling Sarrrko!'

'I can count you out, I suppose?' he asked with a weak grin, dipping his croissant into his coffee and savouring the taste.

'Where will you go?' Véronique's voice was strained, the glow on her face now faded to a deathly pallor.

'Toulouse, most likely.'

Toulouse. Only an hour and a half up the motorway but to Christian it might as well have been halfway around the world, so removed was it in his mind from the cosiness of the Estaque kitchen, the clock keeping time in the corner and the cows lowing in the pastures outside.

'We'll miss you. Especially as that idiot Pascal will be mayorrr.'

'Well, that's not so certain.' Christian finished his pastry and filled them in on the details of his morning meeting with Serge Papon.

'That's a starrrt at least, eh Vérrronique? Having Serrrge in powerrr a bit longerrr. Gives us until Marrrch to perrrsuade Josette to stand!'

A mute nod of the head was the only reply.

'So,' said Christian, looking at the remaining croissant with an eager eye. 'Who'd like the last one? Can I persuade you, Véronique?'

'You have it,' she said, a slight catch in her voice. 'Make the most of Josette's croissants while you can! They won't be as good as these up in Toulouse.'

His hand, already outstretched, hesitated fractionally as her words hit home. Then he lifted the pastry onto his plate and smiled. 'You'll just have to make sure you bring me some when you visit, then!'

Véronique laughed and the conversation moved on to the coming winter, the amount Christian could expect to get for his livestock and the crazy prices outsiders were willing to pay for a farmhouse with a view.

When it came time for Christian to go, Annie let Véronique walk him out to the car while she headed over to the barn with the dogs, saying she needed to check up on a cow that had been under the weather. Which was true, but it was also an excuse as the barn was where she did her best thinking. And right now, she had some serious thinking to do. Because, if she wasn't mistaken, her daughter was unduly upset about the imminent departure of their neighbouring farmer.

Huh! So much for the handsome bear tracker. Seemed like Véronique had fallen for someone much closer to home. Not for long, though. If Christian sold, as he had to, then he would be gone, returning for the odd bank holiday and a few weeks in the summer if they were lucky.

What could she, Annie, do about it though? Not like she had a magic wand that could make his farm viable again.

And what if she was wrong? Went interfering in the lives of young people like the old woman she'd vowed she'd never be, and then realised she'd made a mistake?

She crossed the straw to the stalls and ran her hand over the warm body of the cow, pleased to see that it was on the mend. Funny how confident she was when it came to animals. Knew straight away when one was ailing. Could tell which heifers would turn into good milk producers. And could spot whether a bull had stamina at first glance. But with people it was a different matter. So much more complicated.

Still, she thought, as she straightened up. She hadn't made a mistake. Véronique was in love, that was certain. Because, having known her all her life, Annie had never known her give up a second croissant quite so graciously.

When Véronique wandered into the barn minutes later, she found her mother laughing but unable to explain just what was so funny.

9

Snow arrived in Fogas in mid-December, leaving a thick coating on the ground, layering the mountains in white and making the roads treacherous. It kept Bernard Mirouze occupied driving the snowplough up and down the commune in an effort to clear the routes. It lingered all throughout the festive season, topped up by regular flurries and the occasional blizzard, giving Chloé and the Rogalle twins hours of entertainment sledging down the slopes of Christian's fields. And it made Véronique grateful as all driving lessons with Josette were suspended until the inclement spell lifted.

By New Year, the winter had truly taken hold, its frosty grasp bringing temperatures plummeting to minus ten for a succession of days, causing the river at the back of the Auberge des Deux Vallées to freeze over for the first time in living memory. When the mercury finally climbed back up, it brought with it a sudden burst of rain which fell onto the frigid earth and immediately formed black ice, the worst patch being on the bend in the road which hugged the hillside just past the Auberge.

In the space of one morning it claimed many casualties, unsuspecting drivers suddenly finding their tyres had as much traction as Bernard's beagle on a tiled floor. Some of the cars spun into the lay-by opposite, others slithered to a halt straddling both lanes and blocking the road. And when the drivers went to get out, they struggled to stay upright, slipping and sliding their way to the door of the Auberge where the British owners were doing a roaring trade in coffee. It was enough to make Paul Webster, *aubergiste* and entrepreneur, comment to his wife that perhaps they ought to throw a bucket of water over the road every year at this time.

The arctic conditions, which lasted through January and into February, brought with them an enforced hibernation for the residents of mountain communes such as Fogas. With roads frequently impassable, despite the best endeavours of the *cantonnier*, power intermittent thanks to trees falling on the lines, and frozen pipes a regular occurrence, life in the three villages became centred on the bare necessities. Thus Josette and Fabian saw an unprecedented increase in business as locals walked down to the épicerie rather than risk the perilous journey into St Girons. The bar became the place to grab a morning coffee and catch up on the gossip. And the Auberge, with its new boiler and a generator guaranteeing heat no matter what, saw a sharp surge in the number of restaurant customers, despite its Anglo-Saxon chef.

Needless to say, as woodpiles dwindled outside the houses cut off by the weather, so neighbours began to tire of the confinement which had been foisted upon them and which saw them spending far more time with one another than was usual. Ancient feuds began to resurface, gossip circulated at a faster pace and, due to a lack of fresh material, old scandals were resurrected and embellished, including the one about Madame Sentenac and the curé. Rumour now had it their union had resulted in a love-child, someone claiming that her nephew bore an uncanny resemblance to the banished priest. It didn't take much of a leap to arrive at the topic of Annie Estaque and over that winter period there was much speculation as to the identity of her lover, papa to Véronique. None of it, of course, was on target. Although Jacques, who was party to most of this idle tittle-tattle thanks to his ghostly disposition, had to marvel at the ingenuity of some of the suggestions, especially the one that had *him* down as the father.

It was in the midst of this, in late February, that Eve Rumeau, an estate agent not known for letting mere snow get the better of her, braved the elements to bring a couple of Parisian retirees to view the Dupuy farm. The low temperatures did however put paid to the battery in her Suzuki Jimny and so she was forced to make the journey up to the property in her clients' car which, even with snow chains on, was far from suitable.

'They drove up in that?' Josephine Dupuy exclaimed as a soft-top sports car inched cautiously down the drive, snow crunching under the chain-covered tyres.

'Wow!' breathed Christian, watching the Mazda park next to the barn, long legs swinging out of the passenger door. 'Gorgeous!'

'You can say that again!' André chuckled and got a slap on the head from his wife, who knew that he wasn't referring to the car.

'Bonjour!' Eve's voice reached them from the hallway and the Dupuys shared an anxious look, torn between wanting the viewing to go well and not wanting to sell their home. Then the estate agent breezed into the kitchen, steady on her high heels despite the slippery conditions and followed by a well-dressed couple in their fifties. 'This is Monsieur and Madame Martin.'

They all exchanged awkward handshakes.

'And this,' she said, indicating Christian and his parents who had formed a small defensive huddle, expressions wary, 'is the Dupuy family, owners of the best property I have on my books. Just look at that view!'

As if at her command, the sullen clouds parted and the sun burst through, making Mont Valier sparkle in the distance.

'Spectacular,' pronounced Monsieur Martin with polished Parisian vowels as his wife pulled her fur coat closer around her shoulders.

'No central heating?' she enquired, looking at the antiquated woodburner with a raised eyebrow.

'No need,' Eve replied, before any of the Dupuys could open their mouths. She waved a hand in the direction of the forests through the window. 'With a supply of free fuel outside your door, why would you go to the cost of getting in oil?'

'And upstairs?'

'Electric heaters. Much more reliable.'

At which point, the light overhead flickered and went out and the fridge shuddered to a halt.

'A power cut?'

'Yes, they're working on the lines,' lied Eve with an ease that came from long practice. 'It'll probably be on and off all day. Perhaps you'd like to accompany us with a torch, Christian? In case it goes out at an inopportune moment?'

Christian reached for the torch that hung in the hallway, sharing a complicit grin with his father as he passed. She was good, he had to hand her that. At this rate, she'd have the place sold in no time.

The thought was enough to wipe the smile off his face.

Eve *was* good. She managed to make what felt like a disastrous viewing seem totally routine. When Monsieur Martin had quibbled about the rickety floorboards upstairs, she'd characterised them as having rustic charm. Likewise, the oppressive floral wallpaper that covered his parents' bedroom from floor to ceiling, door included, was passed off as quaint. Objections raised about the lack of an en-suite bathroom and the draughty single glazing were brushed aside by the presentation of building estimates from local companies, though they erred somewhat on the optimistic side in Christian's opinion. And when Madame Martin had been startled by the sudden emergence of a cluster of hens from under the wooden chest in the hall, Eve had waxed lyrical about the joys of self-sufficiency, convincing even the farmer who knew all too well the realities of that life.

By the time they had reassembled in the kitchen and Monsieur Martin dared to say, as he looked out of the window, that it was a pity the barn cut off part of the magnificent view, there was no stopping her.

'Knock it down!' she said, dismissing the utilitarian structure with a flick of her elegant fingers. 'It's of no use anyway.'

'Merde!' The expletive was muttered but audible. Even more audible was the bang of the back door as André Dupuy stomped off across the yard towards the condemned building. A building he had helped his father erect many summers ago. With a scowl cast towards the kitchen, he slammed the barn door closed behind him, causing a large amount of snow to cascade off the roof and onto the sports car below.

Eve didn't so much as flinch, shepherding her charges out of the room and towards the stairs where she encouraged them to have another look at the bedrooms and take lots of photos. As Christian made to follow, she pulled him to one side in the gloomy hallway.

'I seem to have upset your father,' she said, hand on the farmer's muscular forearm. 'It wasn't my intention.'

'It's bound to happen.' A strange tingling sensation ran along his skin where her fingers were gently applying pressure. 'It's not easy selling the only home you've ever known. He'll be okay.'

'As long as you're sure.' She smiled, white teeth visible between luscious red lips. 'I wouldn't want him to be cross with me.'

'He'll get over it,' said Christian, trying to ignore the image that came to mind of his father emerging from the barn, antiquated rifle in his hands as he chased the prospective buyers off his land. 'So how do you think it's going?'

Eve leaned even closer, her hair soft against his cheek as she whispered, 'Perfectly. I have them exactly where I want them.'

'G-g-great, that's great,' stuttered the farmer, her perfume enveloping him and making the circuits in his brain prove as unreliable as the electricity supply to the house. 'You're very good at this.'

'Perhaps you could take me out for dinner one night and I could show you what else I'm good at,' she purred and she brushed her lips against the hard line of his jaw before walking off to join her clients.

He stood there in the hallway, looking at the boots and the coats and the baling twine that was still on the chest. But he didn't see a thing.

'Don't you think, Christian?'

'What? Sorry Maman, did you say something?'

'I said you should go and check on your father. He seemed pretty distressed.'

'Right. Yes. Of course.' And with a sense of shame he couldn't account for, he went out into the cold, the blast of icy mountain air clearing the last remnants of Eve's intoxicating perfume from his senses.

'Knock down the barn, indeed,' he grumbled as he followed his father's footsteps through the snow. 'Over my dead body!'

It was only as he reached the building in question he realised that once it was sold, he would have no say in the matter. The barn, like Sarko the bull, would cease to be part of what was now the farm.

Writhing with frustration at the difficult path he was being forced to take, even the sight of the Mazda covered in a mound of snow failed to raise a smile. Instead of clearing it off, he slipped into the barn and started fiddling with the tractor while his father stripped and cleaned his ancient rifle. They talked about the fortunes of the local rugby club. The impact of the cold winter on the forthcoming fishing season. They even discussed the likelihood of Stephanie and Fabian getting married.

Neither raised the topic of the sale. And neither emerged from the barn until they were sure that Eve Rumeau had left the premises.

'We seem to have an awful lot of bilberry jam,' said Josette, as she unpacked the first of many boxes that Fabian had carried in from the lorry outside. With deliveries unpredictable and sales rocketing thanks to the wintry weather, they'd ordered more than their usual meagre top-up and she was beginning to wonder where they would put it all. 'Quite a few jars of honey too!'

Fabian gave a rueful grin. 'It's Chloé. She's obsessed with bears.'

'She's not giving all this to them?'

'No. She's on some kind of bear diet. Only eating things they eat. Which luckily is quite a lot. She's even asked if we can get some venison or a bit of wild boar!'

Josette laughed. 'And how's Stephanie taking that, being a vegetarian?'

'I think after the events of last year, she's just happy to have Chloé back to her normal lunatic self.'

'Stephanie's right. It's good to see Chloé so interested in something. I heard her quizzing Arnaud last week about one of the bears he's tracking. The one that's pregnant.'

'Miel? Chloé knows everything there is to know about her.' Fabian made a vague gesture towards the mountains visible through the shop window. 'She's been pestering Arnaud to take her up there in the spring.'

'Rather her than me!'

Shuddering at the thought of meeting a bear at close quarters, Josette reached into the next box and pulled out a large plastic tub of what looked like flour.

'Is this for Chloé too?' She peered at the label but Fabian snatched it from her just as she managed to read the first line. 'Didn't know bears needed high-energy drink powder,' she remarked drily as he shoved the container into the bag with Chloé's food.

'It's for on the bike,' he muttered. 'I'll be starting training again soon.'

'And you think drinking that stuff will help you keep up with the Tour de France when it passes through in the summer?' She laughed, amazed at how seriously even the amateur cyclists took their riding these days. In Jacques' era they'd simply got on the bicycle and pushed off!

'Bonjour!'

Fabian groaned quietly and Josette looked up to see Fatima Souquet coming through the door.

'Bonjour, Fatima. Not often we see you in here these days.' Josette smiled sweetly but Fatima didn't rise to the bait. She picked up a basket and began shopping.

The cheek of it! Since last year the woman had barely graced the épicerie, choosing to do all of her shopping down in St Girons. But now that the snow was causing havoc, she turned up. By rights, Josette ought to have shown her the door, but it was a fool who stood on principle in these hard times. Although she noticed Jacques shadowing the thin-faced figure, a grimace of distaste on his face. No doubt he'd have chosen high-mindedness over economics and thrown her out of the shop if he'd had the physical ability. Given his ethereal state, however, he'd settled for harassment, blowing cold air on her neck as he trailed after her.

'I hear you've found a lovely local cassoulet. Are you out of stock?' Fatima called from the back, turning up her coat collar at a sudden chill as Fabian came in with another load of boxes.

'No—'

'Yes!' Josette overrode her nephew who was gesturing at the tins which had just arrived and were stacked at her feet. She pushed them quietly under the counter and his look of confusion changed to a grin. It had taken him a year, but finally he was beginning to understand village politics. Some things were too good to waste on the likes of the Souquets.

'Try the coq au vin,' Josette conceded. 'It's every bit as tasty.'

Shaking his head in amazement, Fabian turned to collect the last of the delivery and collided full on with Véronique.

'Sorry! You okay?'

'No!' she snarled, waving a letter and striding over to Josette. Realising her temper had nothing to do with the collision, Fabian made good his escape.

'Whatever's the matter?' Josette regarded her young friend with concern.

'La Poste!' She thrust the letter over the counter, foot tapping as Josette read it through.

'But what does it mean? Local alternative?'

'It means no, that's what! They're not going to reopen the post office. They've found somewhere else around here to open one.'

'Where? There is nowhere more suitable.'

Véronique threw up her arms in despair. 'I know! But try telling them that.'

'Surely we can appeal?'

'That's what I'm about to find out. I was hoping Christian might be in here.'

Josette shook her head. 'He's got a viewing up at the farm today. You'll have to call him. Or Pascal.'

Véronique rolled her eyes and made a dismissive sound, missing the warning glances coming from behind the counter. 'Pascal? He's the one who promised to sort this out, and look what's happened! That man couldn't organise a fête on Bastille Day. Even with Napoleon on hand!'

'Bonjour, Véronique.' The acid tones stopped the postmistress short.

'Fatima! Bonjour. Didn't see you there.'

'Bad news about the post office, you were saying?'

Véronique passed the letter to Fatima, who read it and then handed it back.

'You should speak to Pascal.' She placed her shopping basket next to the till. 'As first deputy he'll be able to help. Contrary to what you think!'

'I've already spoken to him,' said Véronique from between gritted teeth. 'I gave him my plans for a post office in La Rivière back in November and he assured me he'd get on to it.' She waved the letter once more. 'And this is the result. So you'll forgive me if I place my trust in the second deputy, Christian Dupuy, this time around.'

With that, she flounced out of the shop, leaving Josette to ring up Fatima's purchases in silence.

What a shame, thought Josette as she bent to retrieve the tins of cassoulet from the floor once the épicerie was empty. Neither Véronique nor Fatima had considered Serge as a possible source of assistance. They were changed days. And as she placed the tins on the shelf where they belonged, she couldn't help worrying that things were about to change even more. Not necessarily for the better.

★ ★ ★

141

'What the hell are you playing at?' Fatima spat, the minute she was in the door.

Pascal, who had been watching a recording of *Faust* at the Opéra Bastille, grumbling throughout at the inferiority of the setting, the Palais Garnier being the rightful home of the Opéra National in his mind, leapt up from his chair at the sparks in his wife's eyes.

'Véronique has heard that the post office isn't going to be reopened. Did you have something to do with this?' she demanded, advancing across the room towards him.

'Yes. No. Well . . . sort of.'

'*Sort of?* What does that mean?'

Pascal felt the urge to lie but faced with the scrutiny of his wife, the truth spilled out.

'I may have contacted La Poste.'

'And said what, exactly?'

'Told them about Véronique's plan to combine the post office and the épicerie.'

Fatima looked nonplussed. 'But that's an excellent idea. Why on earth have they turned you down?'

'They haven't.'

'They have! I saw the letter myself just now. The post office in La Rivière is no more.'

Pascal swallowed, his eyes drawn to the television where Faust was being led astray by Mephistopheles. When he spoke, the words were barely audible.

'I didn't suggest they reopen in La Rivière.'

'Then where? Not up here in Fogas? That would be ridiculous . . .'

Something in his face stopped her. It was the same look he'd had the day he'd come home and broken the news about his bankruptcy. The furtive guilt-stricken demeanour of a boy who's broken every pane of glass in the greenhouse. And that was when realisation dawned for Fatima.

'You *haven't*?'

He stared at the television, watching Faust writhe in torment.

'Do you have any idea of what you've done?'

'It makes sense,' he protested. 'Sarrat has a bigger community. It's more viable in the long term.'

'*Viable in the long term*? Is that what HE's told you? Did he also say that Fogas has no long term now, thanks to you? Once the post office moves across the bridge to Sarrat, this commune will be finished. All we'll have left is the épicerie.'

Pascal shifted from one foot to the other.

'No!' Her hands flew to her mouth. 'Not the épicerie too?'

'It was the only way to get La Poste interested. Without the integrated shop and post office, they didn't want to know.'

'Oh my God!' She staggered to the couch and sat down. 'He's totally hoodwinked you. Got you running around doing his dirty work and you can't even see it.'

'But it's what we planned, *ma chérie*!' Pascal dropped to his knees in front of her and clasped her hands in his. 'It will lead to the same result, just by a different path.'

Fatima pulled away from his grasp, her look of horror now replaced with one of revulsion.

'What we planned was for you to use this commune as a stepping stone to greater things. It was never my intention to destroy my maternal hometown in the process! You've gone too far with this, Pascal. I suggest you extricate yourself before you ruin Fogas. And our marriage.'

She stood up and left the room, her husband still kneeling before her empty chair like a penitent refused absolution.

It was too late to turn back. That much was clear in Pascal's terrified brain. So like the bedevilled Faust before him, he convinced himself that all would work out well. While he hadn't anticipated her reaction to the plans for the post office, when Fatima understood the true nature of what was under way she would change her mind and embrace his actions with the drive that had got him elected as deputy mayor in the first place. And she would see that Fogas was a necessary sacrifice. After all, as his ally kept saying, a merged commune combining the strengths of Fogas and Sarrat could only be a positive change for the inhabitants. Despite the mutual antipathy that dated back centuries. And it would prove the ultimate power base for its new deputy mayor, Pascal Souquet, to springboard into national politics.

Even with the latest news that Serge Papon was delaying his retirement until the spring, at the rate things were going Fatima wasn't going to have to wait very long before she realised just how clever her husband had been.

'Did Véronique catch you?'

Christian had only got a foot inside the door of the shop when Josette accosted him.

'No,' he replied, stamping the worst of the snow from his boots on the mats that had been left out for that purpose. 'The power's off up at the farm. Takes the phone out with it. Why, what did she want?'

'She's had a letter from La Poste. Not good news. For her or any of us really.'

'They've refused to reopen the post office?'

'In no uncertain terms.'

Christian swore softly. 'That's bad news indeed. Is she upset?'

Josette simply raised an eyebrow.

'Right, I'll go see her now.'

'Leave that here,' said Josette, taking his mother's shopping list from him. 'I'll get it together for you while you're over at Véronique's.'

'That'd be great. I shouldn't be long.'

Christian turned and retraced his steps, the door chimes sounding muffled in the snow-covered exterior. With the warmth of the épicerie quickly leached away from his body by the bitter cold, he hunched down into his coat and tried to think of summer. The brief burst of sunshine that Eve Rumeau had somehow conjured up for the benefit of her Parisian house-buyers had been replaced with leaden skies, soft flakes drifting earthwards in a premonition of worse to come.

Be surprised if there's not another heavy fall tonight, thought the farmer, scanning the clouds, diminished visibility making the mid-afternoon feel like late evening.

Picking up his pace at the prospect of the drive home, he only glanced up at the old school building when he was almost upon it. Light streamed out of Véronique's lounge on the first floor in a homely welcome, a beacon guiding him in from the raw conditions outdoors. Over a much needed cup of coffee they'd get their heads together and sort out this La Poste business.

Face lifted to catch the yellow glow spilling from between the open shutters, he smiled in anticipation. Which was when the light flickered and Christian found himself plunged into shadow. Someone was standing at the window with their back to him.

Véronique!

He reached down and grabbed a handful of snow, seized by an adolescent urge to make her notice him. Make her jump! He rolled it into a compact ball between his palms and then drew back his arm and fired. It was only as he let go that the person turned and he saw the hair.

It was long, far longer than the shoulder-length locks of the postmistress. And whoever it was, they were much bigger.

Realising his mistake, he threw himself behind an apple tree in the abandoned orchard that lay between the épicerie and the old school just as the snowball smashed against the glass. Heart thundering in his chest, he waited a few beats before peeking out from behind his cover, peering through the gloom as the flakes fell ever faster.

Arnaud. Face up against the window, staring down into the darkened village trying to see who had thrown the snowball.

Christian thumped back against the trunk in annoyance, shaking the tree and dislodging a lump of snow down on top of himself.

Idiot! What had he been thinking? Acting like a kid. Not that he could have anticipated Arnaud being there . . . the bear man . . . in Véronique's flat.

He stood, brooding over the inferences that could be drawn from that fact, drips of thawing snow sliding down his neck, and he realised he was trapped. Having no desire to emerge and continue up to Véronique's, Arnaud's presence somehow making that impossible, equally he couldn't nonchalantly walk away while the bear man watched on. Not without losing some dignity.

He risked another glance.

Still there.

How long, he wondered, before Arnaud got tired and turned back to talk to Véronique? It could take all night! The man was a tracker for goodness' sake, famous for the patience which always saw him succeed.

Christian groaned as a shiver ran the length of his body. He was going to die of hypothermia behind a tree in La Rivière, his demise subsequently becoming part of local folklore which parents would use to warn their children about the stupidity of playing outside in the winter.

He took another look. This time there were two faces. Véronique's very close to Arnaud's.

Perhaps he could take a different route back to his car?

He was on the move before he had time to really think it through. Crouching down like they did in the movies, he made his way uphill between the neglected fruit trees, boots slipping and sliding in the snow. When he was almost at the high fence that partitioned the orchard from Josette's garden, he stopped and looked back.

Véronique had gone. But Arnaud was still watching. However, his gaze was directed down the road, away from Christian.

Feeling relieved, the farmer concentrated on the barrier in front of him. Having last scaled it when he was ten and Monsieur Garcia had been chasing him with a Spanish musket, incensed that the local boys had been scrumping in his orchard, Christian wasn't sure if he could do it again at forty-one. They'd flown up it that day, and then sat on the top throwing the Spaniard's precious fruit back at him from a height. The old man was dead long before Christian understood anything about the civil war that had driven Monsieur Garcia to Fogas. And by then it was too late to apologise for their childish antics, their daring raids a regular torment to the exile who had been equally driven to frustration by his thwarted attempts to grow the oranges of his native Catalonia.

With one of the main reasons why the oranges had never flourished now settling all around, Christian knew he had to act or he would never get home. Using the trunk of a dead apple tree to propel himself forwards, he took a run at the fence and leaping in his last stride, he caught the top edge. But his feet failed to find a purchase on the icy planks. Boots scrabbling for grip, he hung there, the rough boards digging into his fingers, splinters tearing at his face where it was pressed against the wood. It was only as his arms were about to be ripped out of their sockets that he managed to hook his left foot over the top and give an almighty heave, hauling his body up so that he was straddling the fence full length. Which was when he realised, with a flash of intense pain, that the adult male anatomy was not designed for such pursuits.

Trying to breathe through the worst of it, he prepared to clamber down into Josette's garden. He made the fatal mistake, however, of taking a final look back at Véronique's window.

There, still visible through the bare branches of the trees, was Arnaud Petit. Staring straight at the farmer in his precarious position astride the fence.

Panicked, Christian moved too hastily and, as his right leg cleared the top, his left foot slipped off the snow-covered baton it had been resting on, forcing the entirety of his weight back onto his arms. Already tired, they buckled and gave way and his chin hit the fence with a crunch. Then he was falling, arms and legs turning windmills in thin air.

Sure that he was going to hit the ground with a wallop, leading to broken bones at the least, he was somewhat surprised when his fall was cushioned by a soft substance, rather like a gigantic pillow. He lay there for a second or two, catching the breath that had been forced from his lungs on impact and wondering whether Monsieur Garcia was looking down from his orange grove in heaven and laughing heartily as Christian finally got his comeuppance.

Standing gingerly, he brushed off the worst of the snow and walked stiffly past the woodshed to Josette's back door.

'Josette? It's me, Christian,' he called out as he let himself in.

'Christian? You took your time. How's Véronique—?' Josette stopped short as she met him in the corridor, taking in the bleeding chin, the torn hands, the sodden clothing. And the smell.

'Goodness, what have you been doing?' Her nose wrinkled at the odour which was somewhere between rotten and putrid.

'I don't want to talk about it,' muttered the farmer,

stalking through to the shop. 'Just let me have the shopping and I'll head home. And if anyone should ask, I was in here all the time!'

Josette recognised the mood he was in and bridled her curiosity while she took his money and handed back his change. But as he limped out to the car, walking like a saddle-sore cowboy, she couldn't help wondering out loud what had got into the normally level-headed farmer that had him rolling around in her compost heap in the middle of winter. Jacques offered no reply. He was too busy wiping tears of laughter from his eyes, confident that he knew the answer.

For Christian it was no laughing matter. With the heating on full, by the time the Panda reached the farm, the stench inside was overpowering. He stormed into the kitchen, thrust the shopping at his mother and, without a word of explanation, went upstairs to shower and change.

It was as he removed his saturated wallet from his back pocket that he noticed the card stuck to the damp leather. He peeled it off and could just about make out the number on the front, the ink having run into a rainbow of print.

Why not?

It seemed an antidote to the shame, and some other emotion he couldn't quite fathom, that was still coursing through him.

He fumbled for his mobile, surprised to see it still working despite his adventures, and entered the number. The ringtone crackled in the deteriorating weather and he was sure he would lose the signal, but she answered on the fourth ring.

'Thought you might like to go for a coffee sometime?' he blurted before she even had a chance to speak and the sound of her delighted laughter carrying over the static of the weak connection came as a total relief.

* * *

Engaged! Véronique put the phone down and paced across the room to the dark rectangle of window. The blizzard which was now howling outside had brought a premature night and it was only serving to make her more depressed.

Bracing against the blast of arctic air that blew in the moment she opened the windows, she reached out to unlatch the shutters, thinking that perhaps if she closed them despite the early hour, the flat would feel cosier. Fighting the wind which tore at the wood as soon as she released the catch, she managed to pull them to and hook them in place, slamming the windows shut behind them.

That would keep out the noise of the storm. And maybe deter anyone from throwing more snowballs.

Odd that.

She'd just hung up from yet another unsuccessful effort to contact Christian when Arnaud Petit had called round to inspect the fuse box for both flats, which was in her hallway. The frequent power outages had proved too much for his electrics and a couple of fuses had tripped. Glad of the chance to talk to someone after what had been an awful day and exasperated by her inability to contact the second deputy mayor, she'd offered him a coffee and he'd accepted. By mere chance he'd been standing next to the window when the snowball had hit.

Arnaud hadn't seen the perpetrator. Some kid probably, who'd no doubt scarpered. She'd spotted the tracker out in the snow afterwards, bent over, staring at the ground following what must have been prints, and she pitied the culprit because the huge bear man was like a bloodhound. He'd turned up into the old orchard and after that she'd lost interest and had gone to phone Christian. Again.

His landline not working, she'd rung his mobile several times but he'd had it switched off as he always did. Finally, just now, she'd got through, but it had been engaged.

One more try. Then she'd give up and wait until his landline was working.

She pushed redial, hoping to hear a faint ringing sound. But all she heard was a click and then emptiness.

She threw the phone on the couch and herself after it, tears in her eyes.

'Get a grip!' she muttered. 'It's only a job. You'll get another one.'

But the postmistress of Fogas knew the sense of desolation she felt wasn't just because of her imminent redundancy. It was more to do with the ache in her heart that seemed to have become part of her every waking hour.

Despite herself, her fingers reached for the receiver. It was going to be a long evening down in La Rivière.

10

'The problem is, no one wants to know!'
'Have you trrried Serrrge?'

Véronique threw her mother a look of incredulity. 'Are you serious? He's about to retire and everyone knows he's switched off. The closing of the post office is hardly going to spark him back into action.'

'What about the otherrrs?'

'Huh! Pascal has more or less wiped his hands of it, saying that once La Poste has made a decision it's futile trying to appeal. And Christian . . .'

The pasture beyond the kitchen window took Véronique's attention. With March drawing to a close, the field was clear of snow and basking in bright sunshine, signs of spring evident in splashes of yellow and purple crocuses peeking out from under the trees.

For the postmistress, however, the joys normally associated with the coming season had failed to materialise.

It had been a frustrating four weeks since she'd heard the awful news from La Poste. Her endeavours to get more information about their damning verdict had proved universally unsuccessful and she'd been given the runaround whenever she called head office. As for the three letters she'd sent, using registered post of course, they had yet to be acknowledged.

Help had been no more forthcoming in the commune. Figuring that the three-month extension of Serge Papon's tenure was more to appease Christian than a declaration of a renewed commitment to Fogas, Véronique had gone straight to Pascal Souquet. But he'd informed her he could take the situation no further. Which left Christian.

Christian who was now going out with the dynamic Eve Rumeau from the estate agency. As if Mademoiselle Rumeau's long legs and svelte figure weren't enough, she also seemed to have found a buyer for the farm at the first time of asking. With two viewings already, it looked likely that a Parisian couple would be snapping up the property and turning it into a second home. Another one. Not what the region needed.

Clearly with other things on his mind, Christian had been slow to respond to Véronique's calls. When he'd finally got in touch, he'd appeared distracted. Moody even, which was strange given the romance in his life. And she'd got the impression that the situation with La Poste was the last thing he wanted to have to deal with.

'You werrre saying about Chrrristian?' Annie's tone was unusually gentle.

Véronique pulled a face. 'He's in love! Therefore, useless.'

'Ha! In love is he? Frrrom what I hearrr, things arrren't going too smoothly.'

'What do you mean?'

'Andrrré Dupuy was telling me. Chrrristian and that Eve woman have arrrranged two dates so farrr and both have had to be cancelled.'

'Really?' A hint of delight coloured the reply. 'How come?'

'Sarrrko the bull rrruined the firrrst one. Got out of his field and rrrampaged up into the woods leaving Chrrristian rrrunning arrround in the darrrk instead of being at some fancy rrrestaurrrant in St Girrrons. And then one of his cows went into prrrematurrre labourrr on the second.'

'Sounds like Mother Nature is trying to tell him something!'

Annie laughed. 'Well if she isn't, I think Andrrré Dupuy is. He can't stand the woman. Josephine's not too keen eitherrr.'

Véronique tried not to be encouraged by the news. 'Whether they like her or not, she's sold the farm. Which means Christian will be leaving soon, so it's understandable that he doesn't want to get embroiled in our petty squabbles over the post office.'

Annie turned a shrewd eye on her daughter and knew from the hunched shoulders and the brave tilt to her chin that she was only just managing to hold herself together.

'You wouldn't think of going to Toulouse too? Therrre's not much to keep you herrre now.'

'I thought about it.'

'And?'

A shake of the head. 'I can't.'

'Why everrr not? I hope you arrren't factorrring me into yourrr decision, because I can look afterrr myself!' Annie did her best to sound indignant and was rewarded with a weak smile. 'You have no job. No ties. If I was you, I'd jump at the chance of a new starrrt somewherrre else.'

'Would you?' The question was accompanied by a searing gaze, Véronique having inherited her father's ability to see into the hearts of people. 'Honestly?'

'No.' Annie sighed. 'Longest months of my life werrre the ones I spent overrr nearrr Perrrpignan when I was prrregnant. Couldn't wait to get back herrre.'

'What made you go to Perpignan?'

Annie stood up, moving over to the dresser where a row of photos charted their familial history, and Véronique thought they had hit yet again the impasse that seemed to rise between them whenever the background to her birth was mentioned. Prepared for a deafening silence, she was surprised when her mother started talking.

'Society. That's what forrrced me out. I was with child and unmarrrried in a small community. Yourrr grrrandparrrents thought it forrr the best if I wasn't walking arrround with the legacy of my sins visible.'

'But you came back with me. Wasn't that even worse?'

Annie tipped her head to one side and smiled. 'You werrre the cutest baby, Vérrronique. Full of life. No one had a bad worrrd to say once they met you.'

'So you never regretted it? Coming back to Fogas?'

'Rrregrrret? It's not a worrrd I use too often. I did what I did and lived with the consequences. But I wonderrr if you wouldn't have had a betterrr life if I'd left. Which is why you should considerrr it now.'

'I have. But the entire time I was away at college I yearned to be back here. I couldn't bear the idea of not being in these mountains.' Véronique gestured at the crests visible in the distance, hauntingly beautiful in the sunshine. 'That hasn't changed.'

Annie, not normally one to weigh up her words before speaking, took a moment before asking the next question. 'Not even with Chrrristian leaving?'

'Ah!' Véronique hung her head, face flaming. 'Is it that obvious?'

And at that point, Annie, who should have known better, reached across and stroked her daughter's hair. Which was precisely the wrong thing to do with an Estaque in distress. Far better had she laughed at her daughter's folly. Or made light of the infatuation.

But instead, in a rare display of affection, she compounded the mistake by putting her arm around Véronique's shoulders, which immediately began to heave.

'Oh, my child,' Annie murmured as she held her weeping daughter in her arms. 'We'rrre not much good at this love larrrk, arrre we?'

She got no reply.

'Well,' she continued with a return to form, 'if you arrre deterrrmined to stay, we'd best make surrre that bloody post office gets rrreopened. Don't want you moping rrround herrre all day.'

Véronique looked up, eyes red, cheeks tracked with tears. She fumbled for a tissue in her pocket and wiped her face.

'How on earth do you propose to do that?'

Annie stared across the pasture towards the path that linked Picarets to Fogas.

'I think I might know a man who can help. Will you be all rrright herrre by yourrrself forrr a while?'

Véronique nodded as her mother, suddenly full of energy, started pulling on her boots.

'Have lunch without me,' Annie said, slipping into her coat as she opened the door onto the crisp late morning. 'And don't forrrget to feed the dogs.'

With that, a bemused Véronique was left alone at the kitchen table, the longcase clock in the corner ticking away the seconds that remained of Christian's time in Fogas.

It didn't take long for Annie to realise that the path she had walked with nonchalance in her youth posed quite a challenge for a woman of her advanced years. Kicking up from the road, it wound through the woods to emerge above Picarets, providing an unparalleled vantage point for surveying the village. She made the most of it, hand against a young oak as she took a breather and watched Chloé turning somersaults in her back garden, the child no more than a tumble of orange in the sunlit morning. She'd be asking for a hot chocolate to replace all that energy when she called round later, thought Annie, already looking forward to their regular Saturday evening together.

Somewhat revived, Annie continued up the bigger track that linked Picarets with Fogas, a length of hazel serving as a walking stick as the gradient got steeper. Soon Christian's home just outside the village was a mere speck below and when the path turned at the disused quarry, the farm disappeared from view entirely.

Taking measured steps, Annie made good progress and was pleasantly surprised at how quickly she arrived at the pasture that marked the summit. She was also surprised that the thrill she'd felt as a young child on discovering this slice of paradise was no less diminished at the age of sixty-six.

An expanse of green, it rose above the treeline affording spectacular vistas of the surrounding valleys and the mountains that encircled it. She'd first stood here as a seven-year-old and taken in the panorama, convinced that she was at the top of the world. Participating in her inaugural transhumance, when the livestock was taken up to the higher pastures for the hotter months, she'd wanted to stay with the cows on what would be their summer grazing and had thrown herself to the ground, luxuriating in the soft grass. It had taken the promise of an ice cream down at the épicerie for her father to get her moving again.

Although today wasn't quite ice-cream weather, the sharp edge in the air serving as a reminder that winter had yet to retreat, the sun was brilliant overhead and a solitary chaffinch was trilling in the trees below. For the end of March, it was fantastic. Annie took it as an invitation to sit down and have a rest. And to figure out what exactly she was going to do next.

She'd left the house on a wave of emotion, motivated by Véronique's misery. She hadn't possessed a plan for making things right for her daughter. Nor had she formulated one during the strenuous hike up, all her focus on the walking. But of one thing she'd been sure.

The only person who could help Véronique was Serge Papon.

And so her feet had taken her in the direction of Fogas and the mayor's house without a clue as to what she was going to say when she got there. She had to make him interested. Make him concerned about the plight of the postmistress of Fogas. But how to do that when he had lost all enthusiasm for life?

There was only one solution. One key to revitalising the broken-hearted mayor and persuading him to take on Véronique's cause. But wielding it could bring terrible consequences.

She tipped her head back, letting the warmth of the sun wash over her. How good it felt after the harsh conditions of the previous month. As she sat there summoning her courage, she was aware of the irony. For the place where she had decided on a course of action that would possibly wreck her relationship with her daughter was the very spot where her daughter had been conceived.

Late April, Spring dancing across the land leaving blossom and birdsong in her wake and dusting the region with the possibilities of new beginnings. And new life. On that particular day Annie had finished her chores on the farm early and decided to make the most of the evening by walking up to the pasture to watch the sunset. Her disappointment at finding someone already there had been tempered by the fact that it was the deputy mayor, Serge Papon, who was sitting on a rock, waiting for the sky to change colour.

They'd known each other for years, both council members, and perhaps aware that Annie was immune to his notorious charms, Serge had always treated her as an equal, with none of the condescension that she'd grown used to as a woman in the world of farming. So when he'd invited her to join him, she'd accepted.

After a few pleasantries, they'd sat in a companionable silence, the air warm and heady with the scent of flowers in bloom, the budding trees busy with nesting birds and the sound of cowbells carrying up from the valleys far below. Annie had felt a serenity she wasn't sure she'd experienced since. Then everything had changed.

Dipping onto the horizon, the sun had cast a crimson flush across the western clouds and turned the Pyrenean peaks purple, the distinctive shape of Mont Valier a dark cameo on a vibrant canvas. As the sun sank lower, the colours had grown deeper, more sensual, no room for pastel shades in a sky painted with abandon. Finally, in a vain effort to stave off the approaching night, the last rays had broken from behind the mountains, sending strobes of orange shooting into the darkening heavens.

They'd both gasped. And she'd shivered.

It had seemed natural for him to put an arm around her. Natural despite the electricity that was crackling between them.

Spring fever was how she'd termed it as she'd walked down the mountain much later, the path now dark and only her innate sense of direction guiding her safely. She'd arrived at the farm, light spilling out of the kitchen window, and inside she could see Maman setting the table for dinner, talking away as Papa poured wine over at the dresser.

Annie felt the first twinges of shame.

At thirty, she was no innocent. She'd had boyfriends. But the swinging sixties had passed Fogas by and so far, two years into the seventies, none of the inhabitants had shown any inclination to experiment with free love. Well, if they had, they weren't telling. Having a fling with a married man, therefore, was still quite shocking. Especially when he was the deputy mayor.

Brushing the worst of the grass off her clothes and straightening her skirt, she'd taken a deep breath and entered.

'Bonsoir!' Maman had called out, her speech still coloured by the Spanish of her homeland. 'You're just in time, love. Did you have a good walk?'

Annie nodded.

'The fresh air agrees with you.' Papa pinched her red cheek as he passed.

Maman had given her a knowing smile behind his back, no doubt hoping that her only child had finally met someone she would settle down with. Hating the deceit, Annie had determined over the meal that followed that she would forget about the evening as quickly as possible. She would never mention it and no one would ever be any the wiser.

But nature had decided otherwise. Not long after, Annie realised that her sunset rendezvous had led to a permanent reminder of her moment of weakness. She'd been beside herself and in her distraught state she'd had a visit from Thérèse Papon.

It had changed her life. And Véronique's. Because Annie still wasn't sure that she would have been brave enough to be a single mother in Fogas if it hadn't been for the pressure Thérèse had on her to have an abortion. Having guessed who the father was, Thérèse had been terrified Serge would leave her out of a sense of duty for his child, a child that Thérèse was incapable of providing for him. And so she had begged Annie to get rid of it.

Stubborn to the core, with her baby threatened Annie had made a spur-of-the-moment decision. Instead of giving up her child for adoption as she had been considering, she would raise it. But out of sympathy for a woman she had always admired, and in some way to atone for the sin she had committed, Annie had vowed never to reveal the identity of the father.

The secret had been kept between the two women, Annie's parents always believing that Véronique, their adored grandchild, was the beautiful result of a brief liaison with a passing fair worker. Then, last year, after over three decades of silence, Thérèse had made a final request. Dying from cancer, she had asked Annie to tell Serge the truth once she was gone.

Which was what Annie was about to do.

No point putting it off. She stood up slowly, slightly dizzy as the blood rushed to her head. Lifting her face to the sun once more as though to draw strength, she then turned her back on it and walked across the pasture to the woods. One foot after the other, her mind in turmoil, she followed the path down to the ruins of the old mill that lay high in the valley between the two villages. Before long she was climbing the other side and the allotments that marked the outskirts of Fogas came into view.

Lunchtime. He knew because he'd heard the town hall clock striking. So he'd dutifully set the table with a plate, some saucisson on a board and a wedge of cheese next to it. He'd found an old end of baguette and he'd poured himself a glass of wine.

But Serge Papon had no appetite.

He sat staring at the empty chair opposite, not even the letter that had come in the morning post managing to penetrate this dark fog that had engulfed him.

From the Conseil Général in Foix, no less. He'd been intrigued when he'd seen the envelope, wondering what the departmental assembly would want with him. Foix was over the other side of the Col de Port, on the plains that led to Toulouse, and although the capital of the Ariège, it seemed far removed from life in the mountains. Theoretically, the Conseil Général oversaw all the communes but in reality, they had little to do with the day-to-day running of a place like Fogas. Unless you wanted money. Or were in trouble.

Thinking that neither scenario applied to him, he'd read the contents and felt some of his old passion rekindled. Coming from a council presided over by a man known for his anti-bear stance, the letter raised the issue of Arnaud Petit's continued presence in La Rivière. Claiming his occupation of accommodation owned by the commune was tantamount to Fogas supporting the reintroduction of bears, it went on to state that it would be best for all concerned if the tenancy agreement was cancelled.

Although worded in the most verbose manner, full of long-winded sentences and literary flourishes, Serge recognised the veiled threat. The consequences should he refuse to follow its mandate weren't explicitly stated. But Serge had been mayor long enough to know that if he failed to evict the bear tracker, Fogas would have a struggle on its hands should it have recourse to the Conseil Général for grants of any sort.

At first he'd been vexed. How dare they tell him what to do in his commune when he was an elected official! It was uncon-stitutional. A corruption of power. In fact, he'd show them. He'd extend the tenancy and reduce the rent as well.

Thumping the table in indignation he'd reached for the notepad Thérèse had always used for the shopping list, intend-ing to write a reply for Céline to type up after the weekend. But as he drew the paper towards him, he saw his wife's neat handwriting looping across the page. Her last list. He'd left it there for when she came out of hospital, in case there was anything she'd wanted to add to it. Of course, she never had. And as suddenly as the fire had been ignited inside him, it was extinguished.

The reply didn't get penned. An hour later and he'd been still sitting there, looking at the inventory of things she'd deemed essential for their life together. It was only the chiming of the clock that had roused him.

He surveyed the table again, trying to garner some enthusiasm. But it wasn't there. Not for the food, nor for the politics. He'd give the missive from the Conseil Général to Pascal and let him sort it. Which meant, of course, that Arnaud would be given his marching orders.

Serge sighed and picked up his knife. Cheese or saucisson? He had got no further in making a decision when he heard someone knocking.

Who on earth? At lunchtime, too! Grumbling about the mealtime intrusion which was tantamount to sacrilege, notwithstanding that he wasn't the least bit hungry, he shuffled into the hall and opened the door.

'Bonjourrr, Serrrge.'

Annie Estaque bustled past him and into the kitchen before he could reply. Stunned, he closed the door and followed her. Of all the well-intentioned women who'd come calling over the last year, carrying boeuf bourguignon or lapin chasseur in a dish for him to reheat, most of which had made its way to the bin, not once had Annie crossed his threshold. He'd never really thought about it but as he returned to the table, her lack of contact irked him. He only hoped she hadn't come over now to give him some of her famous Estaque counselling because he really wasn't in the mood.

'Have you eaten?' he asked out of habit, gesturing for her to sit.

She shook her head and he noticed she looked fatigued.

'Care to join me? It's not much I'm afraid.'

Her eyes scanned the meagre rations, an eyebrow going up in response.

'I didn't make it to the market,' he muttered before she could comment. 'But I'm happy to share.'

She sat and he set a place for her before resuming his seat. Cutting the stale baguette in two, he presented half to her, and then cut a slice of cheese.

'Rrrogallais?' she asked as he placed it on her plate.

'Of course!' he smiled, it being a standing joke in the commune that Josette never stocked anything but local cheese. 'Wine?'

She made to cover her glass but then something seemed to relax inside her. 'Why not?'

His sentiments exactly.

'So,' he said, raising his glass, 'What should we drink to?'

'The futurrre,' she said, and her voice cracked. 'Yourrr futurrre.'

Bracing himself for yet another lecture from a well-meaning busybody, Serge leaned back and folded his arms.

Up above the Estaque farm where Véronique sat waiting impatiently for her mother's return, way above it, on a mountainside that dropped down from a small tarn, the sun was shining on the rocks scattered in front of a deep crevice. It was warm, a buzzard circling lazily overhead nothing but a dark fleck against the blue sky. At this altitude the trees were still bare, the grass in the clearing just coming back to life. But it was enough.

As the sun reached its highest point for the day, a large shape emerged from the darkness of the crevice. Moving slowly, almost dreamlike, she lumbered out into the bright light and paused, sniffing the air. Satisfied, she moved forward, two smaller shapes emerging from her shadow, taking their first tottering steps beyond the cave that had so far been their only home.

Hibernation was over. It was time to look for food.

II

Annie had never felt more exhausted. When she'd set out from the farm she'd not given any thought as to how she was going to get back from Fogas. Now, as she crossed the road towards the house, her two dogs bounding up to greet her, her feet and her knees were complaining and she knew that her legs would be stiff in the morning.

Not that she'd had much choice but to walk. Having imparted her long-kept confidence to Serge, it hadn't seemed the opportune moment to ask for a lift. And she'd missed the Saturday rush hour down to St Girons, the market ending at midday. So, with the town hall clock striking three, she'd let herself out and retraced her footsteps across the mountains. Despite the aches and pains, however, the return hike had felt less arduous, as though she had left behind a heavy load in Fogas – one she had been shouldering for far too long.

At last Serge knew the truth.

Would it do any good? she wondered. Far from being galvanised by her revelation, Serge had seemed to retreat even further into depression. He'd listened to her unburden her secret in stunned silence, then he'd shaken his head and asked her to repeat it. When she'd finished, he'd sat there mumbling Véronique's name over and over in an incantation of disbelief and then he'd fallen quiet. She'd waited, thinking the inevitable questions would follow. But they hadn't. Finally, sensing he wanted to be alone, she'd left him at the kitchen table, his lunch untouched, gaze fixed on the stale end of baguette on his plate. Shock probably. She'd call him later and make sure he was okay.

'Maman! Where have you been? You've been gone hours.'

Véronique was framed in the doorway, hair falling to her shoulders, a hand on the doorjamb. She looked as beautiful as her Spanish grandmère had before her. But the frown on her face and the set of her jaw were the spitting image of her father. If Annie hadn't been so nervous, she might have laughed. Instead her steps involuntarily slowed at the thought of what lay ahead.

Allowing herself to be led to a chair, Annie also tolerated Véronique pulling off her boots and was happy to accept the coffee that was placed in front of her. She made the most of the fuss. It might not happen ever again.

'So?' demanded Véronique, unable to contain her curiosity any longer. 'Who did you see? And will they be able to sort out La Poste?'

'I went to see yourrr fatherrr,' Annie said, as if it was the most natural thing in the world.

'My . . . ? Did you say . . . ?'

'Yourrr fatherrr.'

'I don't understand.' Véronique had the bemused look of the six-year-old who'd uttered the very same thing in the graveyard all those years ago, when Annie had brusquely told her she had no gravestones to decorate on her father's side. 'He's visiting? After all this time?'

'Not exactly . . . I mean . . . the thing is—'

'Oh my goodness! Is he coming to see me? Today? Why didn't you—?'

Annie reached across to lay a hand on her daughter's arm, gently guiding her back onto the chair she'd abandoned in agitation.

166

'You need to give me a chance to explain, love, and it's prrrobably best if you'rrre sitting down.' Annie braced herself. 'Yourrr fatherrr is herrre. But he's not visiting. He's been herrre all the time.'

'Here? What do you mean, here?'

'He lives in Fogas.'

'But . . . ? But then why hasn't he . . . ?' Véronique blinked.

'He didn't know. I neverrr told him he was a fatherrr.'

The words seemed to hang between them in the charged air, the silence so full it was smothering. With her cheek turned as though she'd been slapped, Véronique's focus was on the pasture outside the window and Annie could see her piecing it all together. When she turned back, her voice was brittle.

'So let me get this straight. All my life my father has been in this commune and you never mentioned it?'

Studying the criss-cross of scratches that marred the table-top, Annie avoided the accusation in her daughter's eyes. 'I thought it forrr the best.'

'For the *best*?' Véronique leapt to her feet, both hands planted squarely on the table as she leaned forward and Annie recognised the stout fingers, the broad backs of the hands brown and freckled. They were the mirror image of Annie's own. Capable. Solid. 'My life was a living hell because of your stupid secret! Did you know that?'

The chair scraped violently across the tiles and there was the sound of a choked sob from near the sink. A foot tapping on the floor, calves shapely, like a dancer's. She'd inherited them from her Grandmère Papon who'd been known to boast she had legs good enough for the Moulin Rouge.

'Did you know the other kids made my every waking moment a torture because I didn't have a papa? Because even my mother didn't know who my father was? They called you a whore!'

Annie flinched.

'So, go on then. Tell me. Let me in on the great mystery at last!'

Finally Annie met her daughter's withering gaze. 'Serrrge Papon.'

Véronique's eyelids flickered as though she were about to faint. 'You're joking.'

Annie shook her head.

'Serge Papon is my father?' Another sob, followed by a harsh laugh. 'Serge Papon! Mayor of Fogas! All that time I was bullied and my father was the most powerful man around. Don't you see the irony, Maman?'

Anger. Annie had known it would come but she hadn't expected it to be so vicious. So justified. She felt her throat constricting, her breath coming in short gasps.

'For my entire life I've dreamt of having a father and he was right next to me all the time. And you *knew* it!' Véronique paused, struck by another thought. 'All those *Toussaint* when I decorated the Estaque graves thinking I had no other ancestors. That graveyard is littered with bloody Papons! How could you do that to me?'

'I'm sorrrry—'

'*Sorry*? That doesn't even begin to cover it.' She gathered her coat and started for the door.

'Don't go, Vérrronique. Not like this. It's best—'

'DON'T!' She yanked open the door. 'Don't ever tell me what's best again. You proved thirty-six years ago that you have no idea what is best for me. None at all.'

Véronique stormed out of the house, slamming the door in her wake. The dresser rattled in response, bouncing one of the photos onto the floor, and at the sound of smashing glass, Annie experienced a rare thing.

Tears. Sliding down her face.

Toughened by the life she'd chosen to lead, she'd long ago stopped crying. So it was a strange sensation to feel the wetness on her cheeks, the sobs racking her chest, and her heart feeling like it was being crushed into a thousand pieces.

She put her head in her hands and allowed the grief to overwhelm her.

Third time lucky. That's all Christian was thinking as he held the door open for Eve – although his thoughts were taken momentarily by the sheer length of leg that dropped from the hem of her dress into towering heels. With two cancelled dates behind them, both thanks to his temperamental animals, he had his fingers crossed that this one would go smoothly. A couple of steps inside the restaurant and he began to feel uneasy.

Swanky was the word Josette had used when she'd heard where he was off to. Perched on a hill on the eastern outskirts of St Girons, it was part of a converted chateau, the former wine cellar now providing the setting for what Eve had said was the best place to eat in the Ariège. Needless to say, Christian had never eaten there before. Neither had René. Nor Josette. He hadn't bothered asking Annie, who never ate out. Or Bernard, whose favourite haunt was Chez Titi, a family-run eatery in the next valley which fed people well but had no pretensions of grandeur. And he somehow hadn't got round to mentioning the date to Véronique.

In fact the only person to express any first-hand knowledge of the place was Pascal Souquet, who'd snickered when he'd found out where Christian was going. Which hadn't helped the farmer's nerves.

As he followed Eve into the dimly lit interior, he could see why it was somewhere the first deputy would enjoy: tables swathed in white linen set back under arching vaults, candelabra softly illuminating the old stone walls, the muted murmur of refined conversation and the chink of fine china, all over-laid with classical music. It reeked of refinement. Christian's shirt collar immediately began to chafe and he felt as out of place as Sarko in a best-of-breed competition.

'It's a bit dark!' he whispered to Eve as the Maître d' verified their reservation.

'Adds to the ambience.' She smiled and ran a hand up his arm, fingers trailing fire and making his collar even tighter.

'This way, please.'

The Maître d' led them to the far corner, Christian conscious of his hulking physique as he carefully negotiated his way through the restaurant. He was even more aware of it when he took his seat. Three glasses at each setting. Multiple knives and forks. A froth of napkins. Crystal salt and pepper shakers. A jug of water with no handle. And a glass vase holding a single rose. It didn't leave much room for the food and for a clumsy man, it was a potential disaster.

He put his ungainly hands in his lap and decided they would only move once the meal was placed in front of him. Which he hoped wouldn't take too long as he was starving. It had been a long day on the farm. He'd been up early with a cow in difficulty, her calf finally born late morning, and then he'd been over to a neighbour to help him repair a barn roof that had been damaged in the snow. By early evening he was already ravenous and had been intending to grab something before he left but he hadn't had time.

'Mademoiselle, Monsieur!' A waiter whipped a napkin under Christian's nose and laid it across his lap.

'Are you going to pull a rabbit out of it next?' asked Christian, laughing. It merited a pained smile in response.

'To commence, the chef recommends the seared duck foie gras with passion-fruit curd, puffed wild rice, glazed endive and puy lentils.'

Christian blinked and glanced at Eve but she was nodding and making appreciative noises.

'And to follow, medallions of venison *au poivre* with apple and celeriac puree and potato rösti.'

To the farmer, the man was speaking a foreign language.

'Do you need to see the menu?'

'Yes!' Christian said before Eve could decline. He didn't have a clue what had been suggested but had a strong feeling that it wouldn't be enough to feed a man who'd done a full day of work outside.

The waiter produced two menus with a flourish, took their orders for aperitifs and promptly withdrew, inclining his head as he did so.

'Did he just bow?' Christian asked with amazement.

Eve laughed at his expression. 'You don't get out much, do you!'

'Obviously not!' He opened the menu, hoping it would make more sense than the waiter, and promptly ran a finger around his collar, now a veritable noose. No wonder the man was bowing. Only royalty could afford to eat here.

'So, what do you fancy?'

Christian averted his gaze from the prohibitive prices and looked at the main courses. He read them. And read them once more. But he was none the wiser.

'Steak and chips?' he said with a wistful tone and Eve laughed again.

'You are funny. Seriously, what are you having?'

Struggling to recognise any of the dishes, he couldn't even tell how they were being served. Everything was pan-fried, chargrilled, lightly smoked, braised or lacquered. And if it survived that, it came with jus, an emulsion, a duxelle or crushed potatoes. Why on earth would you want to crush a potato?

Too embarrassed to ask Eve for a translation, he scanned the page again. Rabbit? No. It said a 'tasting of rabbit'. In his mind that just meant there wasn't enough to go round. Lamb? The last of the five dishes definitely said lamb.

'I think I'll have the lamb,' he said, aspiring to sound confident. 'You?'

'The oak-smoked salmon with crushed peas.'

'Sounds great.' His stomach rumbled loudly.

'You've got an appetite, I see!' Her eyes flashed provocatively and he felt her leg entwine around his under the table.

'May I take your order?'

'Yes!' squeaked Christian, his leg jerking up and clattering the underside of the table, startling the waiter. He cleared his throat. 'Ladies first.'

'The foie gras to start . . .'

Damn! A starter. He hadn't picked a starter. He frantically skimmed the menu again.

'And for you, Monsieur?'

'Erm . . .'

'Try the red mullet, Christian. It's gorgeous.'

'The red mullet it is, then. And the lamb to follow.' He handed back the menu, relieved to be rid of it, and tried not to stare too hard at the basket of bread the waiter had brought.

'And how would sir like his lamb cooked?'

'Rare.'

'And wine?'

Merde! Of course. He was about to ask for a house red but a quick glance around the other tables revealed no carafes, only bottles.

'The Fitou is good,' Eve suggested, saving him the trouble of opening the wine menu. And dying from shock at the cost.

He nodded agreement at the waiter who swept their menus under his arm, bowed and left.

'Sorry,' Christian said, cheeks red. 'I'm not used to all this fuss.'

'I can tell,' said Eve with a beautiful smile. 'If I'd known this place was going to make you so nervous, I wouldn't have suggested it!'

He felt himself relax for the first time that night.

'So,' she said, leaning forward, chin on her elegant hands. 'Tell me how come you're still single.'

'You mean it's not obvious?'

'No, it's not. Not to me, anyhow.'

'Ah! Well that's because you know nothing about farming . . .'

'Do you want me to wait while you go to the house? Seeing as it's dark?'

Chloé rolled her eyes and opened the van door. 'No, Maman. I'll be fine.'

Maman hesitated and Chloé knew she was worried. But it was a short walk to the farm and Chloé had made it many times before.

'Say hi to Annie for me, then. And Fabian will pick you up in an hour or so when he's finished locking up. At about eight-thirty, okay?'

'Yes!' Chloé suffered a kiss and then stood by the roadside, stubbornly refusing to budge until her mother had pulled off. Waving until the blue van was out of sight around the bend, she turned towards the farm.

It had been a wonderful day, ideal weather for practising, and Chloé had just about somersaulted herself out. She'd spent the entire morning perfecting the aerial cartwheel and was managing to execute it successfully more times than not. Only thing was, she was gaining more height than before, so now when she messed up, she really felt it. She rubbed her shoulder, the last part of her body to feel the brunt of failure, the muscle tender to the touch.

A hot chocolate. That's what would make it feel better. And she knew who made the best hot chocolate in Picarets. Well, actually, that was Fabian with his amazing little coffee machine that whipped up the milk into a froth like someone had spent ages blowing bubbles in it. But Annie's was a close second. Especially when Fabian wasn't in. His double duties at the épicerie and the garden centre meant the house in Picarets with the faded Dubonnet advert painted on the gable wall was always unoccupied on a Saturday of late.

Trotting up the path to the farmhouse, she was surprised that the dogs weren't running to meet her. Normally she had to fight her way through a surge of canine affection, the dogs almost as big as her. But today she made it to the farmhouse unscathed. She peeked in the kitchen window where the lights were on but no one was sitting at the table. So she stuck her head around the front door and called out. No answer. Out with the cows, maybe?

She wasn't worried. Not until she approached the barn and saw Annie's legs. They were on the floor, sticking out of one of the stalls. And the dogs were lying up against them and whining. Chloé started running.

'Annie? Annie?' she called as she burst into the barn, able to see Annie's face now which looked old. Grey. Not good. 'Annie? Are you okay?'

Annie raised a hand and Chloé knew she was trying to smile, doing that thing adults always did to a child when there was trouble. She was ten. Eleven in a few months. Didn't they know that she wasn't a baby anymore? Hadn't last year proved that?

'I'll call for help,' she said, reaching for her phone, but Annie laid a hand on her arm.

'No, love. No need.' Her voice was raspy, like she'd been coughing a lot, and she was holding her chest. 'Just taking a brrreak.'

Chloé paused, fingers hovering over the buttons. 'Lying down? Outside?'

Annie shrugged and gave a half-smile. 'It's comfy.'

Confused, Chloé put the phone back in her pocket and instead helped Annie into a sitting position. Which was when she noticed the marks on her face.

'Have you been crying?'

Annie shook her head and grumbled something which Chloé couldn't catch. But the young girl took it as a good sign. It was more like the normal Annie.

'Can you get up?'

'Of courrrse I can get up! I'm all rrrested now.'

'Would you like some help?'

Annie muttered something else but Chloé knew her well. She knelt down and provided a shoulder to lean on. Annie wobbled a bit getting upright, like the early-born calf Christian had up at his farm, legs unsteady beneath her. Then, hand still resting on Chloé, she started walking back to the house, her subdued dogs following.

Once in the kitchen, Chloé insisted on making a coffee, despite Annie's protests. She even succeeded in getting a smile out of her by having to stand on a stool to reach the mugs. Not sure how much coffee went into one cup, she ladled in two spoons, added a good amount of sugar and placed it on the table.

'Thanks.' Annie was looking at Chloé's phone. 'When did you get this?'

'Maman bought it to replace the one you gave me. You know, the one that got broken . . .' Chloé stopped. She'd learnt not to talk too much about last year. About the man who'd attacked her and Maman. It seemed to upset the adults whenever the topic was mentioned. They'd start whispering and mouthing silent words, as if she couldn't understand.

Normally Annie wasn't like that and Chloé could talk to her about anything. Today, however, she seemed frail and Chloé didn't want to make her sad again.

'I know.' Annie nodded, still looking at Chloé's contacts list. 'Is this Chrrristian's mobile numberrr?'

'Yep. He said I could call him anytime,' Chloé added proudly. 'Although he later said it didn't include after midnight unless there was an emergency.'

Sensing some phone-based experimentation behind that comment, Annie actually laughed.

'Anytime, eh?' She looked at the clock. 'Do me a favourrr, Chloé. Fetch me the phone frrrom the drrresserrr and then I want you to feed the dogs forrr me.'

Chloé passed the receiver over and then whistled for the dogs to follow her. They were reluctant to leave their owner's side but she shooed them out and the three of them walked back to the barn. They were almost there when Chloé remembered the dry food. Annie always kept it in the rear porch to stop it getting damp.

Running back to the house, she slipped inside and picked up the bag. Knowing listening to other people's conversations was wrong, she didn't mean to. But it was just that Annie sounded so unhappy. Chloé leaned closer to the kitchen door.

'—Thanks. And let me know if you find herrr . . .' There was a pause and a hiccup. Chloé knew that sound.

She edged round the door to see Annie putting the phone down, tears rolling down her face, and Chloé did the only thing she could think of. She dropped the bag of dog food on the floor and ran over to hug Annie as hard as she could.

★ ★ ★

It was going well, thought Christian as he looked at the dessert menu in Eve's absence, trying to work out which one would be the biggest. He'd got through the first course without knocking anything off the table, although he'd got a bit of a shock when the waiter had started pouring boiling water over his starter. The red mullet had come in a large white bowl and Christian had been sure he was in for a treat when the waiter laid it in front of him. But inside was a square mouthful of fish resting on a small circle of unidentified foodstuffs. The rest of the bowl was empty.

He'd tried not to look too disappointed and had been about to reach for the spoon of yellow paste that was balanced on the edge when the waiter had started pouring water into it. Damn near scalded him!

It was a saffron sauce, Eve had said. Which didn't explain why it couldn't have been made in the kitchen rather than on his lap. And it didn't make the portion any bigger either. He'd eaten as slowly as he knew how, but even so he was finished way before her and had the agony of watching her push her food around the plate without really eating it. Still starving, he'd had to restrain himself from rugby-tackling the waiter as he cleared the table, taking the best part of half her starter with him.

The main course hadn't been much better. His lamb, three puny chops from a runt he would have been embarrassed to send to market, had arrived on some slivers of courgette. A spoonful of creamed potato was next to it and on the far end of the massive plate, a tiny sprig of mint. It was bad enough that he was paying through the nose and his hunger wasn't being satisfied. What irked him even more was that he knew that the price he got for an entire lamb wouldn't cover his half of the meal.

With his stomach growling, he'd endured the sight of Eve

fussing over her sliver of smoked salmon, cutting off small pieces and taking an age to eat them. He'd emptied the breadbasket twice in the meantime. She'd finally taken pity and offered him the rest of her dinner. Which he'd accepted.

If the meal wasn't a success, however, his rendezvous with Eve Rumeau was. She was a lovely woman. Quite witty once you got beneath that polished exterior. The intervals between courses had flown as they talked about the farm, her job, the difference between St Girons and her hometown of Bordeaux. By the time she'd excused herself to go to the ladies, he was having a much better evening than he'd anticipated. But . . .

He couldn't put his finger on it. No one could deny she was attractive. He'd seen the way heads had turned as she walked through the room only minutes before, body wrapped tight in a black dress designed to make pulses race, his own no exception. But . . .

There was something not right. Despite the flowing conversation. Despite the enjoyable company. She simply wasn't the woman for him. He wanted someone more down-to-earth. Someone content to go to the Auberge in La Rivière and trust Madame Webster's *Menu du Jour*. Someone who would clean their plate with satisfaction and think about their figure in the morning. And someone who would be at home on a farm. Even if he wasn't going to have a farm in the future.

He scratched his head, frustrated at this surprising turn of events. He'd asked Eve out in good faith, attracted to her despite his parents' obvious disapproval. Now here he was thinking about turning down a perfectly gorgeous woman. Which was crazy. It wasn't as if he was inundated with girlfriends. But it made no difference. Basically the woman he wanted was . . .

His mobile. Trilling in his pocket. Already loud enough that he was getting dirty looks from the other diners. He'd left it on in case there were any more problems with the calving but had forgotten to put it on mute. Idiot! Spotting Eve making her way back to the table, he signalled he was going out, grabbed the phone and headed for the exit, trying to ignore the disapproving frowns as he went.

'Bonjour?' he said, opening the door and stepping out into the cold night.

'Chrrristian?' The line was crackling, the connection weak.

'Annie?' He walked up the drive, hoping to get a better signal. 'Is that you, Annie?'

'Chrrristian, I need yourrr help.' A hiccupping sound. Was she crying? Annie Estaque? Christian held the phone closer to his ear. Whatever this was about, it was serious.

12

Eve had taken the news really well. She'd immediately suggested that they forgo dessert and leave, insisting she'd get a taxi thus allowing him to start for home. He'd given her a kiss of gratitude and she'd pulled back with a look of remorse.

'It was a lovely evening,' she said with a sigh. 'But I don't suppose we'll be doing it again?'

'Sorry.' Christian looked at the ground. 'It's just—'

She placed a hand on his arm. 'Don't! Never explain to a woman why she isn't the one. I'll be in touch about the farm.'

Watching her taxi drive down the hill into town, he'd felt a pang of regret. Then he'd got into the Panda, which was parked between a BMW and a Mercedes, and had carefully, very carefully indeed, backed it out and driven off. At speed.

Annie had sounded terrible and not just because of the quality of the line. She'd told him that she'd had an argument with Véronique and was concerned about her. He'd pressed her to tell him what they'd fallen out about but she wouldn't say. She'd tried calling her daughter but had got no answer. So all she'd asked was that he drive down to La Rivière and check that Véronique was there.

She hadn't known that he was in St Girons. Hadn't known he was on a date. And he hadn't enlightened her.

Worried about both women, never having heard Annie

Estaque in such a state, he'd hit the road out of town in a hurry, throwing the Panda around the corners as he followed the River Salat up into the mountains. He was willing to take his chances if the gendarmes were doing speed checks at the roundabout at Kerkabanac. At least they wouldn't be able to do him for drink-driving as he'd drunk no more than a glass of the expensive wine, wanting to have his wits about him for his date with Eve.

The trees on the roadside had whipped past, the roundabout had proven devoid of police and in record time he was passing the bright lights of the Auberge in La Rivière and driving on to the épicerie. He parked next to the shop window, threw a wave at Josette inside, and hurried up the lane. If Annie was right, this was where he would find Véronique. Not at home, but in the church.

Skirting round the ruins of the post office, he let himself into the graveyard. It was quiet. Spooky. The two Marys huddled at the foot of an empty cross in the grotto unnerving him with their silent weeping as he passed. He quickly crossed to the church door, pushed it open and stepped inside. A single candle on the metal stands to the left was the only light. The smell of incense filled the air. And the sound of crying came from a pew at the front.

'Véronique?' He moved towards the hunched shape, sliding along the bench until he was beside her. 'It's me. Christian.'

Her shoulders were shaking and he couldn't think what to do. So he put a tentative arm around her and drew her onto his chest.

'Come on,' he said as she folded into him. 'Whatever it is, it can't be that bad.'

A hiccup. 'Shows what . . . hic . . . you bloody know!'

He grinned in the darkness. She would be fine. Just fine. He stroked her hair and waited for her to calm down. Then they could talk about whatever had happened to make the Estaque women so upset.

'Say that again?'

'Serge Papon is my father.'

Christian swore, even the giant Jesus looking down from the cross unable to temper the farmer's astonishment. Then he fell silent, for it really wasn't a piece of news you could instantly react to.

'Yeah,' said Véronique as she dabbed her eyes with a tissue. 'Mad, isn't it?'

Christian nodded.

'And to think Maman's known all this time and never said a word.'

'Does Serge know?'

'I presume so. We never discussed what she'd said to him. I didn't give her the chance.' She balled up the tissue in her hand and shoved it into her pocket, chin at a defiant angle.

'It's understandable. Being upset. The two of you will sort this out. The three of you, even!' He shook his head, still stunned. 'Do you want me to take you back up there?'

'No! I can't face her tonight. I'm too angry. Better if I wait a day or two.'

'She called me, you know. That's how I found you.'

Véronique gave him a sideways look. 'How did she figure out I'd be here?'

'Said it was where you used to come when you were unhappy as a child.'

Her eyes closed and her head tilted forward, a thick veil of hair falling over her face. When she spoke, it was barely a whisper. 'I know she's not a bad mother. It's just . . .'

'A shock. That's what it is. But it could be worse.'

He felt the force of her sceptical stare. 'How?'

'Well, if you had to have a father in the commune, can you think of anyone better?'

'Than the manipulative, scheming trickster that is Serge Papon, you mean?'

The dry tone made Christian laugh and it echoed around the empty space.

'He's not that bad!'

'That's not what you were saying this time last year when he was trying to close the Auberge!'

'True. But at least he'll be on your side now!'

Véronique's lip trembled. 'What if he isn't?'

'What do you mean?'

'What if he doesn't want to acknowledge me? You know, as a daughter.'

Christian laughed again. 'Véronique Estaque, you are the most manipulative, scheming and politically aware woman I know. Of *course* he'll want to acknowledge you!'

Véronique slapped his leg, a small smile dimpling her cheeks. 'Thanks.'

'What for?'

'For coming down here when you could have been at home with your feet up.'

'Actually, I was in St Girons—' He stopped short, kicking himself.

'St Girons? What were you—? Oh!' Her hands flew to her mouth. 'You were on a date! Oh goodness, I'm so sorry.'

'You knew?'

'Everyone knows. It's all your mother's been talking about for weeks. And I've ruined it for you.' Her bottom lip began to quiver anew.

'Actually, I think I may have ruined it for myself.'

And so he told her about the meal. About the tiny portions. The obsequious waiter. The previous failed dates that he'd spent chasing his bull and helping a cow give birth. And by the end of it she was laughing. Proper laughing. Out loud. Inside the church.

'It's probably just as well it came to nothing,' he concluded with resignation. 'Seeing as I'm going to Toulouse soon.'

She glanced down, hair screening her expression once more. 'Yes,' she said. 'Probably is. Hard enough leaving here without the added complication of a relationship.'

When she looked up there was a bright smile fixed on her face.

'Come on,' she said. 'I'll buy you a drink in the bar.'

As they stood to go, his phone trilled again. He was tempted to let it ring but seeing it was Annie, he answered.

'Annie? I've found her—'

He stopped, his back stiffening as he listened to the caller and in the quiet of the church, Véronique could hear a man's voice issuing from the mobile.

'Right. I'll tell her. And thanks, Fabian. We'll head there now.'

'What's the matter?' Véronique asked as he hung up. 'Why's Fabian phoning you from Maman's?'

'He called in to pick up Chloé and thought Annie didn't look so good. Chloé told him she'd found her "resting" out in the barn earlier this evening. So he called the doctor.'

Véronique went pale. 'Is she okay?'

'She's been rushed to hospital. The doctor thinks she had a heart attack and he's taken her in for tests.'

'Right. Well knowing Maman, she won't want to stay overnight so the sooner we can get down there the better. Will you come with me?'

'Of course!'

'I'll drive.'

Christian watched in admiration as she locked up the

church and strode down the street, a mixture of both Serge and Annie, controlling her emotions so she could deal with this emergency on a day that couldn't have been easy for her. She was, he decided as he took his seat next to her in the car, the most down-to-earth woman he knew.

He heard the town hall clock strike eight. That's what roused him. He'd been sitting at the table all that time. Hours had passed and he hadn't noticed. At some point he'd reached out and put on the lamp. But that was it.

What time had she left? He couldn't remember. Couldn't remember what she'd been wearing, either. Had she eaten anything? He looked at the table, at the chunk of cheese and the length of saucisson, but he couldn't tell. The glass of wine was still there too.

She should have eaten. Walking all that way. And he hadn't even thought to offer her a lift home. Hadn't thought of anything but the story she'd told him.

A daughter. He had a *daughter*.

He turned it over in his mind once more.

Véronique Estaque. His own flesh and blood.

What colour eyes did she have, he wondered. He'd never really noticed. Her hair though, that was from his mother. Lovely auburn shade. And her legs! He'd noticed them all right, although he felt ashamed of it now.

Did she know yet? Annie had said she was going to tell her. It would be as big a shock for her. Bigger, maybe.

He sat there for a while before he realised he was smiling.

She was a fine woman. The way she'd given him the flowers at Thérèse's grave. And the way she'd covered for him the day the bear man had arrived in town. He should have known! She was a Papon to the core.

He chuckled, surprising himself with the sound. Then he

heard another noise. It took him a moment to place it. A rumbling, gurgling reverberation.

It was his stomach!

He reached out for the cheese, cut off a corner and popped it in his mouth. The taste nearly felled him. Strong, flavoursome, reminiscent of the high pastures where the cows spent their summers.

Excited, he cut a piece of saucisson and tried that. Smoky, garlicky, the savours of the countryside that he'd grown up in.

He jumped up to check the cupboards, eager for more. But they were bare.

Shopping. He needed to go shopping.

It was eight-thirty. The épicerie would still be open. He drew the notepad towards him to make a list and was instantly reminded of the letter from the Conseil Général.

The bastards! How dare they threaten him. He was Serge Papon, mayor of Fogas!

He jotted down some notes which he would make into a reply tomorrow and take to Céline on Monday. As far as he was concerned, Arnaud Petit was staying. And that was another thing.

He strode over to the ornate sideboard that was his office. Reaching into the top drawer, he pulled out an envelope addressed to the Prefect in Foix. With great ceremony, he slid a knife under the edges and opened it. Then he unfolded the letter inside and promptly ripped it into pieces.

'Resign? My backside!' he exclaimed as he threw the fragments of paper onto the ashes in the fireplace. 'Damned if I'll let that whelp Pascal Souquet get his way!'

Making a note to call his friend who worked for La Poste first thing on Monday morning, he then wrote out a shopping list and slipped on his jacket, noticing how loosely it hung on him now.

'Well,' he said as he closed the front door behind him, 'it's nothing Josette's croissants won't sort out!'

And with the moon shining the way, he got in the car and headed for La Rivière.

Perhaps Annie was right, thought Josette as she stood in the empty épicerie twiddling her thumbs. Maybe she really ought to start closing at six like everyone else? At ten to nine in the evening Jacques was snoring softly in the inglenook and no one had been in for over two hours. Even Christian had failed to materialise and it was over half an hour since he'd parked outside.

It had been a slow day all round. The sunshine and unseasonable warmth had no doubt meant that the Saturday-morning market in St Girons had been busy. But it also meant that people lingered over coffee on the terrace of the Café Bouchon in the market square watching the bustle of the weekly event and so didn't pop into the bar in La Rivière on their way home.

Consequently, she'd sold little more than the regular bread, cigarettes and croissants. And a couple of ice creams to two kids who only needed a bit of sun as an excuse. They'd spent an age choosing, marvelling at the wide array. Which was all thanks to Fabian. She blushed to think that before her nephew had arrived and dragged her and the shop into the twenty-first century, customers would have been offered lollies of an age unknown which they would have had to prise out of the ice at the bottom of the freezer.

Turning her attention back to the *Gazette Ariégeoise*, a newspaper that had been selling well in Fogas since its first-hand account of the fight up at the town hall, she cast an eye over the public notices in a bid to alleviate boredom. She was rewarded by spotting that the épicerie in the next village was up for sale. Retirement of owners, it said. She snorted, making Jacques twitch in his dreams.

Retirement indeed. More like their useless son spent every euro they made on having a good time in St Girons of a Saturday night and they were fed up of it. Still, it wouldn't hurt her business here in La Rivière. One less competitor in the area would mean more customers through her door.

She was about to flick over to the next page when her attention was caught by a planning permission notice right at the bottom of the column. It was for a plot in Sarrat. For a multi-purpose store.

Her fingers froze on the page.

What did that mean, "multi-purpose"? She reached for the pair of scissors hanging from the counter by a string and carefully cut out the square of text. She was still looking at it, an apprehensive frown on her face, when Christian and Véronique walked past, striding purposefully down the road, not stopping at his car and not waving in either.

Odd. Had Christian been with Véronique all this time? Where though? Since the demise of the post office, the lane only consisted of a couple of holiday homes and the church. And as Josette couldn't think of anything that would make the atheist, socialist Christian Dupuy set foot inside the church, she was truly perplexed.

She was still puzzling over this when she saw something even more amazing. Serge Papon pulling up outside and getting out of his car. Smiling.

He was a step away from the door when Véronique drove past, Christian beside her. He waved but they didn't notice, faces serious. Where on earth were they going now and why had Christian left his car in La Rivière? Josette had no time to ponder this latest development before Serge was in the shop.

'Bonsoir, Josette,' he said, greeting her with a kiss.

'Bonsoir, Serge,' she replied and got a lungful of a familiar scent. Aftershave. He hadn't worn that in a while.

'Was that Véronique I saw just now? With Christian?' he asked as he picked up a basket.

'Yes, although I have no idea where they're off to at this time of night.'

'He's left his car outside.'

'I know. Odd, isn't it.'

Serge said no more, simply started loading up his basket with food. Lots of food. Tins of fruit, brioche, eggs, some fromage frais, a jar of honey, a twist of chorizo. He stopped at the fresh vegetables and held a bulb of garlic up to his nose and inhaled. He grinned and dropped it in the basket, followed by a string of onions, four apples and some tomatoes, despite the fact they were Spanish, which normally made him complain.

'Is this any good?' he asked, now holding up a tin of the local cassoulet.

'Superb,' she said. 'As good as your mother's used to be. Try the coq au vin as well.'

He took two tins of each.

'I'll have some saucisson too please, Josette, and some Rogallais and a bit of—' He stopped in front of the cheese cabinet. 'Is that . . . ?'

'Roquefort.'

His eyes lit up. 'Some of that please. Not very local though, is it!'

Josette smiled, well aware that her preference for Ariège cheese had been a long-standing joke. 'You can thank Fabian for that. His idea to stock something different.'

She cut a wedge from the round and went to wrap it, but he stopped her and lowered his head to the cheese.

'Mmm!' He straightened up, face flushed with excitement. 'Amazing.'

'You seem to have recovered your appetite,' she commented, as she started ringing up his purchases. But he was out of hearing, busy choosing croissants. He returned with a full bag and a baguette. And a jar of Nutella.

'Are you sure that's everything?' she asked with a touch of irony, but it was wasted. He was bent over the counter, peering at the notice she had cut out of the paper.

'I forgot my reading glasses,' he muttered. 'Does that say something about Sarrat?'

'It's an application for planning permission. For a multi-purpose store.'

His head jerked up and she took a step back. She knew that look, the eyes narrowed, forehead prominent. Jacques had always described it as the pensive turtle look, tempering the cute description by adding he meant the snapping variety. It usually augured some Machiavellian scheme or other.

'Can I take this?'

'I was hoping to raise it with Christian . . .' She hesitated, realising what she'd just implied. 'I mean, seeing as you . . .'

He nodded. 'As I'm about to resign?'

'Yes. I thought Christian might be able to find out a bit more for me.'

'It does seem a bit unusual, doesn't it?' He tapped the piece of paper. 'Sarrat of all places. And why now, after all these years?'

'It's the threat to me I'm worried about. I don't need another shop opening on my doorstep. Bad enough that Véronique's idea for the combined post office was turned down.'

'Véronique's idea, eh? That's the second time someone's mentioned that today.' Serge paid and then glanced from the bags of shopping lining the counter, out to his car, as though coming to a decision. 'I know it's late, Josette. But how do you fancy telling me all about her plans over a drink?'

'Now?'

'Yes, now. If we're going to turn things around, we need to start acting fast. Because I have a strong suspicion that everything isn't as it should be.'

And with that he crossed to the door and flicked the latch, twisting the sign to *Fermé*.

'Come on,' he said, striding into the bar. 'Tell me what's been going on. And make mine a pastis.'

She followed him through and started talking as she poured his drink, breaking off momentarily when he insisted on taking the open bottle of Ricard to inhale the hallmark aniseed odour and again when he lifted his glass to his lips and groaned with delight at the first sip, waking Jacques with the sound. It had been so long since the mayor had been around that the conversation lasted a while, but Josette didn't mind. She was just pleased that, at long last, Serge Papon was back.

13

By mid-April, Fogas was in bloom. An unseasonably warm spell had resulted in an early burst of blossom in the old orchard and the garden of the Auberge was yellow with the nodding heads of daffodils. Even the wisteria that Fabian had planted on the terrace outside the bar was beginning to show signs of life as the region gratefully shrugged off the shroud of winter and welcomed in the brighter days of spring.

But while Mother Nature could work such a transformation in a couple of weeks, making the flora and fauna overlook the suffering she had inflicted on them in the darker months, those who had lived in the commune all their lives knew that it would take a lot longer for the inhabitants to set aside the latest scandal. The rumour had surfaced like an underground spring, bubbling up out of nowhere, the source never identified, and a fortnight on, not even the repeated theft of sausages from the mobile butcher's van that always parked up opposite the derelict post office on a Tuesday morning could compete with the speculation that Véronique Estaque's mysterious father was none other than the mayor of Fogas. The very mayor who, on hearing the news, had withdrawn his letter of resignation. So it *had* to be true.

Which of course meant that business was booming down at the épicerie and bar in La Rivière, locals calling in on spurious errands, all hoping to catch the latest twist in this narrative that had been running for over three decades. Or even better, to add yet another layer of conjecture to a story that was already stranger than fiction.

This particular day, a Wednesday, was no different. Despite the early hour, Fabian was manning the till in the shop and the bar was bustling with breakfast customers, Josette serving Bernard Mirouze while his dog ran circles through the legs of those sitting at the tables, nose pressed to the floor as he went.

'Incredible,' muttered René as he sipped his coffee standing up, one eye on the demented beagle, his fingers tapping on the counter in the absence of a cigarette. 'Serge Papon. And Annie! How on earth did she manage to keep it a secret all these years?'

Christian shook his head and finished off the last of his croissant, flakes dropping to the ground in front of the appreciative canine who snuffled them up as he passed. 'Think that's the hardest part for Véronique. The fact that Annie knew and never said.'

'But what made her reveal it now? Seems a bit odd!'

'It's not our place to judge,' Josette said from behind the bar with a bite to her tone, never so busy that she couldn't listen in on a conversation. 'Not one of us is perfect.'

'Although René likes to think he is,' chipped in Bernard, as he moved across the room to sit next to the old shepherd.

René scowled at the *cantonnier* with a hair-trigger irascibility that always coincided with his attempts to forswear smoking.

'Still, having a daughter seems to have brought about a transformation in Serge,' continued Christian. 'Not only has he changed his mind about resigning, but when I was up at the town hall yesterday he was using his network of old cronies to find out more about this La Poste business.'

'Did he mention the planning permission?' Josette tipped her head in the direction of Sarrat on the other side of the river.

'He said he's hit a brick wall with that. But you know Serge, he'll just keep throwing his weight against it until it crumbles!'

Josette smiled. 'That's Serge all right. Apparently he received a threatening letter from the Conseil Général about Arnaud Petit lodging here, so he got Céline to type a letter back saying he was considering bringing corruption charges against them.'

Christian choked on the last of his coffee. 'Brave man!'

'Then Arnaud came in the next day and said his rental contract had been extended and the rent reduced!'

Christian and René both burst out laughing.

'Never thought I'd say this,' reflected René, 'but it's good to have him back in charge. Seeing as *you're* forsaking us.' His last words were accompanied by another glare, this time directed at the big man next to him.

'Is it definite then, Christian? Has the farm sold?'

'Seems so. Eve wants me to call in to the office tomorrow to sign the *compromis de vente*. Once that's done, there's no going back.'

René glowered again. 'Christ. It's wrong. Having to sell your home and your livelihood. What will you do with the livestock?'

'I'm seeing the auctioneer tomorrow. Ironic really. We've had our best spring in years, lots of healthy calves and lambs.' The sigh that escaped his lips was enough to silence the other two. 'Ah well. At least I can head up to Toulouse knowing that Fogas is in good hands.'

'Even bloody Bernard in charge would be better than that skunk Pascal!' René drained his cup and turned to see Fatima Souquet standing in the archway that led to the shop.

'Bonjour all. Not interrupting anything interesting, am I?'

'We were just saying how important it is to support local businesses,' said Josette pointedly, knowing that Fatima's sudden conversion to shopping at the épicerie had nothing to do with the superior products that were now on sale. It was a retort good enough to earn her a grin from Jacques in the fireplace and to vex the wife of the first deputy, who shook herself like a wet hen, feathers ruffled, and disappeared into the shop.

'Nice one, Josette!' Christian murmured as he paid.

'Well! She's only in on the off chance she might hear some gossip. And I owe it to Annie not to let that happen. Not in my bar, anyway.'

'How is Annie? Any news?'

Josette's face creased into a frown. 'I haven't seen her. She's not set foot in here and she won't answer my calls. Fabian called in to drop off some shopping the other day and found her carrying a calf out of the barn. He reprimanded her, reminding her that the doctor had said no unnecessary exertion for the time being, and she told him to bugger off.'

'No change there, then!'

'It'll take more than a heart attack to keep that woman down,' said René with open admiration. 'I was on the track above her farm last week and saw her walking up to the ridge at the back with her dogs. She's made of strong stuff.'

'Talking of dogs, is it just me or is Serge getting fat?' Christian nodded at the beagle who was now taking a piece of pain au chocolat from Bernard's chubby fingers.

'Hey, Bernard! You'll have that dog ruined!' growled René. 'He'll be no use to us come September. Not that he was much use anyway. Running around with his nose stuck to the ground but not smelling anything!'

The *cantonnier* took umbrage. 'It's a growth spurt, that's all.' He patted Serge who flopped onto his back, stunted legs in the air.

'He's growing all right,' laughed Josette. 'Just not in the right direction!'

'So what were you doing up there?' Christian asked, turning back to René who was still watching the dog which had resumed its incessant sniffing, coming to rest against René's boots, tail wagging furiously.

'Hm? Where?'

'Up above Annie's the other day. What took you up there? Not like you to go uphill out of the hunting season!'

'Never you mind!' With a dark look aimed at Josette, René scooped up the beagle and stomped over to Bernard.

'Did I say something wrong?' Christian was bemused.

Josette gave a sly smile and beckoned him forward. 'Mushrooms!' she whispered. 'You know what he's like about keeping his patch to himself.'

The farmer rolled his eyes, never surprised by the lengths his neighbours went to over the fungi that grew in abundance in the woods. 'Bit early isn't it?'

'Not if you know what you're looking for. And René is one of the best mushroom hunters around.'

'I'll take your word for it,' said Christian with a laugh, digging out the shopping list his mother had given him. 'Right, I'll get these few bits and be off. Got a man coming to see Sarko this afternoon and I want him looking his best.'

Josette cleared the cups and wiped the bar, and tried to ignore her husband as the big farmer went through to the épicerie. Because she knew that Jacques, like her, would be feeling bereft at the idea of Christian leaving their community and one glance at his sad face would be enough to release the tight hold she had on her emotions. For Christian's sake, she thought as she stacked the dishwasher with an uncharacteristic clatter, she couldn't break down now.

Walking down the hill to La Rivière was the most difficult thing Annie had ever done. It had nothing to do with the steepness of the road or the problems with her health. And while her heart was beating faster than normal, it wasn't because of the exercise. It was because she was terrified.

Once back from hospital she'd remained cloistered on the farm, Fabian bringing her what she needed from the épicerie. He was a saint, that lad. Mind you, she hadn't been best pleased when he'd bullied her into seeing the doctor, nor when it had resulted in a trip to the hospital and lots of tests.

It made no difference what those men in their white coats did. They could stick needles in her and draw her blood and none of it would change a thing. She knew what was wrong with her. She'd felt the pain like a band on her chest when Véronique had walked out of the door. Stubborn, she had refused to yield and had gone over to feed the dogs in the barn which was when she'd blacked out. Next thing, she'd woken up to the angelic face of Chloé leaning over her, phone in hand.

Heart attack, they said.

Broken heart, more like.

She took the turn at the Auberge, Madame Webster waving merrily to her from an upstairs window. Lovely lady. She'd called up last week with a basket of food. Leftovers from the restaurant, she'd claimed. And although Annie had turned everyone else away, she'd opened the door to the young British woman. She'd been rewarded with a quiche, homemade pâté and a divine rhubarb crumble.

They'd talked over a cup of tea, the hotel owner sharing all her news, but not once had the subject of Annie's big secret been broached. Only as she was leaving did Lorna Webster give any indication that the gossip had reached even her non-French ears. Instead of the usual peck on the cheeks that signalled goodbye, she'd gathered the older woman into a hug and told her that if she needed anything, Annie was simply to call and she and Paul would do whatever they could for her.

Annie was at the bridge now, the épicerie visible, Christian's car parked outside. She felt her legs beginning to shake and stopped for a second, leaning on the arch of warm stones to watch the waters tumble over the weir that lay at the back of the Auberge. She was a bag of nerves. It was far worse than when she'd come back from Perpignan with Véronique in tow. Then, she'd had the distraction of a beautiful child to fend off the worst of the gossip, to shield her from the agony of huddled conversations that broke off the minute she walked in the door.

The support her infant daughter had given her by her mere existence was no longer something Annie could count on. Véronique had brought her home from hospital a fortnight ago and had punctiliously visited the farm three times a week to check on her. But she was aloof. A barrier was in place which she wasn't prepared to take down. And Annie had no idea how to break through it. After the headway they'd made in the last year, their relationship growing stronger as a result of the disaster at the post office, Annie felt like it had all slipped away in one afternoon.

Véronique, no matter what connection she managed to forge with her father, would never forgive her mother for the deception she had practised for thirty-six years. And few in the commune would condemn Véronique for that.

Of course, the obvious solution was to reveal everything, to tell them why the secret had been necessary in the first place. But Annie couldn't do that. Not without maligning the memory of a woman already dead. A woman Serge Papon idolised. Having already wronged the man by hiding his child from him, Annie felt unable to compound his pain by this further confession.

So she'd bite her lip and let them all think that she was self-ish. Warped. A bad mother. It wasn't much more to bear than she'd already borne and when it came to the good folk of Fogas, she didn't give a damn what they thought. It was only her daughter's opinion that she cared about. And no tale of a promise made long ago would make right the wrongs in Véronique's mind.

Straightening up, she began walking once more, shoulders back and head held high, unconsciously assuming the exact stance she'd adopted when she'd first walked into town with her baby daughter. All that was missing was the warm bundle of Véronique lying against her chest.

'Annie!' Fabian spluttered into his coffee as Josette entered from the bar. In a panic, he pointed at the small figure heading towards the shop and then towards the bony shape of the first deputy's wife who had her back to the window, engrossed in the label on the tin of cassoulet in her hand. 'Fatima will have a field day!'

'Merde!'

Fabian grinned, never having heard Tante Josette swear before.

'You'll have to distract Fatima,' she continued in a whisper. 'And I'll bring Annie through the shop.'

'How?' he hissed.

'I don't know . . . improvise! And quickly. She's almost here.'

With a grimace, Fabian hurried down the far aisle, past Christian who was skimming the pages of *L'Équipe*. He turned at the bottom, came nonchalantly back up towards Fatima and promptly tripped up. Long legs and arms sprawling, the entire contents of his mug splashed all down the front of the woman before him.

'You *imbecile*!'

The screech was loud enough to mask the sound of chimes as Josette whipped the door open. And the following tirade easily provided the cover needed for Josette to whisk Annie across the shop and into the corridor at the back of the bar, leaving a red-faced Fabian to deal with the irate Fatima Souquet. Last thing Josette saw, he was dabbing at the damp patches on her coat with a tissue as she slapped his hands away, while Christian rocked with mirth.

'Bonjourrr!' a surprised Annie said with a laugh as the pair of them caught their breath out in the garden. 'Wasn't expecting that welcome!'

Josette threw her arms around her and when she pulled back, both of them had tears in their eyes.

'Didn't think you'd appreciate a grilling from Fatima,' she said, brushing her sleeves across her face. 'Go take a seat in the sun and I'll make us a coffee. We've got a lot to catch up on!'

Back inside, the bar was deserted, the scolding that was continuing next door having drawn a crowd of onlookers to the archway. Even Jacques had left his fireside seat to get a better view.

'—And who's going to pay for the dry-cleaning?'

'I'll cover that. It's totally my fault. I'm so sorry—'

'You big oaf. I don't know why Josette employs you. You aren't fit—'

Trying not to laugh at her nephew's noble sacrifice, Josette quickly made the drinks and was about to sneak out when she noticed René walking down the road, Serge the beagle tucked under his arm.

Odd. What was he doing with Bernard's dog?

Seeing that Bernard was engrossed in the spectacle of Fatima castigating Fabian and was seemingly unperturbed by the loss of his faithful companion, Josette headed for the garden. After the darkness inside, the sunshine was blinding. Squinting, she walked up the path to the woodpile where

Annie was sitting with Tomate, the cat from the Auberge, who was luxuriating in the warmth and the unexpected petting she was getting.

'Sorry, no croissants. I didn't want to risk going back into the shop.'

'You mean you didn't rrrescue Fabian? Poorrr lad.'

'I don't know. He seemed to enjoy throwing his coffee over Fatima!'

Annie chuckled.

'So, how are you feeling?'

Josette thought her friend wasn't going to answer, the pause was so long. But finally she sighed.

'I feel old, that's how I feel. Old and tirrred. Even the farrrm is beginning to be too much forrr me and I neverrr thought I'd say that.'

'You have just had a heart attack, remember! Your problem is that you're too stubborn to ask for help.'

'And who am I supposed to ask? Vérrronique? She's barrrely talking to me!' Annie stared into her cup, knowing what the future held before the coffee grounds were even dry. 'I'm such an idiot. I thought I was doing things forrr the rrright rrreason, but now . . .'

'You did the right thing in telling Véronique.'

'Yes. But I did the wrrrong thing in not telling herrr soonerrr.'

Josette didn't answer.

'It's what everrryone thinks, isn't it?'

'Well . . . it is a bit puzzling. I mean, even if you'd told Véronique but not Serge. I think maybe that would have made sense.'

Annie nodded, her eyes following a bee as it flew lazily past them, drawn to the promise of early blossom. When she put her cup down, her hands were shaking.

'Have you spoken to herrr?'

'You mean has she said anything to me?' Josette shook her head. 'Not a word. She does seem a bit lost though, which is natural I suppose. After all . . .'

'Not everrry day you find out yourrr fatherrr is the mayorrr?'

'Something like that!'

'I neverrr set out to lie to herrr. It was just . . . out of my hands in some ways.'

'You don't need to explain,' said Josette softly. 'Not to me.'

'I know. But while I don't carrre what the rrrest think, I want you to know it wasn't a sorrrdid affairrr. He was a frrriend. Nothing morrre. Then that evening . . . Neverrr thought about getting caught. Didn't think about much, rrreally!'

She gave a dry laugh.

'When I found out I was expecting, I just wanted to die. I felt so cheap. Falling forrr Serrrge Papon of all people! The well-known philanderrrerrr. I couldn't bearrr the idea of telling Papa, the shame he would feel. So I was planning on going away. Having the baby and putting it up forrr adoption beforrre coming back.'

'What changed your mind?' asked Josette, shocked to think that Véronique might never have been part of life in Fogas.

Annie closed her eyes. 'It doesn't matterrr.'

'It does to Véronique. Have you told her this?'

'No. Not yet.'

'Well,' Josette said, as gently as she could, 'I think you ought to. And the sooner the better.'

'It won't make any differrrence. She's so angrrry with me.'

'You're underestimating your daughter, Annie. She's one of the most generous people I know, beneath that gruff exterior. Bit like someone else around here!'

Annie gave a small smile.

'And the gossip will die down, believe me.'

'Ha! When? It'll take some doing to beat this.'

'Admittedly you and Serge are causing a stir. Mainly because no one had any money on it!'

Annie laughed and shot Josette a sideways glance. 'Not even you?'

'Nope. Never crossed my mind.' She looked at the back door which was open and leaned in closer to Annie, her voice reduced to a murmur. 'Now that the truth is out, though, I'm not surprised. I should have seen it really. There's not many who haven't succumbed to the charms of Serge Papon!'

'You didn't. Orrr arrre you going to say therrre's still time?' The laugh that was rising in Annie's throat changed to a gasp as she saw Josette's face. 'You *didn't*?'

'No! Never! But I'd be lying if I said I wasn't tempted.'

Annie lowered her coffee cup, complete focus on her friend.

'We were having trouble, Jacques and I. We were trying for a baby and it was causing a lot of tension. Well, Serge came in the shop one day just after we'd had a row. Jacques was out here chopping wood, venting his anger.' Josette took her glasses off and wiped them with the hem of her blouse while she reflected on the past. 'The two of them were such good friends then, Serge and Jacques. They did everything as a pair. Hunting, fishing, the pétanque competition up at the summer fête.'

'Yes! I'd forrrgotten about that,' murmured Annie, recalling the good-looking young men who'd been as thick as thieves.

'Anyway, Serge made some flippant remark about me getting thinner. Gave me a knowing wink and said something about Jacques not doing his duty, you know, implying I should be pregnant.'

She laughed lightly.

'You know me. Cry at the drop of a hat. So I start sobbing

and Serge . . . he was so upset. Didn't know what to do with himself. He came round the counter and put his arms around me and . . .' She blinked, the memories vivid. 'If Jacques hadn't walked in right then, I don't know what would have happened.'

'Did Jacques say anything?'

'Didn't have to. He was still holding the axe!'

The two women burst into laughter, startling the cat out of her morning slumber.

'Serge took off out of there and the pair of them were never the same again. I told Jacques nothing had happened. But he didn't trust Serge. Didn't trust the man's animal magnetism. I always felt awful about it, coming between two friends like that. Of course, Serge went into politics not long after and he and Jacques never saw eye to eye on that either, which didn't do anything to repair their relationship. But I think that day was the catalyst.'

'You darrrk horrrse!'

'Now that is rich, coming from you!'

Annie dropped her head in acknowledgement. 'So you don't think less of me, now you know?'

'Annie Estaque! It wouldn't matter who Véronique's father was. I would still love the pair of you just the same.'

Annie reached across and squeezed Josette's hand and Josette could see she was struggling to keep her tears in check.

'How about I go and see if the coast is clear? Maybe catch Christian before he heads home and get him to give you a lift back?' She held up a hand as Annie began to protest. 'Make the most of it, Annie. He's signing the *compromis de vente* on the farm tomorrow so we won't have the pleasure of Christian Dupuy's company for much longer. By the time summer gets here, he'll be gone.'

'Is that definite?' Annie's face was ashen.

'Yes. He's hoping to sell Sarko today and he's seeing the

auctioneer to sort out the livestock sale tomorrow. I can't take it in really.'

Annie's gaze drifted to the branches of the fruit trees that overhung the fence, the scent of their white flowers soft on the morning air.

'I'll ask him to take you home then?'

'What? Oh, yes. That would be good. Thanks.'

Leaving Annie to her thoughts, Josette picked up the cups and walked slowly down the path, her memory returning to that day all those years ago when a young Jacques had come bursting into the shop. He'd been bare-chested, his muscles taut from the exertion, hands powerful on the handle of the axe.

She entered the bar and saw the present-day Jacques sitting in the inglenook watching Christian with a pensive look, the commotion in the épicerie having subsided. His white hair was still thick, features as handsome more than forty years on. She sat next to him and his face lit up at her proximity.

What she hadn't told Annie, she thought, as she felt the air ruffling her cheek as he kissed her, was that when Serge had fled, Jacques had strode over and locked the shop door for the first time in living memory. And they had spent the rest of that afternoon upstairs like newly-weds, only emerging when the sun was setting and hunger, real physical hunger, had finally overcome them.

She'd never given so much as a second glance to Serge Papon ever again.

She's quiet, even by her standards, thought Christian as he pulled onto the track that led to the Estaque farm. The journey up had been made in complete silence, Annie staring out of the window at the trees as they flashed past. Which was understandable, given what was going on in the commune.

Fatima Souquet wasn't the only one happy to fan the flames of a story that was highly combustible and life for his old neighbour had to be difficult right now.

Plus she had yet to mend her relationship with Véronique.

He glanced at his companion, her face half-turned from him, jawline firm, chin tilted in the same way Véronique tilted hers when she was digging her heels in over something. She looked determined. But she also looked really tired, her normally ruddy complexion tinged with a pallor he wasn't used to seeing on her. Grey was more accurate.

'Can I carry your shopping in?' he asked as he pulled up opposite the door. He was expecting the usual refusal, surprised that he'd even been asked to drive her home as she was stubborn about not accepting lifts. But maybe the heart attack had knocked her back more than any of them had appreciated because she mutely nodded her head and got out of the car.

Inside, the house felt chilly despite the external temperature, the warmth of the sunshine yet to penetrate the thick walls.

'On the table okay?' he asked, gesturing at the bags of shopping as they entered the kitchen.

'Fine. Thanks, Chrrristian.' She paused and looked out at the pasture and when she turned, her colour was back, a streak of red across her cheekbones and a light to her eyes. 'Can you stay forrr a coffee?'

He checked his watch, anxious to get home and get Sarko looking his best. The farmer calling in that afternoon was the only chance the bull had and Christian wanted to do everything he could to give him a few more years of life.

'If you'rrre thinking about that old bull, forrrget him!'

'Sorry?'

Annie cackled and pulled out a chair. 'Take a seat, young

206

man. I'm about to make you an offerrr that will save that contrrrarrry beast's life.'

Baffled, Christian did as he was told and she sat opposite him, hands folded in front of her on the table.

'Now, what would it take to keep you herrre?'

'In Fogas? A miracle!' He realised from her frown she was serious and changed his tone. 'Okay, land. Some extra livestock. And a loan.'

'What's the loan forrr?'

'Solar panels. If I had a small lump sum to combine with the grants that are available, I could install them on the farm buildings and be generating electricity in no time. From the calculations I've done, the amount I'd get paid would more than cover the interest and I'd be debt-free in ten years.'

Annie nodded, impressed. 'And the land? What would you use it forrr?'

'Grazing. That would give me time to get my own land certified as organic. In the space of five years I'd hope to be totally organic and selling my meat directly to local restaurants. But without extra land I can't do it.'

'And the animals?'

'You can never have too much livestock!' Christian said with a grin, making Annie chuckle.

'Is therrre anything else you need?'

Christian's face twisted into a self-mocking smile. 'Well, if you can pull all that off, I may as well ask for a wife! Someone who loves the land as much as I do and someone to work it alongside me.'

'Now you'rrre pushing it!' Annie got up and walked over to the sink, leaning on the edge as she gazed out at the barn, the fields, the cows. 'This is Estaque land.'

She turned back to face him, solemn once more.

'One of the firrrst farrrms in the arrrea and in my family

forrr generrrations. I've loved it the way you underrrstand. It's in my blood. The firrrst thing I think about on waking and the last thing to crrross my mind beforrre sleep. But now, I think it's time someone else took it on.'

'Véronique?'

Annie laughed gently. 'No, son. Not Vérrronique. You.'

He stared at her, mouth open.

'I'm offerrring to lend you the land forrr an indefinite perr-riod. The livestock too.'

'But I can't—'

'Don't starrrt prrrotesting and saying I'm too generrrous. You haven't hearrrd the terrrms yet!' She held up a broad finger. 'Firrrst, I take a perrrcentage of the prrrofit. Not much. But we can sorrrt that out. Second, I'm not to be consigned to the scrrrap heap. I'm not so old that I can't be of use!' She glared at him and he held up his hands to show he wasn't dissenting. 'Thirrrd, if at any point Vérrronique wants to take on the farrrm, it all reverrrts to herrr. And lastly, this is condi-tional on you accepting a monetarrry loan to coverrr the cost of the solarrr panels which I want installed herrre too.'

Christian was dumbfounded.

'Well?'

'I don't know what to say, Annie. I can't—'

'Is it enough? Will it mean you can stay?'

He stood up, made dizzy by the way she had just tilted his world, and crossed the kitchen in three long strides. Taking her up in his arms, he spun her around and planted a kiss on her wrinkled cheek. It was only as he put her back down, she laughing as much as he was, that he remembered the precar-ious state of her health.

'Oh Christ, sorry, I shouldn't have done that. Too much excitement is probably bad for you.'

'Rrrubbish! I'm farrr morrre likely to die of borrredom.'

'No chance of that with the gossip you've been creating!' Instantly regretting the slip, he was relieved to see her grinning, a mischievous glint in her eyes.

'Looks like we'rrre about to crrreate some more,' she said. 'Now get home and tell yourrr motherrr to starrrt unpacking all those boxes. And then call that girrrlfriend of yourrrs and let herrr know the farrrm is no longerrr forrr sale.'

Christian grimaced. 'You haven't heard, then? She's not my girlfriend anymore.'

'When did that happen?'

'The evening you and Véronique . . .'

'When I called you? You werrre on a date?'

'Up at that posh restaurant in St Girons.'

Annie doubled over and he thought for one awful minute she'd had another heart attack but then he heard it. Laughter, rich and vibrant and contagious.

'So when I called . . . ?' She succumbed to another fit.

'When you called we were getting to the crucial part of the night!'

'And instead . . . ?'

'Instead of taking her home and getting to know her better, I came haring back to look for Véronique.'

'And spent the night at the hospital!'

'It wasn't working out anyway,' Christian admitted with a grin. 'She's not really my type.'

'Well, glad to have been of scrrrvice then.'

He sobered up and stretched out his hand. 'You've been of service all right, Annie. This offer you've made me . . . I don't know how I'll ever repay you.'

They shook on the bargain, their hands – one small, one large – both rough from years of working the land.

'I'd best get back and spread the good news. Tell Sarko he has a fairy godmother!'

He embraced her once more and as she watched him walk to the car, his gaze scanning the fields and the buildings as though already planning what he would do with the pasture and where would be the best position for the solar panels, she felt that at least she had got this right.

When the idea had presented itself in the garden at Josette's, she couldn't believe that she hadn't thought of it before. With money set aside and a pension more than enough to meet her needs, it made sense for her to get a caretaker in for the farm, someone she trusted and liked to have around. At the same time, Christian got the land he needed to be able to stay. And Véronique wouldn't have to deal with the trauma of him moving up to Toulouse.

Perhaps, Annie thought, as she started putting away the shopping, she could see about doing something to sort out the last bit of Christian's wish list too.

Once she got her daughter to forgive her, that was.

14

At about the time that Christian and Annie shook on the deal that was to keep the farmer in Fogas, the small red bus that was both dreaded and adored by the youngest inhabitants of the area, depending on the time of day, was winding its way down from the primary school in Sarrat which served both communes. Given that it was Wednesday the mood on the bus should have been jubilant, students only having to endure a half-day in the middle of the week. But as the driver glanced in his rear-view mirror he was surprised to see his young charges clustered at the back, heads bent towards the dark curls of Chloé Morvan who was talking quietly, face serious.

'Kids!' he muttered, turning his attention back to the road as it twisted down to the valley floor. Once across the bridge that divided Sarrat from Fogas, he turned left onto the main road and moments later he parked in the lay-by opposite the Auberge.

'All those for La Rivière and Picarets, off you get!' he called out, as he did at the end of every school day. And as with every school day, Chloé and the Rogalle twins scampered down the aisle and hopped off, followed by Gerard Lourde. The driver was just about to close the door in preparation for the final leg of the journey up to Fogas when he realised there were still children alighting from the bus. In fact, there was no one left in the seats.

'Hey!' he shouted to the group of students who'd gathered by the thicket of trees at the edge of the lay-by. 'What's going on? How come you're all getting off here? Do your parents know?'

They all looked at the raven-haired Chloé Morvan who gave an angelic smile and said, 'We have a school project.'

'Oh. Right. Well in that case . . .'

He shrugged, closed the door and drove off, not one to complain about a shorter shift. Especially when the river was sparkling in the afternoon sunshine and the fish were calling. He'd get an hour in before the wife got home and she'd be none the wiser.

He drove the short distance to his house and parked the minibus in its usual spot. Already feeling the tug of a trout on the line, he started towards the front door.

The splash of colour was what caught his eye. It was enough to make him turn and look at the vehicle he had just left. Enough to make him realise his afternoon would not be going as planned.

'What the—?'

Stickers. Lining the windows all the way around the bus. Every one of them the same: a cartoon picture of a cute bear and some mountains. And underneath, four simple words that were enough to incite a war in these parts.

'This Is Bear Country!'

He was just peeling the last one off as his wife got out of her car and he knew any chance of going fishing had slipped between his fingers.

Véronique wasn't sure she should be driving. She'd had a near miss down in La Rivière, a swarm of kids led by Chloé suddenly dashing out in front of her as she turned up towards Fogas. She'd hit the brakes just in time, nearly causing the cattle truck following her to smack into her boot. But he'd swerved, hooted, sworn and carried on.

Then, as she'd climbed the narrow road up to the town hall, a fawn had leapt out of the bushes and she'd had to swing the car to the left to avoid it. It gave her a startled look before gracefully scampering down the steep hillside to the right.

So Véronique wasn't convinced she was safe to be on the road. Or to do anything, in fact. Her concentration really wasn't what it should be and hadn't been since Maman had revealed the astounding truth about Véronique's father.

Serge Papon, the mayor of Fogas.

All her life she'd dreamed about the identity of her papa. She'd built stories around him in her head, created fantasy scenarios whereby he turned up out of the blue, always with some plausible explanation for why he hadn't been around for the last however many years, which admittedly had been harder to devise the older she got. And in all of them Véronique and her father had immediately forged an unbreakable bond.

When she was a lot younger, she'd even gone so far as to have him fall in love with Maman, culminating in a beautiful wedding with her as a bridesmaid. As she'd hit her teens and realised how difficult a woman Maman was, she'd had to temper this particular storyline and instead had them establish an amicable relationship. By the time she was in her twenties, she'd thought even that was beyond the realms of fantasy and had simply written Maman out of the reunion altogether.

Not once, however, had she envisaged that her father would turn out to be a married man she'd known all her life, thus resulting in her having to reassess every aspect of her thirty-six years on the planet.

No wonder she couldn't concentrate. She was too busy thinking back. Remembering things that had seemed so insignificant but which were now, in this new light, so much more important. Like the time Serge had bumped into her and Maman at the shop one summer.

It had been hot. Dusty and tired from the long walk down from the farm, seven-year-old Véronique had asked for an ice cream, knowing the answer would be no. It always was. So she'd gone outside to sulk, sitting on the low wall of the orchard and kicking her heels against the stones. Serge and Thérèse had pulled up and Serge had asked her what was the matter. She'd told him she wanted an ice cream and he'd immediately taken her by the hand and led her to the old freezer.

She'd been ecstatic and, after unwrapping the lolly, she'd bestowed a kiss on the sweet-smelling cheek of the deputy mayor. Her joy had been short-lived, however, as she'd turned to see Maman in the doorway, face closed, eyes flashing. She'd been berated the entire way home. Lectured on the evils of disobeying a parent and going behind her mother's back.

Ha! Rich indeed coming from Maman, thought the adult Véronique as she turned the last bend and Fogas came into view. But with the benefit of hindsight, it was easy to see why Maman had been perturbed. It was equally difficult to forgive her deception because how much more pleasure would Véronique and Serge have taken from that simple exchange if they'd only known the truth?

With this constant reappraisal twisting her memories and torturing her soul, Véronique was a long way from granting absolution. Truth was, if it hadn't been for the heart attack, she didn't think she would have wanted anything to do with her mother right now. It was all too raw.

'So what am I doing going to meet Serge Papon?' she muttered, as she parked under the looming edifice of the town hall.

They'd avoided each other for just over two weeks. Yet it

had felt as though the stout figure that she knew so well had moved into her flat, such was the extent to which he occupied her thoughts.

Desperate to talk to him and at the same time ridden with anxiety, she had spent the last fortnight getting more and more agitated. She hadn't seen Christian, hadn't been out much, not wanting to face the gossip that was flourishing like weeds in the summer. Nor had she wanted to run the risk of bumping into Serge in some unsuitable place like the bar. Or the market.

Finally, unable to take it any longer, she'd phoned the town hall and made an appointment to see the mayor. Céline had nearly choked when she realised who it was and when she'd asked what the meeting was pertaining to and Véronique had said the post office, the poor secretary had struggled to retain her composure.

But it was the only way that Véronique could go through with it. By meeting him on a formal footing, under the guise of the problems with the post office, there need be no mention of their relationship. Because alongside her intense scrutiny of the past, Véronique was aware that the present might not yield the happy ending that she had always sought. There was a very big chance that Serge Papon would want nothing to do with her, no matter what Christian Dupuy might say.

At least this way, if that were the case, he would be able to seek refuge in his official capacity and by the end of the meeting she would not only know what was happening with her job, she would also have a better idea of whether or not she really had a father.

'She's here!'

Serge wheeled from the window and strode back to his desk. And promptly turned back to the window.

'Should I sit?'

Céline smiled, never having seen him like this before. 'Do what feels best.'

'Right. What feels best. So I should sit.'

He sat and then stood up again, calling to her as she reached for the door.

'Céline! How do I look?'

Arms held out in a mute appeal for support, face perplexed and tie askew, it was clear that for the first time in his life Serge Papon had found himself in waters for which he had no charts. She walked over and straightened his tie, patting him on the shoulder when she was done.

'You look great.'

He nodded and resumed his seat. He didn't even hear the door close behind her. Which was strange as his ears were pricked, waiting for the sound of steps down the corridor.

Véronique. She was coming to see him.

Eighteen days he'd waited and it had been agonising. Not wanting to burst into her life like an uninvited guest, at the same time he was longing to see her, to trace familiar faces across her own features, to know that she belonged. That he belonged.

But there had been no word. He'd asked Josette what he should do when he was down there one evening on what had become a regular visit, the pair of them sharing a drink after closing time. She'd told him he had to give Véronique time. Let her get used to the idea. At seventy-six though, time was relative. And every second was precious.

Still, he'd restrained himself. Even held off from going down to La Rivière too often in case he bumped into her and she mistook it for a deliberate attempt to engineer a meeting. The market had also been avoided as he knew how much she enjoyed the bustle on a Saturday morning. With his newfound appetite, these sacrifices had come at some cost! Although, given that his trousers had recently grown tighter, perhaps it had been no bad thing.

Finally, though, she'd called the secretary and asked to see him. To talk about the post office. He'd fretted over the implications of this. Did it indicate that she had no interest in him as a father? Perhaps was even ashamed to acknowledge him as her papa? Or was it purely a way to break the ice?

After Serge had decided he wouldn't tell anyone about the forthcoming rendezvous, not even Josette, poor Céline had had to tolerate his mood swings for the last week, fielding his questions about the phone call as he made her speculate whether Véronique had sounded happy, or nervous. Or indifferent. He sensed his relentless cross-examination had almost been enough to make the beleaguered secretary resubmit her letter of resignation, which had been locked safely back in her drawer following his political resurrection.

Take it slowly. That's what Céline had said. Slowly. It wasn't a word he was used to.

He heard voices in the outer office and felt his heart pounding. She was here.

'Bonjour,' she said as the door opened and it seemed to take an age before she appeared, head tipped to one side, a high colour making her face glow. And that hair! So like his mother.

'Serge? Can I come in?'

'Yes . . . of course . . . come on in.'

He was striding across the floor before he knew it, his hands reaching out for her shoulders, staring at her, the whole of her. His daughter.

'Bonjour, Véronique,' he said and despite all of his best intentions, despite everything Céline and Josette had advised, he gathered her into an embrace. He felt her starting to cry and when she said 'Papa!' he had a feeling that he had always known her. And that he would never be lost again.

As he pushed the door shut he saw, through the closing gap, Céline reaching for the box of tissues that she kept on her desk.

'Come on, my darling, let's sit down,' he said with a smile as he led Véronique to the seat he had placed next to his, the first person in the long duration of his tenure as mayor to ever sit behind the desk in his presence. 'Let's see if your papa can't sort out this mess with the post office!'

And when she laughed in response, he knew that they would be fine.

'So unfortunately, I don't seem to have got very far.'

Serge Papon leaned back in his chair and watched Véronique scanning the letters, her eyes taking in every detail, brow creased in concentration. Despite the fact that his efforts to get to the bottom of the situation with La Poste had so far been thwarted, he had enjoyed himself thoroughly for the last half hour. He'd not only got to spend time with the young woman whom he was learning to call his daughter, he'd also got to share his devious thoughts with someone who was his equal.

She was every bit as Machiavellian as he was, he thought with pride, as she pored over the latest reply from La Poste.

'But there is no mention here about the application Pascal put in. Not a word about the proposal for a combined épicerie and post office.' She gestured at the letter in her hand.

Serge smiled. 'Exactly my thoughts. Strange, isn't it? I've called every person I know who has any connections to La Poste and no one has heard anything about Fogas applying for a new branch. All they can tell me is that the old post office will not be revived and that our appeal against that decision has been rejected.'

'So the letter I received stating they had turned us down was dismissing the idea of reopening the old post office?'

Serge nodded and waited to see if she would make the connection. It didn't take long, her head snapping up, a grin on her face.

'Well, that means we can send in an application with the new idea.'

'And this time we'll make sure it has the full backing of the Conseil Municipal. I'll call a meeting for two weeks from now. That'll give us a chance to get everything together and make the submission as good as possible.'

'But what about the mention of a local alternative? If La Poste has already chosen somewhere else, aren't we too late?'

'Again, no one seems to know for sure. My sources tell me that somewhere nearby has applied but they can't say where exactly and the suggestion is that things haven't been decided.'

'We still have time then!' Véronique started gathering the papers together. 'Do you want me to come to the council meeting?'

'Of course! You're the expert on all this. You can explain what the changes in services will be, persuade the councillors that it's a good idea for the commune and worth the cost. Besides, you seem to have Pascal eating out of your hand so it wouldn't hurt.'

'Don't know about that!' Véronique pulled a face. 'He was really keen about the idea when I proposed it, took notes and everything. Yet it seems he did nothing with it.'

'Leave it with me.' Serge tapped the side of his nose and Véronique laughed.

'Excuse me,' Céline poked her head around the door. 'Sorry to disturb you—'

'I said no interruptions!' barked the mayor.

Céline didn't even flinch. In fact she was smiling. Broadly.

'Thought you'd want to know this.' She paused, timing her revelation to perfection. Just as Serge opened his mouth to bark at her again, she continued. 'I have it on good authority that Christian Dupuy has taken the farm off the market. Looks like he won't be leaving us after all.'

Both Véronique and Serge looked astounded, heads thrust forward, eyebrows raised. In fact, as Céline declared later that evening to her husband, if she hadn't just found out about them being related she would have guessed it on the spot. Because in their astonishment, they looked the spitting image of each other.

Christian was staying!

Véronique didn't know how she'd managed to control herself when all she'd wanted to do was run around the room screaming with delight. Instead, she'd sat there and let Serge ask the obvious question. But Céline had been unable to tell them what had happened to change the farmer's mind. The only thing she knew was that her sister, who worked next door to the estate agent's office, had happened to see Eve Rumeau taking the details of the farm out of the window. That in itself was no proof but she had also seen Eve ripping up the paper and throwing it in the bin.

Intrigued, Céline's sister had promptly rung the neighbouring office, pretending to be a house-hunter, only to be told that the picturesque farm in Picarets was no longer for sale. She'd hung up before Eve could persuade her to look at a small épicerie in the next valley that had become available.

What could have occurred to effect such a change? wondered Véronique. Christian had been less than twenty-four hours away from signing the paperwork. And now . . .

Now he would be staying in Fogas.

She grinned as she crossed the tiled hallway and let herself out into the afternoon. Life was suddenly looking up. The meeting with Serge had gone well, both of them overcoming the initial awkwardness, and she'd been surprised by how much she enjoyed his company. They'd talked about her childhood and she'd reminded him about the incident with the ice cream.

He in turn had talked about the time Fabian had got stuck in the old quarry. Only a kid, visiting Fogas as he did every summer holiday, the scrawny Parisian had fallen down the steep embankment and hadn't been able to climb out. Christian had sent Véronique for help and she'd flagged down Serge Papon's car. With the aid of a rope he kept in the boot, the then deputy mayor had been able to pull out the snivelling boy. And the larger Christian, who had scampered down to join the poor lad out of sympathy.

Serge had enjoyed recounting the story and it seemed to Véronique that he too was seeing everything through a different lens. One that was sharper. One that seemed to let in more light.

'I thought you were amazing that day,' he'd said to her when he'd finished telling the tale. 'So resourceful, so calm. And at such a young age. I should have known then that you were a Papon!'

But there was a sadness to his nostalgia. The same regret she couldn't help feeling. If only they'd known all along. If Serge Papon was as furious about being kept in the dark as Véronique was, however, he wouldn't hear a word against Annie. When Véronique had muttered something about her mother's ridiculous secret, he'd merely said that in his experience people usually did things for the right reasons. Even if those actions sometimes turned out to be wrong.

Feeling more magnanimous thanks to her extraordinary afternoon, Véronique headed for her car, giving a final wave to the stocky figure watching her from the first-floor window of the town hall.

Papa, she mused, as she swung her legs into the car. That's my papa. And Christian Dupuy is staying in Fogas.

Emotions all over the place, she felt no better suited to driving than she had on the way up.

Serge waved while Véronique backed up the car and drove out of the town hall car park. He continued waving as the small vehicle trundled down the road, the sun glinting off its roof. It was only when it turned the first bend and disappeared from sight that he let his arm fall.

But the smile on his face remained.

It had been a wonderful meeting. Not only had they established the beginnings of a relationship, but they'd also got to grips with the strange goings-on at La Poste. Hopefully, once their revised submission was in, the whole thing would be sorted and Véronique would get her job back at long last.

If he'd had little success getting information out of La Poste, his network of contacts had delivered even less when it came to the planning permission for the multi-purpose store in Sarrat. He'd called in every favour he had outstanding but so far, no one could tell him anything other than that the application had been put in. No one knew exactly where the store was going to be located if permission was granted. Nor what exactly it would be selling.

There was nothing for it but to wait. Which is what he'd be telling Josette when he popped down to see her later on.

Later on? Why was he putting it off? There was no need to avoid La Rivière anymore, now that Véronique had been to see him. In fact, it might be an idea to give Christian a call and see if he wouldn't join him for a celebratory drink in the bar.

Because there could only be good reasons behind this sudden change of plan for the farmer.

He was about to turn from the window when his attention was caught by a streak of colour on the opposite side of the road.

Kids. A pack of them, led by Chloé Morvan, all getting out of an empty cattle truck. They shouted thanks to the driver for the lift and then began walking back down the village, heading for the disused *lavoir* that marked the start of Fogas, its wooden roof and stone washbasins probably providing somewhere they could hang out.

Making the most of their half-day, and who could blame them?

Eager to be doing the same, he gathered his jacket off the back of his chair and crossed the office. He'd call Christian from the bar. Perhaps even treat him to a meal at the Auberge.

It was, he decided as he stepped out into the sunshine, a day that was in need of celebrating.

Up above the Estaque farm, in the forest that led to the small tarn, René Piquemal was doing a bit of celebrating of his own. Well, not on his own exactly, as he had company in the shape of Serge the beagle. And it was Serge who was the reason for the jubilation.

Serge's nose, if one was to be precise.

For that nose, which had intrigued René down at the bar earlier that day, had potential. Having asked Bernard if he could borrow the dog, giving some vague excuse about extra training, René had spent the afternoon up in the forest. Not just any bit of forest but a particular area which he knew well and which he kept secret from anyone else.

He'd passed the time putting the beagle through a series of tests, curious to see if the strange behaviour he'd witnessed down in La Rivière was what he thought it was. And now, as the daft mutt sat pawing at the ground, a patch of ground that showed signs of having recently been disturbed, René was convinced that he had been right.

Serge had a talent. Not for hunting animals. But for finding mushrooms.

Truffles to be exact.

'Good boy!' René bent down and patted the happy beagle on the head before scooping away the earth to reveal a piece of truffle. He let the dog sniff it and then fished in his pocket for another treat. The dog swallowed the biscuit gratefully and then rolled over and offered his belly for adoration.

'You genius,' murmured René, rubbing the chubby stomach. 'You absolute genius.'

Of course, he thought as he straightened up, it was one thing Serge finding bits of truffle that René had planted. The true test was whether he could find one for real.

It had been a long time since truffles were found in these parts. René's great-grandfather had been the last person to discover one, stumbling upon the black lump almost by accident. It had been the talk of the commune but he'd steadfastly refused to say where he'd found it. Not even to his family. It was only as he lay dying, knowing he was heading for the land where rain was always followed by sunshine and edible fungi grew on every surface, that he divulged his secret. To René's grandfather.

Throughout René's youth the subject had caused tension, his father grumbling because René's grandfather refused to disclose the precious location, leaving Piquemal junior to worry that the eighty-year-old, who'd been known to have trouble with his heart, would die up in the woods and never be found. The true tragedy for the Piquemal family would of course have been the loss of the insider information that the old man so jealously guarded, rather than the death of the man himself.

When Grandpère Piquemal's time had come to surrender life, the secret had been passed on to René's father who, mindful of the agonies he had suffered, agreed to write down the location and store it in a safe place so should he come to some untimely mishap and be unable to speak the fateful words, the knowledge would not be lost. And so, a week after his father's death, René had received a letter from a solicitor up in Toulouse. Inside had been a picture, hand drawn. A picture of a view.

René had known straight away where it was. The clearing was unmistakable, the deep crevice in the rocks a place he had scrambled as a child. He had sent the picture back to the very same solicitor with instructions for it to be sent at the time of his death to his oldest son. Who lived in Marseilles and couldn't abide truffles.

Knowing the secret location, however, was only one part of the equation. In the intervening decades not a single initiate had struck lucky. Lots of gorgeous morels; baskets of beautiful brown ceps; delicious chanterelles coming out of their ears – but not a whiff of the bulbous black fungi that were almost as valuable as gold.

There had been many a time when René had cursed his great-grandfather. Many a day in the woods when he'd grumbled that the old man must have stumbled on a truffle dropped by a passing boar, thus meaning that subsequent members of the family had been on nothing but a wild goose chase from that moment on. But try as he might to convince himself that the entire escapade was a waste of time, still that excitement lingered. What if his great-grandfather had been right? What if there really were truffles buried beneath these trees?

He glanced down at the dog which was now writhing on the

forest floor, tail wagging. Well, with Serge by his side, perhaps the answer to those questions would at least come in his lifetime!

Happy with the afternoon's work, René bent to pick up his rucksack and as his hand touched the strap, he saw the beagle flatten itself on the ground, ears down. It made a slight whimpering sound. Funny, thought René, last time he'd seen the dog do that—

Bear! It had been when they'd seen the bear.

He whipped round but there was nothing there. Only trees. And more trees. Still Serge was cowering, eyes looking to the forest behind, making the plumber suddenly eager to get away.

Bloody dog. Had him spooked.

'Come on you daft—'

'Shhhhhh.'

The voice was soft in his ear but filled with menace, a suffocating hand clamped over René's mouth holding him still, fingers digging into the soft point of his chin. He felt everything go grey, the edges of the forest blurring, his legs buckling underneath him, completely at the mercy of his unseen assailant.

'What are you doing here?' A whispered question.

René tried to answer but no sound emerged.

'I'll ask you once more. What are you doing here?'

'Truffles . . .' he spluttered, his weight now collapsed against the solid bulk behind him. 'Just looking . . .'

'And the dog?'

'Training . . .'

Laughter. Gentle, low. Definitely laughter.

'I'm going to take my hand away. Don't make a sound, okay?'

René nodded and as the pressure eased he felt his

consciousness return. Rubbing his chin, he turned, legs still wobbly, and there was Arnaud Petit, finger on his lips and devilment in his eyes.

'Truffles, eh?' he whispered and René nodded, forlorn. The secret. The Piquemal mystery that had been guarded for generations. He'd given it away at the first test.

'Don't worry,' continued the big man with a grin. 'I'll keep your secret if you keep mine.'

Still too afraid to speak, René merely raised an eyebrow at which Arnaud took Serge's lead and looped it around a nearby branch.

'You can come back for the dog,' he said, beckoning René forward. 'Follow me as quietly as you can.'

With that he moved noiselessly through the forest towards the edge of the embankment, glaring at René occasionally as the plumber stepped on a branch or brushed against a tree. It was like tailing a ghost. And when the tracker suddenly lowered himself to the ground, René almost tripped over him. With a dark look of reproach, Arnaud wriggled silently forwards, tipping his head for René to do the same.

René did his best to copy what the big man had done but it was impossible not to make a noise. A branch snagged on his trousers with a whisper and a stone clinked against another. It wasn't much, but enough to warrant a stare in reply. Muttering inside his head that this had better be worth it, he inched a bit further forward until he could see through the small opening in the bushes that Arnaud had made.

It was the clearing. The exact same clearing that René's father had drawn all those years ago. The same trees forming the boundary around the enclave. The same creviced rock that was depicted on the paper lying in the solicitor's safe up in Toulouse. But what the Piquemal picture had failed to show was the bear lying on the grass in the sunlight, her fur brilliant, head lolling back, enjoying her repose in the warmth. And climbing all over her were two small cubs, clearly delighted with life.

'Ohhhhh!' It was quiet. No more than an escape of air from René's open mouth. This time Arnaud didn't frown. He simply nodded, a wide grin on his face.

René had no sense of how long they lay there watching the cubs playing with abandon, tumbling with each other and rolling around, their mother occasionally grunting at them if they wandered too far. All he knew was that he could have stayed there a lot longer, and when Arnaud indicated it was time to leave, it was only because he knew what the big man was capable of that he obeyed. Neither of them spoke until they got back to the tree where Serge was waiting.

'You mustn't tell anyone about this,' said Arnaud as he untied the dog and picked him up, getting a lick on the nose in return. 'In a few weeks my department will announce the new arrivals in the press but I don't want people knowing where to find them. Understand?'

René nodded.

'And I suggest you stay away from here for a while. Give Miel a chance to get over her winter hunger!'

'And the cubs?'

'What about them?'

'Do they have names?'

'Not yet. Why?'

René bit his lip and looked back towards the clearing, the images of the young bears still vivid.

'Morel and Truffle,' he said. 'Think that would be appropriate.'

Arnaud laughed softly and held out a hand. 'It's a deal. And sorry about the commando stuff. But I wasn't sure . . . you being a hunter . . .'

They shook hands and then Arnaud, still carrying a tired Serge, accompanied René back to the track that led to the Estaque farm.

'Thanks,' René said, as the bear tracker handed over the beagle and started to turn back to continue his watch. 'Thanks for showing me.'

Arnaud shrugged. 'It was either that or kill you.'

And then he was gone, his huge shape disappearing into the forest, leaving René to ponder all the way down to La Rivière whether he had meant it, his thoughts only interrupted by the sight of a gang of kids walking up the road, led by Chloé Morvan.

By the time he met Bernard and gave him back his dog, René still hadn't made up his mind as to whether the tracker would have carried out his threat. But at least, he thought as he walked into the bar, pleased to see Christian and the mayor already there, at least his encounter today meant that there really was something special about the place that the Piquemals had been guarding all these years. He was also aware that throughout the entire afternoon, he hadn't once craved a cigarette.

Although the day had been warm, it was still only April and temperatures were quick to fall once the sun dipped below the mountains. By nine-thirty, when Christian and the mayor were finishing their desserts at the Auberge, the sky was already dark and the majority of the houses in La Rivière were shuttered for the night.

It was little wonder then that no one noticed the figure on the ridge that ran at the back of the village. Shielded by a small copse, someone was following the track that began opposite the church, passed behind the garden of the épicerie, the disused orchard and the old school before dropping down at the far end of the village where the road began the long climb up to the town of Massat and the Col de Port. Unaccustomed to the rough terrain and the lack of light, the person tripped and stumbled along the path before emerging out of the trees to cross the road and approach the building opposite, the noise from the river almost deafening at such close quarters. Testing the door at the back and relieved to find it open as had been promised, he slipped inside.

'You're late.' A strike of a match, enough for the boar's head on the wall to flicker in a semblance of life.

'There have been developments,' Pascal stuttered, unnerved by the place and the man.

'So I hear.' An inhalation, features almost visible in the light from the cigarette end. 'And not good ones, I fear.'

Pascal waited.

'Not only do we have Serge revoking his resignation,' the voice continued, 'but the farmer is staying as well.'

'Yes.'

Another inhalation, this time enough to see the eyes. Those eyes. Narrowed against the smoke, the gaze of a hunter.

'I have it on good authority that Serge is poking his nose into our affairs too.'

'He's making enquiries about the planning application.'

'You haven't said anything?'

'No!'

A chuckle. 'Of course you haven't. And the post office – does he know yet?'

'No. He's running around in circles.'

'So we don't have long. We will proceed as we discussed initially, before we got distracted by the mayor's possible departure. If he won't jump, we'll just have to push him.'

'You mean . . .' Pascal stopped, aware of the other man's heavy stare, despite the dark.

'Don't you have the stomach for this, Pascal?' Taunting.

No. That was the honest answer. The thought of what they were planning to do made him sick. But . . .

'When do we start?'

A slap on the back that nearly choked him.

'Good. That's what I like to hear.' Another pause, another drag on the cigarette. 'We start tonight. Have you done what I asked?'

'Yes.' Pascal held up a bag containing the plaster of Paris which he'd driven to the outskirts of Toulouse to buy, not wanting to leave a local trail. He'd paid cash too.

'Then let's go catch ourselves a bear. A couple of attacks on some sheep is exactly what we need to get rid of Serge Papon. And with him out of the way, we can concentrate on our real goal. A new commune.'

The man threw the cigarette to the floor and Pascal heard him grinding the stub into the concrete. And he knew, with a certainty he couldn't explain, that this was the point of no return. For him and for Fogas.

15

It didn't take long, thought Arnaud as he walked up towards the épicerie, a stack of papers in his arms. Only a month since the bears had emerged from their dens and already the complaints were flooding in. Of course, this was the worst time of year, their winter sleep having left the beasts starving and nature not yet providing enough by way of berries and nuts. So the bears did what was only natural. They dropped down into the lower valleys and foraged, feeding on the carcasses of deer or other animals that had lain in the woods over the bleaker months. Or helped themselves to a nice side of mutton or a couple of chickens that just happened to cross their paths.

It was the same every year. Irate shepherds, angry farmers, pressurised mayors. They all beat a path to the door of the government agency responsible for the bears and voiced their outrage. And of course, demanded compensation.

Some of it was legitimate, Arnaud was willing to acknowledge. But the payouts from the government were more than generous and verification of an attack, which was always difficult to prove, was weighted in the livestock owner's favour. Some of it, however, was speculative in the extreme and it was amazing how since the introduction of the compensation scheme the same people who had once complained about stray dogs killing their animals now only ever blamed bears.

In his time working for the agency he'd come across cases

where farmers had used a piece of wood with nails driven into it to make an already dead sheep look like an attack victim. He'd even heard of a man trying to get recompense for his ravaged prize-winning ram, the body badly mauled, only for his ram to turn up in a neighbour's flock some time later. Sold for cash.

But it was the price that had to be paid if the reintroduction of bears was to be successful. And judging by the fact it was still only April and a stack of cases had already been filed, the government was going to be paying out quite a bit this year.

He entered the bar, the old shepherd on a stool in the corner and the man he had come to see already at a table.

'Bonjour!' Arnaud shook hands with the mayor and took a seat next to him, noticing a familiar colourful sticker on the chair.

'Those things are everywhere,' muttered Serge Papon. 'You wouldn't want to sit still too long.' He tipped his head in the direction of the old shepherd whose back was sporting the logo 'This Is Bear Country!'

'Who . . . ?'

'I'd put my money on young Chloé. Seems as though you have a believer there. And she's hell-bent on converting every-one else! The school bus, here, the *lavoir* up in Fogas. Even the hunting lodge. Bloody stickers all over the place!'

Arnaud smiled wryly. 'At least I'll have a receptive audience when I visit the school next month. Just wish others could be equally convinced.' He tapped the papers in front of him.

'More complaints?'

'Lots.'

Serge gestured for him to continue, this regular update the only condition the mayor had imposed in return for his contin-ued support of the tracker, despite the wishes of the Conseil Général. If trouble was coming in the shape of a bear, this time Serge was determined to be the first in the commune to know.

'A dead sheep over in the Garbet valley, a couple of bins knocked over in Massat and a possible footprint across the bridge in Sarrat.'

'Nothing here, then?'

'No. Not yet!'

'Good. We've got a meeting of the Conseil Municipal tonight and I don't want any distractions from the issue of the post office.'

Arnaud's mobile started to ring. Seeing it was his office calling he excused himself and headed for the terrace.

Bears, thought Serge in disbelief. Who'd have thought they could cause so much trouble? He'd had another letter, this time from a hunting association in the department, warning him that if he continued to allow Arnaud Petit to live in La Rivière, the members of the hunting association who lived in Fogas would be advised to vote against Serge Papon in the next election. He'd ripped it up and thrown it in the bin.

He was just finishing his coffee and wondering if he ought to peel the offending sticker off the old shepherd's coat when Philippe Galy stormed in from the shop.

'Bonjour, Philippe—'

Josette's cheery hello was ignored as the bee-keeper made straight for Serge Papon.

'My bees. It's attacked my bees!'

'What's attacked your bees?'

'That bastard of a bear! Ripped the lid off one of the hives, tore the honeycomb to shreds, smashed the frames.'

'How do you know it was a bear and not some vandals?'

Philippe's already puce face turned an unhealthy shade of purple. 'Because there's a bloody paw print right next to the shards of wood which were once a beehive! Look for yourself.'

He thrust his mobile phone into the mayor's hand, the

screen displaying a photo of an imprint in mud. There was no mistaking it.

'I swear, if you're not willing to do something about this, Serge, I'm going to get my gun and—'

'And what?' Arnaud Petit was standing at the door, eyes fixed on the bee-keeper, voice full of menace.

'And nothing,' said Serge, patting Philippe's arm as Arnaud took the phone and studied the photo. 'We'll come up now and see the damage. Get a claim started for you straight away. Won't we, Arnaud?'

'Fine. But I have to go over to Sarrat first.'

'Sarrat? Can't it wait?'

Arnaud shook his head as he put Philippe's phone back on the table and gathered up his papers. 'The agency has just had a call from the mayor over there. One of his farmers lost three sheep last night. They want me to do a preliminary investigation before their expert gets down here later today. I'm afraid that takes precedence over a few bees and a bit of spilt honey.'

He turned on his heel, leaving Serge to deal with the spluttering bee-keeper. It took him a good five minutes to calm the man down and even then, he wasn't sure that Arnaud's parting shot wouldn't be the catalyst for Philippe to carry out his earlier threat.

With promises of a speedy resolution to the problem, Serge left the bar, his feet barely off the terrace before a 4x4 drew up alongside him.

'Care to join me?' asked Arnaud through the open window. 'If you have a strong stomach, that is.'

'I'd love to,' muttered Serge as he pulled himself up into the vehicle. 'Because I have a sneaking feeling that the more I know about this the better.'

As they drove off he saw one of the Rogalle twins running away from Philippe Galy's car which was parked outside the épicerie. Freshly adorning the rear window was a sticker, cartoon bear posing in front of Pyrenean mountains. It would probably, thought Serge, the beginnings of a headache forming behind his left eye, be enough to tip the man over the edge.

'Well? I'm right, aren't I?' A farmer stood glowering at the three bodies sprawled on a flat rock, flies turning their fleeces black. What was left of their fleeces. It was hard to tell that they'd ever been sheep.

'Can't say just yet,' said Arnaud, his camera lens focused on the carnage. 'I'm only gathering evidence. An official investigator from the agency will be here this afternoon. You'll have to wait for him to file his report.'

'And how long will that take?' Henri Dedieu, the mayor of Sarrat, was standing next to the farmer, face serious.

Arnaud lowered the camera and gave a contemptuous look, indifferent to the powerful position the man held. 'As long as it needs to.'

He walked off, body hunched over as he scrutinised the ground, tracing and retracing his steps, bending once or twice to pick up something which he placed in a plastic bag.

'Bloody bear lovers!' muttered the farmer, wisely not loud enough for the big man to hear. 'It's him and his kind I'd like to see run out of here. We'd take care of the bears ourselves after that. In the old way!'

'Agreed. We don't need his sort. Nor those who sympathise with him.'

Henri Dedieu aimed the last comment at his counterpart but Serge didn't respond. He was struggling to hold down the four slices of choc-chip brioche he'd had for breakfast, his reawakened appetite having shown no signs of going back into hibernation. Until now.

He turned away, gazing at the sweep of mountains that

stretched up from the pasture, snow-covered tops pristine. So different from the scene behind him which was making his stomach roil. Bellies split wide open, intestines tumbling out, the glassy eyes, the blood. So much blood.

Taking a deep breath to steady himself, his nostrils filled with a rank odour which caught at the back of his throat, reminding him of the butcher's in La Rivière when he was a kid. No fridge. Meat covered in flies. It had closed before he was a teenager. He raised his handkerchief to his mouth and swallowed hard, fighting the nausea that was threatening to overpower him.

'What's the matter, Serge? Gone soft in your old age?'

The words had enough bite to cause Serge to glance back at Henri Dedieu. Never a fan of Sarrat's mayor, Thérèse had always said the man enjoyed the kill rather than the chase and today Serge could see what she meant. Broad shoulders under his camouflage jacket, muscular legs in good-quality boots and skin tanned from the outdoors, he was a walking poster for *Pêche et Chasse* down in St Girons. But at odds with the nonchalance of his stance, thumbs hooked in his pockets, foot up on a rock, the man's eyes glittered with a disturbing intensity Serge could only attribute to excitement: Henri Dedieu was thrilled by the grisly scene.

Wanting to avoid any further taunts, and the smell, Serge moved away. He'd only taken a few steps when he saw it, embedded in a soft patch of mud on the sheltered side of a boulder. A print.

'Arnaud!' He gestured for the big man to join him. 'What do you think?'

Henri Dedieu and the farmer turned to see what Serge was pointing at and the farmer immediately started grumbling.

'I knew it! Christ! It's massive!'

'Looks like a bear all right,' the tracker conceded, bending down to take photos.

'Of course it's a bloody bear. What else could it be? Damn foreign brutes . . .'

The farmer kept up a monologue of disgruntlement as Arnaud ran his fingers over the indentations, tracing the curve of the foot, the sharp incisions where the claws had rested. It was a rear right print, just like the one in Philippe's photo, and judging by the length and depth it was from a female. But what was curious was the strange tilt to the markings, the weight of the bear on the outside of the foot, the inner pads barely registered. And then there was the size of the centre pad, abnormally large for a female. Odd. He pulled out a ruler and his notebook and proceeded to take measurements.

. . . and what's the point of doing that? Unless you're planning on buying him some shoes next? Considering you've already seen to it that he's well fed. At my expense!'

Ignoring the jibes, Arnaud focused instead on the rock next to the print. Fur, wedged in a slight crack, similar to the samples he'd found minutes before. He dropped it into another plastic bag, a frown forming on his dark face.

'Was the flock unattended?' he asked, straightening up and towering over the other three men.

The farmer bristled. 'No different to normal.'

'So no one was with them?'

'Never been a need until you brought those bears over here.'

'No *patou* or other dog?'

'And how am I supposed to have the time to train one of them?'

'No electric fencing?'

'Pah!' The farmer threw both hands up in the air. 'Look around you. It's grazing land. These sheep are meant to roam. Not be hemmed in by a pen two metres across.'

'You only need to put them in the enclosure at night.' Arnaud slapped his notebook closed and slipped it back in his pocket. 'Not a lot to ask really.'

'*Not a lot to ask?*'

Sensing the farmer was about to explode, Serge intervened. 'So what happens next?'

'We'll carry out a full investigation and should be able to report back within three weeks. If we decide there's conclusive evidence of a bear, then compensation will be paid. If not, it goes to a committee. Which will take a while longer.'

'What more evidence can there be?' Henri Dedieu pointed in the direction of the print. 'You'll be asking for a photo of the beast having dinner next.'

'Well,' said Arnaud, as he started to walk off, 'that would be a help.'

Serge, faced for the second time that day with people enraged by Arnaud Petit, made to follow, thinking that even his famed finesse was not enough to calm the two men from Sarrat. But as he turned, a strong hand gripped his forearm.

'You can tell your pet tracker that I'll be reporting him for this.' Henri Dedieu was staring at Arnaud's back.

'Reporting him for what?'

'Insubordination. Dereliction of duty.' He switched his attention to Serge, lips curved in an emotionless smile. 'If you won't get rid of him, I will.'

Serge shook himself free of the man's grasp and hastened down the hill.

'Don't ever go into politics!' he said, breath coming in gasps as he caught up with Arnaud. 'I'm sensing that diplomacy isn't your strong point.'

'I don't see the need for diplomacy with idiots who can't be bothered to look after their own animals.'

'I'm taking it that's not the official line?' Serge responded drily.

'Thought you would have realised by now that I'm not exactly official material.'

'You don't have any sympathy for the man?'

'Yes, I do. But it's limited by the fact he's done nothing to protect himself. It's like knowing a storm is coming but leaving every window in your house open because that's what you always did when the weather was dry. Difficult to sympathise when everything then gets ruined.'

'You're making it sound so black and white but it's not that straightforward.' Although he'd walked away from life on an Ariège mountain farm, the life his father had wanted him to lead, Serge understood the plight of the farmer they'd just left. 'Some are afraid to take up the protective measures offered by the government. Afraid of what will be done to them by others in the neighbourhood if they're seen to be supporting the reintroduction programme. Look at the pressure I've had put on me!'

Arnaud stopped at the car and leaned against the bonnet, the metal already warm from the sun.

'I appreciate that. But . . .' He stared into the distance, the bell tower of a nearby village church arching into view above a collection of slate roofs. Then he turned and looked at Serge Papon. 'I shouldn't be telling you this. But I think it concerns you. Don't ask me how.'

'Go on.'

'I'm not sure this was the work of a bear.'

Serge gestured back up the hill. 'You mean you think something else could have done that damage and left that print? No way!'

'It's odd, that's all. Two major attacks in one night. Here and at the beehives. Both have clear prints. And yet we haven't had rain for days. Very convenient for the bear to stand in the only place that could conceivably hold a record of its passing.'

'If not a bear, then what?'

Arnaud shrugged. But as they got in the car and began the

traverse across the valley to Philippe Galy's beehives, he became more and more convinced. It wasn't a 'what'. It was a 'who'.

It was all too neat. The unusual footprint. The fur, which he suspected he would find more of at Philippe's. It seemed like someone was making the most of the fact that the bears were out of hibernation. And Arnaud had a terrible premonition that the simmering tensions in the commune, which had lain dormant over the winter period, were about to burst back into life – with Miel, as the only female bear in the region, firmly at the centre of them.

News of the attack spread quickly. The farmer had been on the phone to his neighbours before Arnaud had even arrived at the scene in Sarrat. They in turn talked about it in the épicerie, the post office in Massat, the barbers down in Seix. The yellow van of the postman then carried it even further, passing it on to the woman who drove the butcher's van who stopped to tell the travelling baker. Every customer they served that day heard about the three dead sheep and the presence of a marauding bear and pretty soon Widow Aubert, who had nothing better to occupy her time, was on the phone to Philippe Galy, a distant cousin on her mother's side, to warn him that a bear was on the loose and to suggest he ought to look out for his beehives. She was most put out when the insolent young man let out a string of oaths and hung up, not knowing that she was the fifth person to call him that day with similar, belated advice.

So by the time Arnaud took the sharp bend into Fogas en route to Philippe's smallholding and passed the *lavoir*, still decorated with its colourful stickers, the old men who met on a daily basis at the washbasins already knew where he was heading. And already knew why.

At the town hall, Céline spent the day fielding calls from

anxious members of the public and the school felt compelled to send out a letter to all parents informing them that there was no substance to the rumour that the school would be closed until the bear was caught. A rumour which had travelled faster than the little red bus on which it had originated.

By the evening, tensions were running high.

Down in La Rivière, as word spread, a proliferation of four-wheel drives appeared outside the hunting lodge, groups of surly men, several with dogs, sitting on the low wall that bordered the river hurling insults at any car that drove past adorned with a pro-bear sticker. Too concerned about the state of his beehives to notice his own sudden conversion to the ursine cause, as displayed on his rear window, Philippe Galy was roundly booed by the mob, this unjustified abuse merely compounding what had already been a hellish day for the poor man.

Such was the hostility in the small village that Christian, stopping by to pick up Josette for the council meeting, had advised her to close the shop and bar early. She'd agreed without argument, granting an elated Fabian the unforeseen pleasure of an evening with Stephanie and Chloé.

In light of this, and given what had happened the last time, Serge Papon declared that the council session that evening would be held behind closed doors, all members of the public excluded, with one exception. That exception being Véronique Estaque, postmistress of Fogas.

Ex-postmistress unless the evening went well, she reminded herself as she sat in the meeting room, the mayor's voice echoing around the space where his audience normally sat. Even the U-shaped table hosted empty chairs, the council depleted by the absence of the second-home owner, Geneviève Souquet, who'd sent her apologies, unwilling to make a midweek journey down from Toulouse for something as trivial as a debate over the future of the post office, and Philippe Galy, who was understandably too busy too attend.

If numbers inside were sparse, outside was a different matter. Denied access, a large group of protesters had taken up position in front of the main entrance to the town hall and Véronique had had to push her way through a throng of hunters, farmers and shepherds armed with placards, dogs and hunting horns. The fact that they were neighbours and even relatives of the councillors, Monique Sentenac's son-in-law and Alain Rougé's cousin being among the mob, made no difference. As the members of the Conseil Municipal were forging a path to the door, the demonstrators had jostled and jeered them, incensed about the attacks in Sarrat and Fogas and demanding Serge do something about it.

What exactly he was meant to do was unclear. Although there were calls for the tracker to be removed from his lodgings. And the mayor from his office.

With Serge having decided that Arnaud Petit's presence might inflame an already troubled situation, the bear man was also missing from the night's proceedings. But at least Christian was there, his bulk at the table giving Véronique some reassurance as the crowd in the car park grew more raucous, their shouts audible through the row of arched windows that spanned one side of the room. Catching her looking at him, he winked and she smiled in return, overjoyed anew every time she saw him by the knowledge that he wouldn't be leaving.

When Maman had outlined her deal with Christian, Véronique had almost hugged her, forgetting momentarily the anger she harboured. It was inspired. Maman got to take it easy while Christian got the land he needed. And his plans! She'd only heard about them from Maman, Christian having been preoccupied for the last two weeks with cancelling the obligatory inspections that were part of every property sale, dealing with the estate agent and the solicitor, notifying the auctioneer and emptying all the boxes that Josephine Dupuy had so painstakingly packed. Still, he seemed to have some grand ideas and it looked like he might make the future a lot brighter than the last twelve months.

'With the situation outside,' concluded Serge, finishing the preliminaries as a car alarm went off beyond the window, 'I think we should make this meeting brief. So I'll hand over to our postmistress, Véronique Estaque, who can give you a better idea of the changes we are proposing for the post office.'

Véronique stood, trying to block out the clamour that was filtering through.

'As the mayor said, I'll keep this short and take questions afterwards. Basically, we have to accept that the post office as we knew it is no longer an option in Fogas. La Poste is becoming more and more unwilling to shoulder the burden of rural branches and the fire last year has given them the perfect opportunity to close ours.'

She paused as another car alarm went off and Serge got up to look out of one of the windows.

'Should I continue?' she asked.

'Yes!' he grumbled as he resumed his seat. 'We're not letting those hoodlums disrupt democracy.'

Doing her best to be heard over the racket, she carried on.

'So, that leaves us with two options. Either we apply for a combined facility, using the épicerie as the base for the new branch and taking on rather more of the costs within the commune, or we lose our post office altogether to another local option that is being discussed.'

'Do we know where that is yet?' Alain Rougé asked.

'Not yet. But the mayor is working on it.' She smiled at Serge as a ripple of laughter travelled around the table, skipping Pascal who was taking notes as she spoke. Not that he'd made much use of the last lot, she thought.

'Personally, I think it's a simple choice. The loss of the post office in the commune will have a detrimental effect, not only on businesses like the épicerie,' she nodded towards Josette, 'the Auberge and the garden centre, but on all of us. Many of the residents of Fogas use the post office as their bank, making deposits and withdrawing cash. This would no longer be possible. As for pensioners, they'll be reliant on transport to Massat to collect their pension, making it more difficult for them to reside in the commune past the age at which they stop driving.'

'Josette will be all right then!' René chimed in and got a frown from the learner driver in response.

'Also,' continued Véronique, 'statistics show that communes without a post office are considered less desirable places to live in. This will impact on our chances of attracting new people to Fogas, something that is vital if the commune is to be sustainable. And of course, without a post office, there will be less passing traffic, reduced revenues for the businesses that already exist and therefore reduced local taxes coming in to the council.'

'Christ! Imagine the budget discussions if we have even less money,' muttered Christian.

'Exactly,' said Véronique. 'But it's not just about the money. The post office provides a heart for the community. And if we let it disappear without a fight, then Fogas, and all of us, will be the poorer for it.'

She gave the councillors a chance to digest what they had heard before moving on to outline the proposal for the new post office, one that would be located inside the épicerie. It didn't take long and by the end of her presentation, most of the heads around the table were nodding in agreement. Except one.

'I think my main concern,' began Pascal, 'is the drop in the level of service that we would be able to provide. Am I right that there would be restrictions on the amount of money that could be withdrawn? And that this new facility wouldn't be able to take parcels over a certain size?'

Véronique couldn't believe it. This was the man who had previously been so enthused by her plans.

'As I explained to you five months ago, Pascal, the changes would be minimal and certainly not ones that would be noticed by my regular clientele.'

'But the cost that the commune would have to contribute is significantly more.'

'Not necessarily. Yes, there would be an increase in the percentage that would be paid towards the salary of the employee but there would be some savings on electricity, heating and local taxes owing to the post office being in a shared premises rather than in a single-purpose building. Which was maintained at the expense of the commune, I hasten to add.'

'And what about the cost of renovation? We'd have to install security, a safe. Has all this been factored in?'

'Yes,' said Serge, coming to her aid. 'And it's significantly less than rebuilding the shell that remains of our old post office.'

Pascal shrugged, clearly not on board. 'I just don't think it would work. Sorry, but it's not something I can support.'

'Well, you never set foot in the last one so not having your support is nothing new!'

The retort was out of her lips before Véronique could bite her tongue and the roar of laughter from René coincided with smashing glass outside.

'Right! That's it.' Serge jumped up. 'I'm going to call the police. Christian, vote for me. In favour.'

With a pointed look at Pascal, he hustled from the room and a quick show of hands decided the matter: Fogas was going to apply for a new post office. The motion was carried with nine votes for and two abstentions, Pascal casting both of them, one for himself and the other in proxy for his cousin, Geneviève.

'So what happens next?' asked Alain Rougé as they all stood up, preparing to leave.

'I'll submit our proposal to La Poste, with a copy to the Sub-Prefect in St Girons. And then it's a matter of waiting.' Véronique gave a shrug.

'The police are on their way,' said Serge as he came back into the room. 'I've told the rabble outside but it doesn't seem to have deterred them. So, are we all in favour?'

'Enough are,' replied Véronique.

'Excellent!' He took a step forward, hand held out to congratulate her, when the window above him made a terrible cracking sound, the air glittering with glass for a split second before it cascaded down on top of him.

'Serge!' shouted Véronique, as everyone rushed over to where the mayor was crouched, hands protecting his head, a rock resting on the floor beside him.

'I'm okay,' he said, straightening up slowly, face livid and the backs of his hands grazed and scratched. 'Which is more than I can say for those bastards if I get hold of them.'

Christian was already at the broken window, peering out into the car park, the wail of a police car approaching.

'Huh! They've all gone,' he noted as a flashing blue light cut through the dusk. 'Took off when they heard the sirens. We should have told the police to block the road at the church in La Rivière. They'll have just passed all the troublemakers going the other way!'

'What is the place coming to?' bemoaned René, watching

Véronique and Josette brush the worst of the glass off the mayor's jacket. 'Bloody idiots could have killed you.'

'Thought you agreed with them, René?' Pascal was standing to one side, notebook clutched to his chest, features waxen in the pulsing light. 'Thought you wanted rid of the bears too?'

With a look of disdain, René pulled his jumper up over his protruding stomach, high up until it was under his chin.

'I had a change of mind.'

The laughter that split the room was more than welcome as the stocky plumber stood there with his T-shirt on show. Emblazoned across it, arching over his belly, were the words 'This Is Bear Country'.

The laughter didn't last long. When the councillors made their way outside, they were faced with the damage that had been inflicted on their cars. As before, windshields had been smashed, tyres slashed, paint daubed all over. The police took their time, inspecting the vehicles and taking photos, while Christian, René and Bernard set to and changed wheels where they could, most of the cars only having one tyre damaged. Véronique's, however, had clearly attracted ire, both back wheels punctured and the rear window shattered. As Pascal – the only car owner who'd escaped retribution, having left his Range Rover outside his house at the end of Fogas – had smugly observed, she wouldn't be driving home tonight.

The police had finally left with a warning for the mayor of Fogas, telling him to ensure his doors were locked at night given the escalating rancour. Véronique had been worried about leaving him but he'd brushed aside her concerns, stating that he wouldn't be cowed by yobs who resorted to violence rather than dialogue.

For Véronique, his response had provoked a surge of pride, an emotion she had never experienced in relation to Serge

Papon before. She'd accompanied him down to his house, checked that the cuts on his hands weren't too bad and after making a bit of a fuss over him, which he'd suffered with a big smile, had left, waiting for the sound of the locks to be turned before she walked back to the town hall. With twilight having given way to nightfall, she was reassured to see a familiar frame standing under the lamp in the now deserted car park.

'You ready to go home?' asked Christian, holding open the passenger door on the Panda.

'Yes! Where's Josette?'

'She went with Monique who didn't want to drive down on her own. She thought the protesters might be lying in wait in the woods. Not an unreasonable fear after tonight's performance.'

'Stupid hooligans!' Véronique exclaimed as they drove through the quiet village. 'And there's no chance of anyone being charged as we can't say who caused the damage.'

'No, but a visit from the police might change the minds of some of those who have just been caught up in it all.'

'Let's hope so. They could all do with a René-esque conversion!'

Christian laughed, amused by the about-face of the plumber, the origins of which had not been ascertained as all René would say was that he had seen the other side of the story. It must have been something special, mused Christian, to change the mind of someone who'd been so adamant that bears had no place in these mountains.

He put the Panda in a low gear as they began the winding descent through the trees to La Rivière, the solitary streetlight that stood at the entrance to Fogas soon out of sight and the car swallowed by the night.

It was dark. Which, for some reason Christian couldn't fathom, made him feel awkward. As though he was on a date or something.

Odd. It was only Véronique.

He stole a glance at her and she caught his eye, making him jerk his attention back to the road.

'You did well tonight,' he said, attempting to sound normal. Adult.

'Thanks. Despite Pascal's lack of support. I honestly don't understand the man. He was so enthusiastic in November, and now . . .'

Christian gave a fatalistic shrug. 'Who knows? At least he didn't vote to stop you.'

'I suppose. And hopefully it will mean I get my job back. Or it might be me leaving instead of you!'

He cast another look at her, relieved to see she was smiling.

'About that,' he continued. 'About me not leaving. I wanted to tell you myself but I thought it was best coming from Annie. What with everything . . .'

'I understand. I'm just happy to know you won't be going. We all are,' she added quickly.

'Not as happy as I am!'

'Or Sarko, I suppose.'

He chuckled, his delight at knowing the old bull would be saved still not having diminished. No doubt the next time Sarko escaped would rectify that.

'Has your mother finished unpacking?'

'Not yet. She's using it as a chance to declutter. Throwing out all sorts of stuff from the past while resurrecting things she'd thought she'd lost. And insisting on a new cooker too. She was all set for having some fancy range when we were supposed to be moving.'

'It must feel good?' Véronique was regarding him now, his cheeks starting to burn under her gaze.

'Good doesn't even come close. I know you and Annie have

yet to mend fences but she's changed everything for me with this offer.'

'Maman seems to have turned both of our lives upside down,' she murmured. 'Like tonight. When the window broke over Serge, it was weird. I had this urge to protect him.' She shook her head, bemused. 'Never thought I'd feel like that about Serge Papon of all people!'

Christian grinned at her tone. 'I can't imagine how it feels.'

'Bizarre. Amazing. A bit like your mother, I'm having to go through all my memories and declutter. I keep finding treasures too.'

'And Annie?'

She sighed. 'It's too soon. I can't find it in my heart to forgive her.'

'She's a good woman, Véronique,' he said gently.

'I know. But then you would say that – she's just given you her farm!'

Turning to see the smile he could hear in her voice, his breath caught in his throat. She was looking at him, her hair framing her face, the light at the edge of La Rivière highlighting her cheekbones and her lips were curved in soft amusement.

He managed to pull his gaze away just as they approached the sharp bend that twisted around the bulbous end of the Romanesque church and he had to whip the car to the right at the last minute.

'Sorry,' he muttered, as she was thrown against him, her side warm on his outstretched arm. 'Misjudged that a bit.'

Which was when he realised, now they were in La Rivière and seconds from her apartment, that he didn't want the drive to end.

'I wonder,' he began, as he stopped at the junction with the main road and glanced to the left to check for traffic, 'do you fancy going for a drink?'

'No! Not again!'

It took him a second to realise she wasn't talking to him. She was looking down towards the old school where there were flashing lights and an assembled group of people. Outside her apartment.

The last time it had been like this, she'd lost everything in a fire.

Moments later they were getting out of the car, Véronique racing over to the unmistakable figure of Arnaud who was standing at the back of the small crowd that had gathered to watch the police do their work.

'What's going on?' she demanded.

He pointed at the building which was covered in graffiti, trickles of red dripping down from the freshly painted words.

Kill the bears. Kill the tracker.

Over and over, scrawled on the stone walls which seemed to bleed in the yellow glow of the streetlamp. Then she saw the glass, shards scattered across the ground, refracting the blue lights of the police van.

'The windows?'

'Smashed. Mine, you'll be pleased to know.'

'Any idea who did it?' asked Christian.

Arnaud gave him a sardonic look. 'I think we all know who did it. Proving it will be the problem.'

'Could it be the same people who threw the snowball at my flat in February?' asked Véronique and Christian cringed. 'Perhaps we ought to tell the police?'

'I don't think so,' said Arnaud with a slight smile, while the farmer became very interested in the gravel beneath his feet. 'That was just a kid. Mucking around.'

'Well, if you're sure. Anyway, I'd best go and check everything is all right.' She took two steps away and then turned. 'So your windows are broken?'

Arnaud nodded.

'Then I'll make up the couch. You can stay with me tonight.'

She was gone before Arnaud could refuse or Christian could say goodnight and the farmer felt like someone had trampled on his heart. With boots on.

'She's a woman you can't say no to,' murmured Arnaud as the pair of them stood there, looking at the writing on the wall.

And something made Christian ask; some reckless part of him that was eager to inflict more agony on himself.

'How do you know it was a kid? That threw the snowball?'

Arnaud stared at him, eyes laughing. 'I tracked him. He went up through the orchard and over the fence.'

'Right.' Christian looked away.

'Then he went into the épicerie and came out the other side and after that—'

'Okay! Just thought I'd ask.'

'So like I said. It was a kid. A big kid.' And with a chuckle, the bear man walked off towards the old school. Towards Véronique's apartment. Where he would be staying the night.

Christian spoke to a couple of the policemen, the same ones who had just been up at the town hall, and when he'd established that there was nothing more he could do, he slouched back to the Panda and began the cold journey back to the farm. As he passed the épicerie he didn't glance in. But even if he had, he wouldn't have seen the ghostly form of Jacques who was standing at the window, banging his head on the glass as he shared the farmer's frustration.

Love, thought the old man as he saw the taillights of the Panda disappear up the road to Picarets, never did run smooth.

16

The attack on the old school building split the community. It divided families and tore friendships apart. Philippe Galy, defending the conduct of the anti-bear protesters, claimed they'd had no option but to take direct action to make themselves heard. He'd compared their exploits to those of the infamous reactionary, José Bové, but unfortunately did so in a loud voice down at the market in St Girons. As luck would have it, André Dupuy, an ardent fan of the militant farmer Bové but totally opposed to the violence that had infiltrated Fogas, had been passing and had taken objection to the bee-keeper's words. Things had got heated and by the time Christian managed to pull his father away from the bee-keeper's stall, the fracas had attracted quite a crowd. One that would remember for a long time old Dupuy telling Philippe Galy what he could do with his honey. In detail.

The men weren't the only ones at each other's throats. At her salon in Seix, Monique Sentenac had been colouring the hair of her son-in-law's mother when the woman carelessly made a comment about the situation in Fogas. As the woman's son had been one of the group that had vandalised the cars outside the town hall, and left the hairdresser terrified and out of pocket for a new tyre, Monique was not disposed to share her client's views.

Words had been exchanged. Lots of them. All through the medium of the mirror, Monique with her hand raised holding a brush covered in red dye. Finally the woman in the chair had flounced out of the salon, towel still around her neck, hair not finished, vowing she'd never set foot in the establishment again. But heaven has no forgiveness like a woman who needs a good hairdresser. She'd gone back meekly two days later to ask for the variegated dye-job to be rectified and Monique, horrified to have her name put to the awful coiffure, had agreed.

In Fogas, things were no better. The hunting lodge had become the rallying point for those who were angry with the mayor, upset about the bears or just unhappy in general. Every night large groups of men gathered to light a stack of pallets in the middle of the car park around which they stood with their placards and their dogs. Occasionally they moved out to block the road, harassing any car displaying a Bear Country sticker, as a result of which most locals began removing the controversial signs from their rear windows rather than face such intimidation on a daily basis. Josette was one of the few who dared to challenge the protesters, decorating her car with a long line of bear logos and thus making the Sunday drive yet more of a tribulation for Véronique as the Peugeot crawled through a barrage of insults at the beginning and end of every journey.

Even the mountains weren't neutral territory. When Fabian Servat rode his bike up to Massat, turning at the top of the valley to take the beautiful road that climbed up to the Col d'Agnes, he always took delight in seeing the names of his cycling heroes on the tarmac beneath his wheels. But recently these faded dedications, mementos of the Tour de France's annual visit to the Ariège, had been defaced with fresh messages declaring *NO TO THE BEARS!*

Only in the small school up in Sarrat was there harmony. As Madame Soum pointed out to Stephanie Morvan at the conclusion of parents' evening, Chloé, with her gory tales of the death of Marat and her detailed breakdown of how to tell what a bear had for dinner, had the entire student body in her thrall. And after Arnaud Petit's classroom visit, complete with photos of the new arrivals, every single one of the students was caught up in Chloé's passion for Miel and the twin bear cubs, Morel and Truffle. It was a shame, the teacher remarked sarcastically, that the young girl hadn't shown the same enthusiasm in class. Stephanie didn't reply. It was taking all of her self-control not to burst out laughing as the elderly teacher walked ahead to the door, a colourful sticker adorning her backside.

It was in the midst of this tension, on the Tuesday after Pentecost, that the results of the investigation into the dead sheep came back from the agency. And after four weeks, Arnaud Petit got the news he'd been dreading.

As was to be expected, with the carcasses indicating a strong likelihood that a bear had been responsible for the attacks and this being further supported by other evidence at the scene, the investigator had approved the demand for compensation. Likewise, Philippe Galy was to be recompensed for the loss of his beehive.

Arnaud wasn't surprised. With a clear footprint and a sample of fur, there was no way the investigator could do anything but accept the claims. To do otherwise would compromise whatever fragile progress the bear reintroduction programme had made on the public relations front.

Nor was the tracker taken aback to note that the concerns he'd raised with the investigator about the legitimacy of the attacks hadn't made their way into the official report. There was no mention about the unlikely probability of two such attacks occurring in one night, given the distance that separated the sites. Nor was there anything about the convenient 'proof' that had been found at both locations, and the fact that the damage inflicted on the sheep was in keeping with an attack by stray dogs as much as by bears was glossed over.

But if Arnaud found all of that predictable, given the sensitive politics involved, the final section of the report completely floored him.

It was enough, he thought, as he sat at his rickety table looking out at the serene blue sky that arched over La Rivière, to tip this already unstable community into civil war. And it merited a meeting with Serge Papon.

He reached for the phone, dialling the number for the town hall as he paced up and down the small kitchen, impatient to be up in the mountains instead. Because when this report was made public, Miel and her cubs were going to need every bit of protection he could provide. And he was going to be out of a job.

For Serge Papon, this particular day in the last week of May, despite its proximity to the Pentecost, felt far removed from the gift of the Holy Spirit. Rather than being inspired with the ability to speak in tongues, instead he was struggling to make sense of the two lots of correspondence that had been delivered that morning.

He pushed back his chair and reviewed the letters on his desk. The first was from the Conseil Général, informing him that they had it on good authority that the bear tracker was still residing in the commune. It continued to gently remind him that this could only be viewed as a 'pro-bear' stance which was greatly regrettable.

Greatly regrettable! The mayor of Fogas didn't have to think hard to realise where their information might have come from. No doubt his odious first deputy had been on the phone, anxious to ingratiate himself with the higher powers in Foix.

The other communication was a short letter from the agency in charge of the bear reintroduction programme which stated that as of the end of the month, which was six days away, they would no longer require accommodation in Fogas. Suspecting that political pressure had played a part, he'd called the agency. But he'd been wrong. Sort of. He'd been put through to Arnaud's boss who had explained that due to an ongoing disciplinary investigation which he couldn't discuss, Arnaud Petit would no longer be needing the apartment.

Serge didn't need it spelled out. Arnaud had been suspended. So although the interference hadn't come from the Conseil Général, it was still political. Henri Dedieu, mayor of Sarrat, had obviously been good to his word and filed a complaint. And good to his word, he'd got rid of the bear tracker.

Instead of being satisfied that his problems with the council in Foix had been resolved for him, Serge was aggrieved that the matter had been taken out of his hands. It left him feeling impotent which in turn made him unbearable. So when Céline put through a call to his office, she was glad to be able to remind the mayor that she would be out of the office for the remainder of the morning, thanks to a filling she'd lost to her mother's delicious *veau de pentecôte* the day before. She was especially relieved to be escaping as Serge's old pal from La Poste was on the line and he had more bad news.

'What do you mean, it's been decided?' Serge growled into the phone, overcome with a desire to stretch his hands down the receiver and throttle the messenger.

'That's all I've heard. The head office has said that your application for a new branch will be turned down.'

'But they can't have had time to make that decision. They've only had the submission a matter of weeks.'

The sigh at the other end was pained. 'Sorry, Serge. But

that's not all. I've also been doing a bit of digging about the local alternative that was mentioned.'

'And?'

'You're not going to like this. It's in Sarrat. And it's going to be a combined facility.'

'With an épicerie?'

'Yes.'

Silence. Having known Serge Papon since school, the man at La Poste pictured him with his lips compressed, eyes narrowed, that brain of his making rapid calculations about the implication of this news. And his next move.

'Anything else while you're ruining my day?' the mayor of Fogas finally asked.

His friend laughed, apologised, promised to catch up for a drink in St Girons one day and then hung up, leaving Serge to his thoughts.

They weren't good ones. For as soon as he'd heard that Sarrat was getting a branch of the post office, and that it was also to be an épicerie, the last piece of the puzzle fell into place. He called the planning department in St Girons where he had another contact. One who still owed him a favour.

'Any news?'

'Just in.' The man's voice dropped to a whisper. 'The permission has been granted and Sarrat is going to have a new—'

'Épicerie and post office?'

'You knew already?'

'I put two and two together.'

'Do you want me to send you the details?'

'That'd be great. And thanks.'

Serge hung up and walked across to the window. Fogas. Dead, as always. Disregarding the cabal of old men down at the *lavoir*, it was possible to travel through the village and not see a single soul. And even the group that gathered at the washbasins was dwindling as the years passed.

In his youth, Serge remembered the place being bustling. There'd been a small shop at the top of the road selling essentials like bread and milk. And cheese. The town hall had employed more staff and there had been more farms. More people. He'd been raised over in Picarets, which hadn't been as busy, and had looked forward to the visits his father used to make across the valley, bringing his young son with him to council meetings or to catch up with other farmers.

But as the world changed, so did the village. The small family-run farms became less viable, in competition against the massive agribusinesses in the north, and one by one they disappeared. The local industries also went into decline, the mines that had delivered iron ore and tungsten closed and of the numerous paper mills that had lined the River Salat down in St Girons, only one remained. This meant the young had to leave and it wasn't long before the shop at the top of the road closed. After that there was no reason to visit Fogas, apart from business at the town hall, and pretty soon the once thriving community was quiet.

While other areas were coming out of this long recession, making the most of the burgeoning tourism industry, Fogas lagged behind. It didn't appeal to second-home buyers the way places like Seix did. It didn't tempt people to run chambres d'hôtes or gîtes. And when a company had come looking to set up a holiday activity centre, they had dismissed Fogas out of hand. It was easy to see why.

Without amenities of any sort, and stuck on top of a mountain ridge, it was not ideal. Which is why, thought the mayor, it was vital that he get this latest move by La Poste overturned. At present, the épicerie gave a heart to the commune. If that closed too, which it surely would if a combined facility was allowed to open across the river and enticed customers away, then there would be no stopping the decline of the three villages of Fogas. Attracting fewer visitors and fewer residents, their community would become unsustainable and before long the population would be so small, they would lose the right to self-government. And when that happened, Fogas would get swallowed up by the much larger, much more vibrant Sarrat. With its new post office and épicerie.

Over my dead body! There was no way he had worked so hard for twenty-five years to hold this place together simply to give up now.

A knock at the door roused him from his morbid thoughts and he pulled his gaze away from the empty road to see Arnaud Petit standing before him, a serious look on his face.

'Bonjour,' said Serge, taking a seat and frowning at the young man. 'This had better not be more bad news.'

Arnaud grimaced and placed the report on the desk, open at the relevant paragraph. Putting on his reading glasses, Serge skimmed the text and then looked up.

'Merde. This is going to cause a war.'

Arnaud nodded and sat down. There was a lot they needed to discuss.

'They have permission for *what*?'

Josette's face turned grey and Fabian was sure she was going to pass out.

'A combined facility. Post office and épicerie,' said Serge. 'But don't worry. We'll fight it.'

'But . . . that was my idea.'

The mayor shifted his attention to Véronique who was sitting next to him skimming through the details his contact at the planning department had faxed over. She was just as shocked as Josette.

'I know. I can't say how they got hold of it—'

'I think we know how they got hold of it! That bugger Pascal!'

'Now Véronique, we can't be sure of that,' admonished Serge. 'And he wouldn't hesitate to sue you for slander if he overheard you saying it. But you might well be right.'

'Of course she's right. Who else knew?' asked Josette.

'What I don't understand, though, is why? How on earth does Pascal benefit if Sarrat gets a new post office?'

Fabian's question went unanswered as the three other people in the bar, four if you counted Jacques who had collapsed onto his seat in the inglenook at the news, looked at each other. No one could think of a suitable reply.

'It's just the opposite,' Serge finally said. 'If we lose the post office and an épicerie opens up across the bridge, then Fogas will go into decline. No good being mayor of somewhere like that, with his political aspirations!'

'And he went as far as to abstain from voting for Véronique's proposals at the last meeting because he thought reduced post office services were a bad idea,' added Josette, face puzzled. 'Why would he then do something to jeopardise it altogether?'

'Well, even if it wasn't deliberate, he must have let it slip. I had to do a lot of research to find out about the combined facility scheme as it's brand new. I can't believe that the idiots on the Sarrat council were capable of thinking this up for themselves.' Véronique shook her head and tapped the papers in her hand. 'But you know what else doesn't make sense? The location.'

Serge smiled, impressed yet again by this daughter he'd just discovered. 'Exactly my thoughts.'

'I don't understand,' said Fabian. 'Why is the location of interest?'

'Because it's not practical,' Véronique explained, realising that he still wasn't fully conversant with local geography. 'Unlike here, Sarrat is pretty much made up of one village. Up where the school is. It already has a church, a tennis court and there was once a shop too but way before my time.'

'And?'

'The new post office is going to be across the bridge where the recycling bins are, right on the border of the two communes down here in the valley. Sure, there's a scattering of houses over there but it's hardly at the heart of the community. And there's very little passing traffic.'

'Hopefully it will fail!' said Josette with uncommon spite.

'Who arrre you currrsing now, Josette Serrrvat?'

It was only as she walked properly into the bar that Annie Estaque realised exactly who was present. She was wondering whether it would be rude to leave when Serge stood up and pulled out a chair for her.

'Just in time, Annie,' he said as he kissed her cheeks, acting as if nothing had changed between them. 'We could do with some of your wisdom on this.'

Trapped, Annie sat, eyes avoiding her daughter whose face was scarlet, the first time she'd been in the company of both parents since she'd found out who her father was. It was only as Annie glanced around the table that she realised Véronique was sitting between her and Serge, like a proper little family.

If the awkwardness the Estaque women were feeling was shared by the others, they hid it well as Josette brought Annie up to date with the latest bad news to hit Fogas.

'So you can understand,' Josette concluded, 'why I feel a bit upset. If that shop goes ahead, it could be disastrous for us.'

'Upset? I'd be livid!' retorted her old friend. 'I prrresume you arrre going to do something about it?'

Her last remark was aimed at Serge, who nodded. 'I've already scheduled a meeting for next Wednesday with the authorities at La Poste. I'll take Véronique with me and see if we can't persuade them of our case in person.'

'In the meantime,' said Véronique, a look on her face that was pure Papon as she waved the plans in the air, 'we should make sure news of this circulates around the commune. And quickly.'

Serge laughed and slapped her on the back while the others struggled to catch on.

'You mean they might all unite against a common enemy and forget about this bear nonsense?' he said. 'It could work, given how much we all hate Sarrat.'

Then he remembered his conversation with Arnaud and his face grew sombre. It wasn't something he could share just yet. He'd left the report on Céline's desk for her to file, with a note telling her to keep it under wraps. It would be public know-ledge within a fortnight but that might be enough time for Arnaud to do what he needed to do. When the news got out, however, no amount of shared animosity for Sarrat would unite the commune he loved.

'Right,' said Serge. 'I'd best get back to work or Céline will be sending out a search party.'

Josette got up with him and walked him out to his car, still talking about the developments, while Fabian went through to the shop to serve a couple of tourists. The Estaque women were left on their own.

'Did you want a coffee?' Véronique asked. 'Is that what brought you in here?'

'Actually, I was looking forrr you.'

'Me? Why? Is there something else you've never told me?'

Her mother winced and as swiftly as Véronique's anger had flared, it was doused by contrition.

'Sorry,' she muttered.

Annie waved a hand in dismissal but it had clearly hurt. 'I wonderrred if you'd do me a favourrr. A big one.'

'Like what?'

'I want to do the trrranshumance.'

Véronique's jaw dropped in justified surprise. 'You're kidding?'

'No.'

'But you've never done it. Not in my lifetime.'

'Things change.'

Véronique bit back a stinging retort, thrown by her mother's sudden urge to escort the animals on their annual walk up to the high pastures. 'Why now though? This year of all years?'

Annie shrugged. 'It might be the last time I get the chance. Chrrristian will take overrr the farrrm soon and I'm not getting any youngerrr.'

'So what's it got to do with me?'

'The doctorrr said I wasn't to do it alone.' Annie tapped her chest. 'Afterrr my incident.'

'After your heart attack, Maman. That's what it was. A heart attack. And I'm surprised the doctor has said you can take part in the transhumance at all.'

Annie kept quiet, not having technically asked the doctor. She had enquired whether it was okay for her to walk uphill and the poor man, not being from these parts and not knowing the terrain where she lived, hadn't understood that she was referring to walking up a mountain for several hours with a herd of cows. He'd given her the green light but had suggested she take it easy. He hadn't said a word about having company. That bit she'd decided all by herself. And she knew who she wanted alongside her.

'But if he's said it's fine, I don't see the problem,' concluded her daughter.

'So you'll come with me?'

Véronique stared at her and Annie felt her blood turn cold. She'd racked her brains for a way to break through this veneer of politeness that her daughter had erected between them ever since she'd learnt the truth about her father. But Annie had been unable to see how to do it. Until she remembered the transhumance. It was perfect, she'd decided. And fitting. The reason Annie had shunned what had once been her favourite ritual of the farming calendar was because of the malicious gossip she'd had to endure after she got pregnant. When she'd accepted that she was going to have a baby, going to be a single mother in Fogas, she'd resigned from the council, had stopped going to the market and had never again made the long trek up to the summer grazing with her livestock. All in an effort to stop the rumours and protect her child.

It hadn't worked, of course. And it didn't look as if she was going to be successful now either.

'Are you sure it's wise?' asked Véronique finally. 'Not only for your heart but for us two? Up the mountain for hours on end, just the pair of us?'

'Might do us good.'

Véronique gave a dry laugh and for a second, Annie saw her child again.

'I don't know. I just . . .' Véronique tailed off, a tumult of emotions flooding over her. She glanced out of the window and saw Serge Papon opening his car door. He caught her eye and smiled. A big beaming smile, making him unrecognisable as the man she'd met in the graveyard at *Toussaint*. Clearly finding out he had a daughter had done him no harm. The opposite in fact.

'Okay,' she heard herself say. 'I'll come with you.'

She pretended not to notice her mother letting out a sigh of relief as Josette bustled back into the bar.

'Well,' said Josette archly. 'It's good to see you two talking to each other. And one thing that can be said about today's developments – when word gets out about the post office in

Sarrat, you Estaque women and your secrets will be yesterday's news!'

Annie and Véronique both laughed but Jacques, who was still sitting in the inglenook, was as far from laughing as you could get. The épicerie that his family had worked so hard to create was in danger. And there wasn't a damn thing he could do about it.

Up in Fogas the town hall was all locked up. Céline was still at the dentist, the missing filling proving more problematic than expected. And Serge Papon was in La Rivière passing on the bad news to Josette. But although it was locked, the building wasn't empty. Pascal Souquet had just let himself in the back door, and was trotting up the stairs to collect his sunglasses which he'd left on Céline's desk by mistake on Friday.

His mood was light as he reached the top landing, the repulsion that normally soured his stomach the minute he entered the shabby hallway somewhat abated by the long weekend he'd just spent in Toulouse. It wasn't Paris. But the production of *La Fille Mal Gardée* at the Théâtre du Capitole had been surprisingly good, considering. And the meal afterwards in one of the courtyards across from the theatre had been sublime. Michelin-starred chef. Foie gras to die for. And a 2005 Château de Mercuès Cuvée 6666. That was something to be said for the southerners: they knew how to make good wine.

Seeing as his sister's incredibly rich husband was paying, they'd gone for the *dégustation* menu and each dish had been exquisite. Beautifully presented, intricate flavours and all in an ambience that was a far cry from the restaurants in his current locale. No one had insisted on using their own pocket-knife instead of the cutlery provided. The plates hadn't arrived overloaded with chips and a lump of steak that was inedible.

And everyone had known which glass was for wine and which was for water.

If only he could afford that life, instead of having to rely on the largesse of his in-laws. It was so awkward, not being able to socialise on an even footing. When he'd noticed how taken Pascal was with the wine, his brother-in-law had suggested they all book a weekend at the Château de Mercuès. Only an hour and a half north of Toulouse, an amazing place with an award-winning restaurant famous for truffles. And of course, those wines . . .

Fatima had stepped in to save him. Impossible for them to commit just now, was how she'd phrased it. What with the upheaval in Fogas. She'd managed to imply that Pascal was a truffle-shaving away from being installed as the next mayor, hiding their inability to afford such a luxurious weekend behind the guise of his flourishing career in local politics.

It galled him, though. The deception necessary in order to maintain appearances. The lies they told to conceal the fact that they were unable to live as they used to, a week in Ile de Ré no longer something they could do on a whim, dining out now a rare treat rather than a weekly occurrence. They existed on Fatima's meagre salary and his sick pay. And of course, the pathetic remuneration that came with being deputy mayor. So for now, a weekend at an exclusive vineyard was beyond their means.

But that wasn't going to stop Pascal looking it up on the internet as soon as he got home. It was, he decided, the place where he would celebrate becoming mayor, regardless of the cost. Because once he became mayor, with the future that was in store for this commune, he would be able to spend a little. Live the way he was meant to live.

He entered Céline's office and immediately spotted his Yves Saint Laurent sunglasses perched on the edge of her desk. He hoped she hadn't been trying them on, getting her grubby fingers all over the lenses. He lifted them to the light streaming in from the window and could see a thumbprint smeared across the glass.

'Stupid yokel!' he muttered, as he reached for a tissue. And as his arm stretched across her desk, he saw it. A folder with a note in Serge's unmistakable scrawl.

File immediately. Not for public viewing.

He forgot the tissue. Forgot the offending grease mark on his sunglasses. In fact, he forgot his sunglasses completely, laying them back down next to the tissues as he picked up the report. It didn't take long to read. Only slightly longer to copy. But it was, Pascal knew, the fuel that would set the smouldering discontent in Fogas truly aflame.

He placed the folder back on the desk, made sure that he'd turned the photocopier off and then left the building the way he'd entered, confident that no one would be any the wiser about his visit. Then he made for home, the hours ticking by slowly until he could make the call he knew this warranted.

The next person to enter the building was Céline, jaw swollen, still numb from the anaesthetic. She was far from her usual perceptive self. So when she saw the report on her desk she did as she was asked. Filed it. And when she saw the ludicrously expensive sunglasses belonging to the first deputy mayor sitting next to her tissue box rather than on the edge of the desk where she had placed them that morning, she thought nothing of it. She picked them up, thumb squarely in the centre of a lens, and put them to one side before getting back to work.

When Pascal called in much later that afternoon, she had no reason to doubt his claim that he was just back from Toulouse and had dropped by on the way home to get his sunglasses. In fact she hadn't paid much attention to him at all. Although she had noted with a smile, which was worth the pain it caused her inflamed face, that he'd gone off muttering about the smudge marks all over the lenses.

Arnaud was packing. He didn't have a lot but it was still too much to take. He had to travel light. He stuffed a spare set of clothes into his rucksack and made a pile of all the things he would be leaving behind. Laptop, tent, the meagre food supplies that he'd built up over the last seven months, his winter clothing. He placed it all into a box which Serge Papon would pick up later.

It felt good knowing he was going to be living up there. Nearer Miel and the cubs.

Although, given the news that he'd had, he didn't have much choice! Serge had gently informed him about the letter he'd received from the agency and had suggested it might mean a suspension was looming. Arnaud hadn't been surprised. The report had more or less spelled it out and it wasn't the first time he'd been asked to take gardening leave while the diplomats sorted out some misdemeanour on his part. Always to do with the politics. In this case, Serge suspected that the mayor of Sarrat had taken a dislike to his uncompromising stance in support of the bears and had filed a complaint.

'Sinister' was the word that had gone through Arnaud's mind when he'd met Henri Dedieu. Sinister and malignant. The man had the eyes of a killer, a calculating take on life that harboured no sentiment. Unlike René Piquemal. Arnaud had taken a chance showing the plumber the bears but it had proved right, René now an ardent supporter and even talking about getting an ursine tattoo. Which had prompted Christian Dupuy to suggest the only surface area large enough for it!

After his return from the site of the attack in Sarrat, Arnaud had asked the plumber for his opinion of the mayor from the neighbouring commune and had sensed that it wasn't a positive one. Henri Dedieu pretty much controlled the hunting lodge, according to René, and had made the plumber and Bernard Mirouze the object of ridicule every Saturday when they returned from the hunt empty-handed. René had confided that he was glad the season was over, especially given his recent conversion, and was making strides in establishing a new club, surprised at the expression of interest he'd had from other men who were tired of the macho attitudes prevalent in the old lodge.

But whether or not Serge was right to point the finger at Henri Dedieu, it changed nothing. When Arnaud had returned from his meeting up at the town hall he'd found a letter waiting for him, confirming what Serge Papon had suspected. He was suspended with immediate effect pending a disciplinary investigation. He was to vacate the apartment and return the equipment belonging to the agency as soon as possible.

Which would be difficult, seeing as he was about to head up into the woods. Serge had agreed to cover for him, stall the agency by telling them that Arnaud was incommunicado in the mountains. That should keep them off his back for a while. Give him enough time to get himself organised. Get Miel protected.

He'd thought he was doing that in the autumn when he'd made the decision not to put a tracking collar on her. Instead it had left her open to allegations, left him unable to prove through a record of her movements that she wasn't responsible for the attacks. Which meant she was in grave danger. For if any more accusations were made against the bear, then following standard procedure the agency would give the word for Miel to be killed.

He threw a few more items into his rucksack and lifted it to test the weight. Not bad. He'd make camp out of fallen branches and foliage. Live off the land for a few weeks until the impact of the report died down. And ascertain the truth for once while he was up there. Because he was still convinced that Miel was innocent, despite the evidence to the contrary.

A movement in the street below caught his eye and he saw the hunter who'd been wearing the white bandage at the meeting in November go past, arm now free of its strapping. But it wasn't the man's arm that caught Arnaud's attention. It was what was at the end of it.

A black-and-white dog held on a lead.

'Merde! The bastards.'

It was unmistakable. A Karelian, tail curling over its back, chest stocky, straining at the leash. A beautiful-looking animal. Unless you knew what they were capable of. Famed for their ability to hunt down bears, once they discovered their prey they would hold it at bay, despite the difference in size, running backwards and forwards and nipping at the beast until the hunters arrived. With their guns.

Arnaud pulled back from the window and quickly finished his packing. This changed things. He needed to be up there as soon as possible. Because there was only one reason the hunters had got that dog. And it wasn't for entering the Ariège Dog Show down in St Girons.

He slung the rucksack onto his back and left the apartment, feeling time running out. For him and the bears.

'It's me. Pascal.'

'I know, idiot. I can see your number on my phone. What do you want?'

'The report is back. From the attacks.' Silence, which Pascal hastened to fill. 'I've made a copy. Thought you might want to see it.'

'What does it say?'

'They fell for it. The report blames the bear called Miel. Her DNA was found at the scene.'

'And the tracker?'

'He's held accountable for failing to follow the correct procedures and for refusing to fit the bear with a tracking collar back in November. Reading between the lines, he's been suspended.'

A dark chuckle. 'Well, well, well. Looks like things are finally going to plan. Anything else?'

'The report suggests that any further attacks from the same bear will prompt them to consider euthanasia.'

Pascal heard the intake of breath that went with a cigarette.

'Bring me the copy tonight. You know where. And don't be seen. We're too near the end now to get caught.'

'And then . . .'

A sarcastic laugh. 'And then your job is done. Leave the real work to those of us who don't mind a bit of bloodshed.'

A click and the line went dead.

So, this was it. Serge Papon, the tracker, the bear. All in one tidy trap. As long as he didn't think about how it was going to happen, Pascal was able to live with it.

He poured himself a glass of wine and read once again the delectable menu he had downloaded. In ten days' time he would be that bit nearer to the Château de Mercuès.

17

It didn't take long for the news to leak. By the next day, the contents of the report into the death of the three sheep had become common knowledge in Fogas. Somehow a copy had made its way out of the town hall and as word got round that Arnaud Petit had been apportioned a large share of the blame, so frustration grew amongst those who resented the presence of the bears in the area. Their irritation turned to anger when they realised that their mayor had been shielding the very man who had been criticised in the report. Shielding him against the will of the Conseil Général, as became apparent when a letter from that esteemed body was circulated which clearly advised Serge Papon to distance himself from the tracker.

Understandably, the electorate was incensed. The numbers outside the hunting lodge every evening swelled as those who had previously been sitting on the fence jumped down on the side of the anti-bear protesters and even those who had always been loyal supporters of the mayor began to question the wisdom of their leader.

What was he thinking? Protecting a rogue like Arnaud Petit who was incapable of following orders. A maverick who went off and did his own thing. It didn't take long before the populace realised that these descriptions could well be applied to Serge Papon. When did he ever listen to them? Wouldn't Pascal Souquet, who had at least tried to do something about the situation, make a better mayor?

But if their annoyance at the man in charge was escalating, their outrage at the bear was out of control. The calls from the hunters to kill the beast were now being echoed by the more moderate inhabitants of Fogas. What if it attacked again? What if this time it went for a child? Surely the agency in charge of the reintroduction programme should move to eliminate the risk?

So the anxiety fermented, the sudden arrival of summer exacerbating the tension with temperatures reaching over thirty degrees and villages baking in an unrelenting heatwave. Despite the sweltering conditions, people were afraid to leave their doors open, afraid to let their children play outside – because of the bear. Only Chloé Morvan wandered unattended, her mother having tried to rein her in to no avail, unable to argue against the young girl's firm belief that Miel was innocent.

In La Rivière the long evenings provided the opportunity for the simmering discontent to spread as men convened to add their voices to the already deafening protests. The car park at the lodge could no longer contain the numbers that gathered and so they spilled out onto the road, sitting on the walls of the gardens, lining the verge so that any passing car had to run a gauntlet of abuse.

Then, on the Thursday, just over a week after the report was published and two days before the transhumance, accounts of another attack began to filter through the commune. This time it was one of Christian Dupuy's sheep, stomach ripped open, bones laid bare. Served him right, was the verdict of the anti-bear faction. He'd refused to take their side all along and now he was getting his comeuppance. They were vindicated in their opinions when the investigator arrived and discovered two clear prints which matched those found at the other locations. Despite the absence of fur, it was obvious that Miel had struck again. And accordingly, the protesters called for her to be put down.

The ensuing outcry was enough to catapult the commune into the news. The *Gazette Ariégeoise* had been reporting the story for months and earlier in the week it had been picked up by the regional paper *La Dépêche*. But on Friday, when demonstrations in the village reached a frenzy, a television crew arrived. That evening it broadcast to the whole of France the hostility that had inflamed this small Pyrenean commune, so anonymous to the rest of the country that the presenter of *France 2* news failed to pronounce the 's' on the end of Fogas.

By early Saturday, things were at boiling point. At seven in the morning, as Josette flung open the shutters ready to start another busy day, she noticed that the lodge was already teeming with men. All of them dressed in camouflage. Many of them with dogs. And guns, even though the hunting season was long finished. Perturbed, she called Serge Papon, who arrived just in time to see a convoy of 4x4s drive out of the village, down past the Auberge and turn left onto the Picarets road. He decided he would wait in the bar to see what transpired and ordered a coffee which was to be the first of many.

Up at the Estaque farm, Véronique was greeted at the door by her mother wearing sturdy boots, a length of hazel in her hand and a small rucksack on her back. Beyond perfunctory greetings, neither of them spoke much as they gathered the cows together and started what was to be a long walk. Both of the women were tense although that had nothing to do with the bears.

Way up above them, near the clearing where she'd spent her hibernation, Miel was rolling in the grass, her cubs tumbling next to her, all three of them appreciating the stunning weather. But unlike of late, today they had no guardian angel watching over them. Arnaud, getting wind of the third attack belatedly via a text from Chloé, had left his lookout point and headed for Christian's land to see the scene for himself, in the hope that it would yield some answers as to who was really behind this. One thing was for sure: it wasn't Miel. He'd been following her for the last ten days and could vouch that she hadn't set paw anywhere near the Dupuy farm.

And over them all, the sun shone down from above the mountains, temperature already high despite the early hour, humidity starting to rise. Annie Estaque took one look at the seemingly benign sky and muttered, 'Therrre'll be storrrms beforrre the day is thrrrough.'

She had no idea how right she was.

They left their cars in Picarets. A long line of four-wheel drives. And en masse they set out for the path at the back of Stephanie's house, Chloé watching them from her garden. Men, all of them. In hunting clothes, guns slung over their shoulders. Faces fierce. She didn't need her gypsy heritage to tell her that danger was looming. She raced indoors to send a text to Arnaud. Then she pulled on her boots and made for the door. But it was blocked by Maman. She begged. She pleaded. Tears on her cheeks. She needed to follow them. But Maman wouldn't budge, her own sixth sense telling her that she mustn't let her child out of her sight. And so Chloé was forced to accompany her mother to La Rivière, her head twisted backwards for the entire journey down in the car as she strained to see the hills behind. As though that would save Miel and her babies.

They took it steady. No choice when escorting cows who walked at their own ponderous pace, Annie's two Pyrenean mountain dogs running up and down alongside the herd. It was a glorious morning, thick mist in the valleys below, trees and mountains ethereal as they rose out of it into the cobalt sky.

Véronique checked the time. Eight o'clock. They were making good enough progress. Luckily the road was quiet, apart from all the parked cars in Picarets, which had required a bit of negotiating. With the path at the back of Stephanie's house too narrow for the animals, they were having to go the long way round, following the road up past the old quarry to pick up the broader track to the pasture. But even with regular breaks, they should easily be there by lunchtime.

She glanced at her mother walking alongside her. She looked better than she had for a while, streaks of pink on her rugged cheeks. Maybe, Véronique thought, this wasn't such a bad idea after all.

Arnaud was puzzled. He was staring at two sets of prints next to a small spring on Christian Dupuy's land. Something didn't add up. His measurements for one thing.

Looking at the print on the right, he was convinced it was the same as the one found at Philippe's and on the farm in Sarrat. Well, the top part of it at any rate. He held a photo next to it, ridges identical, spacing between toes the same, impression unnaturally heavy on the outer edge. But yet, it was fundamentally different. According to his notes, this print was ten centimetres longer than the one in the photograph and significantly deeper. Which meant that the bear had undergone an amazing growth spurt in the last month. And it had changed sex.

Because the print in front of him was definitely that of a male bear. Like the one down at the bridge in Sarrat that he'd found in the autumn.

He pondered this discovery as he traced his fingers over the indentations again: a right rear, as before, and this time a left rear too. Now that he had a complete set, he could see that the right print was twisted unnaturally, pointing inwards more than it should as though the animal had a club foot. Which explained the imbalanced markings. And that was triggering something in his memory. Something he'd seen.

Sitting back on his heels he tried to make sense of it all.

There had been three attacks. This one – which Arnaud was pretty sure was genuine given the scat at the edge of the trees – and then the other two, which he had been sceptical about from the beginning.

But if the first two had been faked, as he suspected, why did they share some features with this one? There was no mistaking that the right rear print was identical, except in length and depth. And what about the fur which had firmly placed Miel at the scene? There was none evident here that he could see. Although that didn't mean the investigator hadn't already collected samples.

He pulled out his mobile and called head office.

'Jean-Pierre? It's me, Arnaud. I need a favour. But don't tell the boss!'

By the time Arnaud hung up less than five minutes of whispered conversation later, his friend had passed on all he needed to know and something more besides. There had been no sign of fur at the latest investigation site. Which was interesting in itself. But more importantly, Jean-Pierre was able to tell him that the samples of fur the tracker had provided from the two previous investigations had both shown heavy traces of turpentine.

The fur was the key, of that Arnaud was sure. It was the one piece of evidence he couldn't refute. And the only thing that singled out Miel as culpable. But if the attacks at the farm and the beehives had been man-made, how had they got the fur? It wasn't like Miel was going to roll over and let them comb her stomach for a few stray hairs. Not unless they had a bag of corn with them.

Bag of corn . . . Merde! That's how they'd done it. But he needed proof.

He took off across the field at a jog, anxious to get to his car because every second he delayed was a second closer to the agency ordering a wrongful death. As he started the engine and sped off down the hill towards La Rivière he heard the ping of his phone indicating an incoming text. It would have to wait. What he was doing was far more important and might prove Miel's innocence once and for all. And save her life into the bargain.

Dogs. Barking. Miel lifted her head, trying to place the sound but the wind changed direction and it was impossible to tell. She grunted, calling her cubs to her. They had to move. There was danger coming. Together they headed into the forest, the cubs wrestling and playing, still thinking that life was one long game.

'The dog's found a trail!'

The hunter pointed at the Karelian which was pulling on the leash, barking and dragging the man behind him.

'Excellent. Spread out,' the leader shouted to the rest of the men, signalling for them to make an arc though the trees. 'Guns at the ready. But remember, no shooting. Not unless it's necessary.'

He strained to see through the dense vegetation. Then he spotted it. A lumbering shape, moving away from them. Moving further into the trap.

'We've got her,' he muttered, eyes wild. 'There's no escaping now.'

'Fancy a break?'

Annie nodded and let out a sharp whistle which brought the dogs to heel, allowing the cows to stand and graze the verges of the track in peace. Having passed the turn-off for the quarry a while ago, they were now well into the hills. Another hour, maybe two, and they would be at the pasture.

Sinking onto a rock next to Véronique, she was grateful to be off her feet and glad that they were in the shade. It was ferociously hot, the sun beating down on them, the air thick and heavy. She'd been struggling with her breathing for the last half hour but she didn't want her daughter to know.

'Josette said we'd appreciate these.' Véronique pulled two beers out of her rucksack, condensation on the glass. 'And they're cold!'

Annie grabbed a bottle and rolled it over her face, delighting in the feeling. 'How on earrrth . . . ?'

Véronique showed her a plastic bag with an ice block in it and Annie laughed.

'All mod cons these days, Maman. Not like when you last did this trek!'

'So trrrue! We used to have a bottle of wine and that was it! Not that I everrr rrrememberrr it being this hot.' She fanned herself with her hand as she took a long sip of beer. 'Of courrrse, therrre werrre morrre people then. Big grrroups of us used to head up and we'd have a parrrty at the top once the animals werrre settled. Old Emile Galy would brrring his harrrmonica and serrrenade us all.'

She smiled at the memories.

'So why did you stop going?'

Annie's heart started thumping. If she was going to tell the truth, she might never get a better chance.

'Because I was prrregnant.'

'You weren't able to do it?'

'No, love. It wasn't that.' She took another drink, framing her next words. 'I'd only just found out I was expecting. I couldn't concentrrrate on anything else. So I stayed at the farrrm to give myself some time to think while Papa and Maman took the animals up.'

'And no one knew? No one suspected?'

'No.' She paused. 'Well, that's not trrrue exactly. Someone knew.'

'Who?'

Annie picked at the sodden label on the bottle, intent on peeling it off, and Véronique was sure she wasn't going to answer, but then she murmured, 'Thérrrèse Papon.'

'Thérèse?' Véronique stared at her mother, perplexed. 'But if Thérèse knew then how come . . . ?'

She came to a halt, brain working furiously as the cicadas chirruped against the gentle melody of the heavy bells that hung around the necks of the cows and from the distance came the sound of dogs barking. It took her a minute or two but then she gasped as Annie had known she would.

'That's why!' she exclaimed, gaze fixed on her mother. 'You didn't tell Serge because Thérèse asked you not to.'

Annie inclined her head in confirmation and Véronique shot to her feet and started striding up and down, muttering furiously, the cows shifting uneasily in her wake.

'You'rrre unsettling them,' Annie said softly.

Véronique rolled her eyes but resumed her seat, boots tapping on the grass as she focused on the mountains. It was a while before she spoke but when she did, her voice was sharp with bitterness.

'To think I revered that woman! Everyone did. She was the closest thing to a saint Fogas has ever produced.'

'Thérrrèse *was* a good perrrson, love. It's just she was placed in a difficult position. Thanks to Serrrge and me.'

'Don't defend her! What kind of woman would ask that of anyone? Denying a child the right to know her father and the father the right to even know he had a child? Why on earth did you ever agree to it?'

The fierce regard that accompanied the final question would have made most people quail. But Annie knew her daughter. Understood her temper. And she knew the worst was almost over.

'You've got to underrrstand how it was back then,' she began. 'The stigma. The scandal. Bad enough I was prrregnant. If people had found out I'd had a fling with a marrrried man too . . .' She shrugged. 'And besides, I felt I'd wrrronged herrr. Felt that perrrhaps agrrreeing to herrr conditions and saving herrr marrrriage would compensate forrr having had an affairrr with herrr husband . . . Not that it was an affairrr . . .'

'Spare me the details!' Véronique finished her beer, placing the empty bottle on the ground with great restraint when all she wanted to do was hurl it as far as she could, over the tops of the trees and into the valley beyond. 'Last time I ever put flowers on *her* grave!'

It was such a typical Estaque response that it elicited a laugh from Annie before they both lapsed back into silence.

'You need to tell everyone, Maman,' Véronique said at length.

'No! And neitherrr will you.'

'If you don't, they'll all think ill of you.'

'Like that everrr botherrred me!' She shook her head. 'Telling would forrrever tarrrnish Thérrrèse Papon.'

'So what! You don't owe her anything.'

'Maybe. But I owe Serrrge a lot.' Annie watched Véronique assess the last comment, take in the enormity of what unveiling the past would mean. 'I can't take the memorrries of his wife away frrrom him. Not afterrr everrrything.'

'So Thérèse gets to remain a saint while you get branded a heartless woman. Someone who let her daughter grow up alongside her father without either knowing the other existed.'

'It's not that simple.'

'Huh! So you keep saying, Maman.'

'If it wasn't forrr Thérrrèse Papon,' Annie said quietly as she placed the empty bottles back in the rucksack and stood up, 'you wouldn't be herrre.'

'What do you mean?'

'I wasn't surrre I could cope.' She let her eyes wander across the trees below them to the high peaks shimmering in the heat where a red kite was circling lazily on the thermals. 'Being a single motherrr in a place like this – I knew it would be difficult. So I was planning on giving you away.'

Véronique's hand reached for the cross at her neck. 'What changed your mind?'

'Who, not what. Thérrrèse came to see me. She wanted me to have an aborrrtion. Offerrred to pay forrr me to go overrr to England wherrre they werrre legal.' Annie turned to her daughter and smiled. 'Up until that moment, you werrre just a prrroblem. A terrrrible mistake. But when I hearrrd those worrrds, something shifted. I can rrrememberrr my arrrms instinctively moving to prrrotect my stomach, to prrrotect you. Next thing I knew, I was telling herrr I was going to keep you but that in rrreturrrn, I would neverrr rrreveal who yourrr fatherrr was. To anyone.'

Véronique was staring up at her, face pale, and Annie rubbed a broad thumb along her daughter's cheek, wiping away the tears that had gathered there.

'And you know what, my child, I've neverrr rrregrrretted it. Not once. But I gave up my position on the Conseil Municipal, rrrefused to take parrrt in the trrranshumance and stopped going to the marrrket, because life was easierrr lived out of the spotlight.'

She took Véronique's hand, raising her to her feet and into an embrace and the two of them stood there for what felt like an age.

'You should have told me,' Véronique whispered, pulling away to dry her tears.

Annie nodded, sniffling too, as she searched her pockets for a tissue.

'Perrrhaps I should have,' she said, dabbing her eyes. 'I rrrealise that now.'

And then Véronique kissed her cheek and Annie, thinking her heart could withstand no more, said gruffly, 'Come on, these cows won't walk themselves up that hill!'

She whistled to the dogs and got the herd moving again. The two women ambled behind, sun hot on their backs, both believing that this had turned out to be one of the best days of their lives. The only thing that could mar it, thought Annie as she looked back at the mass of clouds gathering over Mont Valier, was getting caught in the storm that was looming.

They poured it in an arc, liberally dousing the foliage that was already dry from the unrelenting sunshine, the smell astringent on the summer air. Up ahead on the small plateau, the men with dogs were holding the beast at bay as it huffed and grunted, pacing backwards and forwards, unable to escape.

She was bigger than he'd expected, impressive at close quarters, those paws powerful enough to break a man's back with one swipe. What a prize.

He whistled, a shrill sound that cut across the commotion, and the men with the dogs began to retreat. Confused, the bear rose onto her hind legs, assessing the diminishing level of threat, believing herself to be saved.

But when the men were safely behind him, dogs still baying, straining to get back into the fray, he lowered his hand and one of the hunters lit a sodden rag. With a casual flick, the ball of fire fell through space and landed on the soaked bracken. A whoosh of air and flames licked into life, running across the ground along the predetermined line.

And as the smoke spiralled up, twists of black blemishing

the brilliant sky, he smiled, his boar's-head signet ring flickering orange as the blaze took hold.

Arnaud slipped in through the back door and poked his head into the bar, not wanting to walk into a room full of angry hunters. Not that he couldn't take care of himself. Just that he was in a hurry and the fewer distractions the better.

But he was in luck. There was only Serge Papon, sitting at a table looking pensive, and through the archway Josette was talking to someone in the shop.

He hissed softly, catching the mayor's attention.

'Arnaud!' Serge beckoned him forward. 'What are you doing here?'

The tracker crossed the floor in three strides to shake the old man's hand. 'Wasn't sure you'd still be talking to me. Given all the protests!'

Serge slapped him on the back and called for Josette. 'Let's get you a coffee. And when did you last have something decent to eat?'

Arnaud ran a hand across his face, feeling his cheeks protruding, the newly grown beard still surprising him. 'A while ago.'

'Two coffees please, Josette, and—'

'Goodness,' Josette had entered the bar and was staring at the tracker, taking in his gaunt appearance, his grubby clothes and the earthy scent of the forest. 'You've lost weight! I'll get you something to eat as well.'

Serge grinned and gestured for Arnaud to take a seat. 'What brings you down from the mountain?'

'I need my laptop. It's in the box of stuff I left with you.'

Serge slapped his forehead. 'Christ. Clean forgot about it. Which will save you a journey up to Fogas as the box is still in the boot of my car!'

As he hurried out, Josette came back through from the shop with a plate of pâté, fresh bread, cornichons, a glass of wine and a mousse au chocolat. And Christian Dupuy.

'Well, well, well. This rough living suits you,' exclaimed the farmer as he shook hands. 'Good to see you, Arnaud.'

Arnaud nodded as he bit into the bread, the taste amazing after nearly two weeks of woodland rations.

'I heard about the attack,' he mumbled through a mouthful. 'Sorry.'

Christian shrugged, both hands raised. 'That's life. We overlooked her when we were taking the flock up to the pastures and I suppose the bear picked her off. Thought we were being clever getting the transhumance done early. Still, the compensation is good. Could have done with a few more attacks last year when things were tough!'

'So,' Serge said, as he caught the end of the conversation. 'Do you think this one was a genuine attack?'

'You mean the others weren't?' Christian looked from the tracker to the mayor as he sat down.

'That's what he thinks,' said Serge, indicating Arnaud. 'We don't have any evidence and his own agency chose to ignore his suspicions, so I decided it was best not to mention it to anyone. Seeing as what happened with the bloody report.'

The timing of the leak couldn't have been worse. Or better, depending whose side you were on. And it vexed the mayor that he had no idea who'd done it. No one had been in the town hall the morning Arnaud gave the dossier to him – Pascal, the first person who had sprung to mind when Serge was looking for a culprit, had only got back from Toulouse that afternoon, calling in to the office to pick up his stupid sunglasses on the way home, and Céline had been at the dentist. Besides, Serge would trust Céline with his life. Which meant someone from Arnaud's department must have leaked it.

'But that's . . .' Christian stopped, shaking his head in disbelief. 'If you're correct, that's a criminal offence!'

Arnaud nodded again, still chewing. He took a sip of wine and pointed at the laptop in Serge's hands. 'I'm hoping this will prove me right.'

He turned on the computer and began searching through his files while Christian and Serge continued to chat. Something he'd seen up at the Dupuy farm had made him think of some old footage from before the winter that one of the cameras in the forest had captured. But for the life of him, he couldn't think why.

He sifted through the video clips, the grainy images flickering across the screen until he got to the one he wanted. It was from the trap near the quarry, the pictures showing a bear with an unusual gait waddling into the barbed wire enclosure. At the time he'd been positive it was the elusive male. He'd raced up to the trap the following day but had found no clues other than the odd hair, and had been unable to track it beyond the quarry. Now he froze the picture and studied it in detail. Sure enough, the bear's right rear paw was twisted inwards, the result of a birth defect or some injury sustained long ago. It didn't seem to hamper his movement in any way. But it meant he left a very distinctive set of prints.

So, there it was. Proof that Christian's attack was indeed real. But not by Miel. It still didn't solve the question of the others though. How had they been staged, if in fact they had been? As far as he could see, apart from off the animal itself, there were only a few places you could get bear fur from. Especially fur that had traces of turpentine in it. And luckily for him, all of those locations were covered with hidden cameras.

He focused on the laptop again, this time starting with the new footage. He'd been so busy since the beginning of April that he'd stopped checking it, relying on his own observations instead of technology. Consequently there was a lot of film that he hadn't yet seen. Aware it could take some time, he finished his meal as he watched.

He was licking the last sliver of chocolate mousse off his spoon when he saw it. He jerked forward and hit replay. There. Miel, accompanied by her two small cubs, coming into the clearing up at the quarry. He watched her scratch her back against the tree that he kept coated in turpentine, a substance known to attract bears, and then she obligingly dipped under the barbed wire, leaving a large clump of fur behind. Once inside the enclosure, she reached for the bag of corn before shuffling offstage, reward in her mouth. Then the screen went blank.

Arnaud sat back, hand reaching for his notebook. He skimmed through the pages to where he kept a record of his visits to the traps. Then he checked the date on the video. Strange.

The film was taken on April 12th. Yet he'd been to that trap four days later and although he'd found traces that Miel had been there – a half-print, scat and of course, the missing corn – he'd found nothing else. He remembered being in awe of her ability to negotiate the wire without getting snagged. So what had happened to the fur?

He pressed play and within minutes he had his answer. It was the same trap but this time instead of a bear in the video, it was two men, one of them lingering, almost out of the frame. The second was close up, bending over the wire, torch in gloved hand. He looked sideways and spoke to his colleague and then he plucked something from the barbs in front of him. Fur. He held it out to the other man whose hand appeared up against the lens holding out a plastic bag, a boar's-head signet ring where a wedding ring should be. The bag and the hand withdrew and the second man walked over to join him. Walked right up to the camera, his face visible and—

'Any luck?' Serge asked. 'Find anything of use?'

'Nothing.' Arnaud closed the laptop. This wasn't something he was going to share. Not even with Serge and Christian. Because he no longer trusted anyone. Not when Miel's life was in danger.

As the tracker reached for his wine, behind him Jacques' focus was still on the laptop even though it no longer showed the visage of a man he knew well. The ghost stood there, shocked, trying to make sense of it all.

What was Pascal Souquet doing up in the forest in the middle of the night?

Chloé was bored and frustrated. A terrible mixture in any human being, but even more so in a ten-year-old. Maman had made her sit at a table under a parasol inside the gate of the garden centre, potting up cuttings and serving the odd customer. But Chloé was too restless to sit still. Instead she paced up and down between the table and the front gate like a tiger marking the confines of its cage, eyes constantly flicking up to the mountains behind the church. The place where Miel was. The place where the hunters had been heading and where she should be.

It was on one of her outward laps that she saw it. The swirl of smoke looping up into the cloudless sky. She watched for a minute to be sure. And it grew thicker, fatter, darker. There was no mistaking what it was.

Abandoning her station, she ran towards the bar where she knew she would find Christian Dupuy, narrowly missing an oncoming cattle truck as she bolted across the road.

He'd stayed away from the bar. From the épicerie. Not wanting to be incriminated. But he couldn't tear his gaze away from the horizon, waiting for the signal that he knew would come. When he spotted it, Pascal was surprised by how delicate it looked, a twist of grey gossamer on an azure canvas. It was almost impossible to contemplate what was beneath it. What was happening on the ground.

'Is that smoke?' Fatima was at the back door, hand shading her eyes as she stared into the distance.

'I think so.'

'A fire?'

'Looks like it.'

'Don't you think we ought to call the fire brigade?'

'I suppose so.'

'Suppose so? Honestly, Pascal! Trust you to stand around and do nothing when there could be lives at stake!'

She slammed the door shut, leaving her husband to watch the thickening clouds, her assessment of him, as always, accurate to a fault.

The hoot of a horn took the attention of the three men in the bar and they saw young Chloé scampering across the road, right in front of a cattle truck, the driver leaning out to yell abuse at her as she reached the kerb. Before they could pass comment, the girl was in the door and screaming.

'Fire! Fire! Up in the hills.'

Seeing Arnaud, she ran straight to him.

'Miel's up there. With the hunters. And now there's a fire!'

The noise had brought Josette in from the shop and even roused Jacques from his ruminations on the erratic nocturnal behaviour of Pascal Souquet, his face registering concern at the sight of Chloé so wound up.

'Now calm down a minute, Chloé,' said Serge, putting an arm around her shoulders. But she pulled away.

'I can't be calm! Miel is in danger.' Then she whipped

round to confront Arnaud. 'And what are you doing in here drinking wine? I sent you a text about the hunters. You should be up there.' She pointed a hand in the vague direction of the mountain, her voice breaking as her distress got the better of her.

'What hunters?' Arnaud asked, checking his phone where indeed there was a text. Sent several hours ago.

'They went past the house. With guns. Going up the mountain.'

Serge nodded. 'A big posse of them left here in the early hours. Went up the road towards Picarets with their dogs.'

Arnaud got up, face grave. 'And the fire?'

Chloé grabbed him by the hand and dragged him outside, the others following.

'Merde!' Christian muttered, looking at the dense plumes of smoke amassing above the mountain. 'That doesn't look good.'

He turned to speak to Arnaud but the man was already gone, running to his car which was soon screeching past. It spun round the corner opposite the Auberge and headed up the road to Picarets.

'I'll call the fire brigade,' said Serge.

'Best had. And I'm heading up there.'

'What for?' asked Josette. 'Probably some stupid tourist with a discarded cigarette.'

'Because Annie and Véronique are up there. On the transhumance.'

Josette raised a hand to her mouth, her other hand going down to rest on the curls of the young girl who was leaning against her, tears streaking her cheeks. Christian's last glimpse in his rear-view mirror as he turned for Picarets showed them still staring at the ominous grey clouds which had blocked out the sun and turned the tranquil sky violent.

18

Fire. She could smell it. She lifted her nose and sniffed again, a low groan issuing from her throat. Her cubs were up a tree behind her, sensing her fear. One of them moaned and she grunted a reply. Reassured it. Even though she knew they were in trouble, could see orange fingers trailing across the bracken. Fire.

They beat the ground before them, keeping the flames on the other side, focused on the area they'd marked out. With the slightest of breezes at their backs it wasn't difficult. Soon the dry vegetation was snapping and crackling, young saplings consumed, grass devoured and fallen branches scorched.

And beyond it, still visible through the flames, the bear. He watched transfixed as she twisted and turned, trying to decide how to escape. But there was no way out. Before her a sheet of fire and behind her . . .

He laughed. It was the perfect trap. No matter what she did, she was going to die.

'Who authorised it? That's what I bloody want to know.'

Serge could feel his blood pressure skyrocketing as he looked at the billowing smoke. Thick now, spreading out across the mountain in the stillness of the morning. Annie was up there somewhere. With his daughter. He held the receiver closer to his ear and moved away from the door, the worried voices of the group who'd gathered outside the bar drowning out the reply from the man on the other end of the phone.

'One moment while I find the file,' said a harassed Major Gaillard, Chief Fire Inspector for the Ariège.

Serge paced back to the bar, his old friend Jacques watching his every move from the inglenook.

'What the hell . . . ?' the mayor muttered. 'Who on earth would want to set a hill fire on the day of the transhumance? And who would be stupid enough to sign off on such an application?'

He'd called the fire department and when he'd said that there was a fire on the hillside above the old Picarets quarry, his panic had been met with mild amusement. Of course there was a fire, he'd been informed. Someone was burning off their land.

Only problem was, on whose authorisation? Because any agricultural burning had to have permission from the town hall. And he damn well hadn't signed any papers to approve such a thing. Nor would he have on the day of the transhumance when animals and shepherds were liable to wander upon a fire without warning.

So he'd called Major Gaillard, a decent chap at the fire department, even if they didn't always see eye to eye. And he'd asked him to find out who had sanctioned the fire on his patch.

'Hello? You still there?'

'Of course I'm still here,' Serge barked. 'What have you got?'

'I'm looking at the application forms and everything is above board. The farmer applied for permission via the town hall and then it was passed on to the planning department and on to us after it was approved. My boys were notified this morning that it would be taking place in . . . Oh, that's odd . . .'

Serge heard the shuffling of pages.

'You say the fire is in Fogas?'

'Yes.'

'But yet the permission was filed in Sarrat. Which is why you didn't know about it.'

Sarrat! Always bloody Sarrat.

'Have you got the name of the farmer?'

'Monsieur Louis Claustre.'

Claustre. The same man whose sheep had been attacked in the neighbouring commune. Who happened to co-own a strip of land within the Fogas borders which ran down to the edge of the old quarry above Picarets. Steeply banked and ending in a lethal drop, it had never been ideal for grazing, too many sheep having fallen to their deaths onto the rocks below. Claustre had inherited it, along with his three brothers, two sisters and five cousins, from a maiden aunt. With too many owners to make selling it easy, the land had been left untended for years. Why on earth was he burning off up there now?

'And who signed the permission?'

'Why the mayor of course, Henri Dedieu.'

Something wasn't right.

'Is there anything else?' Serge could hear the impatience in the fireman's voice.

'Could you send me over a copy? And thanks. You've been a great help.'

'Will do. Don't hesitate to call if it gets out of control.'

A click on the line and Major Gaillard was gone.

'Out of control,' muttered Serge. 'Things down here are already out of control.'

Still pondering over the bizarre news, he joined the growing crowd on the terrace, watching helplessly as the mountainside became obscured in wreaths of grey.

Véronique was up there somewhere. He hoped to God she was safe.

As if sensing his concern, Josette reached out and stroked his arm, Chloé still leaning against her, a small hand now clasped tight by her mother who'd crossed the road to see what was going on.

'She'll be okay,' Stephanie said to him and he tried to take heart from the fact that she was half-gypsy and rarely wrong in her predictions. But as he saw another belch of smoke spill over the edge of the mountain, he found it hard to believe anything could be okay in that.

The sky had gone dark. The air had turned thick and acrid. And the cows were spooked. They're not the only ones, Véronique thought as they struggled up the hill.

When they'd realised the problem it had been too late to turn around. They'd smelt it first, the unmistakable tang that went with fire. Then they'd spotted the spirals of smoke. Down below them. Right across the quarry road.

'We should turn back,' Véronique had said, nervous.

But Annie had refused. 'If we go back now we'll be walking strrraight into it and the cattle will stampede. Ourrr best chance is to keep going up. Whateverrr the firrre is, it will burrrn morrre slowly once it gets above the trrreeline.'

Véronique had accepted Maman's wisdom but now, with Maman not looking so good, her breath coming in gasps as the conditions got worse, she wasn't so sure. The humidity had increased, exacerbating the effects of the fire, and even Véronique was struggling. She paused, waiting for her mother to catch up, the cows having picked up their pace considerably, no longer needing encouragement to keep them moving. The fire was pushing them onwards.

'Just need a brrreathèrrr,' Annie wheezed.

Véronique handed her a bottle of water and glanced down the hill, immediately wishing she hadn't. The view was now hidden behind a bank of black cloud that was getting closer. Coughing, she focused on the path that stretched in front of them, trying to see through the haze. How much further before they got to the pasture? Another thirty minutes? And then what? Could the fire reach them up there?

'You ready?' she asked, trying to keep her voice calm. Annie nodded and they set off again, the cows now some way ahead of them, their broad shapes indistinct in the swirling smoke.

One foot in front of the other, thought Véronique, as she tucked an arm under her mother's elbow and got a grateful smile in response. Just don't think about what's roaring up the hill behind us.

Fire. An arc of it between the bear and the woods, and beyond it, the dogs. The men. At first the bear tried to rush the flames, but it was repelled by the heat. It turned, retreated to where it had been, on the edge, no way out. Then it tried again. But the blaze was too fierce, the area of safety getting smaller and smaller. The bear grunted and moaned, a high sound that carried over the roar of the inferno. It was trapped.

Following the track that started at the back of Chloé's house, Christian had made good time despite the smoke. It wasn't as bad on this side of the valley, most of it concentrated around the quarry. Which was precisely where Annie and Véronique were.

His concern made him pick up the pace once more, his long legs striding up the hillside, heart thumping in his chest as much with worry as with exertion. He was still some distance from the top when he heard the scream. High pitched, anguished. It stopped him in his tracks.

'Véronique!' he shouted. 'Annie!'

No reply. And then another scream. Piercing the smoke. He started running.

'Stick with it,' he called, surveying the men, knowing some of them would be losing heart. The heat was intense, sweat glistening on their faces in the flickering light as they beat the flames to control the conflagration, the bear just about visible through the wall of orange, her terrified cries audible.

'Not long now.'

He watched her charge at the fire again, only to be forced back. Then a piece of flaming bracken caught on an updraught and carried across the clearing to land on the bear's back. She screamed as her fur caught light, twisting and turning, driven demented as she tried to stop the burning. But in her panic, she forgot the danger, her frantic efforts to save herself carrying her closer and closer to the wall of fire until she brushed too close to a blazing tree.

Another scream, the sound primitive, raising the hairs on his arms. Completely aflame now, she was standing on her back legs, a grotesque parody of the dancing bears of old as she writhed in agony.

He heard someone retch. The man next to him, kneeling, throwing up. The rest of the men averting their eyes from the awful scene, unable to watch.

He faced the fire again and saw the burning shape stagger across the open ground to the furthest point, a zig-zag of flame. It teetered on the edge for a moment as if on a high-wire, limbs flailing. And then it tipped to one side and plummeted down into the quarry.

Like he'd said. The perfect trap.

He only realised he was smiling when he saw one of the men staring at him in horror.

'We're finished,' he declared. 'Let's get this fire put out as quickly as we can.'

They did as they were told. But not one of them would look at him as he passed. Not that it bothered him. They'd done what needed to be done. And now Fogas would be his.

They'd made it to the pasture which was blissfully clear, the air feeling pure and clean as they sucked it in, coughing and spluttering. They collapsed onto the flat rock while the cattle spread out around them, contentedly munching the sweet grass now they were out of the smoke.

For a moment or two they didn't speak and then a sharp wail from below made them both flinch. It was followed by a second agonised scream.

'It's just the firrre,' said Annie, a hand on her daughter's tense arm. 'Gasses escaping frrrom something, prrrobably.'

They waited a couple of minutes but heard only the cicadas and birdsong, as if this day was any normal summer Saturday.

'Chrrrist!' said Annie, head resting on Véronique's shoulder as they watched the thick bands of grey slowly begin to break up. 'Thought I wasn't going to make it.'

'I must admit, for a while there I thought I was going to be left without a mother. Which would have been a shame.'

Annie looked askance at her.

'Well, who else would I have shared these with?'

And like a magician, Véronique pulled two more cold beers out of the bag.

Christian came upon them from behind. It gave him time to ride the wave of relief that washed over him. It gave him time to wipe the stupid grin off his face at seeing them sitting there. And it gave him time to notice that they were laughing hysterically, Annie's head on Véronique's shoulder, Véronique's arm around her mother's waist.

'What's so funny?' he asked and the pair of them jumped and swung round.

They could have been twins. Two fierce Estaque faces, both surprised. And both of them black with smoke.

'Don't suppose you've got another beer with you?' he asked as he sank onto the rock next to Véronique. 'Came up here on a rescue mission for two daft women who got themselves stuck in a fire and it seems I wasn't needed.'

Véronique smiled and passed him her bottle, which was cold, he noted with amazement.

'Us Estaques know how to look after ourselves.' She grinned, all white teeth against the smudges of dirt.

'I'll drink to that,' he said, wiping a dark trace of soot off her cheek and taking a long swig of what was the best-tasting beer of his life.

'If we'rrre that good at taking carrre of ourrrselves,' muttered Annie, 'then I suggest we don't lingerrr up herrre.'

And with a still-shaking hand she pointed at the black clouds tumbling over the Toblerone-shaped Mont Valier. 'That storrrm won't be long coming.'

They'd seen the fire diminishing, the palls of smoke dispersing into mere twists and corkscrews. Gradually the mountain came back into sight and the crowd that had gathered on the terrace entered the bar and started ordering coffee. It was under control. Everything would be all right, they persuaded themselves, as they settled in clusters to talk over the events.

Drama being a known cause of thirst, Josette was rushed off her feet so Stephanie, presiding over a garden centre which had been doing slow business, shut the gates and came to help. With people reluctant to visit La Rivière since the protests had broken out, her decision wasn't likely to impact hugely on her takings and it meant she could keep an eye on Chloé, who seemed to have calmed down and was sitting quietly over by the inglenook, murmuring away to herself.

'She'll be fine,' Josette said in passing, seeing where Stephanie's gaze was resting.

Of course, Josette couldn't tell Stephanie why. Couldn't tell her that Jacques was with the girl, listening to her talking about Miel and the bear cubs. Listening to her relating all the amazing things you could discover from bear poo.

She placed a coffee in front of Serge as he pulled his mobile out of his pocket.

'A text. From Christian!'

The entire bar turned to face him as he read it and then exhaled.

'They're safe!' he exclaimed. 'Véronique and Annie. He's found them and they're okay. Drinking beer up on the pasture. That's my girls!'

Everyone cheered and Serge called out, 'Drinks on the house! We're celebrating.'

Rushing to get back to the bar, Josette didn't see the car pull up outside. Didn't see the man walk wearily up to the doorway. The first she knew was that everything fell quiet and then as she turned, she saw Arnaud Petit, face smeared in black, shoulders slumped. And those eyes. They held centuries of pain.

'What is it?' Serge asked.

'The bear.' Arnaud shook his head, unable to say any more.

'Dead?'

'In the fire.'

Josette would remember the silence afterwards. The weight of it. And then the wail of a child.

'Miel!' Chloé screamed, jumping from her chair and making for the door. Arnaud caught her around the waist as she passed and lifted her into his arms, where she started sobbing uncontrollably.

'She needs to go home,' said Stephanie, hurrying round from behind the bar to take her daughter. No one spoke. There was just the heartbreaking sound of Chloé crying. And then the words that would haunt their dreams for that night and many nights to come.

'But what about her babies, Maman? Who's going to care for them now?'

As they left the bar, Chloé's face buried in her mother's neck, a fork of lightning split the sky and thunder rumbled down the valley. Then the first heavy raindrops began to fall. Too late to save the bear, the storm that Annie had predicted first thing that morning had arrived to extinguish the fire.

19

'She's inconsolable.' Fabian placed the metal tray on the table and began to distribute the beers to the subdued group on the terrace in front of the bar, their glum faces at odds with the profusion of wild roses scrambling over the fence from the abandoned orchard. 'She's lost weight. Can't get her to eat, not even her bear diet sparks an interest in food. And for the first couple of days, she burst into tears all the time. At least that seems to have stopped, but she's not herself.'

He glanced across the road to where Chloé Morvan was sitting under a parasol inside the gates of the garden centre. Schoolbooks lying neglected on her lap, the young girl was staring into the distance, Tomate the cat curled passively at her feet.

'Poorrr thing,' remarked Annie Estaque.

Fabian shook his head in despair. 'It's her birthday soon. Stephanie says she's normally given a long list of present demands about now. This year, not a thing. Chloé doesn't even raise a smile when we ask her about it.'

'She's not the only one without a smile around here,' said Christian Dupuy. 'It's been a tough couple of weeks since that awful business.'

As though providing a suitable backdrop for the horrific events that transpired above the quarry, the storm that had begun that afternoon had hung in the twin valleys for the rest of the day and on into the next, the force of the thunder rattling roofs, the lightning scorching the ground in several places. As was always the way in such meteorological conditions, the power had gone out for prolonged periods as the heavy rain lashed the countryside, swelling the creeks and streams that had previously been almost dry. The water washed down the mountains, poured over the hillsides and thundered into the river that ran behind the Auberge until the weir was no longer visible beneath the torrent that cascaded over it.

On the second day, when the tempest ended, the clouds had cleared and the sun had emerged in a pale blue sky, the air fresh with the smell of summer and everything touched with the promise of a new start.

The atmosphere that pervaded the commune of Fogas, however, couldn't have been further from this natural revival. The fallout from the incident up above Picarets hung over everyone, a heavy shroud of collective guilt oppressing the inhabitants despite the beautiful weather. For it had been confirmed, and widely reported across the French media, that a bear had been unfortunately trapped by agricultural burning and had fallen to its death in the quarry. The body, identified by Arnaud Petit as that of Miel, the female bear, had been removed to the headquarters of the bear reintroduction programme awaiting formal identification from DNA comparison. Although considering the state of the carcass, the recovery of DNA was not a given as the charred remains were unlikely to yield anything conclusive.

So it was that when the rain lifted and the sunshine returned, the hunting lodge in La Rivière remained quiet, no protesters gathering outside its doors, no one lining the walls along the road. Some argued that the heart had gone from the demonstrations, the need for protest nullified by the death of the bear. Others argued that the burly men who had been so vociferous had been tamed by quieter voices, smaller people:

their children. For it was well known that the youngsters of the commune were in mourning.

Led by the Rogalle twins, the kids had taken to wearing black armbands adorned with a 'This Is Bear Country' sticker. Their faces perpetually sad, they sat morosely on the little red bus as it ferried them up and down for the last few weeks of school. The summer holidays, which normally dangled so tantalisingly in front of them with guarantees of swimming in mountain lakes and roaming the hills and eating plump bilberries straight off the bush, were banished from their thoughts as they agonised over the fates of the little cubs, Morel and Truffle.

In turn their grief was transmitted to their mothers who worried about the lack of appetite, noticed the lethargy and the fits of tears. And who were equally anguished at the thought of two young bears orphaned and alone in the big forest. Despairing, they turned to berate their husbands, many of whom were the very men who had been part of the group up at the quarry. Even the hardest of hearts, those who believed that what they had done was right and were prepared to carry on the protest, faltered before these women with their fury. And began to question their actions when they saw the misery of their children.

Slowly the tide turned. The stickers abandoned at the height of the disturbances began to reappear in car rear windows, thick black circles drawn around the outside to mark the passing of Miel. An enterprising soul at the market started selling T-shirts proclaiming a love of all things ursine. There was an upsurge in the number of farmers applying for grants for electric fencing and Pyrenean mountain dogs, regardless of the opinion of the anti-bear lobby. And that very morning, marking two weeks since the death of the bear, there had been a march down in St Girons organised by the children of the commune accompanied by their mothers. Walking silently through the town, their mournful appearance contrasting with the gaiety of the Saturday market, they were joined by throngs of supporters; no chanting, no hunting horns, it was just a dignified demonstration to show their revulsion at what had happened.

Chloé Morvan, however, had taken no part in these public lamentations. She hadn't been to school since the day of the fire. She'd barely left the house. And when she had, Stephanie kept a close eye on her as Chloé repeatedly expressed a desire to go and find the two motherless cubs, something Stephanie knew her daughter was capable of attempting if she got the chance. But perhaps the biggest indicator of her distress was that not once since the awful day had Chloé turned a cartwheel or performed a somersault.

It was no wonder, then, that the friends who'd converged outside the bar were so disheartened, the glorious June sunshine failing to lift them.

'Those responsible should be hanged!' muttered René as he shook a cigarette out of a packet and lit it, watching the smoke curl upwards towards the wisteria-covered trellis that arched over them, squares of blue sky visible between the patches of green. Along with the others at the table, he'd attended the demo that morning and was still feeling emotional.

'It's not that straightforward. We have no evidence that they knew the bear was there, so we'll never be able to prove that the death was anything but an accident.'

René glowered at Christian's voice of reason.

'Even though it took a group of hunters with guns to set the fire,' he grumbled. 'And a special dog trained to catch bears!'

He'd felt the death more than had been anticipated, turning up at the épicerie on his way home from work that fateful day, oblivious to the drama that had transpired in his absence. Christian had broken the news, expecting him to be shaken, as they all were, but not expecting the fury.

René had gone rushing out of the bar and down the road, heading for the hunting lodge where the four-wheel drives had reappeared. Armed with nothing but his fists, he'd stormed in the door and by the time Christian caught up with him – an enraged René fleet of foot for his size – he'd already lunged at the nearest man. Who happened to be one of the biggest in the room.

The farmer had been sure the pair of them would be beaten to a pulp. But instead the man simply absorbed a few punches, mostly to his solar plexus as René couldn't reach much higher, and then gently lifted René up and walked him to the door. The rest of the hunters watched passively, faces blackened, reeking of smoke, their eyes unable to meet Christian's as he followed his friend outside.

The guilt had been palpable.

Thinking he'd be relieved to have escaped a beating, Christian had been surprised when René tried to get back in the lodge. Despite the farmer's attempts to restrain him, René had wriggled out of the bigger man's grip and flung himself at the door. But it was locked. And no matter how much he pounded and roared, it hadn't reopened. Eventually he'd collapsed on the floor. It was when Christian bent to help him up that he noticed the plumber's shoulders shaking with grief.

'She was so beautiful,' René whispered. 'And the cubs. So young. What's going to happen to them?'

They'd walked slowly back, René confiding in the farmer the miracle behind his ursine conversion, the sheer beauty of seeing the bear and her babies in their natural habitat. He'd also made his friend swear an oath of silence on two counts: that he would never divulge the fact that René had seen the bears and that he would tell no one he had seen him crying. Conscious of the rage he'd just witnessed, Christian had eagerly agreed to both. They'd entered the bar in a sombre mood, and a fortnight on, it had yet to lighten.

'What we all know happened up there and what we can prove are two different things,' Véronique said, siding with Christian. 'So I wouldn't be expecting the police to charge anyone if I were you.'

'Huh!' The plumber took another long drag on his cigarette, fingers playing restlessly with the packet.

It was affecting them all in different ways, reflected Véronique. Having made great strides in his long-running battle to quit, the death of the bear had seen René start smoking again. As for herself, she found that her nights had become an endless torment as she relived that dreadful transhumance over and over. In her nightmares, her mother fell behind and was consumed by the flames, Véronique unable to help her.

At the mere thought of it she reached out a hand to touch her mother's arm. It merited a smile in return. They'd been lucky, that much Véronique was sure of. A bit later setting off, perhaps even a bit longer talking at their break, and their transhumance story might have had a different ending. As it was, it had been tragic enough. But Véronique had to admit, the heart-to-heart that day had done wonders for her relationship with her mother. While it would never be perfect, given all that had happened, she now understood some of the decisions Maman had made and could better accept the consequences that had arisen from them.

'Well, at least the demonstrrration has made the news,' Annie said. 'Perrrhaps that will turrrn a few souls who have always sided with the anti-bearrr faction.'

'It's already happening!' Josette was leaning out of the open window and she tipped her head towards the dark recesses of the bar behind her. The old shepherd was sitting in the corner nursing a pastis, a T-shirt from the market on his wiry torso outlining the top ten things about bears. 'Just goes to show. You can get a point across without resorting to violence.'

'Don't know about that,' muttered Véronique. 'We don't seem to be having much success with La Poste.'

It was already several weeks since she'd visited the regional headquarters with Serge, the pair of them putting their case for a post office in Fogas in person, and still they'd heard nothing back. She'd had bad dreams about that, too. Now she was beginning to fear they were about to come true.

Josette's face clouded over as the gloom settled once again on the group. 'It would be great,' she said with unusual venom, 'if for once things could just go smoothly in this commune.'

High above the downhearted group that was clustered on the bar terrace in La Rivière, Serge Papon was having the very same thought. He was labouring his way up the short track that led from the road end, where he'd left his car, to the top of the hill that loomed over the épicerie, a basket in his hand. The sky stretched blue from horizon to horizon, not a cloud in sight, and when he reached the summit, face scarlet from the effort, the view was breathtaking.

He left the basket on the small camping table that he'd already carted up the hill, along with two folding chairs which were now sitting empty as though awaiting guests. He must be mad, he decided, as he took a moment for his heart to stop thumping, hands on hips, chest rising and falling rapidly.

Before him, rolled out like a bumpy green carpet, layers of hills gradated in a procession of crests, each higher than the previous one until they scaled up to the towering peaks that dominated the valleys. Now late June, the snow that had draped the mountains since the end of autumn had melted, no more than sparse patches remaining. He always felt the mountaintops looked harsher at this time of year, their grey edges brittle against the brilliance of the sky, and was probably the only person in the area, apart from the owners of the ski resort at Guzet, who relished the first heavy snowfall after the summer that would leave the tops with a dusting of white once more.

But despite the stunning vista, Serge had Fogas matters on his mind. He'd finally heard from La Poste that morning and the answer had been a resounding 'no'. Despite the pleading and the appointment he'd wangled with the regional office, the decision had been made; Sarrat had been awarded the contract and would be opening an épicerie with post office within the following six months.

'Bastards!' he fumed, his anger fogging his vision momentarily. Not ready to sit down and mark this special day, he strode across the open space to look out upon La Rivière. It was like a toy town, cars tiny on the road, the church insignificant from this height. And if he lifted his head he could see the hill that lay directly behind Picarets, while to his left he could just make out the clock on top of the town hall in Fogas.

It was his favourite place in the commune. The only place where he could stand and watch all three villages at once, as though that would somehow cement the fragile relationships that bound them into a political whole. Thérèse had loved this spot too. So much so, that every year on her birthday they'd come up here for lunch. In the early years they'd thrown a blanket on the ground and spread out a picnic. Put the blanket to good use after they'd eaten a few times too, he remembered with a grin. But as they'd got older and Thérèse's health had started to fail, he'd taken to bringing a table and chairs despite the hassle of dragging them up the hill.

He'd done the same today, even though a blanket would have sufficed seeing as he was alone, his efforts partly to honour her memory by keeping things the way they had been but also to prove to himself that he was still fit. Now that he had a daughter, he found he was contemplating his mortality more than before.

Thérèse's birthday. The second one he'd celebrated without her. But what a change since the last one. His depression seemed like a half-forgotten nightmare, something that had happened to someone else. And he owed his new lease of life to Véronique.

Well, to Annie Estaque actually.

He shifted uneasily, aware that his infidelity during Thérèse's lifetime had led to him getting over her death and also aware that there was something not quite right in that. Something that perhaps he shouldn't be celebrating on this day of all days. But still, he'd known Thérèse better than any other person. And he was sure that she would have been overjoyed to see the change in him, perhaps would have loved to know that he had a daughter.

While he could never be certain of that, he knew without a doubt that she would have been furious with his present preoccupation with work, this having always been a time when he'd agreed to leave town-hall-related matters at the bottom of the hill. Bad enough that he was running late, the lunch hour long past, but as he looked out over the region he was responsible for, he couldn't put business matters aside. The black cloud that had settled above Fogas the day of the fire may have lifted when the flames died down, but it had left behind a veil of despondency that was tearing the commune apart. It was his responsibility to work out how to lift it.

So far, he hadn't been doing a very good job.

It irked him that he hadn't got to the bottom of the incident up at the quarry, none the wiser as to whether the bear had been killed in a genuine accident as was claimed by those present, or if it had been premeditated murder as most, including the press, seemed to think. In the days following the fire, the controversy surrounding Miel and the unknown fate of her cubs had been blazoned across the papers, and the city-dwelling journalists had taken great delight in depicting Fogas as a backwater populated by bear-hating peasants and governed by inept officials.

For Serge Papon, the unjust portrayal of his beloved commune hurt more than the accusations of incompetence levelled against himself and his colleagues because, if truth be told, he felt the latter had some legitimacy. Still fuming over the fact that the authority for a fire in his jurisdiction had in effect been granted by the mayor of Sarrat, he had yet to ascertain the reasons behind it. When he'd called Henri Dedieu, the man had patronised him insufferably, telling him that it was nothing to get so upset about. After all, the farmer, Louis Claustre, had the majority of his land in Sarrat and it being the bigger commune of the two, he'd naturally presumed that was where he should apply for permission to burn off.

Serge hadn't been able to argue. By then he'd received a copy of the application from Major Gaillard and as the fireman had said, everything was above board. The farmer had stated that he intended to carry out several controlled fires, mainly on his land in Sarrat, and only mentioned the tract of land by the quarry in the last paragraph.

From an administrative point of view, it made sense for Sarrat to have authorised it. But still, it rankled Serge that his counterpart had been so reckless as to allow an agricultural fire on a day when livestock was being accompanied up to the summer pastures, the place where the fire was set cutting across the only route up to that particular grazing. At the very least Henri Dedieu should have notified the town hall in Fogas and it was only thanks to good fortune that the bear had been the only one killed.

He sighed, thinking how quickly the euphoria he'd felt at hearing Véronique and Annie were safe that day had dissolved into worry and stress. And now he was going to have to call down and tell them that their battle with La Poste was lost. Even worse, he was going to have to watch as Josette's business went under and Fogas was dragged down with it.

As if he wasn't cross enough already, to crown his terrible morning he'd received a condescending letter from the Conseil Général commending him for revoking the rental contract with the bear tracker.

'Bastards,' he muttered again.

'My sentiments exactly.'

'Christ!' Serge whipped round to see Arnaud Petit standing next to the camping table. 'How do you creep up on people like that? And how did you know where to find me?'

'Bonjour, Serge.'

They shook hands, both sombre, and Serge indicated for him to take a seat. If Arnaud found it bizarre that the mayor was presiding over a table laden with enough food for two on top of a hill, he never said so.

'How are you?'

The question was superfluous. Serge only had to look at the man settling his large frame into a folding chair to know. Thinner, with a tension to his jawline as though his teeth were permanently clenched, his eyes stared out from his unshaven face with a brittle gaze. Arnaud was a whisper away from losing control.

'I hear you've resigned?'

A shrug. 'No other option. The agency and I don't see eye to eye over what happened.'

'Their hands are tied by politics,' replied Serge, understanding only too well the balancing act involved when negotiating a path through opposing factions. 'You know they can't go rushing in demanding criminal charges when it's impossible to prove what really happened.'

'We all know what happened,' Arnaud retorted, face darkening. 'They murdered that bear.'

'Most likely you're right. But how do you prove it? A big group of men. None of them willing to apportion blame. It won't be the first time a bear's been found dead in suspicious circumstances. And I daresay it won't be the last.'

'They're not even willing to prosecute,' fumed the tracker.

Serge gave a weary sigh. 'What's the point? Look what happened when that bear Cannelle was shot back in 2004. The man who pulled the trigger claimed self-defence and walked away without any criminal charges.'

'You're forgetting he had to pay damages.' Arnaud's voice dripped sarcasm. 'And he didn't even get to keep the pelt.'

'Like I said, sometimes you have to know when it's worth fighting. And when it's not.'

'Which is why I've made it easier for the agency by resigning.'

The intimation being, thought Serge, that the tracker had done or was about to do something that might have precipitated his departure anyway.

'Well, you're welcome to return to the flat if you need somewhere to stay while you work out what to do next.'

'I know what I'm doing next.' The menace was manifest.

'I don't think I want to hear,' Serge interrupted. 'Not if it could implicate me later. Although my gut instinct is to help you find the thugs that did this and hold them down for you while you give them the hiding they deserve.'

Arnaud's lips twitched.

'What?' Serge retorted. 'You think I'm past it?'

The man opposite raised his hands to placate the mayor. 'Nothing of the sort. But I didn't come here to ask for help. I came to offer my services.'

'How?'

'La Poste.'

Serge shrugged dismissively. 'They've turned down our final appeal.'

'And you're going to accept that?'

'I don't think anyone around here has the heart for another battle. Not after . . .' He gestured vaguely towards Picarets and the quarry. 'The entire commune is like a ghost town. Everyone walking around with long faces, talking in whispers. And the children . . . It's awful.'

'So a battle is exactly what this place needs,' growled Arnaud. 'Something to focus on.'

'And you're offering to help?'

Arnaud glanced around and then looked enquiringly at the delicious spread before him. 'Do you have time, or are you expecting someone?'

Serge laughed. 'It seems like I was expecting you. Why don't you join me and we can talk over lunch. Bon appétit!'

He tried to politely ignore the light that shone in Arnaud's eyes as he started piling his plate with saucisson, soft goat's cheese and chunks of crusty baguette. Serge poured them both a drink and waited for his unexpected guest to take a few mouthfuls, the man clearly ravenous. Finally Arnaud sat back and took a sip of wine.

'So this help you're offering,' began Serge.

'I'm offering you more than that. I think I might have found a way to kill two birds with one stone.'

He leaned in over the table and despite the fact they were totally alone and at the top of a hill, he began to whisper.

Down in La Rivière, René, Christian, Annie and Véronique were still outside the bar, talking in hushed tones and occasionally joined by Josette and Fabian as their work permitted. By four in the afternoon, business had eased off and finally Josette took a chair and put her feet up on the low wall that divided the terrace from the road.

'Has anyone heard from Arnaud?' she asked.

'Not a thing.' Véronique nodded towards the flats. 'He's not been back there since the end of May.'

'I heard he'd been sacked,' said René. 'That he'd moved on.'

Christian shook his head. 'Rumour has it he's still in the woods.'

'Chloé had a text from him,' piped up Fabian as he collected their empty glasses before going through to the shop to serve a customer. When he returned some minutes later with their coffees, his audience pounced on him.

'You can't just say that and walk off,' exclaimed Josette, still not used to her nephew's way of passing on news. 'What did it say?'

'Told her not to worry about the cubs. That they'd be able to survive.'

'And did she believe him?'

'Not a word. She brought down one of the books she has out of the library on bears and pointed to a section on infant mortality. Those poor things don't stand a chance. Probably dead already.'

Véronique groaned. 'I can't bear to think about it. The pain she's feeling and the suffering those cubs are going through.'

They all looked across the road to where Chloé was now serving a customer, placing plants in a bag with a face older than her years.

'So, did you find out anything else? Any idea what he's doing, if he is still here?' demanded Josette, convinced there was more to harvest from Fabian's store of gossip. But her nephew simply shook his head and sauntered back into the bar.

'Hopefully he's plotting revenge!' said René. 'If anyone can find out what happened up there, Arnaud can.'

Christian murmured agreement. 'I wouldn't like to bump into him on a dark night if I'd been involved, that's for sure!'

'I still don't know how they had the stomach to go through

with it. Those screams . . .' Véronique shuddered and René reached for another cigarette.

They fell silent, each burdened with their own thoughts, their own memories of the day. In the background the chirp of cicadas was high-pitched against the roar of the river as it tumbled over the weir and drifting across the air, the scent of honeysuckle came rich and sweet. If it wasn't for the gravity of their expressions, they would have looked like any other group of friends, enjoying a summer's afternoon.

'No point sitting here moping!' called a loud voice, startling them all from their reveries. 'There's work to be done.'

They turned as one to see Serge Papon striding towards them, his sleeves rolled up and an all too familiar mischief in his eyes.

'Christ,' Christian stood to greet him. 'I know that look!'

So did Jacques Servat who was inside the bar by the open window, his alternative life form not allowing him to venture beyond the perimeters of the business he had once run. He watched his old friend pull up a chair and he rubbed his hands in anticipation. This was going to be interesting.

'So you're thinking some kind of protest?' asked Christian when Serge had finished talking some time later. 'But something focused on La Poste specifically?'

Serge nodded and sat back, giving the group a chance to take in what he'd said.

'Well, we can't do a sit-in. Not unless you want to spend a day clambering around the lumps of charcoal over there!' Véronique pointed in the direction of the ruins of her old workplace.

'Doesn't carry much weight when the business is already gone, does it,' agreed Josette. She pushed her glasses up her nose, thinking hard but getting nowhere, not very good at the subterfuge that seemed to come so naturally to some of her friends.

'What about another demonstration?' asked René. 'Down in St Girons. Or even over in Foix. We could take a leaf out of the anti-bear protesters' books and throw something at the departmental offices!'

'Like what? Stamps?' Christian grinned and René thumped him.

It's working, thought Serge, watching the group become animated. Arnaud was right after all!

'Whateverrr we do, we need to get good coverrrage. Something that would attrrract the TV camerrras.'

Véronique stared at her mother and Serge could see she'd got it.

'What if they were already here?' she asked, as Fabian sat on the wall to join in.

'Why on earth would they be here? They couldn't get out of the place quick enough once things died down over the bear and showed no interest in the children's march this morning.'

'Josette's right,' added Christian. 'Once in a lifetime that was, Fogas on the evening news.'

'I'm not thinking about the evening news,' Véronique said and Christian noticed how her eyes were now shining in an uncannily similar way to her father's.

'What then? When else do we get the honour of being on the tele—' He stopped and slapped his head. 'Of course!'

Véronique nodded, clapping her hands with excitement.

'Hope you'rrre going to sharrre it with the rrrest of us!'

'The Tour de France, Maman. We can disrupt the Tour de France.'

Fabian, who had just taken a well-earned sip of coffee, was only saved from choking by a resounding slap on the back from René.

'You can't do that!' he protested once he'd got his breath back. 'The Tour is sacrosanct. It's the greatest sporting event on the planet. You just can't . . .'

The passionate cyclist spluttered to a halt as he took in the faces of the people looking back at him. Radiant. Focused. And determined. And that didn't even include the face he couldn't see, that of Jacques, one time semi-professional bike rider who, like the others, was already weighing up the options this amazing opportunity offered them. Live coverage on national television. Just think what they could do!

'It's been done before,' offered René as an act of concili-ation. 'They had to change the start of a stage one year in the Alps because of protests about the reintroduction of wolves over there.'

'And I heard of a case where farmers blocked the road using tractors and manure, to protest about falling meat prices,' added Christian.

René's eyes lit up. 'Manure! Now there's an idea.'

'But . . . but . . .' The Parisian was lost for words at what was being suggested.

'Fabian, you need to understand.' Serge spoke for the first time, putting an avuncular arm around the young man's thin shoulders. 'This is a matter of life or death. If we do nothing, this commune will disappear. And the épicerie along with it. That's how important this is.'

'I understand that. I do. But it's just . . . the Tour . . .'

'The Tour will survive. And we will become part of its legend.'

'And no one will get hurt?'

Serge let his silence be understood as consent, unwilling to speak an untruth. He had plans that might include Sarko the bull and whenever that beast was involved, it was impossible to say nothing would go wrong.

'Well in that case . . .' Fabian paused, not quite believing he was condoning such a thing. 'But there's only one problem. The Tour doesn't come up this part of the valley this year.'

Expressions fell around the table.

'Nowhere near?' asked Christian, knowing that sometimes La Grande Boucle, as it was known, swept through St Girons without even a passing glance at the mountain roads around Fogas.

'It comes over the Col de la Core and drops down into Seix, and then goes over La Trappe and down the Garbet valley.'

Heads picked up again, hearing that the cyclists would be riding over two mountains to emerge in the next valley.

'But then it turns off for the Col du Saraillé, coming out onto our road much higher up in Massat.'

'So it effectively cuts out our corner altogether?' asked Josette.

Fabian nodded.

'Well that's that ruled out then,' conceded René as he reached for another cigarette.

The group looked to Serge as if to say 'What next?' but rather than being disappointed, he was grinning. And so was his daughter.

'What?' asked Christian. 'Can you see a way round this?'

'Oh yes,' said Serge. 'Most definitely. But it will take some organising. And complete secrecy. And possibly a bit of danger.'

He surveyed the faces around him.

'So who's in?'

Seven hands shot into the air. But of course, Serge could only see six of them.

Across the road, Chloé didn't even notice the huddled group, the contained excitement on the terrace. She was miles away, eyes fixed on the hills behind the church where the fire had started.

She needed to get up there. The orphaned cubs needed her help. But how was she going to do it when Maman was watching her all the time, never letting her out of her sight?

'Chloé, do you want to go and get an ice cream? You're owed something after working so hard!'

Maman was holding out a five-euro note, head tipped to one side as she studied her daughter. She was also using 'that' voice. The one she'd been using with Chloé since the day Miel died. As if Chloé was too fragile to be spoken to normally.

Chloé shook her head. She had no desire for ice cream. She wanted to be allowed up into the mountains. Maman sighed, returned the money to the till and continued sorting out the greenhouse where the plants were growing vigorously in the perfect conditions.

Putting a hand to the pocket of her shorts, Chloé felt the comforting rectangle that was her mobile phone. It was days since Arnaud's text. She'd sent a reply but had heard nothing back, not even knowing if he was still up there. Hopefully he'd found the cubs by now if he was.

She kicked her heels against the chair in frustration. It was so unfair. All the people in the commune were talking about how awful the fire had been, how terrible it was that Miel had been killed. Yet no one was doing anything about Truffle and Morel.

Would they still be alive? Her throat clenched and tears stung the back of her eyes. Not now. She couldn't cry here. Maman would start fussing over her again like she was an invalid and she'd never get away.

A simple connection fused in her ten-year-old mind.

Maman was only treating her like this because she knew Chloé was upset. If she thought Chloé was better, then perhaps she wouldn't be so strict.

That was it! She was going to have to pretend she was happy. Make out that she had forgotten all about the cubs. It was like the reverse of the way Josette had to pretend that Jacques wasn't around anymore.

She fixed a smile on her face, her cheeks stiff from lack of practice. Too much? Maman would suspect if it was too sudden. So she tempered it, feeling her lips with her fingers to make sure it was about right. Then she strolled over to the greenhouse.

'I've changed my mind, Maman. Can I have an ice cream?'

Maman put down the flowerpots she'd been arranging and embraced her child.

'Of course you can, love,' she murmured against Chloé's curls. She leaned back and stroked the pale cheeks before her. 'It's just wonderful to see that beautiful smile after so long.'

Chloé managed to keep her expression fixed while Maman gave her the money. She even managed to maintain it as she crossed the road.

'Ice cream, Chloé?' Fabian called out at the sight of her.

And she nodded, all eyes on her as she walked into the shop behind the tall Parisian. It was only Jacques who saw the shift of mood, her lips falling the minute she thought no one was looking. But as soon as Fabian started asking how she was, she lifted them again.

She hoped, as her muscles began to tense under the effort, that it wouldn't take long to convince Maman that she was no longer sad. Because Chloé didn't think she could keep this up for very long.

20

Colour. That was the first impression as you drove into La Rivière from Massat on the thirteenth of July. Starting at the hunting lodge, twisting around the lamp post and then over to the old school, crossing to the garden centre and then back to the épicerie, round another lamp post, looping over the gutter on Josette's garage, over the last streetlight, a string of red, white and blue bunting zigzagged down the village. And at the very end of it was René Piquemal, at the top of a ladder, attempting to tie the final bit to the Auberge des Deux Vallées.

'Hold it steady now!' he warned as he stretched out a short arm to reach the metal bracket from which hung the sign for the Auberge.

Given the difference in stature, really it should have been Christian Dupuy up there, but the farmer's severe aversion to heights rendered him more useful as the man at the foot of the ladder. Something René was cursing as he tried once more to poke the end of the string through the bracket and catch it on the other side. But it was no use. Every time it slipped out before he could grab it. He glanced down, making sure that Christian was paying attention, and then leaned precariously to the left. Nearly there.

At that precise moment Véronique walked across the bridge, wheeling a barrow full of geraniums. She parked her load opposite the Auberge next to wooden barrels filled with soil that Alain Rougé had brought down earlier. Christian didn't even know he was doing it, his eyes sliding from the view of René's backside to the much more seductive sight of Véronique Estaque, trowel in hand, her jeans curving beautifully as she leaned over to plant the flowers. And he forgot all about the plumber up above him.

'Christiaaaaan!' Having stretched a fraction too far, René felt everything tipping sideways, the bracket looming close enough for the bunting to thread through it with ease.

'Sorry!' Christian jerked his attention back to the ladder which had slid drunkenly to the left and gave a heave to right it, nearly toppling René off it in the process.

'Merde!' he fumed, glaring down at the red-faced farmer, Véronique laughing at the pair of them in the background. 'You nearly killed me!'

'Sorry,' the farmer mumbled again. 'But at least you got it tied.'

René finished off the knot, tugged on the bunting to make sure it was secure, having no desire to go back up the ladder for a while, and climbed down.

'It looks gorgeous!' announced Véronique, trying to mollify the seething plumber.

And it did. The bunting had lifted the whole village and was complemented by the red and white geraniums that Stephanie had procured which had been placed in bright blue window boxes, some in glazed blue pots and the others in the wooden barrels that Véronique was preparing. The atmosphere was definitely festive.

It had been a manic three weeks. Under the guise of a fête to celebrate the fourteenth of July, Serge Papon had encouraged, cajoled, bullied and terrorised the population of La Rivière into tidying up the village. Shutters had been painted, gardens tended, roofs patched, windows cleaned, and the anti-bear graffiti that had adorned the old school building since late April was finally scrubbed off. The lay-by got a makeover too, the trees and bushes that encircled it falling victim to Bernard Mirouze and his hedge trimmer. Even the hunting lodge was targeted, the hunters putting up no resistance when asked to clear up its grounds and give the woodwork a lick of paint.

With the festival to celebrate France's national day traditionally held up in Fogas in the car park of the town hall, naturally questions had been raised about this sudden relocation. Pascal Souquet was among those curious to know the reasons for the changes but Serge had shrugged him off, saying it was about time La Rivière shared in the celebrations. And what celebrations they were going to be!

The mayor himself was standing in the gardens of the Auberge, watching Alain Rougé and Monsieur Webster, the owner of the hotel, erect a marquee, the white sides flapping like sails in the breeze. Nearby, Madame Webster and Stephanie were busy wiping down tables and chairs while Tomate the cat darted in and out between their legs, adding to the commotion.

All this preparation, but would it work? Serge felt a knot of tension in his stomach. The one thing he couldn't predict was how the inhabitants would react when they realised what was really going on, which was crucial. Because if they didn't endorse it straight away, the idea was doomed.

Of course, it would be far easier if he could tell them the truth, but he didn't dare. Didn't trust them. Not all of them and most certainly not his first deputy. Serge remained sceptical about Pascal Souquet's involvement in the whole post-office business, suspecting that he had let slip to the mayor of Sarrat the excellent plans that Véronique had come up with. Which meant that Serge couldn't take the people of Fogas into his confidence just yet.

Instead he'd had to circumvent the problem. First he'd made sure that everyone heard about the latest knock-back from La Poste through the vine of gossip that connected the three villages. He'd even had Céline make up a newsletter which had been distributed to all houses, stressing the need for them to fight this rejection which could threaten the very heart of their commune. But when pressed to say what exactly he meant by fight, he'd remained deliberately vague. Murmurs had begun, some of them started by the small group in the know, suggesting that a protest ought to be mounted. An idea favoured by many. But still Serge Papon held back, telling them that they needed to wait for the right moment.

And that moment was tomorrow. He would have a window of about two hours to get them behind him and organised. Could he do it?

He had to. There was no alternative.

Satisfied that preparations were under control, he wandered back out to the road where Christian and René were putting a ladder on René's roof rack.

'All done?'

Christian nodded.

'And the other thing? Our Plan B?'

'He's on his way. I hope you know what you're doing!'

Serge chuckled. 'Not a clue, actually.'

As he walked off under the canopy of red, white and blue flags, Christian could well believe that was true.

'How beautiful! Wait until Chloé sees this!' Stephanie Morvan exclaimed as she emerged from the Auberge garden and took in the sight of the fluttering bunting.

'How is she?'

Stephanie wrinkled her nose. 'A lot better. But sometimes I catch her unawares and she still seems so lost.'

'She's not with you today?'

'No, she's up with the Rogalle twins. It's her birthday and she begged to be allowed to play with them so I relented.'

Christian rolled his eyes in dismay. 'Her birthday! I completely forgot. I'll pop in later with her present, okay?'

'She'd love that.' Stephanie waved a hand and followed the stout figure of Serge Papon up the road, secure in the knowledge that her daughter was on the mend.

Chloé Morvan was nowhere near the Rogalle twins. Although her mobile phone was. Afraid that Maman might try to check up on her, she'd given them her phone and told them to say she was doing cartwheels if it rang. Not that she'd turned a cartwheel in ages. She'd done her best to convince her mother that all was well, smiling when spoken to, eating the food that was placed before her though it tasted of cardboard, and sometimes even asking for seconds. She'd only managed that once or twice and had been nearly sick afterwards.

The only thing she hadn't been able to fake over the last three weeks was her acrobatics. When Maman has asked why she wasn't making the most of the beautiful weather by practising in the garden, she'd claimed to be injured, telling her mother that her shoulder hurt too much to do somersaults. As if! There'd been many days before the fire when she'd gone outside to work on her skills with her body still bruised from the session before. Not once had that deterred her. But lately it had proved a useful excuse.

She pushed aside bracken and branches on the track she was following, the foliage encroaching thanks to an amazing growing season. It had taken her longer than she'd anticipated to gain enough freedom to mount a search for the orphaned cubs, Maman not fully believing the façade of the happy child Chloé had created. And to be honest, Chloé no longer had the energy to maintain her pretence. So she needed to make the most of this precious stolen time. She had to find them today or give up all hope of them surviving. But of course, finding them was proving a lot more difficult than she'd expected.

Already halfway towards the quarry, there had been no sign of bears. Thanks to the books from the library and a school project that had verged on a dissertation, Chloé knew what to look for. Scat, for one thing. Which was just a fancy word for poo. And then fur on trees, snapped branches that might indicate the presence of a large animal and imprints in any area of soft soil.

So far, nothing. Pausing to shift the small rucksack on her back, she felt its weight disproportionate to its size. She'd forgotten to bring water and was already feeling thirsty, the heat heavy in amongst the trees where the cooling breeze didn't blow. She was about to set off again when she felt it: a sense that she wasn't alone, like she got when she was near Jacques.

'Bonjour?' she called out, trying to sound confident.

No reply, only the sound of a stream burbling over to her right.

But it was still there, her gypsy awareness telling her that someone else was present. She was thinking about running when he stepped out of nowhere; one minute the forest was empty, the next he was standing right there in front of her.

'Arnaud!' she squealed and ran towards the big man.

'Shh!' He clamped a hand over her mouth, smiling down at her. 'Keep your voice down!'

She nodded to let him know she understood and he released her.

'What are you doing up here, young Chloé?'

'Looking for the cubs.'

'All by yourself?'

'No one else seems interested.'

He studied her, stroking his beard which was now quite full, giving him an older demeanour. 'I thought I told you not to worry about them?'

She sighed, hand on her hip as she gave him a look of derision. 'I looked up their chances in one of my books. It's not good. Left alone, cubs that age can't survive.'

He raised an eyebrow, impressed with her knowledge. 'So how did you get up here without your mother knowing?'

'It's my birthday. I asked if I could play with some friends and she couldn't refuse. Especially as I've been so upset.' She gave a cheeky grin and Arnaud laughed softly.

'Well in that case . . .' He looked around as though checking they were still alone and then slipped the rucksack off her shoulders, his face a picture as he felt the weight.

'What have you got in here? Rocks?'

'Jars of honey, some bilberries, a bit of chicken from the Rogalles' fridge as we don't have much meat at home because Maman's a vegetarian, a tin of tuna and some popcorn.'

Arnaud stared at her, a smile lighting up his dark features.

'It's for the cubs,' she explained. 'I thought they might be hungry by now. But I forgot to bring water. Could I have some of yours?'

He passed her his water bottle and when she'd had a drink, he took her hand.

'So where are we going?' she asked, falling into step beside him.

'Somewhere you can't tell anyone about.' Arnaud Petit looked down at the small girl and wondered at how the residents of Fogas kept making him break his silence when it came to bears. But he'd made the right decision with René Piquemal. He was confident he'd made the right decision now. Besides, it would be common knowledge soon enough.

★ ★ ★

Which way would it fall? That was the question preoccupying Bernard Mirouze a couple of hours later on a hillside above the Garbet valley, some distance from where Chloé and Arnaud had been walking.

He stood back from the ash tree and looked at the road again. If he wanted the tree to fall to the left, should he make the first incision on the right? Or did he make it on the left? He scratched his head, painfully aware that as a *cantonnier* he really ought to know this stuff. But he'd never been confident when it came to using the chainsaw, which was why the communal Christmas tree was always such a sorry specimen; his options were limited by his inability to fell anything that couldn't be cut with a bow saw.

So he'd listened intently when Christian Dupuy had explained the science of felling to him in a whispered huddle in the bar. It had sounded so straightforward. Make a notch. Make a deeper cut opposite it. And wham. A fallen tree.

Only now, as he stared up the length of trunk that stretched above him, it was difficult to remember exactly what the farmer had said. And if he got it wrong, Serge the beagle could end up an orphan like those little cubs that were roaming the forest pining for their dead mother.

Tears sprang to his eyes, as much for his dog as for the bears. Even though he knew René would take him in, having developed a sudden affection for the beagle, taking him for long walks in the forest which Serge clearly enjoyed.

He sniffed, and wiped his T-shirt sleeve over his face.

So, what was it to be: a left cut or a right cut? And did it make a difference that the tree was leaning downhill slightly? As long as he was prepared to move quickly, he decided, it wouldn't matter either way really. One more tree down in the forest wasn't exactly going to draw attention.

He placed the chainsaw on the ground and gave a sharp

yank to the pull cord. Nothing. Another tug and the engine turned over but stalled. Flexing his shoulders, he gave it one more go. The motor roared into life, shattering the tranquillity, and Bernard approached the trunk. Standing uphill from the base, he touched the bark with the saw and it was only as splinters started flying that he remembered his safety goggles were in the car. Which he'd parked down in the village of Oust to deflect suspicion.

Squinting to avoid the worst of it, he persevered and made the notch as Christian had advised. Now to make the cut opposite. He stood back, turned off the saw and as he prepared to change sides he heard an almighty crack. Instinct was what saved him. Leaping backwards, he felt the whoosh of air as the tree toppled over, the bottom kicking up before his face as the trunk fell down the hill.

Merde! He hadn't been expecting that! He picked himself up and inspected his handiwork. Not bad, but totally in the wrong place. He scratched his head again and chose another victim, this time going for one that wasn't on such an incline.

The chainsaw started on the first attempt, teeth biting into the wood with ease. Again he made the notch, going no more than a third of the way through. Learning from his mistakes, he stepped promptly back once he'd finished and waited a few seconds to see if anything happened. The ash remained standing.

He was getting better at this, he thought, proud of himself. He waddled round to the other side, started the saw and made the straight incision, cutting two-thirds of the way through and just above the point of the notch that was already there. He felt it begin to move as Christian had said he would, the gap around the saw widening as the tree began to fall. Only thing was, he thought with bemusement as the top of the ash crashed into the forest, it wasn't the way he needed it to go.

Which was just as well, he considered as the branches settled on the floor, because he'd been standing exactly where he'd wanted it to be.

With a sigh he walked back onto the road and surveyed his achievements. So far, two felled and he still hadn't got any closer to doing what he'd been told. He was going to be here all night.

'Seems like you need a hand.'

The voice was right next to him, deep and menacing and enough to make him drop the chainsaw and scream.

'Christ!'

Arnaud Petit watched the reaction with amusement. Only Chloé Morvan seemed able to sense his presence, the rest of the inhabitants of Fogas repeatedly mistaking him for the Messiah.

'Where did you come from?' demanded Bernard, wincing as he realised that the chainsaw had landed on his foot.

Arnaud flicked a hand at the depth of forest behind him. 'Serge said I might be of help.'

'Do you know anything about cutting down trees?'

The tracker reached for the chainsaw, a smile curving across his face. 'Just tell me where you want them.'

It took nearly two hours but by the end of it the result was better than the *cantonnier* could have hoped for. Bernard had even been trusted to fell the last tree on his own, although he'd noted that his mentor had stood some distance away throughout the process. Still, it had been successful, the final bit falling into place exactly as Serge Papon had wanted.

They'd even added the *pièce de resistance* using the paint Christian had given him, Arnaud's interpretation intensifying the overall effect. It was amazing. And it was bound to work.

'We all done then?' asked Arnaud, edging back towards the forest.

'Well . . .' Bernard began. 'If you have time, do you think you could teach me how to sneak up on people?'

Arnaud took in the rotund belly, the wide backside, the moonlike face which was staring at him with open admiration.

'Sure,' he said, beckoning the man forwards. 'Why not?'

While Arnaud was trying to teach Bernard the basic skills of stalking and wondering what the Iroquois Indians would make of the lumbering *cantonnier*, across several hills, below the scar that marked the old quarry, in a small cottage with vibrant shutters two people stood at the window, arms around each other. They were watching a slight figure in the garden, a blur of colour as she performed somersaults, back-flips and even landed three aerial cartwheels in a row for the first time in her life.

As she stood upright, facing her audience, a wide smile transformed Chloé Morvan back into the child they'd once known.

'I don't know where she's been,' murmured Stephanie, as she watched her daughter begin her routine once more, 'but she's home now.'

'She was at the Rogalles',' replied Fabian in his customary prosaic way, having no sixth sense at all.

Stephanie smiled and drew him down for a kiss which Chloé spotted out of the corner of her eye, just as her feet were suspended over her head. She lost her concentration and collapsed in a tangle of arms and legs, issuing a groan more of embarrassment at the adults than at the shock of her landing.

Her complaint wasn't loud enough to be heard down the road where the forest gave way to a small plateau that led to the Estaque farmhouse. But even if it had been, the inhabitants were too busy to have noticed. Annie and Véronique were sitting at the kitchen table which was covered with paint pots, paper, glue, scissors, a sewing machine, fabric and wool. A pile of cardboard boxes marked 'William Saurin Coq au Vin' and 'Café Grand-Mère' was stacked to one side. They chatted quietly as they worked, Annie paintbrush in hand while Véronique bent over the sewing machine that had occupied a lot of her time for the last few weeks, the whirr of the needle punctuating their conversation. They discussed the transfer of the farm to Christian, the plans Serge had for the following day and of course, the news that Eve Rumeau was now dating a civil servant over in Foix.

While the two Estaque women laboured away, down at the Auberge the wooden flooring was being put inside the marquee and Paul Webster was up a ladder, tying an enormous piece of fabric to the PVC roof of the big tent. It had taken his wife, Lorna, two days to make it. But it was worth it. Grinning at the thought of the impact it would have tomorrow, he raised a thumb to René down below and then descended. Lorna was standing at the foot of the ladder, face pale, one hand on her stomach. He gently folded her into his arms.

'I'm thinking it's a boy,' she whispered with a smile. 'Only a male could make me this sick!'

Just up the road, Christian Dupuy was also feeling nauseated, but not for the same reason. His was the usual gastric complaint that Sarko the bull always seemed to bring on. He'd finally got him corralled for the night after the obstinate beast had led them all a merry dance, escaping from his makeshift quarters in the old orchard twice before they decided that an electric fence was not going to be enough to hold him. At a loss as to where to put him, Josette had come up with the idea. And it was brilliant.

As long as no one walked in on him by mistake!

The farmer closed and bolted the graveyard gate, tying a rope around the post to make sure no one could open it accidentally. He pinned the warning sign he'd made to the wood, a rudimentary drawing of a bull accompanied by a skull and crossbones, and then waited to make sure Sarko was settled. Ignoring the feed and fresh hay that had been left for him, the stocky bull was contentedly grazing the far extent of the enclosure where the land was still covered in grass, patiently awaiting the next batch of inhabitants to die. Christian had taken the unusual step of tethering him with a long chain attached to a thick neck strap but it didn't seem to be bothering him.

Hoping his animal would pass a quiet night and not destroy too many gravestones, and that tomorrow they would have no need to use him, Christian walked towards the shop. As he came down the alleyway by the ruins of the post office, Serge Papon emerged from the bar, hands on hips, eyes narrowed, like a general on the eve of a battle.

Unaware he was being observed, the mayor of Fogas looked out at the village and knew there was nothing more they could do until tomorrow. But what they had done was excellent and he felt an immense surge of pride for this Pyrenean community that had elected him as leader.

Josette didn't disturb his thoughts as she gathered up the last glasses from the terrace, wiping a cloth over the tables and chairs. But when she saw his expression, and saw Jacques standing in the window next to him in exactly the same pose, she knew that the following day would go down in Fogas legend.

'We're ready,' Serge muttered to no one in particular. And Jacques nodded in agreement.

21

*D*omestique. Stupid word. Better to call him a slave. A chattel. A drudge, even. All were more suited to his present position than the soft-sounding *domestique*.

Cédric Dupont, youngest rider in the peloton of the Tour de France at the age of twenty-one, was feeling irritable. With just under two weeks in the saddle, the sun beating down on his back and a tough day of climbing ahead, many would have forgiven him for feeling tetchy. But they would have been surprised to know, perhaps, that it wasn't that aspect of his chosen profession that was annoying him.

Nor was it the fact that for the last twelve days he'd ferried water up and down the long snake of cyclists, dropping back to the support car and then returning to his team-mates with eight cold bottles shoved down his jersey. He'd also been responsible for making sure that the food bags handed out by assistants at the side of the road were collected and distributed and he'd lost count of the number of times he'd had to sacrifice a wheel for a team-mate with a puncture. Which meant that when he finally got a replacement from the team-car, he had to ride like the blazes to catch up with the peloton again. Still, this hadn't bothered him.

As he'd expected, after racing every day he was last in line for a massage at the hotel, last in line for second helpings at dinner and first up for a shower every morning. On top of this, he was sharing his room with someone whose snores could trigger earthquakes.

All of that was normal, to be expected by the new boy. He'd even accepted that despite his willingness to play his role, to sacrifice himself for the sake of the team leader, he was being belittled at every turn.

No, it wasn't any of this that was upsetting the young man. But if he got called a bumpkin one more time, he was liable to throttle someone with a spare inner tube.

Born and bred in the Ariège-Pyrénées, his rural upbringing was a cause of mirth for many of the other riders. From the very first day in Belgium, where the rain had poured down and soured moods already fragile at the prospect of three weeks of riding a bicycle, he'd been the butt of the jokes. If they weren't calling him 'Methodical Jacques' after his famous cycling namesake and fellow Ariégeois, Jacques Dupont, who'd won Olympic gold in London in 1948 and to whom he unfortunately bore no relation, he was being called 'bumpkin'. Or 'yokel'. Or 'peasant'.

He'd thought when they'd entered the Pyrenees it would stop. Had hoped that when they'd scaled the Tourmalet, the Aspin and the Aubisque they would be too tired to rib him. And he'd naively believed that when they entered the beautiful Ariège, his homeland, they would be too awestruck by the scenery to tease him anymore. Fifty kilometres from the border and it didn't seem like it would be the case.

'Hey bumpkin!' The voice hailed from the front, its owner wearing the yellow jersey that marked him out as the race leader. 'Which one of these was your girlfriend?'

A snigger went up from the pack as they sped past a herd of grey cows which Cédric could have told them were Gascon. If he could have been bothered. Instead he bit his tongue and concentrated on the wheel in front of him, the countryside flashing past as they left the start town of Bagnères-de-Luchon behind. Soon they would be climbing, the first of many cols for the day, and that's when he would come into his own.

'Merde!' The man frantically reached for his mobile as he got out of the car and walked to get a better view of what had prompted his expletive. In his many years as an organiser of the Tour de France, he'd never come up against anything like it.

'We have a problem,' he said into the phone, not quite believing what he was seeing. His colleague was beside him now, aghast as he took in the scene.

'How big a problem?' came the reply, the sound of horns and traffic coming down the line.

'Big enough that we may have to change the route.'

He held the phone away as a stream of curses rained down on him.

'Sorry,' he said when the person on the other end finally paused. 'But that's how it is. We have an obstruction on the Col du Saraillé and there's no way we can move it in time.'

Aware of his colleague jabbing at the map he had brought from the car, he leaned in to see what he was pointing at.

'But I think I have a solution. Tell the publicity caravan to ignore the turning for the D17. They should continue on the D32 down to the roundabout at ... what's it called? ... Kerkabanac. Then turn right up the valley to the village of La Rivière. If we carry straight on up, we can pick up the route just before Massat.'

'What's the name of the village again?' The sound of a pen scratching across paper carried through the phone despite the other background noises.

'La Rivière. Obviously you'll need to ring ahead and get the roads closed. Wouldn't hurt to get the mayor onside too. You know how these provincial politicians can be about their little kingdoms.'

'So what exactly is this obstruction?'

The man stared at the road. Trees. Everywhere. But not standing upright. Instead they were criss-crossing the path in front of him, expertly felled so that the road was impassable. Apart from the odd one or two which had clearly fallen nowhere near their intended target.

'Someone has blocked the route with fallen trees.'

He heard more curses.

'But that's not all,' he added, his eyes now drawn to the crude paintings that were splashed across the tarmac. 'The road is covered in anti-bear slogans and there's even a gruesome picture of a teddy bear with a gunshot wound to the stomach.'

A deep sigh emitted from the phone. 'Bloody protesters. I didn't think they'd go this far.'

There was a pause and the man knew the race director, for that was who was on the other end of the phone, was thinking.

'It's time we taught these bastards a lesson,' the race director finally said. 'Get the helicopter to hover over the scene and broadcast it to the whole nation. Then they might think twice before interfering with my Tour again.'

The man hung up and smiled. His three children, who had still not recovered from the news that the bear Miel had been killed in this area leaving two orphaned cubs, would be watching TV back home in Paris. They would be overjoyed to know that finally someone was taking on the thugs who were probably responsible for her death. And even happier to know that their Papa had been involved.

He took photos of the scene, made the call to the TV crews to alert the helicopter and then he and his colleague got back in their car, turned around and drove away. It was only when the sound of their engine had faded to a putter that Arnaud emerged from the trees. He sent a quick text and began making his way across the hill to La Rivière. There was going to be a demonstration and he wanted to be part of it.

The call came at midday, as Serge had known it would, having already received a text from Arnaud Petit alerting him that things were under way. The mayor of Fogas answered on his mobile. A panicked representative of the Tour de France squawking down the phone about a problem with the route. Apparently there was something wrong with the road up to the Col du Saraillé in the next valley.

Serge made the right sympathetic noises. Then he offered assistance. Of course they could detour and come through Fogas. He would make sure the good people of the commune were assembled to greet them. No, it was not a problem. He would personally guarantee them a welcome like they had never had before.

He hung up and winked at Véronique who was standing to one side. Then he stepped forward to speak to the locals who had descended to La Rivière en masse expecting an afternoon of Bastille Day celebrations. There were children running around, parents, young couples, a large number of pensioners, a handful of teenagers and of course, a phalanx of second-home owners grouped around Fatima Souquet. Quite a turnout for such a small commune. And he was about to make the most important speech of his tenure.

'I have a bit of news,' he began, addressing them from the front steps of the Auberge. 'I've just been told that the Tour de France has had to make unforeseen changes to its itinerary. As a result, we are to be honoured by having it come through here this very afternoon.'

While the crowd erupted into excited chatter, he saw Christian shake his head in amazement, the mayor having delivered on the promise he'd made three weeks ago which the farmer had thought impossible.

'Now, before I go any further, I have to tell you that I have been keeping a secret, which isn't like me!'

A ripple of laughter came back to him.

'It's about the post office. And the future of this commune.'

Puzzled silence as the population failed to see the connection between the two topics.

'As you all know by now, La Poste has refused us a contract for a replacement branch. To add insult to injury, they have instead agreed that Sarrat will be the location for the new post office.' He paused, timing impeccable. 'And épicerie.'

They were muttering now, shooting dark glances across the river to the neighbouring commune.

'It doesn't take a genius to work out what that will mean for us here in Fogas.' He held up a stout hand and began ticking off fingers. 'Fewer visitors; a loss in revenue; a disastrous impact on our businesses; a disastrous impact on our pensioners; reduced local tax income.'

He gazed out across the upturned faces.

'Ultimately, it will lead to the death of this commune.'

A couple of gasps from some women and a sneeze from the old shepherd who was plagued with hay fever.

'A few of you have approached me over the past couple of weeks and asked what I was going to do about it. What *we* were going to do about it.' He swung his arm around to encompass the beautified village, the flowers, the bunting. '*This* is what we are going to do. We are going to welcome the Tour de France to our community. And then, live on national television, we are going to mount the most spectacular protest this country has ever seen! I couldn't do anything about someone killing that bear. But I'm damned if I'm going to let La Poste kill our commune!'

Stunned silence. A couple of claps. And then a shout of approval from Fatima Souquet.

René Piquemal, who was standing next to her through accident rather than design, did a double-take. And then he joined in. Which carried along the person next to him and their neighbour and Widow Aubert who was alongside a cheering Philippe Galy, and André Dupuy who momentarily forgot that he'd tried to throttle the bee-keeper down at the market not long ago. Soon they were all voicing their support, even the second-home owners who normally shunned local politics.

'So,' Serge roared, the din growing steadily, 'are you ready to fight?'

A thicket of arms shot into the air and Véronique and Annie stepped forward with the placards and outfits they had spent so long making. While they armed each inhabitant, Christian and René divided them into three groups: women, men and children. And in separate huddles they were told what to do.

Serge slowly exhaled, releasing the breath he felt like he'd been holding for weeks. The worst was over. Somehow, after twenty-five years of service, he still had the touch needed to bring these people together. Although he had to admit, he hadn't expected support from the likes of Fatima Souquet. He could see her already taking charge of her little brigade, face fierce, the rest of the women too afraid not to do as she asked. She was so different from her spineless husband. Which reminded him.

He searched the groups but there was no sign of Pascal Souquet. Yet he had definitely been present because Serge remembered him moving away from the old shepherd when he sneezed, a look of distaste on his elite features as though he feared he might catch some deadly disease.

But now he was nowhere to be seen.

Serge put it out of his mind. He had more to be concerned with than his stupid first deputy. In less than three hours, the world's biggest live sporting spectacle would be rolling into town. And there was still work to be done.

The phone rang unanswered, Pascal hopping from one foot to the other with agitation as he stood next to the ruins of the post office.

It was a master stroke. So typical of Serge Papon. The grand gesture that always turned out right. And now that he couldn't get through to his ally, Pascal risked being politically isolated, left in no-man's-land without support on either side. He'd seen his wife's reaction to the mayor's rallying call. Seen the group that normally cast their votes in his favour siding with Serge. So he knew the risk was real.

He paced across the small road to lean against the grave-yard gate, concentrating on his mobile and so failing to notice the piece of paper pinned to the wood behind him. He needed to think. This latest trick might ruin his plans. If Serge was successful today, which was a long shot but given the circum-stances might come off, then the post office and the épicerie would remain in Fogas and the commune would continue as it was with Serge at the helm. Possibly even prosper. In which case, the promises Pascal had been made would amount to nothing. Not yet, anyway.

If on the other hand the protest failed to change the opinion of La Poste, then things continued as before. Fogas would gradually fade and, using the new laws giving powers to local councils to merge communes, it would make sense for the failing community to be adopted by its larger, more prosper-ous neighbour to form a new political district. One which would have a thriving new épicerie and post office at its heart down by the Sarrat bridge. And a new deputy mayor.

So what to do?

Nothing, he decided. Or rather, not enough to cause suspicion. With Fatima behaving as she was, no one would guess that he was plotting to kill off the commune.

Happy that he'd resolved the quandary, he slipped the phone in his pocket and pushed himself off the gate. Which was when something smashed into the side of his face. It came out of nowhere and with enough force to knock him to the ground.

What on earth . . . ?

Rubbing his jaw, he picked himself up off the floor and looked to see where the blow had come from, only to find Sarko the bull tossing his big ugly head over the graveyard wall. Knowing his reputation for escapology, Pascal initially presumed the animal had arrived there by accident, especially as there was a length of chain hanging free from his neck strap where a tether had been snapped. Then he saw the warning sign he'd missed earlier. And the rope looping through the gate and around the gatepost.

Were they planning to use Sarko in the protest?

They must be mad! The bull was completely unpredictable and liable to be more of a hindrance than a help. Especially if he got loose.

Pascal rolled that thought around his mind a second time.

If he got loose. It could undermine all of Serge's planning if Sarko caused real damage. Maybe even injured a cyclist or two?

He didn't take time to think twice. Checking no one was around, the first deputy untied the rope and slid the bolt quietly back, leaving the gate unlatched. Then, in a moment of inspired cunning worthy of his nemesis, he ripped the warning sign from the pin and threw it over the wall before turning on his heels to flee.

It wouldn't take long for the crafty Sarko to work out he could push the gate open. And it might just prove the undoing of the arrogant Serge Papon.

Pleased with his efforts, when he got to the Auberge where Christian was marshalling the men into small groups, Pascal reached into his pocket for his mobile, intending to try one more call. But the phone emerged in his hand with a shattered screen, a busted case, and when he pressed the buttons, nothing happened.

He was well and truly on his own.

The announcement filtered through the peloton slowly. Already over the gruelling ascent of Portet d'Aspet, the riders were strung out along the road, trying to take on as much fuel as they could, chewing energy bars and swallowing isotonic gels in the hope they would reap the benefit on the next mountain. Needless to say, their preoccupation with getting their meagre rations down them hampered the speed with which they would normally have passed on such momentous news.

When it reached Cédric Dupont's ears, it was already old. Having got fed up with the cries coming through the radio from his *directeur sportif* in the team car who'd been screaming for him to stay with their team leader, a veritable elephant when it came to climbing, the young cyclist had flouted the team rules and pulled out his earpiece. Not seeing himself as a modern-day Hannibal, Cédric had decided that rather than nurse the team leader over the cols, instead he was going to do his own thing. This was his region and he was determined to try and win the stage with a breakaway. Even if it meant getting into trouble later on.

Free of distractions, earpiece bobbing on his chest, he'd moved forwards in the peloton and had managed to position himself in the lead group, holding his place over the steep climb. So it was that he first heard about the route change from the man next to him who, between bites of a banana, informed Cédric that the road up the Col du Saraillé had been blocked by anti-bear activists and a new route had been decided which would take them through the small village of La Rivière.

Cédric shrugged. It didn't change much. Just one less climb and knowing Col du Saraillé well, while it was a stunning ride, it wasn't much of a challenge. He ripped open a gel and squeezed the paste into his mouth. A far cry from his mother's cassoulet, still, a couple more of them should get him as far as the start of the Col de Port where he planned to make his move. Having grown up in the area, there wasn't much these mountains could throw at him that he wasn't already expecting.

22

A cacophony of horns split the tense silence. Then the publicity caravan came around the corner and for those on the floats that were the precursor to the race, tasked with giving away freebies to the waiting crowds, La Rivière was exactly like any other mountain village they had travelled through that week. Narrow roads, slate roofs, grey houses. And the villagers lined the route, shouting and cheering, ready to kill each other for a free sachet of coffee or a packet of washing powder. There was nothing to make the pretty girls on the back of the promotional vehicles think twice as they smiled sweetly and threw out packets of sweets to the excited children. Nothing to make them suspicious.

Although, perhaps if they had thought about it a bit more, they might have marvelled at how many people had turned out for an event that had been announced at such short notice.

As the last of the floats pulled out of the village, the passenger in the official race car that accompanied them called the race director.

'It's all gone smoothly,' he said, allaying the fears of the stressed man on the other end. 'In fact, the mayor should get a commendation. Big crowds, no trouble and the place is beautifully decorated. An excellent welcome all round. You're going to love it.'

He hung up without a backward glance and so was unaware of the mad dash behind him as the spectators left the roadside and took up their battle positions. And as he passed the slightly tatty-looking building at the end of the village, he was too busy making notes on the possibility of future Tours visiting this quaint community to spot the solid brown shape that was lurking there, chain dragging on the ground behind it, its baleful gaze tracking the car up the road.

The peloton had followed the new route without a hitch, most of the riders overjoyed at the thought of one less climb. Apart from the reed-thin man who wore the polka-dot jersey to signify he was King of the Mountains. He'd been hoping to extend his lead by grabbing yet another summit but instead, they had a long drag up a dull valley to reach the next col.

On the plus side, the detour had given the riders who'd been strung out at the back a chance to catch up and, as they turned right at the roundabout at Kerkabanac, all one hundred and eighty cyclists who had managed to survive the Tour so far were grouped together.

Cédric was quite content as he tucked in behind a bunch of older men near the front, legs pistoning up and down as they tore up the gentle gradient on a narrow tree-lined road, the steep sides of the mountains rising above them and the clear waters of a river rushing in the opposite direction to their left. They swung past a bridge with a sign pointing to Sarrat and then they were round the bend and the village of La Rivière lay before them. And an elderly lady was standing in the middle of the road waving a red flag. From farming stock himself, Cédric immediately knew what it signified.

'Slow down!' he hollered as loudly as he could, gesturing with his left hand at the same time. The cyclists around him reacted with lightning speed and the peloton was brought to a crawl.

'Therrre arrre sheep up ahead!' the woman called, standing to one side as they passed.

'What did she say?' asked the Yellow Jersey, perplexed by what was effectively a foreign language to his Breton ears.

'She said there are sheep on the road. That's why she's waving the flag,' explained Cédric.

'Bloody hell! Sheep. Trees. Dead bears. What kind of place is this?' muttered the race leader, looking around at the sleepy village with its auberge which didn't appear to have more than a handful of rooms.

Two minutes later, he found out, as they crossed a small bridge and were confronted with a flock of sheep which emerged from a small alleyway by a shop and blocked the route ahead. Only, the sheep were all on two feet and some of their fleeces looked a bit hastily made, bits of wool already coming off.

Sensing there was no point trying to ride through them, the sheep having formed a barricade strung out across the road, the riders came to a halt, the snap of shoes being clicked out of pedals ricocheting down the group as feet hit tarmac for the first time in hours.

'Get an official up here!' the Yellow Jersey yelled into his radio mike.

But Cédric could have told him to save his breath. For behind them a herd of black and white cows, equally walking upright, had materialised from the far side of the Auberge. Some with bells round their necks, tails swishing, they took up positions behind the bikes, arms folded over their chests and one of them, shorter than the rest and stocky with it, was even smoking a cigarette. The cyclists were trapped. Isolated. No official cars had made their way through. Or were going to.

'We mean you no harm,' shouted the nearest sheep with a woman's voice and a face that was a younger version of the lady who'd been waving the flag.

'Placards!' yelled another with ferret-like features and an

expression that could turn the sweetest summer milk. Suddenly the sheep whipped out placards from behind their backs as miniature shepherds, complete with crooks and berets, and some with drawn-on moustaches, scampered down a side lane and started weaving through the bikes with trays of drinks and canapés. And Cédric knew that on his very first Tour de France, he had stumbled into one of its legendary protests.

This fleeting thought was quickly followed by a fierce pride in the fact that it was taking place in his very own Ariège.

The helicopter pilot basically did what he was told to by the camera crew. Sometimes he would circle above a castle so they could get pretty pictures. Sometimes he would fly past a well laid out exhibition on the ground, a bicycle made from haystacks say, or a field of cows all dressed in yellow. But never, in all his years working with the Tour de France, had he been asked to hover over a thin ribbon of tarmac in the middle of a forest in the Pyrenees so that the cameraman could film a road that had been blocked by trees.

He glanced out of the side at the scene the man was focusing on and shook his head. What were they thinking of, the hooligans who'd done this? The whole nation would see straight away that they were idiots. Murdering idiots at that. Even if the country didn't already suspect the Ariège anti-bear faction of having killed that poor creature the other week, the perpetrators may as well have signed a declaration with the picture they'd scrawled on the ground next to their rudimentary protest. It was crude. It was brutal. And it was about to incense the whole of France. On Bastille Day when the Tour got its biggest viewing figures.

'Okay. Got it. Now let's get over to La Rivière.'

The pilot swung the helicopter effortlessly over the tops of the trees, and veered left. A couple of blade rotations later and the grey slates of a largish building came into view.

'That'll be the Auberge des Deux Vallées,' he heard the cameraman say as he consulted his notes. 'Get in closer and let's see if there's anything worth showing our viewers.'

It was to become a standing joke between them for the rest of their working lives. For as the helicopter cleared the final hill and the village of La Rivière was revealed to the audience of *France 2*, there, on top of what looked like a marquee, was a gigantic banner, which the camera just had to zoom in on.

FIRST OUR BEAR WAS KILLED – NOW LA POSTE IS KILLING OUR COMMUNE!

'Christ!' muttered the cameraman. 'This is going to cause a few ripples.'

'Possibly a few more than you think,' replied the pilot, pointing at the mêlée of riders down below who had been penned in by what looked like herds of sheep and cows. Only, the animals were all walking on two legs and holding placards and if he wasn't mistaken, the cyclists were being offered drinks from trays held by pygmy shepherds.

'Now *that*,' declared the pilot with a dose of Gallic pride, 'is how to hold a protest!'

Serge knew he wouldn't have long. The police were already on the scene, trying to get the herd of human cows out of the way. But inspired by André Dupuy, veteran of many protests in his political youth, the placard-wielding bovines had all sat down, making it much more difficult for the officers to move them. And then the children had arrived in their shepherds' outfits with glasses of wine and bites to eat and somehow the whole thing had taken on the air of an impromptu party. Cyclists were leaning over their handlebars and chatting away, the children were vying with each other to get autographs and the local police were busy taking photos, which Serge suspected were more likely for their family albums than for any official investigation. And all of it was being filmed on live television. On Bastille Day.

But the man talking to him was far from being in the festive spirit.

'This is unacceptable,' he was saying, his face tense. 'I'm begging you to kindly move out of the way so that the race can proceed.'

'I'm sorry,' said Serge, genuine for once as he stood there in his best suit with his official red, white and blue mayoral sash draped around his right shoulder and tied on his left hip, shoulders drawn back and ramrod straight as he held his ground. 'But you must understand that for the inhabitants of this commune, the loss of their post office has far graver consequences than a delay to the Tour de France. Even if it is the greatest sporting event on the planet.'

The impact of the words he'd stolen from Fabian was clear to see, the race director preening himself at the praise. He looked over Serge's shoulder at the mass of people beyond and he sighed.

'So, how can I help?' he asked.

And Serge repressed a grin. They were exactly the words he'd been hoping to hear.

Christian was a panicked cow. Not because of the protest. That all seemed to be going to plan, which was amazing, considering how little time they'd had to get the inhabitants ready. The placards were in full view of the cameras, the slogans ranging from the emotional *Keep Our Way of Life Alive – Say No to La Poste's Changes!* to the pragmatic *Give Us Back Our Post Office!* And of course the ones that implicitly linked the closure to the death of Miel were getting great coverage.

Nor was he worried about tensions in the peloton; the cyclists were all taking the dramatic events in their stride, making no move to push through the line of human sheep that still blocked the road. If anything, they were enjoying themselves, touched by the hospitality they were being shown and revelling in the adoration of the children. And Fabian. He'd come across an Ariégeois in the body of professionals and was busy reminiscing about some cyclist called Jacques Dupont whom he was adamant must be a relative of the youngster he was talking to. In fact, so amicable was the whole situation that most of the male inhabitants of Fogas had abandoned their posts, their job being done for them as the way back down the valley was now thoroughly blocked by team cars and press motorbikes, and so there was the incongruous sight of lots of men dressed as cows talking to lots of men dressed in Lycra.

Of course, with everything going so smoothly, the good news was that they'd had no need to resort to Plan B, which would have involved the road being blocked by Sarko the bull, a rather more threatening sight than René Piquemal dressed as a cow, handlebar moustache and all.

But that wasn't enough to lift Christian's mood. For despite all of these great efforts, he had just discovered something that could scupper everything they had worked so hard to achieve.

It didn't help matters that the bloody cow suit was so hot! He pushed back the hood, blond curls springing out, and wiped a hand across his sweating brow.

'Christian?'

He turned to see a beautiful sheep, face framed in fleece, her hand on his arm.

'Are you okay?' asked Véronique.

'I can't find Sarko,' he whispered, face ashen.

353

'What do you mean, you can't find him? Surely he's in the graveyard.'

Christian shook his head and Véronique's hand instantly moved to her throat where normally her crucifix hung, but today she felt only tufts of wool.

'I went up to check on him and he's not there.'

'But how . . . ?'

'The warning sign was gone. I mustn't have fixed it properly. And someone obviously went into the graveyard, not knowing, and didn't latch the gate after them when they left.'

'They were probably in too much of hurry once they realised their mistake!'

Christian groaned softly.

'Come on. We'll both start looking for him. But quietly. We don't want to start a panic before Serge has a chance to wrap things up.'

'We might not get the time,' muttered the farmer, taking in the multicoloured cycling jerseys that surrounded him, shades of pinks and reds and oranges and right at the front, the vibrant yellow of the leader. 'You know how Sarko likes bright colours. Merde! Why couldn't they all be wearing black!'

His shoulders drooped and Véronique's heart went out to him.

'Don't worry. I'll ask Arnaud to help.' She gestured towards a rather large cow that stood out from the herd, his towering form too big for his outfit, thus giving him the appearance of a bovine whose hide had been through too hot a wash. 'He should be able to track Sarko down in no time. And by the looks of things, Serge won't be much longer.'

'Let's hope not. Because I'd hate for things to go wrong after all this.'

Véronique turned to go, and some impulse – afterwards he thought it was the stress – made Christian reach out and pull her back towards him, the jostle of the crowd pushing her into his arms.

'But even if it does go awry,' he added with a smile, 'it was worth it all just to see how lovely you look as a sheep.'

She laughed, her eyes sparkling. 'And you make a very fetching cow, Monsieur Dupuy. Now let's go find this missing bull.'

She gave a tweak on his tail and they separated, Véronique making a beeline for the tracker and Christian heading for the opposite end of the village, head turning as he kept an eye out for the one thing that could ruin the day.

In Saint-Germain-en-Laye, a genteel suburb located to the west of Paris, a middle-aged man was sitting in front of his television. Having already received the Ordre National de Mérite for exceptional services to the state, he was widely rumoured to be in the running for the prestigious Légion d'Honneur; it was a rumour he was doing everything he could to perpetuate.

So it was with great shock that he turned on the television, anticipating an afternoon of spectacular cycling, only to see some tiny village in the middle of the Pyrenees was holding a protest. Fair enough. Very French, and in keeping with the spirit of Bastille Day, one might say. But not if you were the Director General of La Poste and you had dreams of pinning that red ribbon with a white cross to your chest one day. Which he was and he did.

His eyes took in the placards, the cute children dressed as shepherds, and that terrible banner draped across the marquee which the helicopter cameraman insisted on focusing on. For whatever reason, the protesters were drawing links between the suspected murder of some bear down there, which he vaguely remembered someone talking about at the tennis club last week, and his own august institution. And it was enough to take his dreams away from him.

His hand was just reaching for the phone when it began to ring.

'Bonjour?' he said. He didn't get to say much more, other than 'yes' and 'I understand' and 'straight away, sir'.

'Bloody politicians!' he muttered, once he'd hung up. And then he called his subordinate and repeated the conversation verbatim. Only, this time, he was the one doing all the talking.

It was some time before he got back to the television but by then his bank holiday had been well and truly ruined. And if this little matter didn't get resolved quickly, then his career might not be long after it.

'I've done what I can,' the race director said, putting his phone away. 'But I can't guarantee it will be enough.'

Serge took his hand and shook it enthusiastically.

'We can't ask for any more than that,' he said. 'Now, let's get you back on the road.'

Winding through the collection of bikes and bodies, he began making his way to the front where the battle line of sheep, under the command of Fatima Souquet, was still standing firm, spaced out across the road and blocking any access.

Having enlisted the help of Arnaud who had immediately gone up to the graveyard to start tracking the bull, Véronique had also returned to the front of the gathering, eyes searching nervously for signs of the missing animal. Over the heads of the throng before her she caught Christian's gaze and he gave an exaggerated mop of his brow as Serge arrived beside her. She grinned in return.

It looked like they'd got away with it. The protest was over and once the peloton was out of the village, they could find Sarko at their leisure.

Standing facing the crowd, sheep behind him, the mayor gave a shrill whistle and the cows disentangled themselves from the bikes, ushering the little shepherds before them as the click of shoes on pedals bounced off the stone walls. A frisson of excitement ran through the crowd, accompanied by a raucous cheer. The race was about to start again.

'Right,' shouted the Yellow Jersey, taking control as a leader should and addressing the mass of cyclists behind him. 'Rolling start, no jostling for position and no racing for the first kilometre or you'll have me to answer to!'

'Are you ready?' asked Serge, proud beyond measure to be starting the resumed Tour de France.

The Yellow Jersey nodded and Serge stepped to one side, gesturing for the sheep to do the same. On a command from Fatima, Serge realising that they no longer took orders from him, the sheep parted like a woollen Red Sea. And that was when they saw him.

Sarko. Standing in the middle of the road, facing the cyclists, like a lone gunslinger who'd wandered into town intent on causing mayhem.

'Bull!' yelped the Yellow Jersey from his vulnerable position at the head of the peloton. Which was probably what triggered it. Or perhaps it was the sudden sight of so many colours. All shades which were guaranteed to send him crazy. Either way, Sarko lowered his thick neck and pawed the ground, snorting as he tossed his head to and fro.

Véronique could see Christian struggling to get through the mass of people, his powerful physique hampered by bikes and little shepherds and cows that were straining to get a better view while those in the front line were pushing backwards, trying to escape the ferocious beast and further hindering the farmer's progress.

He's going to be too late. That was her only thought as she

saw the bull paw the ground once more, his malevolent gaze firmly fixed on the bright yellow object in front of him.

And then, just as Sarko started to move, head shaking from side to side, causing the Yellow Jersey to whimper with fear, the young cyclist with the local accent Véronique had heard speaking to Fabian earlier stepped out of the peloton.

'Come on now, there's a good bull.' He walked forwards, hand outstretched, body slightly angled away and Véronique felt the crowd hold its breath. He was so slight, bony shoulders jutting out through the thin covering of Lycra. It looked as though the bull could toss him aside on an exhalation alone. But he wasn't afraid.

'Why are you causing all this fuss?' he asked, his voice firm but gentle, rising and falling in a singsong.

Sarko snorted, but Véronique saw him relax, the high ridge of his back collapsing as he started to calm down. By now the cyclist was close enough to touch him. But he didn't. He just kept speaking to him, one hand carefully extending to gather the loose ends of the chain that were hanging from Sarko's collar. And then he slowly walked to the side of the road, the bull, the cantankerous beast that was a legend in the commune of Fogas, meekly following him.

The young man was tying Sarko to an apple tree in the abandoned orchard by the time Christian reached him.

'Thanks!' the farmer said, slapping the cyclist on the back. 'That was incredibly brave of you. Or stupid! I'm Christian Dupuy. Owner of Sarko.' He jerked a thumb at the now passive bull.

'Cédric Dupont.' They shook hands.

'How did you know what to do?'

Cédric shrugged. 'We had a bull at home when I was a teenager. That's what used to work with him.'

Christian's eyes narrowed as he recognised the accent. 'Are you from round here?' he asked.

'Over towards Mas-d'Azil.'

'The Dupont farm! Of course!' He laughed. 'That's where I bought Sarko. Your bull was probably his father!'

Cédric smiled as his day took another unexpected twist. 'Well now you know what to do if he gets like this again.'

They walked back to the waiting cyclists and as the young man entered the group of his fellow professionals, the Yellow Jersey winked at him.

'Come on, Cédric,' he said. 'You're holding us all up.'

With a clatter of shoes on pedals and shifting gears and shouts of 'Allez! Allez!', the great spectacle that was the Tour de France got back on the road after its brief but interesting hiatus in the commune of Fogas. And for Cédric Dupont, as he twisted his head back to catch a last glimpse of the village, everyone waving, Sarko the bull lying down amongst the apple trees, it was a day he would never forget. It also marked the last time anyone in the peloton called him bumpkin. At least within earshot anyway.

The Director General of La Poste was not the only one contemplating his career. At the far end of the village, Pascal was waiting, his foot tapping the ground anxiously, afraid that he would get caught.

Using the mayhem in La Rivière as cover, he'd snuck inside the Auberge to make a call on their payphone, sensing that the situation necessitated it. And the man had insisted on coming down to see things for himself. Which was the reason Pascal was tense. Because if they were seen together, then everything would be out in the open and their plans would be destroyed. Along with his career. For if the good people of Fogas knew with whom he'd been collaborating, they would never forgive him.

'Nervous, Pascal?'

The first deputy mayor whipped round to see the cold, calculating eyes of the man who had led him this far.

'It's over,' he blurted. 'Papon has won. It's best if we just walk away and forget we ever planned this.'

A sardonic smile greeted him. 'It's not over until I say it is.'

The man inhaled on his cigarette and then blew the smoke straight into the first deputy's face, making him splutter and cough in response.

'We will continue as planned. Through official means. If Serge is still in place, even if the post office stays in Fogas, it makes no difference. It will just take more time. But time,' said Henri Dedieu, mayor of Sarrat, 'is something I have plenty of.'

He made to walk away and then turned back and leaned in to whisper in Pascal's ear.

'And in case you're thinking of having a change of heart, remember the bear, Pascal. Remember the bear.'

He laughed harshly and sauntered off, Pascal immediately collapsing to his knees and retching onto the dusty ground outside the hunting lodge.

Fatima had been right. He was in way over his head. And now there was no way back.

23

By French standards, where bureaucracy crawls slower than an escargot towards a dinner plate, things moved fast that afternoon. The inhabitants of Fogas had just enough time to change out of their now redundant animal costumes and gather in the gardens of the Auberge when Serge Papon's mobile rang and silenced the excited chatter.

Véronique watched him listening intently to the caller, his brow furrowed, lips pursed, and she realised she was holding her breath, the entire commune looking on in a similar state of apprehension. It had been a long shot but the protest had gone so well that they'd dared to believe they might have been successful in persuading La Poste to change its mind. But perhaps, given the solemnity of Serge's expression, it had been too much to hope for.

The mayor hung up and turned to address the anxious faces gathered before him.

'Josette,' he said, seeking out the petite owner of the épicerie who was standing next to Fabian, nervously clutching her hands to her chest. 'You have a new business partner. And Véronique,' he continued, a grin stretching across his features as the crowd started to murmur, 'you've got your post office back. La Poste has done a U-turn!'

Pandemonium broke out.

Christian grabbed Véronique and swung her around, her feet only just back on the ground when Serge was by her side and pulling her into a warm embrace, both of them in tears. He released her and Maman was there, laughing and crying, and they just hugged each other. After that there was Josette, and René, and Stephanie and Fabian and even Bernard Mirouze. All of them hugging and kissing and going mad while Philippe Galy started playing "La Marseillaise" on his accordion, everyone joining in with the rousing chorus in a celebration of Bastille Day and of their achievements. And then, out of nowhere, he was standing before her, Arnaud Petit, clean-shaven, long mane loose and a shy smile on his face.

'Fantastic news,' he said as he kissed her on both cheeks, his hands warm on her shoulders.

'Arnaud!' Christian shouted in delight, striding over towards them. 'Are you staying for the party?'

Arnaud let his gaze linger on the reinstated Postmistress of Fogas before replying, 'I wouldn't miss it for the world.'

What a party it was! Everyone assembled in the garden of the Auberge, each family bringing a basket of provisions, and soon the main table in the marquee was straining under the weight. There were quiches and onion tarts, homemade pâté and pickles, salad and pungent tomatoes fresh from Stephanie's greenhouse, olives, home-cured ham, saucisson and meltingly thin slices of magret de canard, delicate rounds of goat's cheese, thick slabs of Bethmale, some Roquefort which Josette brought just for Serge, enough bread to satisfy the hordes outside Marie Antoinette's window and a delicious salade niçoise contributed by Josephine Dupuy, who thereby proved that she knew how to boil an egg at least.

Despite the amazing food, Paul Webster was still greeted with a roar when he came out of the Auberge with a massive pot of moules marinières, Lorna right behind him with an equally large container of frites. They were closely followed by

Christian and Bernard carrying trays weighed down with flutes of champagne.

Such was the good-natured chaos as people jostled for seats and got ready for the meal that no one noticed Bernard Mirouze pause next to the bear tracker. No one but the *cantonnier* saw the vial of clear liquid that was tipped into one of the glasses. And if anyone thought it odd that the plump waiter insisted on serving Pascal Souquet with champagne before anyone else, nothing was said. When everyone was holding a glass, Serge Papon stood to make the toast and a hush descended over the rows of tables.

'It's been a long year. And at times I haven't deserved to wear this,' he began, touching the official sash of red, white and blue that still graced his torso, cutting a very different figure to the forlorn man of the previous winter. 'I know I've let you down since the death of my wife. Badly. But you stuck by me and I can't thank you enough for that.'

He cleared his throat as many of the female members of the audience hastily reached for tissues.

'While I've always known it was an honour to represent you, today you have shown me how amazing you really are. Each and every one of you. Together we have pulled off an incredible feat – by sheer people power we have made one of the biggest institutions in France do an about-face. And we have wrestled our post office back from our thieving neighbours!'

A tumultuous roar split the air, accompanied by a variety of gestures aimed in the general direction of Sarrat on the other side of the river.

'So,' said Serge Papon, 'without further ado, I propose a toast. To this commune, which embodies all that is great about our nation on its national day, and to my daughter, who just happens to be the postmistress of Fogas! *Santé!*'

'*Santé!*' called out the crowd and like cowbells across a Pyrenean meadow, the clink of champagne glasses chimed across the garden.

In the way typical of that region, the repast lasted well into the night, the sky having darkened by the time the last fork was laid down and the umpteenth belt loosened. With the serious business of eating concluded, the tables were stacked away and the chairs moved to one side, Christian and Arnaud having to carry an inebriated Pascal Souquet in his as he was unconscious despite the early hour, much to the disgust of his wife and the amusement of everyone else. They deposited him in a far corner where he remained slumped over a table for the rest of the festivities and would wake the following morning with a dull head and no memory of what was to be one of the best parties in commune history. Although he would suffer terrible earache for a couple of weeks thanks to his prolonged proximity to the music system which had been set up by one of the second-home owners, the speakers large enough to make sure the inhabitants of Sarrat could hear the people of Fogas enjoying their victory.

'How are you coping?' Paul Webster asked Lorna as she came to stand with him at the edge of the marquee, watching the revellers twisting and turning on the wooden floor to yet another Johnny Hallyday song.

'Tired!' She grinned. 'But happy.'

'Have you told anyone?'

She shook her head, hands crossing over her stomach. 'Not yet. It's a bit early. But Stephanie knows. And Arnaud Petit. They both came up to congratulate me! Stephanie I can understand, what with her gypsy background. But Arnaud? How on earth did he guess?'

Paul shrugged. 'I suppose he's used to working with pregnant animals.'

The glare from his hormonal wife was enough to tell him that honesty wasn't always the best policy.

'Never seen Pascal that drunk!' he quickly said, diverting Lorna's attention to the comatose first deputy mayor who was still sprawled in his chair. Fatima Souquet was administering the odd slap to his face, although whether as a remedy or a punishment, it was difficult to say.

'Not like him to lose his cool,' agreed Lorna. 'Chloé on the other hand seems to be back to her chirpy self.'

She pointed towards the group of children sitting on the ground some distance from the big tent, all of them listening to some story Chloé Morvan was telling. Whatever the subject, they were transfixed, and as she drew to her conclusion the band of youngsters who had been so sombre for the last three weeks started laughing and hugging each other, one or two of the girls even crying.

The outburst of noise caught Serge Papon's attention as he sat to the side watching some of the younger adults dancing. He turned to see the children leap up and begin tearing around the garden, Chloé Morvan at the front, flanked by the Rogalle twins.

'Those kids would follow herrr anywherrre!' remarked Annie as she took a seat next to him.

'She's a born leader. Bit like our Véronique.' He watched her face to see how she would react.

She smiled. 'Yes. She gets that frrrom you.'

He reached for her hand and as the music slowed, the first notes of a classic Edith Piaf song drifting across the evening air, he impulsively led her onto the crowded dancefloor, surprised when she didn't resist.

'That's fitting!' Arnaud Petit appeared at Véronique's side just as she was taking in the strange sight of her mother dancing with the mayor. Who also happened to be her father.

'How do you mean?'

'The song. It suits them both to a tee.'

She laughed, catching the strains of the Little Sparrow declaring she regretted nothing.

'Come on,' he said, catching hold of her arm. 'Let's join them.'

And before she knew it she was dancing with him, her cheek pressed against his chest where she could hear his heart beating rapidly. It felt weird. But right.

'I'm leaving,' he murmured in her ear as the plaintive 'La Vie en Rose' began. 'I only came to say goodbye.'

She pulled back in his arms to see his face. He was staring down at her with an intensity that caught her breath. 'When?'

'Tonight. I can't stay here. I have things I need to do.'

'Will you return?'

He shook his head and pulled her back into his embrace and she felt a terrible sadness welling up inside her that was at direct odds to the euphoria she'd experienced only hours before. They'd succeeded. She'd regained her job. The village had fought off the threat of a rival épicerie. She'd found her father. And Christian wasn't going to have to sell the farm. All of this in the space of nine months. She should have been rejoicing. And yet she was distraught. To think that this gentle giant who had come into their community and made them all think differently about the wildlife that surrounded them was going to be gone from their lives for good.

'You could come with me.'

He said it so quietly she thought she was mistaken.

'Sorry?'

'Come with me.'

He was looking at her as if she were the only woman who walked the earth.

Christian was having a fantastic evening. The food had been amazing. His mother's salad had gone down a storm. He'd learnt how to control his cranky bull. And both his problems and Véronique's were solved. She had her old job back and he was going to be expanding the farm.

And to top it all, Pascal Souquet had gone out like a light after a solitary glass of champagne and was now a standing, or rather a sitting, joke. As if that wasn't bad enough for the poor man, not only was his wife furious but the kids, egged on by Chloé, had raided one of their mother's make-up bags and had drawn a lipstick-picture of a bear on one of his cheeks and a love heart on the other.

'Couldn't happen to a nicer person!' exclaimed René as he joined the group of men standing to one side, near enough to the marquee to be part of the fun but not near enough that their wives could nag them to dance. 'Just what we need to crown a brilliant protest. And great news about the race too!'

'What news?' asked Christian.

'You didn't hear? The young lad that dealt with your Sarko. He got into a breakaway with some other cyclists just outside Massat and then jumped them on that short descent as you leave the village. Took off up the Col de Port and was in Foix before any of them knew what was happening.'

'He won the stage?'

René nodded. 'Now you'll always be able to say that a stage winner of the Tour de France taught you how to tame your bull!'

The group burst into laughter.

'Someone else that needs taming right there!' remarked André Dupuy, gesturing towards the dancers.

Christian turned round and felt a sharp pain in his chest. It must be how Annie had felt when she took ill, he thought, as his eyes tracked the tall man and his partner across the floor, her dark head resting on his broad shoulder as they whispered to each other.

'That Serge Papon,' continued old Monsieur Dupuy, unmindful of the fact that his son was watching someone different entirely. 'What a sly dog!'

'They make a lovely couple,' someone else chipped in.

But Christian didn't hear. He was still staring at the tall man and the woman in his arms who were dancing in the crowded space. The way he was looking at her. The way she tipped her head back and laughed, the cross glinting in the beautiful hollow below her throat. Christian wanted to run over there and tear them apart. Tell him that she was his.

Which was when he realised. He was in love with Véronique Estaque.

There was no blinding flash. No magic revelation. Just a sense of knowing, like it was something he'd always been aware of, a fleeting image at the corner of his vision that had suddenly come into sharp focus. But as the pieces all fell into place, he was consumed by the dreadful awareness that, stupid idiot that he was, he may have diagnosed his condition too late. With a dull ache he watched Arnaud lead Véronique across the floor, out of the marquee and off into the dark that had settled on the village.

'He could teach you youngsters a thing or two about romance!' André Dupuy added, fascinated by the mayor.

'Romance!' René scoffed and beckoned Christian. 'Come on, let's go catch the highlights of the Tour. Our protest should be on it. That's more romantic than anything going on out here!'

And Christian Dupuy trailed after the rotund plumber and the group of men, past the snoring first deputy and into the Auberge, one foot plodding after the other as his soul screamed in agony at the thought that he had lost her.

'Good timing,' announced Paul Webster, as the first images of the valley came up on the TV in the bar.

Christian watched in a daze. He saw the shots of the banner flapping on the marquee roof. Saw the pictures of them all in their ludicrous costumes. Saw the cyclists and the children and the bull and the restart. And saw nothing but the face of Véronique Estaque.

The way her eyes creased when she laughed. The way her nostrils flared when she was annoyed. That habit she had of touching her cross when she was worried which made him want to hold her and tell her he'd fix all her problems. And the way she'd looked when she'd followed Arnaud Petit out of the gardens of the Auberge. Like she was disappearing out of Christian's reach for ever.

'I hear Arnaud's left,' remarked André Dupuy, as a shot of the tracker came on the TV.

'Already?' René sounded hurt. 'He didn't say goodbye.'

Paul slapped his head. 'Sorry. He asked me to give you this.'

René took the envelope the Auberge owner was offering him, slid his finger under the flap and pulled out three photographs.

'Jesus!' Tears sprang to his eyes as a grin formed beneath his moustache. 'The bastard!'

He passed the photos around to general gasps and exclamations.

'But are these from before the fire?' asked someone, puzzled as they stared at the pictures.

'After. Look at the date!' The plumber pointed at the top corner. 'She's been alive all this time!'

'So . . . what about . . . ?'

'But there was a bear . . .'

'In that case . . .'

And so it was that the others gathered around René with

lots of head-scratching and bemusement as they tried to make sense of the different perspective the photographs cast on recent events, leaving only a dazed Christian Dupuy to see the final images of La Rivière on the television in front of him, taken from the helicopter as the Tour de France left town. Even in his love-stricken state, he recognised the features of Pascal Souquet, first deputy mayor, caught deep in conversation with someone on the far side of the hunting lodge. The side furthest from the village where, but for the helicopter, the clandestine meeting wouldn't have been seen.

Christian squinted at the screen but it made no difference. He couldn't see who Pascal was talking to. All he could see was the man's shadow. Then the first deputy mayor collapsed in a heap on the ground before picking himself up and walking slowly away. It was strange. Very strange. And in a way that marked him out as a true leader, a man willing to put the concerns of the community before his own failed concerns of the heart, the farmer forced himself to concentrate.

Why would Pascal Souquet be meeting someone in secret on the very day that Fogas needed every hand on deck? And could the mystery person be the same man who'd orchestrated the protests up at the town hall back in November? Whatever it was, Christian concluded, it was unlikely to bode well for Serge Papon. Or for himself.

But then, he mused, ever pragmatic, it wouldn't hurt to have more political machinations for him to concentrate on. It would stop him from dwelling too much on his broken heart.

The crack of fireworks sounded overhead and with a resigned sigh he wandered out with the rest to watch the colours bursting over the hills, flowers of red and blue and gold shooting up into the dark sky to commemorate the beginning of the French Republic and to mark a momentous day in the history of Fogas. And for Christian Dupuy, as the pyro-technics burst into a brief technicolored brilliance before fading into the night, they mirrored the way he had fallen so spectacularly in love. Only to have his dreams dissipate into nothing.

For Jacques Servat standing at the window of the épicerie, the exploding fireworks served to give him enough light to see a young couple wandering up the road.

Romance! He grinned. It was the perfect night for it. A warm breeze, a wild party after the events of the day. Ideal conditions for declaring love.

He watched the couple with interest, her head on his shoul-der, his arm around her waist. It was only when they got closer to the shop that he realised who they were and he started slap-ping his head with frustration.

Véronique and Arnaud! That wasn't supposed to happen. What on earth was that dolt Christian playing at, that he couldn't capture a woman on a night like this?

God! If he was mortal again he'd show the farmer a thing or two. Teach him how to reach out to a woman and never let her go. Like he'd done with Josette all those years ago. Taking her to dance after dance when he knew that she envisioned a life far from Fogas, knew she had plans to escape to the brighter lights of Paris and beyond. He'd let his feet do the talking, seducing her on the dancefloor, waiting until she started to swoon with desire before asking her on another date. And it had worked. He'd made her his.

Of course, he was blithely overlooking the fact that he'd been enslaved by her the first afternoon he'd set eyes on her, waiting at the lay-by for a lift into St Girons, her hat tipped back on her head like a French Audrey Hepburn.

Back in the present he saw the big tracker lean down to kiss

Véronique. And he banged his forehead against the glass in annoyance at the ineptitude of modern youth.

Véronique Estaque was oblivious to the frantic ghost in the épicerie window as Arnaud kissed her. She was only aware of the tracker's lips on hers, the way her body tingled in response and the clichéd fireworks exploding overhead.

'Are you sure?' he asked as he pulled away.

She was and she wasn't. 'Yes.'

He sighed and caressed her face with a broad hand, making her shiver. 'Then there's something you should know.'

She waited for him to continue.

'The snowball, that night.' He leaned down and kissed her on each cheek, her skin burning at his touch. 'It was Christian who threw it. I think he thought I was you.'

And with one last embrace, he said goodbye and walked away.

She watched his huge frame disappear into the night and wondered if perhaps she had just made the biggest mistake of her life. Why had she stayed? She glanced around at the dark houses, the entire population of Fogas down at the Auberge.

Was this worth giving up love for? Was it worth turning down Arnaud Petit for?

Then her eyes came to rest on the épicerie, soon to be home of her new post office. And she smiled.

She had friends here. She had a job here. Amazingly, after thirty-six years of fruitless searching, she'd also finally found her father here. And from what she'd witnessed under the canvas of the marquee, he seemed to be renewing his friendship with her mother!

But for the postmistress of Fogas, most importantly of all, she had Christian Dupuy here. Even if he did go around throwing snowballs at her like a teenage kid.

Still puzzling over the nugget of information she'd been handed, she walked slowly back to her flat, too worn out to return to the festivities. A good night's sleep. That's what she needed. Then tomorrow she would contemplate all that had happened on this incredible day.

In the unlit window behind her she couldn't see the spectral presence doing a jig of delight, heedless of the fact that his back wasn't quite up to it anymore. For Jacques Servat was throwing caution to the wind, so confident was he that given a bit of time, everything would come together for the postmistress and the farmer. It always did in Fogas.

Epilogue

Dawn. Up above the commune of Fogas, high up in the forests of green that graced the sheer mountainsides, a man was crouched in thick bracken, concealed from the objects of his attention.

They were safe now, Arnaud Petit reasoned, as he watched the three bears breakfast on bilberries, Miel holding the higher branches down for the young cubs to reach.

They'd been lucky the day of the fire. Across the hillside from where it had started, Miel had had the sense not to go any closer. From the tracks he'd found, it seemed like the three of them had waited it out, the cubs up a tree while their mother kept guard.

Of course, the day had still been tragic. When he'd arrived at the quarry and had seen the burnt and twisted carcass down below, he'd known it wasn't Miel. The size for a start. And the clubbed rear foot. He'd worked out straight away that the hunters had killed the male bear that he'd been trying to find since the autumn.

Still puzzled by the attacks he'd been investigating, convinced by the evidence he'd discovered on his laptop that they were fake, he'd felt that there was something more to this brutal murder than a bunch of hunters and shepherds whipped into a frenzy over a few dead sheep. Oh, they'd been stirred up all right; it was the motives of the man controlling them that Arnaud couldn't figure out. Or his identity.

So it only took the tracker moments to make the decision. As he stood there gazing down at the mangled body, rage boiling through him at the callous act which he knew had been no accident, he'd realised he could use this innocent death. Use it to gain more time. And use it to protect Miel and her babies.

Even though it would mean losing his job.

He'd lied. He'd deliberately identified the dead bear as Miel and had remained in the hills making sure that no one suspected a thing. Guarding the bear and her cubs from the killers who had set the fire.

But it was time for the truth to come out. While those at the agency were still struggling to get a DNA sample from the dead bear, he knew they'd get there eventually. When they did, they'd realise it matched the records of an unnamed male, records compiled from a clump of fur that Arnaud had sent in for analysis at the start of the winter. And from that they would know that Miel was still alive.

Thanks to Arnaud, however, at least they would now know that she was innocent.

Along with his resignation, which he'd tendered knowing that his actions over the last few weeks had breached pretty much every rule in the agency guidelines, he'd sent them his report on the attack at the Dupuy farm. It contained clear proof that the sheep had been killed by the bear that had subsequently perished in the fire. He'd also sent his theories on the other attacks.

It had taken him a while to work it out. And it still sounded preposterous. But it appeared as though the imprints at the beehives and the farm in Sarrat had been made using a fake foot; a foot that had been created from the mould of a partial footprint left by the dead bear. Adding Miel's fur, which they'd collected surreptitiously, the perpetrators had made the evidence hard to refute. In fact, Miel would still have a death sentence hanging over her if it hadn't been for one little mistake.

With only half a print to work with, those responsible had improvised. But in doing so, they'd made the fake foot too short. They might have got away with it if it hadn't been for the subsequent attack at the Dupuy farm. A real attack. From a real bear. With the same prints but a longer foot.

So Arnaud had detailed all this in his report and while it would be enough to lift the threat of euthanasia for Miel, he didn't expect the agency to withdraw the compensation they'd paid out. Diplomatically they wouldn't dare. Plus there was no suggestion that either Philippe Galy or the farmer in Sarrat had staged the attacks. In fact, Arnaud had stated in his conclusion that he could offer no clues as to those responsible.

Which wasn't entirely true. He knew that Pascal Souquet was involved. Had video footage of him gathering Miel's fur to prove it. But he also knew the man was a patsy. So he'd excluded some information from his final analysis. Had made sure that the incriminating video would never be seen by the agency. And had mentioned none of this to Christian Dupuy or to Serge Papon. Because he was convinced that one day Pascal Souquet would eventually lead him to understand what had prompted the attacks in the first place. And from that he would discover the identity of the man who wore the boar's-head signet ring, the mastermind behind the violence.

Then Arnaud would exact revenge for the terrible death that had been inflicted on a creature that had done nothing to deserve it. A revenge far more dire than a dose of tranquilliser in a drink like he'd administered last night to the first deputy mayor.

In the meantime, although he'd grown attached to the

commune of Fogas, more so than to anywhere he'd ever lived, it was time to move on. Gradually the news about Miel would spread through the commune, Chloé having already told the children about her wonderful birthday spent watching the bears in the forest, and Arnaud was sure that René would show the photos around that he'd left for him – snaps of the cubs Truffle and Morel playing with their mother. And after yesterday's protest where the anti-bear movement had suffered hours of negative publicity on national television as had been the plan, he felt confident that public opinion was strong enough to prevent an outrage similar to that which had happened on the day of the transhumance from ever occurring again.

As for Véronique, she'd made the right decision, thought the tracker ruefully as he carefully stood and began to move away. The big farmer would make her a far better husband. Once he plucked up the courage to accept he was in love.

With a smile on his face, hair loose around his shoulders, Arnaud Petit moved deeper into the woods. He was on his own again. It was, after all, easiest that way.

Miel heard the slightest of noises. A twig breaking, perhaps? She lifted her nose and sniffed. Nothing. No danger. Her cubs were playing in the patch of sunlight that dappled across the forest floor and she lifted her head to take in the warmth of this summer sun. Above her the trees fluttered in the breeze, a canopy of green that spread across the hillside and up the steep angles of the mountain that formed just one of many peaks in the long stretch of serrated edges that was the Pyrenees.

Acknowledgements

No author is an island and as always I am indebted to a range of people for answering my questions – which were often naïve and usually numerous. As before, I listened to all advice offered but am solely responsible for how I chose to use it . . . So, for their generosity, patience and wisdom, I send the following a bear hug and some of Josette's croissants:

Dr. Pierre-Yves Quenette, leader of ONCFS bear team – a man with a difficult job who found time to answer odd questions about all things ursine; Ian Maxwell, tracker extraordinaire whose zeal made me want to change profession; André Clare, Président du Syndicat des Trufficulteurs de l'Ariège and yes, he knows his truffles; Kevin Jack, old school friend and forensic expert who didn't balk at being asked to apply his knowledge to the world of bears; Richard Prime, an Ariège devotee and wildlife expert; Gillian Elizabeth, another who shares my love of the region and a gardening guru; Jennifer Palmer for imparting her (and her deputy mayor's!) understanding of the dreaded 'Code'; Ellen McMaster and Matthew Brown for fearless and accurate input; Claire Jones and Brenda Stickland for being passionate first readers; my parents, Mícheál and Ellen, whose enthusiasm and support never waivers; the amazing team at Hodder, including my *two* editors, Sue and Francesca, who made the editing process a joy (honestly!); my agent, Oli Munson, who was brave enough to take on a Coventry City supporter; and lastly, Mark: I think it's finally my turn to cook dinner, *mon amour!*